Copyright © 2022 Mia Thorne

All rights reserved.

No part of this book may be reproduced, distributed, or transmitted in any form or by any electronic or mechanical means, including information storage and retrieval systems, without written permission from the author, except for the use of brief quotations in a book review and certain other noncommercial use permitted by copyright law.

THE FALLEN KINGDOM

A LOST REIGN

MIA THORNE

★⁺₊★ ☾★⁺₊★

To everyone who's fighting their own battle.

TRIGGER WARNING

This book contains explicit content, mentions of blood fighting, swearing and death. Readers discretion advised!

Prologue

Life isn´t always black or white.

It took a lot for me to realize this. It could be a near-death experience, a loss, or just the flapping of a butterfly´s wings.

Whatever it is that triggers the thought, the sooner it does the better.

Because as far as I know, there´s a hell of a lot gray in between black and white.

"I didn't do anything I swear!"

I hate fucking liars.

"Huh, that's pretty weird because you know, Ellister, you are a wanted man. If you knew what I get paid to get rid of you, you would probably kill yourself."

The knife slides through my hands elegantly as I trace a circle around the wooden chair. My eyes wander over the ropes that constrict the greasy-haired man, the chair groaning when he tries to free himself.

His head flies around, waiting for my next step and I gauge his reaction closely. The way sweat drips down his chin, even though outside dances the fresh wind of winter.

His eyes are hidden behind the blindfold out of expensive silk, robbing me of the sight of them. The eyes that are the gateway to every man´s soul, the eyes which I looked into and saw nothing but darkness.

Ellister Gerard is a dangerous man despite his pretending of a pathetic stance. If he weren´t pure evil I wouldn´t have gotten the tip to trace this bastard down and let my clean blade slit his throat in pure excitement. Someone wanted to see this man dead and paid a high price for it. Which means there are no questions asked. Just actions that are done.

Even though the man is blindfolded I made sure to wear my mask to be sure I wasn't seen, until the beating of this cold man's heart stopped. The silk lining of the material familiarly cools my skin, hiding my identity from curious eyes and dirty looks. The lining fits perfectly to the royal blue, velvet cloak I make sure to wear every second. It swallows my body, hiding the curves and dips, keeping it a secret.

The moment the people in town take a glance at the color they turn their heads, knowing it is better to not have seen me.

They always pretend not to see me and keep on going, hoping, praying the blue shadow doesn't visit them that night.

"That's not true! You know what we have to do to survive here!" He protests again and I sigh lightly. It all comes down to begging once they get tied to a chair and it's embarrassing that they don't have the guts to die with pride. It makes all of this so much more boring, and predictable.

I swing my arm registering the sound of the air whooshing around me but instead of hearing the satisfying sound of a throat-slitting, I ram the knife into the table. The wood splits lightly around the blade, small splinters flying around it.

I walk over to Ellister, bending down, even though he can't see me. I grab his chin harshly and pull his head towards me, his hands clenching against the rope. He reeks of liquor and dirt, of dark sins and forbidden places.

He reeks of the streets of the capital.

"Who are you?" His voice is quiet and I can hear the tremble in it. His skin is pale, sweat tripling off his forehead in fear.

What a pathetic look this man gives. Hurray to the male species.

"The question we have to talk about is, who are you, Ellister? I have heard bad things about a man building some kind of army. What exactly was your plan with a group of men which were recognized for their excellent killing, for their lack of mercy, and their hearts that seemed to be fed by chaos and death? Do you know how hard it was to track them all down and kill them?" I ask him my face close to his.

My voice is barely a whisper. A voice carved out of cold stone and blood.

"No, no. You're lying! You couldn't have killed them, no one can!" He screams at me and I step back when some of his spit lands on my face. Bastard.

I clench my hand and ram my fist straight into his stomach, making him bend over and groan before I swipe the spit off my cheek with my gloves. Now I have to get them fucking cleaned.

If someone would see my bare hands they would know where I'm from.

Elegant pale hands that are clean, no burns and scars to see. Just a person living at the royal palace could have the chance at spotless skin like that.

To many, it was a sign of power or wealth, purity in its finest form. What they didn't know was that it was a curse because even the purest-looking hands can be stained by blood.

"You can say a lot of things about me, you bastard, but I'm not a liar. I take my job very seriously and tracked down every member of your small, arrogant, little group. It was easy to kill them, you know? They were driven with arrogance and their pride was their death blow."

I slide a greasy strand out of his face before I continue.

"You should've heard them. How they begged and pleaded for their life."

I mock him lightly while he shakes his head throughout my whole little storytelling. I have to smirk at the disbelief etched into his face, almost wishing to see his pale eyes and the fear in them.

"I am telling the truth. These men were all killers and if they wouldn't have underestimated a woman so foolishly maybe they would've stood a chance. Well, even then they wouldn't have but it would be much more of a fun fight against somewhat of an equal enemy." I tell him, this whole thing is dragging out longer than I wanted and I still didn't get anything out of him.

My eyes fly towards the clock ticking on the wall.

I'm wasting my fucking time.

"You're. . .you're crazy."

His words drop into sobs and I roll my eyes at his dramatic ants. It is time for him to die and yet, I can't. I still didn't get the information that I wanted because—crippling death or not—these bastards were loyal. They didn't tell me one thing about why they were recruited and what they were preparing. Ellister is the last one and I left him for last on purpose. The weakest member in the chain, hoping he would break easily and it seems like I have to handle his annoying little cries if I want to find out what the hell has been going on these last weeks.

I grab a chair and sit down in front of him, putting my arms on the rest. I carefully grab the blindfold and push it up on his forehead. The moment the light hits his eyes; they narrow and squint, warding the source off. I watch his pupils dilate once they adjust.

The pale blue almost vanishes in the warm light of the candle.

The knife is still driven into the wood of the table where his eyes instantly land on. I watch them widen for a moment, his throat bobbing hard with his next swallow.

"Now listen, Ellister, this can go two ways. One; you tell me what I want to know and you will die within a second, no pain, no feelings at all. Two; you'll be difficult, refuse me any answers and I will have to torture you all night long until you die an excruciating death."

His icy blue eyes place themselves on my face, widening with every word I tell him. I would love to enjoy this moment so much more, grinning at him like the predator I am but I don´t have enough time tonight.

"I don't know what you want." He says quietly and my suspicions are confirmed. Even though Ellister was the one to recruit the killers he's not the mastermind behind this. He's far too scared and easy to get captured to lead an army.

"That's because I didn't ask you a question yet, so I guess you'll go with option one?" I ask him and after a moment of hesitation, he nods.

I smile satisfied while I watch the sweat run down his forehead.

"Why are you recruiting these men?" I cut straight to the chase making him grimace. His head drops while he shakes it. His greasy hair hides his pale eyes in the process, protecting him from my stare.

"Why are you recruiting these men, Ellister?

Answer me or we'll have to do it the hard way, do you want to go the hard way?" I ask him and he quickly looks up, eyes wide.

"It's not me okay? I told him it was completely crazy but he wouldn't budge, gods he knows my family! I have a small daughter, I couldn't just do anything?" His voice breaks through his words pathetically.

I arch my brow.

"When you say him who are you talking about, Ellister?"

"I can't tell you, he would kill me!" He protests and I raise two brows now. He's going to die anyway.

"You don't understand, he's cruel, I never talked to him just his guy. I don't even know his name but if I tell you who, he will not just go after me but my family as well, I have a—"

"Daughter, I know, I know. But what makes you think I will not go after her, if you don't tell me?" I say in a threatening voice. His eyes almost fall out of their socket.

I'm not going to do anything to his daughter, I am not heartless but he needs to spill the information because I'm getting impatient. The ticking of the clock in the dark living room seems to be getting quicker with every passing second.

"I´ll tell you. But I need to start from the beginning." He says and I nod before I motion for him to go on. "It practically started one night. I was in my favorite bar and this creepy man walked in, he was dressed in a cape that hid his face and his boots were kind of weird they had metal attached to them and he was wearing a funny—"

"I don't care about a fashion analysis, Ellister, get to the point." I interrupt his stupid description impatiently.

"Yes, yes sorry. Well, he didn't belong in that bar, anyone could see it. He caught wind of my business and talked to me. He said he saw potential in me and wanted me to recruit Aerwyna´s best killers. He never told me his name or any locations; if he wanted to talk he would find me. Once I understood his plans I wanted to get out, believe me, I did but then he threatened me with killing my wife and daughter. I know what he's doing is wrong but I couldn´t. . ." His sentence ends in another sob.

I sigh again, impatient and he pulls himself together before he continues.

"I heard the rumors, they are all over town. It's just whispers and secrecy and I don't think many people heard of it but it doesn't make it less true. The guy I helped, was associated with the Dark Prince."

A sharp intake of air echoes around us. It takes me a second to realize it was mine.

Everyone knows the Dark Prince. Stories—no—nightmares are told to every child in Adalon when they didn't behave well, that the Dark Prince would come and get them, torturing them with dark magic and sins they couldn´t even dream of.

Nightmares turned into legends and legends into memories. Memories that are told by the elders living in Aerwyna and even adults and the most dangerous soldiers were scared of the stories of the cruelest man on this continent.

You were lucky to avoid the wrath of this creature.

Because that is what he is, no longer a human of flesh and blood but more like a crazed animal, ready to paint the world in red.

It was a tell-tale but there's always some truth in stories like that. The dark magic part and sins were utter nonsense but I didn't underestimate the facts that the legend stemmed on.

"The Dark Prince wanted to build what exactly?" I ask him because it doesn't make any sense. The Dark Prince was rumored to have an undead army trailing his every step, unable to be killed. It was a curse and a blessing, to be immortal and endure death from others but never their own. But why is he starting a riot with these third-class killers, who can't even fight against me?

"How would I know? The guy just told me to gather the cruelest men of Aerwyna in the name of the Dark Prince. I. . .would never do it on my own accord I told you—"

"Don't repeat yourself Ellister." I threaten him and stand up from the chair, pulling the knife out of the dark wood. I start to circle it in my hands, distracting him while I dive into my thoughts.

Someone is being cautious about this. I don't like that at all.

"Please, I told you everything I know; don't kill me I'll do whatever you want me to." He begs me, his eyes trailing my every step around the room.

"You said you have a little daughter?" I ask him while I walk behind his chair crouching down to grip the ropes that are holding his wrists together. I'm going to regret this.

"I do, she's five years old and she's my everything. You can't kill me, my wife and her wouldn't survive."

~ 14 ~

I know they won´t, not just because they wouldn´t find any way to get money but Ellistor is a wanted man and if he won´t pay his debts, I know his family is the first people they will go to.

I sigh and set the cold metal of the knife against his wrist. His whole body freezes in horror.

"No, no you can't—!" He protests loudly before I make the cut and his wrists are free. He gets up from the chair and turns around, eyes wide. I arch a brow and let the knife slip back into my boot to show him I'm not going to hurt him. He starts to rub his wrists still amazed and I roll my eyes at his dramatics.

"Before I let you go, you need to do something for me, Ellister."

"Anything, I'll do anything!" He says, his hands clasped in gratefulness and I walk over to the table to get my bag and strap it back around my torso. I grab the other knives and sheath them to their places while I organize the information and thoughts in my head.

The Dark Prince coming into this chaos is not good news and when just dirt like these killers know of it I'm sure a spy of my father told him about it. Then why isn't he doing something about it?

"I want you to prepare your family for your departure in a week, there is going to be a ship full of workers who will be deported to the crystal mines of Oceanus, where no one will notice you. Because once you stop your plans for this so-called ´associate´ of the Dark Prince, he's going to kill you and your family. I'm giving you this one chance to do the right thing. If you promise me to meet the man again before you leave." His eyes widen horribly at my words.

Gods, what must've scared him this much? Ellister surely isn't a good man and he has seen a lot in the capital. He is known for assassination, corruption, and robbery. Just to name a few.

Still, he looks like he came in contact with the brush of death's hands.

Like a scared animal waiting to be escorted to the slaughterhouse.

"But how am I supposed to do that? I told you if he wants to meet me he decides to come. I don't have the opportunity to contact him—"

"He is going to talk to you, Ellister, believe me. I killed every single one of his men and made sure to leave a mess, so he will meet you." I interrupt him and catch his Adam's apple bob when he swallows hardly.

"And what do I tell him when he asks me about. . .the men?" He asks while I adjust my gloves, ready to get the hell out of here. I walk close to him and stop to look into his scared eyes.

"You tell him that the Red Saint wants to meet him, on the night of the red blood moon ball, she'll see him at the coast of the lost," I whisper. The temperature drops in an instant and I practically see how a shiver runs down his spine. One corner of my lips tips up before I brush his shoulder and leave this poor excuse of a house.

I don't need to see his face or notice the sharp intake of breath to know that he put the dots together.

So I leave his dump as quiet as I came and make my way into the darkest alleys of my kingdom. The Red Saint is just a legend as the Dark Prince and yet she exists. I'm sure Ellister will do as I told him because if not, the Red Saint needs to kill the father of a daughter. If Ellister tries to run before he told that bastard of a man that I want to meet him, I am going to kill him the second I lay my hands on him again.

And this time I will show no mercy.

Once I reach the old brick building I swing myself up on the stones poking out of the uneven wall. My boots have the perfect material to give me a steady grip and I make my way up on the roof like a shadow in the dark. I know my way around the capital like the back of my hand, which makes me take off my mask because the hood around my face is enough to cover it in the dim lighting of the town.

Most lights are already out, the streets filled with the occasional drunk man, or the beautiful and deadly women, dressed in deep red gowns, waiting for their next victim to fall right into their trap. The courtesans are waiting for rich lords to slip their way into town, looking for distraction and fun while their wives sit at home carrying their babies.

I make a small grimace when I watch one of them, a beautiful dark-haired girl, make her way over to a group of men and turn my head quickly jumping onto the next roof. It's not like I judge them, I judge these men not being rightful and loyal enough to stay at home and love the women they married.

But in the end, everyone needs to own their money. In one way or another.

I shake my head and concentrate on the next roof just to stop at all when I see a hooded figure leaning against a building not far from mine.

My body freezes for a moment at the sight.

I quickly crouch down and narrow my eyes to see the figure dressed in shadows, spying on a man not even a street away.

The face is slightly covered, with expensive silk. If they would turn their head I could get a glimpse of just the eyes.

Broad shoulders carry the cloak elegantly like a royal, metal glinting at the belt around a narrow torso. The thief is heavily armed, ready for whatever they planned.

Despite them being covered I easily notice that it is not an amateur. The air seems to bend around the figure, adjusting to the power it oozes.

I trace my eyes from the figure back to the man it is watching. He seems to be in a rush and looks every few seconds over his shoulder. He's carrying something in his hands but it´s too far away to let me see so I whip out a knife and fling myself down the wall of the building, the blade screeching lightly against the wall as it slows down my fall. Once I see a balcony move in my way, I drop down on it while making no sound. Oh, how I love these fucking boots they make life so much easier.

It seems to be some kind of bag in his hands but the form of it is weird, I can´t even make out if it is a solid object or not and I know I'm still too far away to see his face so I swing myself to the side and grab the vines of ivy climbing down to the next roof of a smaller house. My eyes fly to the wall the hooded figure stood at seconds ago but I'm met with an empty spot.

"What the heck—"

I stop myself when I feel a presence behind me and turn in one swift motion, the knife clasped tightly in my hand. I miss the person by just an inch because they duck down and out of my hit. But I don't give them a second of rest as my leg kicks out but the person dodges it like they were swiping a piece of paper. A soft growl of frustration escapes me.

I get out another knife from the strap at my thigh and start to lunge again just to get all my hits parried by them.

For a second my eyes fly to theirs to catch a glinting pine-green color and this second is my downfall because the figure surprises me with a hard hit against my wrist. It has the desired effect and makes me drop the knife with a hiss.

The sound of the blade cluttering against the ground beneath us disturbs our ragged panting. I look around for a way out, just to notice the fact that the figure had me right where it wanted me. My heels come into contact with the edge of the roof giving me a nauseating picture of the ground beneath me.

A sixth-floor fall at least.

If I don't move now I will experience what it feels like to kiss the ground just like my knife did.

"Fuck." The curse leaves my lips in a whisper.

I won't survive this fall no matter how amazing my boots are.

And if I die tonight my father will make sure to bring me back to life just to kill me himself again.

But it seems like the hooded figure has no intention of shoving me off the roof so I take a few daring steps forward.

The green eyes glint with something close to amusement and anticipation. But I´m not sure if I´m imagining things.

I gather all my focus and squat down swooping long legs underneath the figure with one of mine. A gruff curse leaves their lips in a masculine voice before he lands on his knees. I don´t give him time to process and ram my fist into his hard stomach, making him drop to the ground while I hold my second knife against his pale throat.

The throaty laugh that escapes causes a shiver to run down my spine.

I question my sanity the moment goosebumps cover my skin. My eyes meet green glinting, emeralds and I bite my lip when I see the amusement in them.

For a moment it knocks all the breath out of me, realizing I´m holding a knife to a strange man´s throat. A tall dangerous man with hard muscles—that I can feel—and a big—not the right moment.

I don't think I ever fought against someone equal to me. Somewhat close to curiosity flickers inside of me but I quickly push the emotion away, my chest still heaving with heavy breaths. The air fizzles again when his pants meet mine and a hiss starts to move around our bodies.

It is a moment of distraction in his favor.

A moment where he kicks his knee into both of mine and rolls me over, my back colliding with the roof.

A pained breath escapes me before a cold hand wraps around my throat.

The moment our skin comes into contact a wave of electricity moves through my body.

The gentle touch of his hand squeezing could be confused with the touch of a lover and the hard press of his muscles against my soft curves like a whispered promise.

"Who the fuck are you?" I hiss, straining at the searing touch but it only makes my chest brush his hard muscles and I completely freeze when he shoves his thigh between my legs.

A harsh swallow sits in my throat as my heartbeat picks up. It crashes against my ribs and transcripts to his pulse.

A soft brush of his thumb against my throat makes me part my lips and when our eyes clash for a moment the panic subsides.

A small flicker shines in those eyes and even though my body yells at me to not move, to bathe in this stranger's touch I do the only sane thing.

My knee flies up against his groin in one second and he falls right off of me.

"Fuck."

Comes the hoarse groan of his lips and I am quick to straddle his waist, another blade against his throat.

I brush his groin in the process, both our eyes widen and I tighten the hold of the blade against his skin before I slide up to straddle his ribs.

I ignore the rough laugh that somehow makes goosebumps rise on my skin and press the blade harder against his throat while I rip off the cloth around his nose and mouth. A breath escapes me when I recognize the familiar face and quickly take my blade from his throat.

His head follows as if he wants to feel the cold metal, somehow finding amusement in this situation.

"Cassian?" I breathe out and slip the hood off of my head while his lips turn into a crooked grin.

He leans in and lets his luscious lips brush against mine, his hands grab my waist and pull me back down against—oh gods he is so turned on.

"It's nice to see you again, princess."

1

"You're so quiet this morning. Did something happen last night?"

I stare at the reflection of olive skin; trace the worried lines and curves of plump lips. The lines on my friend's forehead tell me that she's going to bug me until she has what she wants. Edlyn is, besides me, one of the most stubborn human beings I know and I would be foolish to think I could trick her into telling her a lie. Doesn´t hurt to try though.

"Just tired," I tell her and even I hear the tremble in my voice, indicating that I´m telling her a weak lie.

She's the only one who knows about my nightly adventures, she disapproves but she knows nothing can hold me back.

Still, I don't feel like telling her about Cassian. Gods, I still can't believe it was him last night, and the fact that he recognized me made me feel on edge for the whole night and this morning.

I didn't stay long after he recognized me and made my way off the roof, disappearing as fast as I could. I don't know if he tried to follow me and I was just too fast, or he didn't even try. But there's been no word from him since last night, no letter, no visit and I'm sure if he told my father I was wandering around Aerwyna and the capital at night, I would be in a very much different situation than I am in right now.

It´s bad enough that he caught me completely off guard. I was also surprised by his hard hits and skills almost throwing me off the goddamn roof.

"You're holding off again." Edlyn sighs while she pulls my hair back and puts it up with the sapphire pins she laid out organized on my dresser. The blue color shines magically when the sunlight hits through the windows in my chamber. It represents the deepest ends of the ocean that connects to the kingdom. Small little reflections shine on the dresser and I can't help but hold my hand up.

The reflection of the gems travels between my fingers as I move them slowly.

"It's to your best; you wouldn't want to know how it is out there it's not a place for a woman."

"You are a woman Katarina. You are the regent of Aerwyna, the princess to be exact, so technically you should be the last one traveling the streets." She protests and I keep my mouth shut.

I'm not a woman when I'm out killing people, that's when I'm the Red Saint. But it's hard to explain and I don't have the nerve or patience to tell her. My mind is too scattered, the prospection of last night scratching at the back of my mind.

If Cassian even thinks about exposing me I'm dead. I will not be left alone by any guard and my father is going to lock me up until I'm married and ready to be controlled by my husband. I can already hear his words echoing in the back of my mind.

You're the next rightful regent of Aerwyna, Katarina. Take some responsibility; you could be the key to the rebuilding of Adalon.

Whatever the hell that is supposed to mean. I don't see how a marriage, let alone a husband, could be the reason or the solution to the retreat of the protestants.

No one thought that Adalon could ever rise again after the war of the three kings thousands of years ago. Magic that once flooded these lands is long gone, the gift of the gods forgotten.

The story of the continent Adalon is a tale you'll learn in first grade and from then on it is recurring every year, reminding you of the losses and the past rulers.

The story is told about four siblings, three princes, and one princess exactly. They lived a long time ago and no one of the folks now can remember. It is a tale that exists since before the eldest lived in our world and is going to exist long after the youngest of us are dead. It is a story about a once powerful continent that was ruled by dark magic.

No one believes the magic part, it is just a part an old sailor's man added to entice it more I guess.

But it is rumored that the descendants of the so-called blood witches, live in the darkest forest, hidden from innocent and naïve eyes and that they are still able to use the ancient magic that once flooded the lands. But that could be another nightmare story.

Add it to the list of many legends in this kingdom.

But what I do know is true is that these siblings existed. They were sent by their father Adales—yes ironically close to the name of our continent I know— to come and part Adalon into four equal pieces and name them after their birth names and houses. They were supposed to keep the balance in nature, with every king or queen ruling differently.

Polyxenus was the youngest of the four; he was known and loved by many to be a gentle and wise king. He married a woman that was so beautiful that many men dreamed of her every night.

With golden locks and brown skin, eyes as blue as the ocean. She was a known healer, a great addition to their kingdom.

When their first daughter was born they named her after his kingdom. Polyxena. It was said he had the most courageous army led by the strongest soldiers ever seen.

Oceanus was the second youngest and got his kingdom by the coast, making his ships the strongest and fastest in our world, his intelligence and cleverness brought him to be the richest king in history. He made the world codependent on his fishing such as export and import, with his quick ships. He didn't marry, too big was his greed for bigger things, more gold, more developments. His lineage got carried on with his lover Shania, a princess that was supposed to marry his oldest brother.

Demetrus was the oldest of the four and he was the darkest of them. His kingdom was feared and respected by its strong king and shiny, dangerous weapons. His men were just like their king, relentless and cold.

But his army made sure that their continent stayed feared and safe from others, no one dared to go against him and so the people thanked him for the safety he provided. While Polyxenus' powerful army was fighting for rights and peace, Demetrus was going to keep their enemies in fear. His planned marriage to Princess Shania was not made out of love, Demetrus was too cold of a man to feel something even close to love and when Oceanus got a son from the princess Demetrus was raging.

He was cursing his younger brother and his foolishness to go after the woman he was supposed to marry.

Almost nothing stood in the way of his wrath and the people feared that a big war might disrupt the continent. Though he didn´t love her, it was said that the Moreau men were to be possessive of their women; feeling threatened by any other being trying to take what is theirs. So the only thing standing between him and his brother was his beloved sister, Aerwyn.

She was the second oldest of them four and loved by all of her brothers, even Demetrus. He trusted her with his whole heart and listened to her even in his darkest hours. They said she was the last string of his humanity and when she told him to forgive Oceanus, he did. War was no longer on his mind and the kingdoms lived in peace for a few centuries.

Until the only light in his life went out.

When Aerwyn Sebestyen was murdered coldly and unknowingly, peace was long over in Adalon and the kingdom broke into many pieces that could never be fixed again. Demetrus turned into a cold monster feared by everyone and not Polyxenus nor Oceanus could help his soul to stay pure anymore.

He was raging, destroying lands and innocent souls in his way. Well, what a great ancestor of Prince Cassian Moreau.

Since then many lands of our continent are ruled by Protestants and the descendants of the four siblings, me included. We could win back pieces of their land but it's not enough. The protestant groups are growing with every day that we live and my father thinks the key to destroying them is with a strategic marriage with one of the other descendants with me.

He thinks that my marriage could save a whole continent from crumbling just because I'm the ancestor of a queen that was killed million years ago.

As if the Protestants would put down their weapons once I am married.

They couldn't care less about a girl who hasn't even seen her whole kingdom.

"Gods, you're distracted today."

I flinch when Edlyn's words get to me and look back at her through the mirror. She's finished pinning up my hair and I see a delivery boy standing at my opened door.

"Sorry, what is it?"

I turn around to look at them both, the boy blinking nervously.

"His Majesty requested for your company at breakfast in his royal quarters."

My mood deflates immediately.

"Of course he does," I mumble before I get up and give Edlyn a small smile. She's dressed in one of her lavender gowns again, contrasting beautifully with her darker skin.

"If I don't come back after thirty minutes, he most probably murdered me."

"Stop being ridiculous and we're not finished with our talk!" She says threateningly making me smile at her smugly, happy I'm escaping her watchful eyes. For now.

"Thank you, you can go now," I tell the boy and he curtseys before sauntering off again. Poor boy, he is probably scared to death by my father's request.

Usually, my father dines alone at every meal and lives while ignoring my existence. He likes to think that the professors and maids are responsible to keep me company. Unless something serious needs to be discussed. I wring my hands as I pass through the halls of the castle thinking about what he might want to talk about.

The sound of my shoes echoes against the ground and accompanies the rhythm of my quickening heartbeat.

A small voice in my mind reminds me of last night and that a very dangerous person now knows of my secret.

If Cassian told him about me, my life could be threatened, potentially. Gods I should've stayed and given him a lie about my nightly adventures. Now I'm going to get caged in and never let out again.

To no doubt, he must've told him. No matter how far away our ancestry might be, we still carry parts of their characters in our veins.

I pass various guards and take the right wing which leads me to the royal quarters of the king.

My mind spirals with every worst-case scenario that could happen from now on. I feel the weight of my ruby dagger strapped to my thigh, knowing it won't do me any good once I'm standing in the wrath of my father.

Reaching the big wooden doors with ornaments carved in, the guards greet me and I hold my breath.

My body acts on its own as I raise my fist and rap hardly against the door. It takes a few seconds before I hear the familiar deep voice that tells me to come in.

Here I go into the lion's den.

2

I shoot a longing look down the hall that leads to my chambers and prepare myself for war to be started once I step through the threshold.

"Close the doors behind you, Katarina."

Very warm words that I'm greeted with when I step into my father´s chamber, but I nod anyway before I close the doors quickly.

Once they're closed I meet his eyes without any hesitance. Royal 101, never let your enemy notice your fear.

Chin high and shoulders back is the way to win any fight. No matter if physical or mental. The eyes are the gateway to the soul, they are one's greatest power.

Besides the fact that my insides feel like they turn into burning lava, I make sure there is nothing in my physical appearance that indicates the inner tumult.

Until he tells me himself that Cassian reached out to him I will not say anything. Still, I can´t suffocate the feeling of needing more air, the corset around my upper body squeezing my lungs painfully.

These damn things are going to be the death of me.

"Sit." He says, offering me the chair that stands opposite him from the elongated table that is filled with various deliciousness of Aerwyna.

This time I don´t have the pleasure of eyeing the sweet honey-drizzled quarters, or the scent of fresh bread accented with butter.

I grab the hems of my dress and walk over to the chair before I sit down elegantly, looking at my father. He looks the same as he always does; I don't think he changed the slightest bit over the years, physically. He still has dark sapphire eyes that are filled with familiarity and safety. His hair is the same dark brown, the waves caressing his neck, both things I inherited from him. His beard is neatly cut but is struck with a few grey strands. Even Daragon Sebestyen is unable to outrun everyone's enemy, time.

The only thing different is the lines on his forehead that have multiplied over the years. The task of being a king lies heavily on his shoulders and without his wife, it seems almost impossible to master.

Sometimes I can see him soften up and it almost seems like I see a flicker of the remains of my mother in him. I don't remember much of her, time took away the few memories that I had, tinting them with pictures I can't decipher from reality or imagination.

"You wanted to talk to me?" I speak up after a beat of silence while his eyes focus finally on the unopened letters by his side. A short breath of relief escapes me, restrained by the tight stay around my lungs.

He grabs his iron dagger from his belt and starts to open the first letter.

"Yes, I have very serious matters to discuss with you and thought it would be better if I ease you into it."

Ease me into it?

"Okay. Shoot."

That earns me a disapproving look from him, regarding my words but I ignore it and wait for him to continue. Even now with no eyes watching he contains his act as a royal leader.

"As you must know your birthday is coming up—"

Not this again.

"If this is about the party, we already established that you can't stop me from inviting more than fifty guests. I promise we will behave but it is my eighteenth birthday and for once I want to spend it as I want. I'm not fancying any dinner parties or celebrations with a dozen lords I don't even know—" I shut up the second he lays his eyes back on me, raising a brow and I paddle back completely.

"But that's not what you wanted to say—sorry," I say quickly realizing that I've been trying to convince him even though I don't have to.

The former anxiety of my secret being revealed is long gone because if the prince told him, he would react very differently.

"Can I talk now?" He asks me his brow still raised and I nod before I motion to zip my lips and throw away the key.

It's not a very princess-like motion but it does the job.

"The day you turned four, your mother and I thought about the security of our kingdom and how the future was tainted by uncertainty because our firstborn child was not a boy."

It seems like that is the only important topic in this kingdom. That my mother got a girl as a firstborn and that even though two years later she got pregnant with a boy, I was the one who was going to rule over Aerwyna once my father was too old to do it.

The people don't trust a woman to rule on her own—no—she needs to be directly wed to another prince to even take on the responsibility. I can promise every one of my subjects that I am going to be a better queen than any man who could be a king.

The lack of royal consorts speaks of the male line in this kingdom.

My father made it a task of his to invite as many lords, viscounts, and even distant cousins to the castle. No one even captured a glimpse of my attention.

There is no need for a man to stand by my side and annoy the hell out of me.

"So we made a deal with the King of Demeter, that the second you turned eighteen and weren't engaged to a different regent, you'll be promised to the king's son, based on how good you two got along when you were little."

My mouth drops open at his words. Is this happening right now? I mean what is he even saying? I'm not just some object you can promise to be possessed by something or someone. I was four for heaven's sake!

"You've got to be kidding me. This is a joke right?"

The first words that escape me sound wobbly and shaky, I bite my tongue in embarrassment.

The look on my father's face darkens as he puts the next letter he was about to read down.

Not a good sign. Not a fucking good sign.

"Do you think I would be kidding about something so important? You knew this was coming sooner rather than later, Katarina.

You must marry a royal, preferably a prince, to strengthen our lands and ensure our kingdom's safety."

"But I thought if I had to marry a prince at least I could choose which one. Zayne and I didn't get the slightest bit along!" I protest while I grab the material of my dress tightly to release the tension in my hands and keep the anger inside me hidden tightly between locked doors.

But the movement in his face struck deep horror inside me.

"You are talking about Zayne. . .don't you?" The question escapes me quietly. I never prayed in my life, was never the religious kind, even though the gods were sacred in our kingdom.

But if there is a perfect moment to convince me of godly power it would be now.

Because the flicker in my father's eyes is concerning and I am sure I would wish to marry Zayne just to escape his words.

"Zayne might be the first in line for the Moreau throne but he abdicated the throne a long time ago. Which means the contract falls to the next in line."

"That doesn't mean I can't marry him, he would still be a great ally." My voice sounds desperate.

My father's eyes narrow into slits and I know it's my downfall. Why take a royal prince when you can have the regent prince? The soon-to-be king.

"Zayne wouldn't do fit form the age gap as well and it came to my ears that Cassian would be delighted to ally with our kingdom."

I groan at his words and let my head fall back.

Tears prickle my eyes as the painted ceiling blurs in front of them.

Please don´t let this be real. Please, please, please.

"Prince Cassian and I can´t stand each other, gods."

"You haven't seen him for years, Katarina. Cassian became a handsome young man, respected by his people, he is an excellent warrior." My father uses his diplomatic voice but he's not going to win this argument. Not in a thousand years am I going to marry that boy that is closer to the devil's spawn than any other human being. If he is even human.

"Do you think I care if he can kill people easily? He was always cruel and completely egoistic. On my sixth birthday, he was so bored that he blew out the candles of my birthday cake and dunked me face-first into it.

When he was over with Zayne one time they made sure to find all my dolls and burn them in front of my eyes just so they could see me cry.

He was the one who sabotaged my arrows at the yule party when I was twelve!" I talk myself into such a rage that I have to stand up, making my father follow my movements as well.

"That was childish nonsense back then, Katarina. He has grown as much as you have and he is a respectful man, he will be a great addition."

"He will not be a great fucking addition because I won´t marry him."

The king takes a step forward, crossing his hands on his back.

"Is that so? And who are you to decide?"

"I am the one who has to endure that bastard!"

"Carina." My father scolds my language and I take a short breath to calm down.

"What is it that he has that you need?"

His sapphire eyes flicker at my question. I hit the nail on the fucking head.

"This is just to your liking. It isn't about me or my well-being. It's just your wish, your greed, for more power.

Instead of working with what we are good at and helping solve problems of the people in the capital, you want someone threatening at my side so they will stop complaining and shut up!" I start to yell angrily when he turns his cold eyes on me. The same eyes that look at me every day through the mirror.

I fist my hands at my sides, my nails digging small crescent patterns into the delicate skin.

He wants someone that can keep me under control like some stupid girl.

He could've chosen anyone and technically he did choose Zayne.

Why did that asshole need to abdicate?

I'm sure he never did it for his reasons but just to torture me even more.

That is what the Moreau brothers always did, bathe in my misery.

"I don't expect you to understand, Katarina, you were never able to see it from the right point of view. Power is what brings the kingdom its safety and a safe kingdom is equal to your safety. He will be strong enough to protect you and I don't need to worry—"

"I can protect myself!"

Oh, how I wish he knew how much I can protect myself. That these clean, pale hands can kill any evil man on this continent.

I even defeated this disgusting bastard of a prince on the roof last night.

"I swear, I—"

"ENOUGH!"

His voice booms through his chamber as his palms collide with the table, making the glasses on it clink. I flinch and straighten up, my chest heaving with every breath I take.

"You are going to marry Prince Cassian if you want it or not." His voice is quiet again, steady. The thunderstorm left as fast as it came.

"Are you ordering me as my father or as the king?" I ask him, my eyes stinging with unshed tears as I clench and unclench my hands. He can't expect me to go along with this. He just can't.

His face softens at my words and for a second he closes his eyes and pinches his nose between his fingers. A humane gesture I never expect from him.

"I know you can't see it right now, but it's for the best." He says softly but I don't even care what he says, nothing will get rid of the deep betrayal I feel. My father is selling me off like an object to a boy I despise.

Unless. . .

"You said the deal was about me getting engaged with Cassian if I wouldn't be engaged already by eighteen. I still have over a month until then." I offer while I take a few steps toward my father. His brows arch in interest and I know that if I do this right I can wind myself out of chaos. A sliver of attention from the king is the only thing I need. And I know he will bite, I lived with this man my whole life and when the interest sparks in the sapphire eyes, I know I have him.

"I'm listening."

3

"Careful princess!"

"Sorry!"

The thrown apology travels with the gush of wind that I leave behind me, almost knocking into a maid. The enormous tray in her hand tips for a moment before she regains her balance.

Trying to run in a floor-length gown is harder than it looks. But I'm sure to catch the deliverer before he leaves to send the afternoon letters.

I carefully wrote three letters after I left the chambers of my father addressing every living regent in Adalon.

I addressed the prince in Oceanus, inviting him to settle in our castle for over a month before joining my birthday party. I made sure to underline how much of an honor it would be if he joined and let me be his host for the upcoming weeks. I never met Marrus personally but I heard he was a lively person and I wonder why my father never kept in contact with the King and Queen of Oceanus.

The almost identical letter to the prince in Polyxena is gripped in my other hand and I know for sure that they are not going to decline.

Both kingdoms have been left with much smaller lands and they will be interested in a marriage with a strong kingdom like Aerwyna's. Even though Prince Hector of Polyxena is technically king of his lands due to his father's passing, I know he will be at least interested to visit my court.

Officially his title is still the one of a prince because somehow the coronation of his is being dragged on.

But he is the one currently ruling over Polyxena, his mother, the former queen, helping him with the tasks and duties.

I rush around the next corner and down the various stairs so I can get to the post office of Mr. Rubain. These damn heels are the only obstacle from making me sprint down the steps and it's not the first time I wish for my trusty boots which I wear at night.

I'm hoping to Adales that Mr. Rubain is still here not because of the letters to the prince of Oceanus and Polyxena but because of the last letter.

It differs from the other two and I didn't let anyone read over it.

Anyone who'd put their eyes on the rude words would scold me for my foul tongue. But the receiver doesn't deserve any politeness.

If it were up to me I wouldn't even send the third letter. I'm perfectly fine with sharing my time with Hector and Marrus if it wasn't for my father.

One condition of the king is that as long as Cassian is invited to our palace, the two other men can come as well. So even though I have no intention of marrying Cassian I had to write this stupid letter.

Doesn't mean the words have to be particularly nice to him.

We must invite him because he has a right to get to know me, to fight for my interest which to me sounds ridiculous.

They have no right over me; I am the one who is going to decide in the end and no one else. But if he has the desire to make a fool of himself I will enjoy the show.

I can't imagine the other two princes being equal to me, from what I know we never really shared the same interests. But a girl must do what she has to in other to escape marriage with the literal devil.

Because of my latest night adventure, I needed to alter his letter from the other two.

I want to talk to him in person before he travels straight to the court and I'm sure he's still staying in Aerwyna for an unknown reason to me.

That's why I don't just owe him answers but he owes me some too. For example how long he has been residing in Aerwyna and why he didn't tell my father he saw me last night.

It would be much to his advantage to reveal my forbidden adventures and the fact that there is nothing but silence keeps me on edge.

I don't want to be in anyone's debt, especially not Cassian Moreau's.

When the post office comes into view I see that the lights are still on. A small sigh leaves my lips before I slow down. I'm sure I've walked myself through a few blisters on my way here.

I addressed the letter for Cassian to his captain of the guard because I have no idea how else to reach him and I hope that the time I gave him to meet me is enough.

Uneasiness spreads along my skin while I wonder what he is doing here. I can't help myself and imagine worst-case scenarios.

"Mr. Rubain?" I ask the second I knock softly against the wood his office door ajar and spot the older man sitting at his desk, sifting through papers.

He looks up at my voice and quickly stands up, curtsying.

"Your Highness, what can I help you with?"

"I already told you to call me Katarina," I tell him with a small grin while I motion for him to sit back down.

"And I told you to call me Arow." He says with a smile, making me grin again.

"Yes you did, I'm sorry, Arow. Are you busy right now?"

"Not busy enough for you, Your Highness."

I ignore the title and put the letters down in front of him, the claws on the seal of Aerwyna shine in the last sunrays of the day.

"I wanted to add these three letters to the daily mail and make a small request about this one." I motion for Cassian´s letter, amber eyes looking at me intently.

"It's of a serious matter and if possible I would like the addressee to receive it tonight. Do you think you could manage that?"

"Of course, I will send my fastest rider for you and Prince Cassian will receive this letter tonight." He says seriously and I can see in his eyes that he is curious.

It is none of his business and even though Arow is one of the few people I like in this castle, I don't know if he can keep his mouth shut. The maids and soldiers are the biggest gossips some could imagine. There is no secret safe from their ears and it is bad I´m prioritizing Cassian´s letter over the other two.

It's bad enough that the people think that I can't rule alone even worse if they know I send letters to the prince to who I have been promised.

It is called improper as a princess to contact any man without letting my advisor read over the words as if I would be poisoned by it.

"Very well, I take you by your word," I tell him and smile.

"Are there any other deliveries I could help with?" He offers and I shake my head politely.

"That would be all, thank you, Arow."

He curtseys and I make my way to leave but stop at the entrance.

"I need that letter to reach the prince tonight."

I press again and he gives me a serious nod.

"There is no need to worry, Your Highness, it is in the best hands."

My eyes drop to his hands for a moment and I arch one brow before nodding.

"Have a nice evening, Arow."

"You too, Your Highness."

I don't stop again and leave his office to rush up the steps. I need to talk to Edlyn as fast as possible and inform her about my plans.

"Prince Henri! You need to be careful!"

A voice makes my steps halter and I close my eyes, sighing before I turn around. I know that voice all too well, knowing I won't get any peace if I don't tend to it.

Seems like I won't be able to talk to Edlyn until getting into bed tonight.

I focus on the way that leads into the Royal Gardens to catch sight of maid Agnes running after what seems to be my escaping brother.

The maid's face is flushed in anger, her brows drawn close as she tries, emphasis on tries, to catch the prince.

His dark, long hair is flying in the wind just like his robes that shine in a deep red color. I know if I could see his face I'd notice the mischievous look on him as he again tricked his maid into racing him through the castle grounds.

This boy is nothing but trouble.

I could just ignore this and rush to my chambers so I can talk to Edlyn but the screech of maid Agnes makes me rush down the steps again, almost stumbling over the hem of this dress—which I'll make sure to never wear again after today.

Skipping down the path of cobblestones I ignore the beautifully made rose hedges for once, to see Agnes' blue dress disappear into the path of the maze. I can't help the un-lady-like groan from escaping me. She will not be able to find him once he's deep enough, I don't know why she even bothers to try.

With my light steps she doesn't hear me once I appear beside her and make her jump in the air.

"Oh by the holy ghost of Adales, I didn't hear you, Your Highness." She says while she doesn't stop running beside me and I smile.

Sweat is already dripping down her forehead, even though she should be accustomed to these kinds of situations. Poor lady.

"Seems like you have a little problem, Agnes, why don't you wait here and I'll get my brother," I ask her not the slightest bit out of breath and once she nods gratefully I run through the hedges leaving her behind me.

"Every single time. . ." Her mumbled words disappear with the sound of rushing air in my ears.

My steps are so quiet that I don't hear them myself, as I listen to the laughter of my brother.

I pick up my speed holding the skirts of this damn dress and rush around the corner to see a flash of bright red disappear again. This little idiot is fast.

I don't even bother to call his name because I know he's not going to stop and instead of rushing behind him I take a shortcut no one knows about.

Jumping over a miniature wall and through a small puddle of water, I cringe, well that gives me an excuse to get rid of this dress later.

I finally step into the major path again stopping my run.

The shortcut gave me a few seconds to gain my breath.

I wait, crossing my arms in front of my chest because I know he's going to run past here and it doesn't take long before I hear his untrained steps a few hedges away from me.

If I were a predator Henri would be dead by now.

His steps are too loud and heavy and he has a slight drag in them. Something must be stuck to the underside of one shoe because you can hear it collide with the stones every time they meet.

Henri flashes into view and I put out a leg, making him stumble right over it and I hear his gasp of surprise. Before his face can collide with the ground I grab his elbow and hold him up.

Once he realizes he's not kissing the floor his eyes open again and fury moves through them.

I let go of his arm as he furrows his brows and his green, intelligent eyes move to me.

Eyes so different from mine and yet they are the most familiar color I know.

"What the hell was that for?" He snaps and I roll my eyes before I turn my back and start to make my way through the maze again.

When I don't hear his steps I freeze and speak up again.

"Follow me, Henri, now." There is no place for discussion in my tone. He still doesn't move and I raise my voice slightly.

"Now."

I hear him grumble something but he finally follows me and steps up beside me.

His form towers over me even though he's barely fifteen years old and still, I could knock him off his feet without him even realizing it. "You're taking away all my fun."

"I am not. I'm looking after you and running around the garden aren´t tasks a prince should go after."

"You sound like dad." He says stubbornly and I move my face towards him, my lips in a straight line.

That´s the worst thing someone could say to me but I know he´s not being serious.

He raises a brow and I nudge his shoulder lightly, making him grin.

Henri inherited the charm of my father and the looks of my mother. His green eyes are light and playful, reflecting his creative soul.

His chestnut hair tangles always in chaos, no matter how much Agnes tries to tame it. I´m happy that she can´t because I like how it flies in the wind, reflecting his refusal of being caged. His figure is tall and lanky, making him look like the young boy he is but I know if he would put some effort into it, Henri would have the tactic brain to be a great soldier.

"I know it can be hard, believe me, I do. But you need to listen to Agnes, be cooperative and things will be easier."

"I listened to Professor Bernath talks about the history of Adalon for several hours. My brain feels fried and I can't do it anymore. It´s not like I don´t know the story but all of these people are dead, they can´t help me in life anymore." He whines while we walk out of the maze, Agnes watching us from the palace.

Her face is a mask of utter fury and Henri grimaces when he notices her.

"But it is our history; I had to go through these lessons as well."

To be honest I didn't listen much to my teachers just like him but if I tell my brother that, he will just feel validated in his decision.

"Yes but you are going to govern Aerwyna in a few years. That means you have to know that, but I don't. I want to travel, to see the continents past Adalon, I've been here for long enough."

His voice is so desperate that I stop walking to look up at him.

It's almost ironic that Henri wants to leave and travel and if he were a girl they would let him because they wouldn't see him as someone to govern as a second-born girl.

And if I would be a boy they would let me govern now without a husband or in that case wife.

The sad truth is they are keeping Henri here in case I fail. In case I don't marry strategically and that's the only reason for me to go along with this plan.

If I do marry and govern alongside my husband, Henri will be able to go. At least one of us can be happy then. I want him to see every place he yearns to go to and the sooner I marry, the sooner he gets to do that.

"You need to be patient okay? I promise you will see every place you want to. Until then you need to at least try to go after the rules." I tell him seriously. The only answer I get is the sagging of his shoulders.

"I already heard about it." He says and I furrow my brows at the sudden change of topic.

"What do you mean?"

"That you're inviting the princes. And I find it highly ridiculous that father thinks you couldn't rule by yourself. I'm sorry for the poor man who has to marry a stubborn girl like you." He says and I hit his arm lightly.

"Hey!" I protest making him smile shortly before it drops again.

"You don't need to marry to govern, Carina. If you want help we're going to convince him to let you rule alone." He presses, the fire of determination burning in his young eyes again.

"It's not just him Henri, it's the whole kingdom, it's all of the kingdoms. They're not going to accept me if I'll govern alone. Sooner or later I'd have to choose a husband."

"Well, then it should be later. You are seventeen." He presses, panic tainting his jade eyes.

"Mom was sixteen when she married our father," I tell him with a small smile and he sighs.

"That´s different."

His voice is small, unsure.

"How would that be different?"

I know it is. Our parents loved each other. But love is a luxury in our world; it is the exception to the rule.

"It´s just a load of bullshit. I couldn't imagine a better queen than you. You're stronger and smarter than any of the guards. You can sneak in and out any time you want and no one notices. You don´t need a man to rule."

At his words, I take a surprised step back.

"Why do you think I can sneak out?" I ask him suspiciously. His eyes widen for a moment, caught in his mistake. My brother shoots me a sheepish smile as he scratches his neck.

"Edlyn told me."

"What?" I gasp making him hold up his hands.

"It's not her fault! I turned up at your chambers one night and wouldn't let it go. Please don't be angry with her. And stop changing the topic. I don't want the princes here and neither should you. Make up a fight and convince father, I know you can because if anyone can it's you." He tells me and I cross my arms in front of me, narrowing my eyes lightly.

How could Edlyn tell my little brother that I can sneak out at night if I want to? It´s not that I don´t trust him but he´s not old enough to understand why I´m doing it and I don´t want him to think that I can leave and he can´t.

It wouldn´t be fair to him.

"Hey back to your lessons, Henri." Maid Agnes calls angrily from afar, her cheeks red and puffed up.

Henri ignores her.

"The Carina I know wouldn't go down without a fight."

"Don't you think I tried?" I arch a brow and he offers me a grin.

"If you have tried you wouldn't marry, Carina."

My brother tells me before he jogs over to Agnes.

I clench my jaw at his words knowing that he's right. I won't go down without a fight, I never did, never will.

That's why I need to get to Edlyn now.

4

"You were pretty busy this afternoon."

"I needed to organize a few things and met Olah for the upcoming banquet in a week," I tell my friend while I watch her sort through various herbs and liquids. Olah is the head of the maids and needed me to figure out the food options and glass and cutlery designs as if that would be of importance. It´s just another show of my father to make sure everyone knows how much he possesses. Who has the biggest jewels in the whole Aerwyna, Daragon Sebestyen.

Instead of staying in the castle and talking to Edlyn, I offered her to go into town to her favorite shop, filled with various herbs and potions.

Edlyn is talented in the healing department and the knowledge of venoms.

She taught me everything she knows and supplies me whenever I go on my killing sprees with things I need. It is handy to know how to kill an enemy, without being suspected or to torture with certain herbs that are venomous but not deadly enough to kill someone.

"I was surprised when I heard about your plans and I couldn't stop wondering what the hell you're doing, Carina." My friend looks up from the vials using the nickname only my close ones use. Her brown eyes place themselves on my face, raising a perfect brow of hers.

I didn't have the time to completely tell her everything and I don't know if now is the right time as well but it´s the only time we're not surrounded by the enormous walls of the castle.

Well almost.

I look at the two guards following us close behind and with a nod, I tell them to stop trailing us before I grab Edlyn's wrist and pull her into the back of the shop. My head is already turning dizzy with the different scents and I wonder how my best friend can stand to be in here so often.

When I feel like we've put enough distance between the few customers and the guards, I stop. Edlyn's eyes meet mine with a curious glance. After another small glance around the place, I lower my voice as much as I can.

Better safe than sorry.

"When I went out to talk to Ellister last night I met someone."

"I knew it! You acted so weirdly this morning—" I put my hand over her mouth my eyes wide in panic but when I look back at the guards I see them standing at the entrance waiting for us. No sign that they heard her.

"Why don't you yell louder so the whole kingdom can hear you?" I ask her and she mumbles an apology against my hand.

I let go of her mouth and start to talk again.

"I was finished with talking to Ellister and on my way back to the palace I caught a man spying on another. I didn't think much of it but I was curious so I followed him. Turns out I kind of lost him and the next second he's on the roof behind me." Her attention is focused on me and at my last words, her mouth drops open. "What do you mean he was suddenly behind you? How could you not hear him?"

"He was—dare I say—good at what he was doing. We fought and I admit it was hard, he was an equal opponent but at last, I got him pinned to the roof my dagger against his throat."

"That sounds kind of hot." She interrupts me again and I furrow my brows at her comment. It was likely for her to romanticize a situation like that. Still, I feel the tingling sensation low in my stomach when I think back. Familiarity sparks when I think of my opponent and his stupid green eyes but I quickly shake my head, focusing.

"If you mean fighting for your life is hot you need to see a healer, Edlyn," I tell her with a serious look, making her grin. "I mean this is a big deal! The first opponent who is equal to you. He managed to surprise you that is kind of hot. But that's not important right now, go on." She ushers me on and I sigh before I speak up. It seems like my friend isn´t grasping the seriousness of the situation. "Well, I got rid of his cloth and realized who I was fighting against."

"Who? Who was it?" She asks and I have to chuckle lightly at her investment.

"Cassian Moreau," I tell her, making her mouth close and her brows furrow. She almost looks disappointed at the name I give her.

"Cassian Moreau? You mean. . ."

"Cassian asshole Moreau."

I´m pretty sure that´s not his middle name but I´m not one for sentiments. Edlyn curses badly and my brows raise at the words.

"The Prince of Demeter was the equal fighter? How disappointing." She tells me and I nod telling her I think the same.

"But I believe that it was just him catching me off guard. I had different things on my mind." She raises a brow at my words a thoughtful look on her face.

"Why would he even be in Aerwyna?"

"Great question. That´s what I should´ve asked him." I tell her with a frown.

She starts to walk through the back and I follow her while she picks up a few vials, eyeing the liquid inside.

"Well, did you? What did he say or do after he realized it was you? What did you do?" The questions slip past her lips in a rush her cheeks flushed in panic.

"I ran," I say sheepishly biting my lip in shame.

She shoots me a surprised look before a small chuckle bubbles out of her. "That's surprising."

"I panicked; I didn't know what to say, I was completely caught off guard by his presence. But it seems like he didn't tell anyone or my dad would've—"

"Locked you away in your rooms forever?" She offers and I nod exhaling lightly. It feels good to talk to someone about it. I didn´t realize how on edge I am with all these events happening. That´s why she is my best friend. It doesn´t take long to explain things because she finishes the thought process herself.

"It´s kind of weird. It seems like no one knows that he's in the kingdom besides you and when you say his face was hidden behind a cloth, it means he didn´t want to be identified."

"That's what I'm curious about as well. And that's why I send his general a letter and hope to meet him in two days so I can make sure my secret stays a secret. But that's just the tip of the iceberg, Edlyn, believe me." I tell her making her eyes widen.

I shoot another look at my guards who don't look the slightest bit bored or impatient and decide to tell her the worst part as well.

"My father told me this morning that I was promised to marry Prince Cassian if I won´t be engaged before my eighteenth birthday."

The next vial she grabs slips out of her hand when the shock reaches her and I quickly catch it making her blink.

I let the part out where I originally was promised to the older brother, it seems like the former information is enough to shake her.

"Oh shit." She curses again and I nod before I hand over the unbroken vial.

"Wait, that's why you invited Prince Hector and Prince Marrus to court? You think you want to be the wife of one of these men?" She asks me skeptically and I shake my head.

"Gods no, I'm not stupid. But if I invite them I can make sure that Cassian´s father sweats a bit and isn't so sure of his decision. I can't believe they think I would let myself be married off to a stupid boy who can't govern or expand his kingdom."

"But they're never going to let you rule alone." She tells me and I nod.

I'm still thinking about that part and I'm going to figure something out. Whatever it takes I'm not marrying anyone. I need to make sure I seem responsible and maybe, maybe if I make these princes look all like incapable losers they will listen to me and give me a chance.

"Let that be my problem. First, I need to meet my dear old childhood friend and make sure no one knows of my secret."

"This is a really dangerous game you're playing, Carina." She tells me, her voice a warning as we walk to the register.

She is right it is a dangerous game. I won´t be that stupid to underestimate my enemy. But there is no chance for me to win any kind of freedom if I don´t fight. Whatever it takes I will make sure that I won´t go down quietly.

I watch her pay for everything she picked up and think about her words.

I know what my role is in life and I was prepared for it for seventeen years.

I am not saying I won´t ever marry but if the gods somehow think it is funny to marry me off to Cassian they are delusional.

How high this fire might be I won´t let it scare me off with a cocky grin and glinting eyes. If it means I have to get my hands dirty to survive this I will do it. It wouldn´t be the first time anyway.

5

"Another one."

The bartender eyes my masked face for a second too long and I slam three gold coins onto the bar so he'll give me another drink.

One quarter for the drink, the other two for not asking any questions. A woman shouldn't be in a dirty bar like this, lingering around on stools that are stained with questioning liquids and men with wandering eyes, like waiting wolfs.

My face is hidden behind the same mask I wear every night when I'm out, the hood of my cloak pulled over my head securely. I'm not out today with a task of the Red Saint but my clothes give me some kind of confidence, it's like a veil I put on that gifts me to turn into a different person. It makes certain situations and tasks easier, and more bearable.

I couldn't stop myself and visit Ellister on the way here and was met with an empty house which made me smile satisfied. There is no trace left, the furniture covered in white sheets like there was never a family living in the house.

He packed his bags and left just like I told him and he left a note for me with two words.

Blood moon.

My plan works flawlessly, the stranger believed Ellister.

The blood moon is at the end of this month, which gives me about two and a half weeks to find out more about this and the Dark Prince. Whatever his plans might be I won't let him destroy my kingdom, not as long as I live. If there is a sliver of possibility that my father knows of this and isn't doing anything about it, I feel even more protective over the people here.

I can't imagine him overlooking something important like this while he's the one who's always talking about a safe kingdom, feared by any enemy.

The bartender slaps another glass in front of me and I nod as thanks before I motion for him to come closer.

He leans forward suspiciously and I move my red-painted lips into a soft smile.

I bat my eyes for a moment, playing the unsuspecting woman.

"I was wondering if I was at the right place to get some answers to questions?" My voice is soft like velvet.

The gruff bartender moves his eyes around before focusing them back on me.

"Where did you hear this from?"

"That's not important. What do I need to do to get my questions answered?"

"You don't have enough money for that." He tells me rudely, crossing his arms in front of his chest.

It makes his arms bulge and I almost laugh out loud at his trying to intimidate me but I keep quiet. If he knew I could slit his throat without him even noticing, I wouldn't get any questions answered.

So instead I tilt my head and try to look as stupid as I can so he doesn't view me as a threat.

"You might wonder how much money I have. Tell me your price." I say and he wavers for a second. Ponding, if I'm telling the truth because there are just two types of women who come into this bar.

Women who search for prey and women who are lost and out of their minds.

Tonight I want to be viewed as the hunter and that's why I choose a tight-fitted silk dress, dancing around my body and accentuating every favor of my female curves.

"A dozen of gold coins." He says almost daringly and my smile widens as I pull out a small sack of gold and put it on the counter between us.

His tiny eyes widen for a second before he moves his hand to grab it but before he can, I ram a knife into the expensive wood right between his fingers and the sack. Okay maybe I didn't need to do that but everyone wants to show off once in a while. The small flinch that I notice is satisfaction enough.

"First my answers, then you can have it," I say, making his widened eyes flicker to my face.

"Who are you?"

"I believe I am asking the questions, no?"

He grumbles some incoherent words before he finally nods. He inches his fingers into the distance from my knife and I have to smile mentally at the move.

"What do you know about Ellister Gerard? Has he ever visited this place?"

His pupils dilate in recognition of the name.

"I heard of a rumor. A man coming here often, he was dressed in the most expensive materials, hiding an arsenal of weapons beneath it. Ellister met up with him a few times, poor guy looked like he was trembling just talking to that man."

"Do you know the name of that man?" I press but he shakes his head.

"He pays me far more than you do to keep my mouth shut."
I furrow my brows while I go and grab for another sack but
his hand wraps around my wrist, stopping me. My eyes drop
to his dirty fingers around my skin and I arch a brow. The
hold immediately slackens.

"A lady like you shouldn't ask these questions. They're
better left untouched or else you will come into contact with
death and I don't think that's what you want." He whispers
while his grip tightens for another second as if to underline
his words. If he knew how often I came in contact with death
already, it would make his skin crawl.

It's weird to see men like him be so afraid of the Dark
Prince. It's like a warning I keep in mind, I should be
worried some of his men are wandering around the town.

"But why is he here? What wants the Dark Prince with an
army of killers?" I hiss back making his little eyes widen
again.

"Don't speak his name, don't even think about him. He is
one of the most dangerous men I know and the second he
knows of your existence, you're going to be dead." He
finishes his words and finally, lets go of my wrist and I
furrow my brows because it seems like I am as clueless as
before.

"He's just a fucking myth. Who knows if this man even
exists?" I ask my voice higher than I intend it to be.

"A rumor always has a spark of truth in it. Now leave and
don't ever come back. I am not going to be responsible for an
innocent death and I won't go against him. Not in a lifetime.
Take your money with you." He nudges the sack but I shake
my head and get up from the barstool.

What a total shit show.

"Keep it. Maybe it will soothe your ridiculous paranoia."

I step through the bar and into the night sky of the capital.

The stench of liquor and sweat finally leaves my nostrils while I curse these men for being so afraid of a myth.

The moon greets me high up in the starless sky, mocking me and my intentions. As if someone would tell a woman of things that are as old as the legends of the four siblings. Some people say it was him who killed Aerwyn and even though I mostly don't believe in stories like that I can't shake off the thought of it.

Still what a pack of pathetic, superstitious idiots.

If they're not corruptible how the hell am I supposed to unravel this? The blood moon is two too close and I want to come prepared for it.

Not let myself fall blindly into what could be a trap—no what will be a trap. If these grown men are scared what could this person do? Or be to make them this scared?

I need to figure this out later because I have something far more important set on my agenda tonight.

I scan the street in front of me which is mostly empty and decide to go by foot; it's not a long way from the bar.

I strip off my hood to let the wind hit my masked face gently, my hair pulled back in a braid that Edlyn did for me.

She packed me up with new vials and herbs, even though I told her that tonight I wouldn't need any healing ointments or venom. At that she let her brows wiggle lightly, a smug smile on her face, which I ignored completely because I have to focus tonight.

Tonight was an inspection tour and a meet-up with my past.

My stomach is twisting uncomfortably when I think about Cassian and the fact that I'm going to see him in minutes.

I have my words planned out neatly and organized, I made sure to talk with Edlyn to come up with a plan so I could get answers from him. Most important is that I am not the one talking, especially not about my whereabouts at night. Whatever made him stop telling my father about our run-in, it has to be something calculating or cruel. That's how his mind works. Cassian doesn't do anything if it's not somehow playing into his cards.

As ridiculous as it sounds, if you don't prepare for meeting the Prince of Demeter, you will spill more secrets than you intend to.

I turn around the corner greeted by a small group of women, the same from the night, dressed in suggestive clothes.

My eyes fly over their tightly laced corsets and for a second my eyes fly upwards to their cleavage making my cheeks burn up when I meet the gaze of a woman. Her eyes are surrounded with dark coal, complementing the ice blue of her gaze. Her lashes are long and seductive, her lips plump and luscious. It's like the gods created her to be a weapon, to fool with any man's or woman's mind.

Her penetrating gaze doesn't leave mine and I finally get uncomfortable enough, diverting my eyes from her. I pick up my speed and ignore the suspicious looks from the women and when I round the corner and get out of their sight I let out a big breath.

"Gods, I'm ridiculous."

"Why? Because you can hold a dagger to my throat with no remorse but are scared of courtesans?"

I whirl around at the voice, a knife already in my hand, ready to fight. A dark figure steps out of the shadows, the lean body moving slowly as if the shadows are clinging to it. Embracing every step he takes. I don't have to look up to know who sneaked up on me but I know eventually I have to. So I brace myself and lift my eyes to meet my opponent for tonight.

~ 6 ~

"Fuck. Would you stop scaring me, I almost cut your face off."

"You're exaggerating." He shoots back in a bored voice and I put my knife back into the holster, while my eyes fly over this familiar and yet so unfamiliar face.
For a moment I´m frozen watching the man in front of me.
The round, boyish cheeks of the younger prince are long gone and replaced by high cheekbones that contribute to the hard look on his face.
Once his hair was in a light hazel color but it gradually turned into dark curls that spring around his face playfully. His lips are reddened and sinful making my eyes flicker quickly to the only thing that stayed the same.
The clever green eyes are still filled with playfulness. They always looked like they hold a big secret that could change your world in a second. Turn it upside down.
They´re framed with lashes as dark as his hair and for a moment it seems like the green softens a bit.
I take a step back so I don't have to crane my neck so much because he's grown to be taller than me. And not just a few inches, he's towering over my form with a few heads, which I didn't even notice that much when I fought against him two days ago.
Still, I remember the hard muscles my fist met and saw how fast he could move no matter his height. He is lean and agile like some kind of panther. Dark like the shadows, blending in and lurking in them. It is almost entrancing and for a moment I feel respect for his skills. Just for a moment though.

"Finished with your ogling?" His voice makes me look back up at his face, where a smug smile sits on those damn lips.

"I wasn't ogling you, don't flatter yourself," I say while I watch him take a few steps towards me, brushing his hood off in the process.

He's in the same clothing he was that night. Curiosity about what he's doing here sparks, wondering what his business might be, dressed like a thief. If people knew that the Prince of Demeter was running around the streets of the capital, unprotected, he would be in a lot of trouble. He is fast and a good fighter but can he fight off a whole group of men at once and alone?

He's still walking toward me and when he stops right in front of me I have to tilt my head lightly to keep looking into his eyes. Green as vibrant as expensive emeralds that lay in the treasury of my father.

"Ogle as much as you want, princess, it is my pleasure." He says quietly before he raises his hands and grabs the edges of my mask.

My body freezes at his touch ready for any form of attack but to my surprise, he just gets the mask off and takes a step back looking at me.

His gaze is apprehending, flickering over my face for a moment. It's like his eyes are soaking into my exposed skin, caressing every curve and every line.

I need a second to reorganize my thoughts and decide to look down at his chest which is covered in black, expensive fabric.

"You wanted to talk to me? Now talk." He tells me and I exhale quietly before I look back into his face.

The cruelty is burned into every cell of his being and I'm sure he didn't change since he was younger and at our court. This means I need to be careful with what I say.

"I'm sure you heard about the news, now that the letters have been sent out."

I speak the first thing that comes into my mind.

"You mean the fact that you're inviting those idiots to your court?" He says his voice hard and I nod before I raise my chin a bit. I don't like the tone he's speaking in. He´s already got an advantage with his height but I won´t be the slightest bit threatened by it.

I could take him out with a blink of an eye.

"You're invited to come as well and I wanted to tell you in person because it seems like last time I was too caught off guard to think."

"When you ran away you mean?" He says with a smug smile that awakens the wish in me to deck him in the face.

"When I left, yes. I'm grateful that you didn't tell anyone—"

"Yet." He interrupts me again and I let out a low snarl.

His smile widens even more and I take a step forward my hands clenching into fists. A stupid small dimple appears on his left cheek.

He notices my rage and looks even more satisfied. That sick bastard.

"Would you listen to me for a moment without interrupting me?" I ask raising a brow and he motions for me to go on.

"What I'm doing at night is none of your business but I'm willing to do you a favor for your secrecy."

"'What you´re doing at night?' I would love for you to specify that, princess. Even better if I could join your nightly activities."

I clench my teeth with my next answer.

"I wouldn´t think you´d be interested in these activities."

He arches a black brow.

"How would you know? I would find it highly interesting to get a look into your world."

"Sorry to disappoint you, prince, but as you said it is my world. So tell me what you want to keep your mouth shut."

I don´t bother to cover my rudeness.

He frowns lightly as he takes a step forward.

"I must say I´m disappointed in our reunion, I would´ve hoped for you to be a little more enthusiastic about seeing me again. After all this time."

"I forgot the welcome back flowers at the castle."

He grins at my answer and I narrow my eyes.

"If you´re this delusional to think I would jump into your arms the second I see you again, you need to see a healer. Now get to the fucking point." His green eyes glow in amusement at my words.

"You want to bribe me so I keep your little adventures a secret. What would your father say if he knew about it?"

I am going to choke him. I swear I am.

"Listen you little shit, I don't care if you're a prince or if our parents have a stupid deal to make us marry, it's either me bribing you or killing you. Believe me, I won't hesitate with the second option." I hiss at him and he starts to chuckle.

"Princess, even if you would want to, you couldn't kill me."
His tone is so arrogant that it makes me clench my teeth,
fighting to keep a cool head.

"I think two nights ago proves you're wrong. I beat you." I
tell him with a smug smile and his face hardens visibly.

"You caught me off guard, that's not going to happen a
second time."

"Bullshit." I shoot back while we both take a step forward
not backing down.

We stare at each other for what feels like an eternity while
the fire continues in our eyes, ready to win once the other
looks away.

Finally, he sighs and his eyes flicker down to my lips for a
moment before green meets my eyes again.

"You are lucky I don't have the intention of revealing your
secret. You would be chained up and locked away in a tower
if anyone knew and that's not really in my favor."

"I'm aware of that," I tell him as waves of relief crash
through my body.

He's not going to tell anyone, that's the only thing that
matters. That was easier than I thought.

"And your little idea of inviting the princes is not going to
work. You were promised to me, Carina, and that's final." He
says with a steady voice and to my annoyance, it reminds me
just of my father. Arrogant and full of himself, typical for the
Moreau men. It makes anyone with a sense of mind sick.

I let out a humorless laugh before I take a step forward
jabbing his chest with my index finger.

"If you think I'm going to marry you in this or any other
life you're stupid," I tell him, and instead of him getting

angry, his lips form that crazy smile again. I don't see his move coming when his long fingers wrap around my wrist and pull me closer.

I stumble over my own feet in surprise, my heart stuttering with the movement. The soft scent of honey and morning dew envelops me.

"If you think that you're not going to marry me, you are the fool, princess." He whispers and I furrow my brows.

Is he so greedy for power that he would marry me without a complaint?

I know my hate towards him was always mutual in the past and that the only good thing coming out of this is a bigger kingdom.

I know what an arrogant asshole he is but I never thought he would go this far.

"I still have over a month to get to know Prince Hector and Prince Marrus. Anyone will be better than you are, I'm sure of it."

A grunt escapes his lips as his brows draw together.

"But are they going to ensure safety for your kingdom? The protestant groups are growing every day and you need an army. Strong and cruel soldiers to promise your subjects that they are going to live and be safe."

He's right I do need that but he's not the only one with a strong army.

"You need more than an army to be a great king, Cassian. You never had the gentleness and control to govern a kingdom with love and care. You're not able of any other emotion than anger and hate." I tell him and rip my wrist out of his grip.

My eyes flicker down to the tender flesh of my wrist checking if his scorching touch somehow left marks. It didn´t.

"A kingdom doesn't need a weak king that's seeing stars and hearts everywhere. We two could be perfect together. They would swear their loyalty to us and worship us, Carina." I stiffen when he uses my nickname again, his words a whisper like something he promised himself a long time ago.
I shake my head at his words. He sounds like a satanic man.
"You're wrong. They would fear their king and queen."
He takes a step forward clouding me in his scent.
"What is so bad about that?"

"A leader reflects on their kingdom. What would it make us when we ensure our subjects stay safe but fear us?"
"It makes us leaders with a kingdom that is alive. Do you want to rule over subjects that don´t exist?"
I have to scoff at his words and shake my head slightly.
His eyes search mine for a moment.
"What?"

"You haven´t changed a bit from when we were kids. Power hungry and arrogant enough to think you can do and get whatever you want."
"Is that why you´re putting up that whole show? Because you think I´m arrogant."
My eyes narrow at his small smirk.
" I´m not ´putting on a show.' I don't refuse to ensure the deal because you´re arrogant but because I never want to marry a man I despise." My words bathe in the silence, leaving a small echo.

I watch his eyes darken before they narrow a slight bit. When he takes a step forward I take one back. The playfulness is wiped away from his face in an instant, his ugly character shining through like it always does when he gets angry.

The mask drops and just like I predicted his true inner self is as ugly as his outer appearance is beautiful.

I instantly feel the cold wall in my back and curse myself for not meeting him in a crowded area with witnesses. The look on his face speaks and I don't know if he's angry or disappointed. What I do know is that his proximity makes something flare up, deep inside me and the feeling is so close to hate that I can't decipher what it is. I need to get out of here before he completely loses control.

Because even if I did fight him on that roof and somehow managed to win I won't be foolish enough to repeat it. I'm no one to underestimate my opponent.

"Did you expect me to welcome you with open arms after you tortured me in our childhood?"

He scoffs at my comment.

"I didn't torture you, we were children having jokes."

"Well, I didn't find them funny and I refuse to marry a man who can't own up to his faults. Do you want power that bad?" I take a step closer but he doesn't shift back. His eyes fly over my face, scanning my emotions.

"Do you want to be feared by your subjects so bad that you overlook your hate for me and my hate for you?"

I try to make sense of the forming lines on his face.

Even though he is the same person I was with in my childhood it's hard to read him now because the emotions are flickering so quickly.

It´s like he can´t settle on a certain emotion that is worth his time.

"You don't despise me. You won't if you give me a chance. I can give you more than just a safe kingdom, things you don't even know you want right now," His voice drops, and I swallow hard while I stare up at him. "And who says I still despise you?"

Now it´s my turn to scoff and shake my head.

"I´m not even going to address what you just said."

"Because you´re scared." He breathes out the words in seconds and I meet his eyes again.

"Scared? Of what exactly?"

"Of whatever you felt on that roof two nights ago. I know you felt it."

My voice dies down in my throat but when the smirk appears on his lips again my features harden. He´s doing it again, he´s playing with my head. Cassian is a master at getting into someone else´s head.

If I´d still be as naïve as I was in my childhood I would believe him. But I know better than that.

"I am giving you a chance just like the other two princes," I tell him quietly at his proximity and I hope to the gods that he can´t hear the slight tremble in my voice. Or the thundering of my heart.

I don't know what's happening but his closeness makes my body buzz weirdly.

I try to concentrate, to somehow focus but I can´t stop the images of him moving on that roof that night. Tender and quick. His moves flowed elegantly like he was born to be a predator. Years of training are the only answer to his skills.

I have to blink multiple times to get rid of the feeling while he finally takes a step back. This is Cassian, the stupid, arrogant spoiled kid who always got what he wanted with a snap of his fingers.

He might look like he is carved by the gods of beauty and faith but I´m sure his inner self was created by death and sin.

His jaw clenches as he pulls up his hood again hiding his face in the shadows of it.

"Try to earn your place at the court and maybe we can leave our past behind us." I try to sound generous even though I know it is a lie.

"So you expect me to watch this morons court you while I stand by?" His question is hard, his jaw clenching. I can feel the anger ooze off his body but don´t acknowledge it.

"You can either watch or don´t come at all. I prefer the latter but it is up to your choice." I shrug a shoulder lazily and cheer mentally when I see him narrow his eyes. The hood slips lower on his face and conceals the striking green eyes.

"I won't tell anyone about your secret and you shouldn't forget about the favor you owe me. I'll see you soon, princess." His lips tip into an evil grin before he leaves the alley and disappears into the shadows.

I catch myself staring after him for a few minutes before I shake my head and pull my hood up, scolding myself for all the miserable thoughts and imaginations in my head. He´s not going to tell anyone about this and still I don´t feel the slightest bit relieved because the cruel Prince of Demeter has now a favor I owe him and that can´t be good for anyone.

7

I don´t linger after I pull myself together and make my way through the dark forest that leads out to the lands of the Sebestyen castle. My swirling thoughts are my only company and I wish I had taken my horse with me tonight which would´ve made my journey much faster.

The moon is up high, hiding between a few stray clouds that hinder me from my only source of light. People say you should stay out of the forest and use the common paths towards the court but I don´t want to be seen tonight, even if I´m masked. I need the time to rethink my decision and can´t help myself but wonder over the prince.

Instead of asking him any questions, it feels like I got tricked by him again, distracting me from what I had to do. Ask him why he was in my kingdom. How could he even stay unseen with all the dirty people in the capital who seem to know everything about everyone?

I had to fight hard and learn to keep my identity hidden, choosing the name of the Red Saint on purpose because I know the people. They believe anything once you give them a good story it makes their transparent minds think they would be less scared once they have a name.

As if it would give you some kind of power over the person which it doesn´t.

To my luck the forest stays as quiet as it should, my footsteps soundless and it takes me over half an hour until I see the high peaks up in the sky, dark bricks in neat rows forming a wall around my home.

I take out my two knives and start to ram them into the wall, making my way up without having to fear being noticed. It is so late at night that even the soldiers are dozing off, their eyes drooping lazily as I make my way over the brick wall like a thief in the night.

Instead of worrying about my marriage, my father should make sure to have enough soldiers so the ones we have, could take humanly shifts and secure the walls.

There is a small door at the back of the castle that I once registered during the many walks in the garden which I make my way through, darkness meeting my eyes.

It seems like the whole castle is asleep which makes it very easy for me to take the regular path, I don´t choose often until I use a hidden path through one hall. I think it was once made for maids and deliverers to get to the chambers of the royals. But they´re long forgotten which is perfect for me.

I follow the path and end up in front of a door, making me pull the handle that sits on the left and it opens with a small creak.

Stepping through the threshold I slip right into my chamber without anyone noticing. I don´t bother to dress correctly and just get rid of my clothes. My limbs are aching, sleep sitting tightly in my bones as the weapons clatter and clunk against the hard ground.

I make sure to kick everything under my bed safely, closing the secret pathway that is covered by a bookshelf, and slip under my covers.

I sigh at the cool sensation as the fresh scent of lilacs engulfs me.

The moon is sinking lower and lower in the sky and while I fall asleep I wonder where he might be right now, hiding from curious onlookers, wandering around the kingdom.

~

"Are you excited?"

"Excited, no. Nervous." I say as I watch the rose petals flow around me in the milky white water. For a moment the color blurs and it looks like drops of blood against milky white skin.

Edlyn makes herself comfortable on the tiles of the bath chamber, a book about healing potions hiding her face. Her fingers are dusted with black paint. The coal pencil resides in her hand, occasionally scribbling something down into the pages of her notebook. She didn't put that book down for weeks and I'm wondering if there is still anything she can learn about it. I don't bother to ask because I always end up with a scolding look and her infamous words; There is never enough to learn, Carina.

She always reminds me of my former professor when she does that. The knowing smirk stretching onto her lips always tells me that she is quite aware of that fact.

"I wonder if Prince Hector is as charming as they say. I heard he's just as gentle and lovable as his ancestor Polyxenus was." She says and I furrow my brows before I swim over to the edge, my arms propped up on the rim of the bathtub. The water swirls lightly when I put my cheek on my arms, watching her.

"Those are stupid stories."

"Do you think so? Cassian reminds me in every way of how they talk about Demetrus."

I shake my head at her words because there is an important difference.

"Demetrus had a soft spot, his sister. She could keep him calm and his cruelty was at bay. I don't think Cassian has anything that could make him be a better person."

The irony is, Cassian does have a brother, Prince Zayne— whatever his middle name is—Moreau but instead of keeping him at bay he always edges him on, making him prove he can be as evil as their father.

Zayne is mostly the spark of the fire that Cassian held in their childhood. You could handle one of them but both were unstoppable.

Maybe I was quite lucky that Zayne wasn't interested in the throne, I fear what kind of king he might've been. Even worse what kind of husband he would be.

"What if he would fall in love with you? That would be so romantic, he would try to be better for you." Her voice is dreamy and makes me laugh lightly. Edlyn is the only one naïve enough to make this nightmare I'm in look the slightest bit romantic.

She looks up from the book at me brows furrowed.

"What?"

"Sometimes I wonder if you even hear what you're saying."

"Who knows? You said he hinted he could give you pleasure; I don't think someone just says that if they don't find the other person attractive."

"He doesn't find me attractive, he's just a man like any other and he's trying to get into my head. I'm sure he would never touch me and I would never let him, even if he tried."

We won't take the night on the roof into judging, that was an accident.

"Well, it's working. I think he already is in your head." She says sheepishly and when I shoot her a look she maneuvers her eyes on the letters in the book again. I narrow my eyes.

"What is that supposed to mean?" I ask her suspiciously and she just shrugs her shoulders.

"Tell me." I press when a smile moves on her lips.

"As your princess, I order you to tell me!" I say and splash her with bits of the rose water I'm bathing in.

"Hey! My book is getting wet!"

"So? I'll buy you another one. Tell me why you just said that."

"Because I know you, Carina. You're going to resist and curse him for a few days and eventually, you're going to let him do all the things you secretly dream about."

My mouth drops open offended by every single word of hers. I dream of nothing but killing the prince slowly and painfully. As if I would be as stupid to make up scenarios in my head differing from making him feel anything other than pain!

Never in my life would I desire Cassian Moreau and whatever he would do to me.

I fist my hands under the lukewarm water banning the scenarios that fight to get into my head. I must be completely brain-dead if something like that happens.

"That is so not true!"

I sit up splashing the water angrily.

"Then why are your cheeks turning red?"

"Because I'm so angry, I might strangle you any second."

She chuckles and gets up, placing the book on the turquoise sink.

"Well, if you're not curious I sure am. That's why I talked to a few maids about Cassian and it seems like he is all grown up now. He's rumored to be very popular and he doesn't make a secret out of his liaisons. And it is told that he's damn good in bed." She speaks the last words with a wiggle of her eyebrows and I roll my eyes.

"I don't care about him or what he's doing. I invited the princes to avoid Cassian and make sure I will never marry that idiot."

Her brows arch for a moment as a devious smile moves on her lips. "Are you sure?"

"Of course I am! I loathe that asshole."

She just stares at me with that stupid smile. I feel the need to speak up again, to somehow ensure that she believes me.

"It's bad enough that I offered him a favor for keeping my secret, but I will deal with that when the time comes. Now I need to make sure to make it look like I'm interested in a marriage with Prince Hector or Prince Marrus."

Edlyn puts her hands on her hips leaning her back against the sink.

"I still have no idea how you're going to get out of this."

Well, that makes two of us.

Before I can give her a witty answer a soft knock interrupts us.

"Come in," I call, and a maid dressed in blue gowns steps in, curtsying before I tell her to speak up.

"I'm here to prepare you for the banquet. The princes have arrived and are ready for dinner to greet you." She says and a satisfied grin forms on my lips.

"Perfect."

I stand up from the cold water and let her wrap me up in a towel. When I shoot a look over at Edlyn I see her focus back on her book.

"You can leave and get ready yourself."

"Me?" She says surprised and I nod.

"Of course, I'm not going to do this without you," I tell her with a smile.

My friend smiles right back before she leaves the room, the book clutched tightly in her hands.

She seems weirdly attached to it. I might let my curiosity get the best of me and sneak it out of her hands once she's distracted.

I shake my head and focus on my task.

I chose a dress in the deepest turquoise color that resembles the depths of the ocean limiting against Aerwyna. The material shines which gives the illusion that the dress is moving on its own just like when the sun plays with the waves in the water.

Millions of small little blue topazes are sewn onto the expensive silk, making it sparkle with every turn.

The same stone is attached to my ears and a dainty necklace is placed around my neck when the maid starts to carefully pin up every lock of my dark hair.

It's a long process and I know it would be much easier for me to just cut them off. It surely would make my nightly adventures much more practical but I can't help but hold on to the length.

I remember playing with long, soft hair in my childhood. Braiding the strands back from my mother's face when she allowed me to. Somehow the length gives me comfort, reminding me that I have something of her.

I watch myself in the mirror, the reddened cheeks the maid accentuated, my lashes elongated with the black ink she used. I almost look like the princess everyone wants me to be if it weren't for the stern look that seems to be branded on my face forever.

I try to relax to get rid of the lines but it somehow ends in a weird-looking grimace.

"Did you see them when they arrived?" I speak up to distract myself from the nervous knot forming in my stomach.

I want to leave an impression when I meet the princes. They need to see it is a favor that they can marry me, not a necessity for me.

Woman or man, I am perfectly capable of governing on my own and they should see it.

"I'm sorry, Your Highness, I didn't. But I heard a few maids talking about it; they said the princes were thrilled to be here at the Sebestyen court." She tells me while she offers me a soft smile through the reflection of the mirror.

I return the favor and continue to watch her; she looks like she's not much younger than me, maybe fifteen or sixteen.

Guessing she was born in the palace, due to her family serving the Sebestyen court but I'm not sure.

Many maids are born into the tasks, others are chosen from the capital, willing to come here and serve the royal family. I made sure that those born here could choose between staying and leaving.

I don´t want anyone around me who doesn´t want to be here, I know the feeling of being trapped.

This is why I will make sure that everyone receives their choice. The choice that I never had.

"What's your name?" I ask her which seems to catch her off guard.

"Marianna, Your Highness." She says while she finishes my hair.

My neck is bared for curious eyes now and it makes me feel vulnerable.

Still, it makes my shoulders look elegant, the skin soft and shining light with the sparkly liquid she put on minutes ago.

I get up from the chair, the skirt of the beautiful dress swinging around my legs. The cold blade of the dagger presses against my ankle. The added weight assures me, makes it easier to breathe.

"Thank you, Marianna," I say gratefully as I look at myself in the mirror.

I look like a mystic creature descended from the sea, ready to fight her battles. It feels like that is what I´m about to do, fighting, instead of making nice acquaintances.

"It is my pleasure, Your Highness, you will have the princes right on their knees." She says and my cheeks tint at the weird picture that's forming in front of my eyes but I nod.

That's not exactly my mission but it's close enough.

"I hope so," I say anyway to keep up the facade.

I walk over to the doors of my chamber, my heels clicking against the floor with every step I take. I push my shoulders back and place my hands in front of me, my chin held up high. My lungs feel already crushed by the stupid corset that´s limiting my breathing but it is tradition and the proper way to dress which means I have to endure it for this dinner.

"Do you wish for me to escort you, Your Highness?"

"Thank you, Marianna, but there is no need. You can rest now. I don't need your help tonight after dinner." I tell her with a smile and she nods before she opens the doors for me. I´ll make sure to rip this corset off the second I´m done or I will pass out.

I step out of my chambers and make my way through the cold hall of the palace.

My steps echo against the stone walls and I try to go over everything I planned, keeping my breathing controlled.

The prospect of meeting the other two princes is not what makes my skin itch.

They won't even be a handful to worry about, I'm sure they're going to be friendly. It is more the presence of Cassian that is worrying me. He is inscrutable and I´m not in the mood to practice any damage control.

I´m hoping he will keep himself from strutting around, announcing that he feels not the slightest bit threatened by any male who could catch my interest. It makes my skin sweaty to see him in formal clothes and in a space that is so open, yet there is no way to flee.

I always had the reassuring parts of the shadows in my back, the hood hiding my face partially and it was some sort of comfort to be in the dark.

The streets we met felt more like home to me than the cold walls of this palace ever could.

The proposition of him staying here for a little over a month should be worrying. But technically he doesn´t even need to talk to me because he gets to marry me anyway if I don´t find a suitable partner. There couldn´t be anything he says that makes me marry him and choose him over any other man.

Even if my plan doesn't work to somehow rule on my own, I rather marry any other prince than him.

I will not curse my existence to spend the rest of my already damned life with a person like him.

It is like volunteering to reside in the Abyss for the rest of your life.

The double doors of the dining hall come into view and the guards standing in front of it greet me with a nod while I stop right in front of them.

I take a deep breath which isn't that deep due to the corset that's sitting snugly around my ribs.

Why do I feel so nervous about this?

I can fight against the evilest men, slitting throats, and ripping out hearts but I know I am not good at seducing someone. And I´m even worse at being the elegant, quiet princess my father wants me to be. Nonetheless, I have to try.

"Open the doors."

8

A second after my request the guards move to open the doors to the dining room. I fear my hands would be too sweaty, slipping right off the handle of the big doors.

I push my shoulders back again and my chin high as I step into the hall. I can do this, I have to.

My eyes fly over the elongated table the people are seated at and the first thing that springs to my eyes is that the chair of my father is empty.

Where the hell is he?

He insisted that he would be here and now I have a table full of lords and ladies that I know of just by names because these are his people, he knows them not I.

They all stand up and before I can even take a step a dark-haired man rushes over to me.

He is dressed in a vibrant green dress shirt, tucked neatly into his breeches, a stitched vest over it.

His face looks mature and elegant, his eyes the same color as my turquoise dress. It takes me a moment to organize my thoughts when I meet the intensity of his ocean gaze.

"Princess Katarina, I am Prince Marrus, it is a pleasure to finally meet you."

His gentle voice tells me once he stops in front of me. He must be a little older than me maybe Zayne's age which is why he's trained properly, his manners on point. Confidence is oozing from every pore of this man.

I raise my hand and he doesn't hesitate to take it, pressing a kiss against my knuckles, while his eyes stay on my face.

Damn those are some blue eyes.

"I'm delighted you accepted my invite, was the journey here alright?" I ask out of politeness and his lips stretch into a smile, gifting me with a set of sparkling white teeth.

"It was just fine. Your kingdom is astonishing, from what I could see on the journey." He tells me and offers me his arm. I put my hand on his bicep and let him accompany me to walk towards the table. What a weird picture we make. A storm of blues and turquoise colors, against magically looking green as if it was all planned.

I register how the loud chatter turns into murmurs, most of the lord's and ladies' eyes probably propped on us.

I see Prince Hector standing at the empty chair that's supposed to be mine, a charming smile on his lips. Honey eyes sparkle when they meet mine like a quiet invite to dive deep into the ends of it.

He will earn his proper title of king once the ceremony is planned but until then he is still a prince governing his lands due to the loss of his father.

"Prince Hector," I greet him once I let go of Marrus's arm and he takes my hand as well, placing a warm kiss against my skin.

"Princess Katarina, it is my pleasure." His voice is warm and sweet like honey. It is everything I expected and more. The contrast between him and Marrus is so obvious it makes me want to laugh. He is impressed, dare I say, in awe of me. His honey eyes are almost translucent in the candlelight, the smile on his lips oozing charm.

I smile and turn to the rest of the people looking at me. And while my eyes search for a particular person that I was so nervous to meet I just come up with an empty chair.

Did Cassian think the better of it and stayed away from the castle?

Maybe he saw the obvious distaste in my face, the anger, and hate directed at him. But more importantly, where the hell is my father?

"Well, originally it was my father who would greet you all and I'm very sorry to let you wait this long but I'm happy to be surrounded by your company tonight and more than honored by your presence," I say and motion for them to sit down while they smile at me.

My heart thumbs hardly in my chest while I hope that Edlyn will make her way here quickly before I hyperventilate.

Assassin or not I won't endure a meal with all these people on my own. I can already feel their scrutinizing eyes on my skin, judging if my spine is straight and my shoulders pushed back. To my luck, I don't need to. Before anyone can move the doors fly open and in steps my father, a stern look on his face. His hair is dark as ever, his sapphire eyes burning as he struts like the king he is.

But the weird thing is not his dark stance. I can't remember the day my father stepped into the room with a smile gracing his lips, anyway. A man walks behind him, a playful smile on his lips, a dark green dress shirt contrasting against his skin.

It makes the color of the darkest forest in his eyes reflect mysteriously.

The weird thing is that my father, the king, is entering the dining hall with Cassian by his side talking as if they were the best of friends.

"I'm sorry to have made you wait, gentleman." My father says as the lords and ladies curtsey and sit down when he does. I won't address his lack of using the proper introduction to men and women.

I sit down as well, narrowing my eyes when I see that Cassian sits down right beside my father, not even sparing as much as a glance towards me.

What a fucking, lying, sly bastard.

~

"The beaches are mesmerizing. They will entrance you the second you'll see them."

"I'm sure they will, I always wanted to visit the famous beaches of Oceanus but you know how busy a day can be," I tell Marrus with a charming smile and he nods quickly.

My eyes fly over to my father and Cassian again who are in deep conversation with the Lord of Nayland and his wife.

The slimy smile on the dark-haired male makes me sick to my stomach, my hands clenching into fists.

Thankfully Edlyn made her way into the hall quietly during dinner and is occupying the chair beside me, to hinder me from climbing over the table and strangling the young prince with my bare hands. Her presence is the reason I get ahold of myself, knowing she can interfere and get me out of this horrible banquet.

Even if it is called improper I consider the option of fleeing multiple times during the meal.

A few musicians were ordered to play soft music accompanying in the background and still I'm not distracted enough to not stare at the cause of my hatred.

The arrogant look on Cassian's face makes my fists tingle again and I have to bite my tongue not to speak up and gain his attention. But it seems like he notices my burning gaze and his dark eyes place themselves on my face over the table. I narrow my eyes when his lips twitch before his eyes fly to the prince beside me, who's still babbling about fish.

Yes, fish.

He's been talking about it this whole evening and my brain is close to exploding. Instead of charming me with his matureness, he has been talking nonstop like a child who can't control his excitement. I'm all for having a passion in life but you don't need to always share it to this extent.

He is living in the south at the ocean. Most of his gold is earned by fishing but I'm tired of talking about how 'beautiful and inspiring' creatures they are when my knife is currently slicing through a dead one.

It makes me so sick to my stomach that I can't actually continue eating the dead fish and instead nibble on the potatoes dished aside them.

I hope for Prince Hector to cut in some time but it seems like he is more the 'listen and watch' type.

When Cassian's lips stretch into a smile at my obvious annoyance I grit my teeth, my chair just moving the slightest bit.

My attention gets snatched when I feel a kick to my shin and I divert my eyes towards Edlyn, whose own eyes are wide and motioning to the place beside me.

To the place where Prince Marrus sits, looking at me questioningly, his lips sealed.

Shit did he ask me a question?

"Sorry, I missed the last part," I say with a charming smile and he blinks repeatedly before repeating his question.

"The ocean here in Aerwyna is it as cold as it's told?"

Right. He's still talking about water.

"Yes, sadly it's too cold to go for a swim but it's still a peaceful place to go after your thoughts," I tell him with a smile before I focus back on Cassian but to my surprise, my father suddenly gets up earning my attention.

He didn't speak one word with the other princes and me. I need to talk to him before he leaves.

"I'm sorry, I wanted to have a word with my father tonight before I go to sleep. We will see each other tomorrow and I´m sure my friend Edlyn will tell you everything she knows about my kingdom." I tell Marrus and Hector the latter gifting me a silent smile. Edlyn shoots me a look with narrowed eyes and I know I´m kind of leaving her in the lurch but I promise her with an apologetic smile that´ll I owe her for this.

She rolls her eyes and motions for me to go which I do without hesitation.

I grab my skirts and quickly get up trying to leave the hall as calm as possible but still fast enough.

It seems like it´s not fast enough because when I step out into the corridor there is no sight of my father.

"Where did he go?" I ask one of the guards who looks at the other unsure and I furrow my brows angrily.

"Tell me now!" I order them and one of them caves.

"He has serious matters to return to."

Serious matters my ass.

"What is that supposed to mean?"

"It means it's no business of a princess." I turn angrily at the voice to snap at whoever thinks he's funny and stare straight into the last face I want to see right now.

"You mean the future queen." I hiss at Cassian who steps out of the dining hall, the doors closing behind him.

His hands are shoved lazily into his breeches, his dress shirt hanging out. Oh, how I hate my stomach for tumbling at the view he's giving me.

His lips twitch lightly as if he notices my slight slip of attention before he speaks up again.

"Emphasis on future." He says and anger bubbles up deep inside of me. Anger at my father, at myself but mostly at this stupid asshole who treats me like a child as if he has all the power over me.

It doesn't take long for me to burst. It's as if he knows right where to push so I'll explode. Well, one could say it is his fault for what's coming next.

Before I can stop myself—or any of the guards—my fist flies out and collides straight with the face of that stupid prince.

The skin on my knuckles tears painfully but the satisfaction of finally hitting him is more than worth it. As is the groan that leaves the prince's lips when he holds his nose. I arch a brow before I turn around, dismissing his presence, and strut down the hall.

Gods, that felt fucking good.

It was improper, yet it felt fucking good.

"That was a hell of a hit." An amused voice pipes up and I turn to my left narrowing my eyes. Cassian's long strides match mine easily, catching up to me in a second.

"Are you offering me a second hit?"

"Even if I would—which I'm not saying I am—you wouldn't have the heart to destroy the handsome face of your future husband."

A cold shiver runs down my spine and I stop my walk. My eyes narrow as they meet his but I don't have the strength to discuss it with him again. My brain feels like mush thanks to Marrus's educational talk about all different kinds of fish and water.

He arches a dark brow at me and I wonder how such a small movement can flare the anger right back up in my veins.

I have to leave. Leave now or I will seriously hurt him this time.

I start to walk again hoping that he will get the rude message. He doesn't.

"Already regretting your idea?" His tone is light as he walks beside me and I wonder how he can be in such good spirits after I punched him in the face.

When I don't answer his question he speaks up again.

"What? Now you're ignoring me?"

"Why? Is it bothering you? It's not like you were talking to me during dinner either?"

When I get a dark chuckle in return I immediately regret my words. I bite my tongue until I draw blood reminding myself that I need to keep my stupid emotions at bay.

"I wanted to give the other princes a little head start and even with that they're not going to stand a chance against me."

I stop walking at his words and look up at him and his stupid smug smile.

"You're full of yourself you know that?" I snap and his smile widens.

"Well I have every right to be, haven't I? I think you've got more than a feel of my assets on that roof. We did get very close."

To my horror, my cheeks flush at his suggestion. I hate that I know exactly what he's talking about. His grin widens.

"Most women find that—"

"Repulsive? Arrogant? Disgust—"

"I was going for pleasing but it seems like you have a lot of adjectives that define your thoughts about me." He interrupts my angry speech and I scoff again continuing my way to my chambers.

"Believe me, I'm not spending a single thought on you."

That's a lie. But it's just thoughts of me slitting his throat. Mostly.

"I'm sure you do." He says and I clench my hands, close to hitting him. Again.

He doesn't leave my side even though I don't speak up.

It's best to ignore him and don't fuel his stupidity. Or my anger.

"I'm sorry I didn't talk to you during dinner, if I knew you craved my company so much I would've requested to sit beside you."

"I don't. Stop talking bullshit." I snap my breathing clipped.

If I don't calm down the corset will make it very hard to breathe and I don't look forward to passing out. To be in such a vulnerable state in front of this cruel man would be a curse.

"What a dirty mouth you have, princess, does your father know you talk like that?" He mocks me again and I take a deep breath while I rush down the stairs.

I need to get some fresh air into my lungs or I'm going to explode.

"What do you want, Cassian? I don't have the time for your games. You already have what you want; you don't need to fight for my attention."

"I know I don't need to, I have your attention anyway. But you're blind with rage to see the advantage you could have with me." His words make me stop at the entrance to the gardens and look up at him.

A chilly breeze passes us and the moonlight creates a weird shadow on his face.

"What are you talking about?"

"I am willing to be your alliance, Carina, if you let me be."

Those are the weirdest words I ever heard come from his mouth. The sincerity is confusing my hazy brain which seems to be dysfunctional with the little oxygen I´m getting into my blood.

I don´t dare to think his voice sounds almost gentle.

"You want to be my alliance with what exactly?"

"I can be your spy at court. You would wonder what you hear while walking through the corridors at night." He says ominously making me wonder how he knows this when he just arrived today. For a second I consider his words, having him as my ally but then I remember the second he walked into the hall beside my father. He made clear which side he is on and I'm not letting him trick me into one of his traps. No fucking way.

So after a minute of silence, I shake my head.

He sighs and his jaw hardens again.

"Call this stupid thing off, Carina. You look exhausted after just one conversation with the fish prince and the other one has no courage or interest to speak to you at all."

"Oh, and you think you're a better match? I'm close to having a heart attack every time I talk to you!" I snap and his lips grin suggestively.

"Not the way you think you pig!" I say and want to push against his chest but he doesn't move one inch, his chest hard as a stone which makes my hand lay against it awkwardly.

I quickly pull it back while his eyes follow my hand.

"I want to help you if you want to believe it or not."

He takes a step closer cornering me in. I exhale surprised when his voice drops a few octaves.

"You're going to learn it sooner or later because believe me, princess, one thing I'll make sure of is that once you're in the white dress, I'm the only one who's going to take it off of you after the wedding."

~ 9 ~

"Can you believe him? As if he would be my ally, he did ignore me during dinner and was focused to gain my father's trust. What a slimy idiot."

Pure rage rushes through my veins.

"Sit still, Your Highness."

"And then he dares to talk bad about the princes like he's so sure he's going to marry me, which I will never do!"

Over my dead fucking body.

"Your Highness, please sit still."

I get up from the red chaise longue and walk over to Edlyn because she's focused on that book again instead of listening to a word I'm saying.

"Edlyn!"

She looks up surprised while another voice speaks up. I refrain from stomping my foot on the floor like a small child.

"Your Highness?"

"What?" I snap and turn around to glare at the artist.

"You got up from your position. . ." He trails off unsure and I look at the chaise longue where I was supposed to sit for three hours. My eyes flicker back to the frail-looking artist, his eyes wide. He looks like he´s expecting me to rip out his throat at any second. Which I might consider due to the anger still rushing through my veins.

My father ordered the best artist in our kingdom to paint my portrait. It is tradition to paint the portrait of the regent once they turn eighteen. It´s part of the birthday gift and it´s a symbol of a teenager turning into an adult, a girl turning into a woman.

As if anyone cares about that. I sure don't.

I don't need a painting to tell me that I turned eighteen either. It's wasted paint and gold if you'd ask me but whatever the royals want, they get.

"I apologize, would you give me a minute? You can take a walk." I tell him with a friendly smile, dropping the angry demeanor for a second. The artist sighs before he gets up and leaves the room.

I'm not sure if he'll come back the way I scared him with my yelling like a lunatic.

I turn back around to my best friend who looks at me with raised brows.

Great that she didn't feel the need to speak up and rather observe this whole thing.

"Are you finished with your fit?"

She arches a brow, making her look weirdly devilish for a moment.

The anger returns because the expression somehow reminds me of the Demeter Prince.

"Do I look like I'm finished?"

She doesn't answer the question. She doesn't need to.

"Your father is not going to be happy if he hears about this." She gestures around, meaning that I send away the artist. I roll my eyes and cross my arms in front of my chest.

"I don't care. He didn't even talk to me last night and today. Just a simple little note that says 'you're going to get painted in the salon', no good morning or how are you. And to top that off Cassian wasn't at lunch neither was my father. They're plotting and I don't like it at all. Meanwhile, I think that my father just agreed to this whole charade to talk to

Cassian and plot the upcoming marriage." I huff out exhausted. Sometimes it feels like the whole court is plotting against me to make everything I plan even harder to play out. I huff out a small breath.

"Sounds awful."

The careless words of my friend make me look up at her.

As expected her eyes are trained on the book in her hands, which are stained with coal again. Her brows are drawn in, her hair building a hazel curtain around her. Great, she didn't listen to a word I just said.

Enraged by everyone lately, I narrow my eyes.

I walk over to her and snag the book right out of her hands making her protest.

"Hey! What are you doing?"

I quickly dash away holding the book up high. Her notebook slips out from the book and meets the ground with a soft thud.

"Why are herbs and potions more important than your best friend's problems? I'm going crazy over here and you're reading about—" I trail off slowly when I pick up the notebook from the ground.

She was indeed reading about herbs and potions, a complicated formula drawn onto the pages.

But it's not the formula that makes my cheeks grow hot and my eyes widen, it is her notes.

Or what is supposed to be her notes.

Instead of words, I stare at a drawing made out of coal, some lines soft and curving, others hard and straight.

It takes me a second to realize that two humans have been drawn into a most compromising situation and I don't refrain from flipping the page.

My cheeks turn crimson.

A girl is on her knees, her long hair black like coal as she hovers in front of the hips of an unknown man.

The notebook slips right out of my hands as if I've burned myself.

"What kind of obscene drawings are these?" I look at my friend with wide eyes, who stopped trying to get the book back, staring at it on the ground.

Her jaw locks her eyes trained on the floor. I don't even know what to say, that's how offended I am by her activities. My eyes fly back to a new drawing that has flipped open and I have to swallow when I look at the next drawing. I gasp when I realize who is who and what they're doing. Holy fuck.

The woman is on all fours, her back arched as someone plunges into her from behind, her long hair fisted in his palm. I don't want to but I can't stop noticing the details. The way her head is thrown back, or the muscles that ripple in the man's back, hard and prominent. I angrily pick up the notebook and slam it shut, containing my anger.

"I don't even know what to say right now."

"Great, then don't say anything." I turn my eyes on her sharply and raise a brow.

"Oh sorry, I'm going to give your dirty images back to you. How could I think it was any of my business?" I spit out sarcastically.

She narrows her brown eyes at me, her facial expression becoming sharper.

"It isn't any of your business. It's not like I'm doing something forbidden."

I scoff.

"It's not that bad and while being at this court nothing happens, I need some kind of entertainment."

'Nothing happens? Nothing happens?'

The kingdom is in the process of being stolen by an arrogant little prince and she dares to say that nothing is happening and that drawing sketches, which are as dirty as the horse's barns, are more exciting!

"Do you know what happens, if someone found out you were drawing these kinky things? No one would be ever willing to marry you." I grip the notebook hard in my hand while I try to reason with her. To make her see how ridiculous this is.

It's not like I want to forbid her from drawing these things, she can do it but at night alone in her room. Where it is secure and no one can catch her. She can't carry this thing everywhere she goes.

People will think she is a harlot and she will be banned from the palace. She won't be able to find a job and even I can't protect her from the shame she will be met with once something like that gets into the open.

"Who says I want to marry?" Her voice has a dark edge to it.

"You never objected when we were talking about the topic." I shoot back and she shrugs her shoulders.

"Because we were talking about your marriage."

"Edlyn, this is not just about marriages, you know that."
A hard sigh leaves her lips.
I know women that occasionally read stuff like that and draw to fuel their fantasy but they're married and nothing bad can happen to them.

"I think I´m old enough to handle the consequences."

"Are you? I don´t think it has anything to do with age to endure the pain of a whip."
She flinches at my harsh words and my shoulders immediately slacken.

Her mouth screws shut at my words but the determined look stays on her face. For a moment I don´t recognize my friend.

"It´s not like I am the first one to do it, there are plenty of books with pictures in the royal library, Carina."
There is something weird in her eyes, a glint I have never seen before.

"As far as I know we don´t even have the allowance to wander the darker sides of the library."

"Well, we aren´t." She arches a brow knowingly.

"Who?" I order immediately.

"I don't know. She was dressed in a red gown, a beautiful woman said she was here on order of a lord. Anyway, she gave me a few books and I couldn't put them down. You put it out as something dirty but it isn´t. It´s sensual and enlightening."

"Enlightening." I have to scoff before I break into a humorless chuckle.

"It´s not something to be proud of, Edlyn." I protest and she groans making me furrow my brows.

"You´re not getting it."

"I don't need to get anything, I'm not the one risking my life. I will make sure to burn every book like that in this castle!" I interrupt her quickly not interested in any word about these dangerous books. If she's not able to care for her life it is my job to do so.

"Sometimes you're such a stuck-up!"

I narrow my eyes at the childish insult.

"I'm not a stuck-up, I'm the future queen and I'm sorry if I want to ensure that we both live long enough to finally have a happy life!" I shoot back at her while she crosses her arms in front of her stubbornly.

"Well, could you for one damn day not be the queen!"

I ignore her comment as my facial expression locks up.

"You can draw and read any kind of dirty things you want once I'm the queen. Your life is too valuable to end it over something like this."

"My life is not valuable. And how can I have a happy life when I'm caged in? When I can't even read what I like—"

"—if that's what you like, you lack in taste, my friend."

"How would you know, you've never experienced anything like it!"

Are we fighting over stupid drawings of acts we shouldn't even know about?

How can she not understand how dangerous this is? Just a little slip—someone could've seen her and she would be dishonored.

Edlyn grew up in the palace she would never survive out on the streets and I would never let her endure it.

And that would dishonor me even if I'm the princess of this kingdom.

"I don't want to fight about this." I sigh finally but the stubborn look doesn't leave her face. I don't think I've ever seen her this angry.

"Can I have it back?" She asks clipped.

"Not in a lifetime, these drawings are going to be nothing but ashes in a few hours and I swear if I see you with one like this again I will—"

"You will what? You don't need to repeat yourself, Your Highness." She asks me daringly and the anger flares right up again. She is mocking me, using my title to get the best of me, she knows better than to do that.

"I will marry you to a lord and will not pay any attention if he's to your liking or not."

She looks at me wide-eyed and I regret what I said the second I look into her eyes. I try to contain my stern mask, even though I know this is her worst nightmare.

"You wouldn't." She says shaking her head, any trace of anger long gone.

"Do you want to test me?" I offer her even though everything inside me yells at me to apologize. To step forward and promise her that I would never do such a thing.

She glares at me the last time before I hear her retreating steps and the door slamming shut once she's gone.

I relax my tense shoulders and let out a small sigh pinching my nose between my fingers. The minute she is out of sight a big lump of guilt grows inside my stomach.

My temples start to throb immediately, greeting me with a headache. I still have to go a few hours of things I have to do. The stupid notebook is still clutched in my hand and I promise myself to make sure to burn it this evening in my chambers where no one will see it. Until then it stays with me because no one can order from me to know what I'm writing or drawing about.

I close my eyes and a picture of Edlyn's face forms in my mind, disappointment, and anger written all over it.

I hate it when people order me around and tell me what to do as if I couldn't decide on my own and I know she does too.

And I just did that with her. I treated her like everyone is treating me and I could kick myself for that.

I'm not forbidding her to do it, I just want her to be smarter about it.

Another exhausted breath leaves my lips before a knock sounds against the doors.

"Come in," I call and clutch the book in my hands while I turn around. Maybe the artist got enough courage to come back but I doubt he would.

The wooden doors open again and I half expect Edlyn to rush in and apologize, saying how stupid our fight was but it's not her.

Instead, I'm greeted with honey eyes and a gentle smile when Prince Hector steps into the room.

He curtseys quickly and I follow his move before I wait for him to explain his appearance.

"Am I bothering you right now? I wanted to see if you care to go on a walk, I saw the Royal Gardens last night and was immediately entranced." His dreamy voice says and I believe this is the first time I heard him talk this much.

"No, you're not bothering me. It seems like I scared off all my company so I'd love to go on a walk with you." I say with a sweet smile and when he offers me his arm I walk over to him. My heart thrums nervously as I approach him, the sound of my shoes against the marble floor matching the rhythm. The weight in my hands is not forgotten but I try to hide the notebook as well as I can.

My fingers wrap around his offered arm and I shoot him another gentle smile.

Maybe a walk right now is the perfect solution to calm down my nerves, with a prince as silent and gentle as Hector is told to be. It gives me some time to ponder my decision and spoken words. And hopefully, I will come up with the best apology I can muster because I realize fully that I acted like the stupidest asshole today.

"Whose idea was it to build these beautiful rose hedges like a maze?" Hector asks me as he walks beside me, his eyes on the red petals of the flowers.

They're blooming beautifully this time of the year, making the soft scent waft around the air, tickling my skin. Edlyn always uses them for my baths; she claims it has a calming sense to them.

"My mother's actually. The king said it reminded her of the rose hedges in a city far from Adalon. I guess it felt like a little escape from the cold walls of the palace." I say while I look over at the enormous castle that limits the royal gardens. I surely can understand the motive behind it. Even if you were born in the palace the walls around you feel suffocating most of the time.

It is my favorite place outside, not just because it feels like you can walk endlessly without anyone stopping you. But it feels like I'm left alone outside. Far away from any duties to accomplish. No one comes to see me, to order me around and give me tasks I don't want to do and most importantly my father doesn't come outside.

I think the memory of my mother is too painful for him to step just one foot outside, which makes it my safe space.

"A brilliant idea, it makes the place look magical. I wouldn't mind getting lost in them a few times."

I have to smile lightly at his words.

It has been nice talking to Hector, he's a good listener.

Very quiet and yet it seems like he says much just by listening and watching.

I get why people like and respect him as the current prince and soon-to-be-crowned king. My first expression of him was right and I have to laugh mentally at what Cassian said about him, that he was not courageous to speak up which is ridiculous.

Hector chooses his words wisely as if he has just a limited amount and it makes me cherish every spoken word so much more.

"I think she had a great eye for it, for things to be beautiful."

Hector looks down at me the amber in his eyes almost liquid.

"Some people have that gift. It´s amazing how many people are blind to the eye. Blind to the beauty our world can still offer."

Why does everything he says sound so sensual?

It´s like he´s the complete opposite of Marrus.

While Marrus feels like a whirlwind of a man, who never stops talking but he says so little. Hector is like a soft breeze on a hot summer night, who says much by saying little.

"Do you remember her?" He asks after a moment of silence.

"Not really. There are little slips of memories but I never know if they're real or not, sometimes it feels like I'm just clinging to the imagination that I made up in my mind." We walk out of the maze.

The sun stands low and I know it's soon time for dinner but I don't feel like leaving yet.

I want to bathe in his presence for a little while longer.

"Did you try to talk to your father about it? If anyone could tell you it would be him if these memories are real."

A small laugh escapes me.

His brows raise confused and I shoot him an apologetic smile.

"The king isn't transparent about his thoughts and emotions, especially not about my mother," I tell him with a smile and he furrows his brows as if he can't imagine that.

"He's just really secluded and tries to focus on his tasks as a king. His idea of a mighty king revolves around strength and the ability to make hard decisions that aren't always good for everyone." I tell him and he stops walking to look down at me.

His eyes reflect the orange sunlight in them while it seems like he searches for something in my face. The look on him is almost adorable.

"But can't a king be mighty while still talking about his feelings? I mean with all these pent-up emotions I wouldn't be able to concentrate." He tells me and I smile gently.

"He doesn't think it's possible but I think there are many kings in your lineage that prove him wrong. Including you."

There is no denying that Hector's kingdom is healthy and safe and it is thanks to his ruling skills.

It is weird how alike we are to our ancestors sometimes and then again there are exceptions. As far as I remember my mother was like Aerwyn it is weird how she fell in love with someone like my father.

"Yeah, it seems that way," Hector says and I watch how his cheeks blush lightly.

When he doesn't speak up again I follow his line of sight to see my father rushing out of the castle and to no surprise Cassian is right beside him.

They round the Royal Gardens as if it is a disease and I´m relieved that we are this far away from them. There is no way we will catch their eyes and weirdly it makes me exhale relieved. I don´t know if I´m in the mood to meet Cassian´s unyielding gaze again, it seems to burn up my stupid body every time.

Is he being his lapdog now?

My father can't be that desperate to marry me to the prince and take him wherever he wants to.

I thought Cassian´s whole purpose to join the court was to get to know me.

I watch them meet up with the captain of our guard, their expressions cold and somehow alarmed.

"Prince Cassian seems to be in liking of your father."

"Maybe he wishes to marry him. I certainly wouldn´t object to that."

I say and look back at the prince who has a small grin on his face before it turns thoughtful.

"I heard he was often here at the court in your childhood."

Someone did his work correctly.

"Yes, his brother as well. It's just because his kingdom is the closest and often you get lonely as a regent child." I tell him and try to sound as diplomatic as I can.

I don't want him to think I favor Cassian in any way just because we know each other for so long.

My feelings for Cassian are strongly led by hatred and despise but I can't tell him that so openly. For most of my life, I thought the Moreau brothers stayed at our court because the distance wasn´t that far. But now with my new knowledge I know it was because both the kings were plotting. Watching me interact with the Moreau heir. I feel violated thinking about it.

"You can tell he's very comfortable here," Hector says making us both look back at my father and Cassian. They both stand with their chests jutted out, their shoulders proud and open. The latter has caught us standing close to each other in the garden, his green eyes focus on us directly making me inhale. I hold my breath for a moment which makes my ribs push painfully against the corset.

Even from this distance, he's causing me discomfort.

"Maybe a bit too comfortable," I murmur while I watch his brows furrow, anger flashing on his face. I narrow my eyes and arch a brow at him.

It feels like I can almost touch the tension that seems to be oozing from him, which makes my heart jump hastily. I turn my attention back on Hector, trying to ignore the burning gaze on us. I will not let him get the best of me.

"Would you like to see the Night-crawlers next? I breed them myself because they are my favorite flower." I say with a smile and he nods and lets me hold onto his arm before we start to walk again.

I know it's childish but if Cassian can see us I make sure to place a very satisfied smile on my lips. I am offering the Prince of Demeter a loud and visual fuck you.

~ 11 ~

The best feeling at the end of the day—besides ripping off the suffocating corset—has to be able to put down my hair.

I sigh the second I take out the last pin, letting my locks cascade down my back in a storm of tangles and chaos. I don´t mind it tonight, the sensation of pulling at my scalp is finally gone.

Marianna is currently opening the laces of my too-tight corset as I hear the smile move on her lips.

"Exhausted, Your Highness?" She asks me and I nod.

"It feels like every bone in my body is burning, yelling at me to rest."

Not just exhausted but deeply frustrated. I didn't see Edlyn the whole day and when I went to her chambers after my walk with Prince Hector, the guards told me she was out in town. That was an obvious lie but I respect it.

I can't even be mad at her for not wanting to speak to me, she needs distance and I am willing to give it to her.

To my excitement, it meant I had to spend dinner with Prince Marrus who didn't stop talking for one second. I had no way out and Hector was being his usual quiet self, so he was no help. I occupied myself—with the company of Marrus babbling in the background—with watching the two empty chairs opposite the table.

It seems that my father and Cassian didn´t find it necessary to join us for the meal.

Whatever it is they're doing—I don't like the tiniest bit of it. I can handle my father and I can handle Cassian but just on their own. I don´t like them together and the feeling of them plotting makes another tense muscle move into my back. Even though I already stretched a thousand times this day to keep myself from crumbling into a pathetic pile of disappointment, the muscles stay taught.

If these two cunning men go behind my back it means trouble and I won't let them do that. Usually, Edlyn is the one to help me reveal plotting but with her being angry at me I'm left in the dark.

I'm too hot-headed when something concerns the Prince of Demeter and usually, that makes me too impulsive and I overlook obvious hints.

An idea pops into my head and once Marianna gets me out of the thousand skirts and lets me slip into my silk night dress I turn around to look at her.

Her dark eyes are open, sparkling in the candlelight. It makes her look terribly young.

"I have a question, Marianna."

"Of course go ahead, Your Highness."

I hesitate for a moment.

"Maybe I have two. First, you can stop calling me 'Your Highness' and just call me Carina?" I ask or more tell her. I liked her presence so much that I told Olah, the head of the maids, to assign her to be my second maid when Edlyn isn't available. It's weird if she'll continue to call me Your Highness it always makes me feel cold like I'm not a real person.

"I don't think I would be comfortable with that."

She says wringing her hands and I sigh.

"I would be delighted if you tried, it would mean a lot."

I don't expect her to immediately follow it but I hope that with time she will ease into the feeling of just calling me by my name.

"And your other question?" She asks now.

"Do the maids. . .sometimes hear things they're not supposed to hear?" I ask her cautiously. I don't want to scare her away so I busy myself and sit down at my dresser. I grab the prepared cloth and dip it into the bowl of warm water to clean my face off the paint she applied so carefully this morning.

I see her eyes widen in the mirror and she quickly shakes her head no.

"I don't know what you're talking about—"

"No need to panic, Marianna, no one is in trouble. I'm just asking, hypothetically, if I wanted to know something who would I have to ask?" I smile lightly to make sure she doesn't go back into her stuttering self. I continue cleaning my face even though I'm sure it is already clean. It gives her some time to think.

"You could ask the person directly. I don't think anyone would forbid the princess a question." She states clueless and I stop cleaning my face and turn around to look at her.

"The king can," I say and her eyes widen before understanding washes over her face. For a moment she hesitates but to my relief, she nods afterward.

"Do you mind finding out why he and Prince Cassian are always talking in secrecy or not appearing at meals?" Something glints in her eyes when she nods at my request.

"But make sure that you are safe at all times, if it seems too dangerous you leave it be, alright?" I ask of her with a serious tone because as much as I want to know what the two men are plotting, I don't want her to get into trouble.

"I understand, Your Highness."

I muster her for a moment, relishing the fact that she somehow reminds me of myself.

I don't want her to get hurt and I might be the one who's getting her into trouble with this.

It feels awful but I don't know what else to do.

"Thank you, Marianna, you can leave now," I speak up after a moment.

"It is my pleasure, I am happy to help." She gives me a small genuine smile, making her whole face light up beautifully.

I give her a small one back before I watch her curtsey and dismiss her from my chambers.

I hope she can conduct some information on this because I can't stand it when someone keeps something from me. Especially my father. It's like a start of an omen, washing through the castle walls.

When I finish cleaning off my neck I walk over to the big windows, turning on a few candles with the matches lying beside them. A soft glow stretches into the room and I hum lightly at the feeling spreading in my chest. I am ready to get in bed and sleep a whole day before I have to face the people living in my castle again.

Placing my eyes out the window I watch the moon already high up in the sky, shining ominously on the Royal Gardens.

My Night-crawlers are surely opening up to the darkness now, their beautiful blue-purple petals shining and shimmering.

When I was little Edlyn and I repeatedly snug out of the castle at night to watch the rare flowers open up their petals. It is unusual how I always had a liking towards the flowers like I was enchanted by the beautiful view. Edlyn always said I inherited the eye for beauty from my mother.

I hope she stays in the castle and doesn't wander around the dangerous streets out of anger. Maybe I should've gone to her chambers one last time before getting ready for bed.

No, I think what she needs right now is a little bit of space. I was out of line and shouldn't have said anything.

At that thought, my eyes fly over to the loose floorboard beside my stack. With a few steps, I cross the room towards it. The soft padding of my feet echoes and gifts me some kind of comfort.

I hid the book after my walk with Hector so I could burn it tonight. I didn't know Edlyn had such a talent in the arts, she never indicated it. Even though the sketches she draws are inappropriate, even a blind person could see how talented she is. If she would just use her talent for more common paintings, paintings you could show to someone.

I wonder whatever lady she talked about wandering the royal library. I get on my knees and pull at the loose board making it pop open, revealing the thin pages of Edlyn's sketchbook.

Pulling it out quickly, I push the board back in before I walk over to the burning fire.

The flames are up high, crackling with secrecy as I bend down to feel the heat against my face.

My eyes wander from the orange light to the cover of the book and for a moment I consider opening it up just to take a peek. It is filled with one of the most dangerous feelings I know and never felt in my life. Desire.

It is such a primal, natural feeling, close to hate and anger and I still can't imagine the feeling of it, even though I'm so familiar with rage. For a moment I remember the fight with Cassian and can't deny that I might have felt a spark of desire. The feeling to wrap my hands around his throat and squeeze was still prominent but somehow the lines washed away. Did I want to choke him because I hated him or because I wanted to hear that beautiful sound his throat would make? It would be deep and vibrate against my skin.

I shudder at the thought and push it away. I am messing up things. I don't desire the prince. All I feel is hate, distaste, nothing that could ever please me.

I slowly stand up again not realizing what I'm doing while my hand slowly opens the cover and—

I almost get a heart attack when a knock sounds against my chamber doors.

Shutting the book, I turn around in panic while I search for a place to hide the forbidden drawings. There's no way I can get them back under the loose floorboard in time.

My throat closes up when a second knock appears and I still haven't found a hiding place.

I am so fucked.

"I know you're awake, princess, I can see the light."

Some muffled curses are heard.

"The princess is ready for bed—"

"I don't care, fuck off."

Oh no not that voice, please not that voice.

Panic flares up; my cheeks flush with the forbidden drawings in my hand. I can't stop pacing around the room, my eyes searching, hoping to find a place for hiding the pages. How can I not find anything, I spend every day in this damn chamber?

I turn again and decide to hide it under my bed covers but the doors to my chamber fly open and I quickly hide my hands behind my back when my eyes fly towards the doorframe.

"I'm sorry, Your Highness, he wouldn't stop." The guard apologizes and moves to escort Cassian out but I shake my head. I ignore the murderous look on the prince's face.

"It's alright, you can let him go," I say quickly while I feel my cheeks warm when the guard's eyes linger on the sheer dress I'm wearing.

A low rumble vibrates through the room and I realize it was Cassian, snarling at the guard and his lingering eyes. The man's spine goes rigid and before I can dismiss him he's already curtsying and out the door. It is highly inappropriate to stare at me for either of them. Cassian shouldn't even be in this room at this hour of the day or rather night.

The servants, lords, and ladies will know that a prince has been in the chamber of mine, in the evening while I am dressed in nothing more than a scrap of fabric.

My eyes focus on Cassian who's staring at me strangely and I raise my brows waiting for him to speak up. The scrutinizing look on his face makes my heart pound like it's going to burst through my ribcage at any second.

The cover of the book slips slightly in my warm hands but I tighten my grip not willing to let it slip down even further.

"You have. . .lousy guards."

Cassian's eyes finally move upwards to my face while I start searching the room with my eyes. I need to get rid of the sketches right now. My spine goes rigid when I finally meet his gaze and realize he has been staring at me. The hard beat of my heart stumbles now for a completely different reason.

"Is that why you're searching for me in my private chambers at eleven in the night? Because you're concerned. . .of my guard's skills?" I ask him, trying to fight for countenance. I narrow my eyes and meet his gaze even though I feel exposed in my dress.

"Maybe I missed you?" He offers and with the smile on his lips I know he's back to himself, whatever he was just seconds ago.

The dark fire in his eyes vanishes and he straightens his shoulders.

I roll my eyes and try to move towards my bed to put the damn sketchbook away.

"You can ask for an audience tomorrow, like the others when they're missing me," I say with a raise of a brow.

"But then I would be robbed of you looking this. . .delightful." His eyes flicker down the dress and I inhale sharply, angry that he's staring at body parts he isn't even allowed to see. I grit my teeth angrily.

"Shut up," I say narrowing my eyes while I'm almost at my bed. I need to put these damn sketches away and stop letting him provoke me.

"You're weird today. What do you have behind your back?" He asks me suddenly. He starts advancing on me and I stop moving. A small breath escapes me as I pray to the gods that he won't notice the tremor in my voice.

"Nothing. I just find it inappropriate that you're in my room while I'm not dressed properly. It makes me uncomfortable."
I swallow when he stops right in front of me.
I tilt my head to look up at him, cursing his tall figure. I'm trying to keep as much dignity as I can be dressed like this, knowing I have to protect the book with my life because I can't imagine what happens if Cassian's sneaky fingers get a grip on it.

"In a month I'm going to see you in much less." He says, his eyes boring into mine. There is that stupid glimmer again making a lump form in my throat, he needs to stop looking at me like that.

Gods, this is the fucking enemy.

I narrow my eyes at his words and shake my head.

"Not in this life, Cassian."

When I say his name, his eyes wander to my lips and I take another step back.

"So you're offering it in your next life?" He arches a dark brow and I swallow.

"I don't know if your frail ego could manage the answer." I take another step back when he chuckles darkly.

His eyes flicker to my hands behind my back and I curse myself for even picking up the sketches.

That's what I get for being curious and not burning it immediately when I could. I was as naïve as Edlyn for a second and now I'm going to be the one who gets punished for it.

"Come on, princess, show me what you have." His voice is a soft purr, it almost sounds unearthly. I am sure it is the voice that convinced so many women to share their beds with this monster. It is the perfect trap.

"Stop calling me that," I say angrily while he corners me and my back hits the cold wall of my room. A shiver runs down my spine out of fear or anticipation I am not sure.

"What? Princess? It's your title."

"But you're using it as an insult," I say raising my chin again, determined that he's not going to get these pages. The cold wall digs uncomfortably against my back, sending a rush of pain through my spine.

His eyes flash at my words and he moves even closer and I take in a ragged breath. It feels like my body is on high alert, able to notice many things at the same time. The crackling of the fireplace turns louder with every second or maybe that's my heartbeat pumping in my ears?

My eyes fly from his down to his lips for a second and I catch myself wondering what they would feel like. If they're soft and gentle or hard and unyielding.

I squeeze my eyes shut and am greeted with a low chuckle of his.

It travels all the way through my body flaring up feelings that I've never felt before and before I can move I feel the pages slip right out of my weak hands.

My lids open in panic and I watch Cassian move away from me the sketchbook in his hands. It feels like I'm bathed in cold water, realizing what he just did.

That manipulating, little bastard.

"Hey, what are you doing!" I protest and already move, following his tall frame.

"Finding out what you're hiding so desperately." He says as he escapes my hands and I feel the panic spread through my body like hot prickles of a needle as I rush after him but he's so tall that he holds it up while flipping open the first page.

Please no. By the power of Adales or anyone who hears me right now, make up a hole and let it swallow me right now!

I jump and try to reach it but his only answer is a delighted chuckle. When the first page comes into view the smile drops and I stop jumping defeated, when I see the realization dawning on his face.

He flips to the next page, revealing the girl on her knees.

The next has three parties on a bed, one of them watching the male and female in the act.

I close my eyes in horror when I hear a rushed breath escape him.

When I open them again I watch his arms sink slowly, his throat bobbing with the hard swallow he takes.

"What is this?" His voice sounds breathless and when his arms are low enough I rip the pages right from his hands.

"It's none of your business." I hiss as I curse my friend for her stupid drawings.

"Did you draw these?" Another breathless question and my lips part in surprise.

"Of course not! I was just about to burn it!" My cheeks flush when his green eyes place themselves on me. The look in them burns right through my skin, edges itself into my bones and soul.

Gods, it could've been anyone else but it had to be him, who found this book.

"You can tell me the truth I won't judge you." A weird glimmer shines in his eyes and I look at him as if he's crazy.

"I don't care the slightest bit about your judgment but I'm telling you the truth. These. Are. Not. Mine."

"But you were looking at them?"

He takes a step closer making my heart stumble.

"I was about to burn them." It feels like I'm repeating myself.

"Sure, that's why you were about to lie down and do what exactly, Carina?" His voice is deep as he takes another step toward me and I shake my head panicked to make him understand that I'm not responsible for any of his accusations.

"Nothing, okay? Even if it's none of your business I would never do something like this." My voice is quieter than I intend it to be.

He reaches me with two big steps and I hold the book at a safe distance but instead of going for the book he stops in front of me. His head tilts to the side and his curls bounce for a moment. I can see his fingers twitch before they meet my skin. The tips of his fingers wander over my arm, a feather-light touch, barely noticeable.

I exhale when I feel the heat from his skin ooze through me. This is not what I should do I need to push him away now.

But when his fingers wrap delicately around my wrist and he pulls me closer, gauges my reaction, I am unable to move.

"What are you doing?" My voice is barely a whisper as my heart almost jumps out of my chest.

I thought he hated me as much as I hated him, he shouldn't touch me.

And why the fuck am I not moving?

"Trying to stop you from walking right into the fireplace, princess." He says and his lips slip into a smug smile when I realize what he's saying.

I turn my head confused and see the fire right in my back.

A few steps and I would've walked right into it.

"Right." I breathe out and take a step away from it, his hand drops from my skin with the movement.

Thank the gods.

My eyes follow his retreating hand.

"You should go now," I say embarrassed.

I take another step away from him and he watches me carefully as I place the book on my nightstand. I can deal with it later. He needs to leave first.

"I came here for a reason." He says and I shake my head quickly.

How can he look so unbothered now?

"I don't care. I'm going to sleep now and I want you to leave." I tell him stepping close to my bed. I won't let him get close to me again because it seems like my body is my enemy.

It's as if my brain stops functioning when he's this close and that's a prospect I neither like nor want to think about further.

He ponders over my words for a second and nods but instead of leaving he walks toward me and I can smell his scent for a short moment.

He smells like snow and shadows, something dark mixed into it and I hold my breath when his knuckles graze my arm as he places something on the nightstand behind me. I don't dare to move this time. I´m close to squeezing my eyes shut, hoping that he will just disappear once I open them again.

"Have fun with those pages. Sleep tight, Carina." He says quietly before he leaves the room.

I watch his retreating form, surprised that he followed my request.

I don't move from my spot until a few minutes after the doors closed and when I do, I turn around to look at the dark velvet box he placed on the book that got me into so much trouble.

The velvet shines in the flickering light a promise or a warning for why he is here and that he is not going anywhere before he has what he wants and that is my crown.

~ 12 ~

I leave the velvet untouched not daring to burn my fingers with it being cursed or Adales knows what. I don´t take Cassian as the quiet murderer, he would probably make a show out of it but still, you can never be sure.

I don´t even look at the small box designed for jewelry when I go to sleep.

No amount of curiosity that resides inside me can convince me to open it.

It doesn´t mean I am not thinking about it. I spend the whole night wondering, barely getting an eye shut. When I do fall asleep I wake up a few hours later exhausted and with new determination.

Lately, it feels like I'm digging my own grave, I´m losing control over someone like him. Marianna doesn´t mention the purple color residing beneath my eyes when she brushes my hair and we both decide to bathe in silence this morning. She gets me ready for breakfast before I send her off to spy on my father—who´s currently looking anything but suspicious as he chats happily with Prince Marrus.

He never shows any interest in the princes besides Cassian but I arrived so late to breakfast that I don´t know if Marrus went and spoke to the king on his own accord.

It wouldn´t surprise me.

Well even better for me, means I have some thinking time over breakfast.

My father looks bored and I don't even think he's listening to the babbling Prince of Oceanus, who has not the slightest clue of how annoyed the king is. I'm sure he's telling him another thrilling story about fish and the water they live in.

My stomach starts to churn uncomfortably when my eyes flutter just a bit to the left, to look the person right in the eye, sitting beside my father. Cassian's stare is relentless and it is not the first time that I wish to know what is going on inside of his head.

I try to focus on buttering the bread in my hands but continue to keep glancing at him.

My cheeks heat up involuntary and when he gets up from his chair and makes his way over to me, my heart crashes against my ribcage repeatedly. No, not again, I'm not ready for another confrontation when I didn't even process the one from last night!

"Do you feel alright this morning, princess? You look a little nauseous. . .and heated." The chair beside me scrapes against the floor when Cassian sits down.

A waft of his fresh scent greets me and I narrow my eyes.

Damn Marrus for leaving his spot. Damn Edlyn for not wanting to talk to me.

I would much prefer to babble about fish any day over Cassian's intrusive eyes.

"I'm fine."

I force a tight smile and watch his eyes fly towards my naked hands.

Something close to displease flashes in his eyes and it gives me the satisfaction to smile lightly and relax a bit more. I could relax further if this damn corset wouldn't be squishing my organs around my body.

"Didn't you like it?"

"You mean the pretentious ring? That you're trying to buy me with?" I say not looking at him. I mentally pat my back for my stubbornness. The ring is sitting discarded in the velvet box in my room and it will sit there for eternity if it gets a rise out of him.

"I am not trying to buy you; it's your engagement ring if you want it to be. I added the amethyst myself I thought it would remind you of your flowers." My eyes fly over his face surprised at his words.

There is no stupid smug smile on his lips and I narrow my eyes at him. Suspicion crawls its way over my spine.

"How do you know about them?"

"Your father told me you were growing them. It was no surprise to me when I think about the obsession you had when you were little." He tells me quietly and for a moment I fall for it.

Fall for his stupid trap where Cassian is caring and thoughtful, wanting to make this stupid deal as easy for me as it can be. But I remind myself who I'm speaking to and give him a cold smile.

"We're not engaged, Cassian, and we're not going to be. I'll give you the ring back and you can give it to your future wife."

He narrows his eyes. I blink innocently.

"What? Don't know the feeling of rejection?" I mock him and watch his jaw clench. It's fascinating how easy I can rile him up.

"The ring is yours, Carina."

His words are tense and I scoff.

"Just because you're walking in here, reminding me of our childhood it doesn't mean you can do what you want. Because as far as I remember I hated you then and now. Take the ring back."

I take a bite out of my bread smug and satisfied. He keeps on staring at me and I arch a brow. "Was there anything else? Because I would like to enjoy the first hours of my morning." He shakes his head at my words and gets up. I tilt my head back to look at him.

"The ring was made for you and it is yours no matter if there is going to be an engagement or not." With that, he leaves the dining hall and I watch his retreating back until he's out of sight.

What the fuck.

Is that part of his play? Now he's pretending to be the hurt boy who got rejected by his childhood crush. An evil premonition makes its way to the surface and I realize that this game is going to be far more dangerous than I thought.

~ 13 ~

"So how are they?"

"Who?" I grunt while I take the next step, swinging my sword so hard it clings loudly when it collides with my brothers.

"Your little guests—ow." He hisses when I jab him with the wooden sword in the side.

"Don't get distracted," I tell him and attack again making him huff when our swords collide.

Beads of sweat are trailing down his forehead and even though he could use his height to his advantage to corner me, he's not focused enough. He never is and I doubt that he ever will be.

"You're dodging my question." He protests and I squat down swiping one leg out which makes him stumble and land on his back while I quickly hold my sword against his throat, defeating him.

His wild eyes flare up and he pushes the wooden blade away from his throat. I relax.

"They're alright," I say and hold out my hand for him to help him get up.

He takes the offer and gets up with a groan making me roll my eyes. I lightly grazed him nothing serious.

These swords are made out of wood and he likes to think I slice him open every time we´re finished with a fight.

If he had been listening to me he could easily beat me but to my dismay, Henri thinks sword fights and shooting arrows are boring.

He doesn't need to be a perfect fighter but you never know what or who is waiting around the corner and maybe if my mother knew how to fight she would still be here.

At least I'd know she wouldn't have gone down without a fight.

"Alright means they're horrible."

We walk over to the wall filled with various weapons and put the swords back into their bracket. My body buzzes happily with the adrenaline rushing through, my back soaked in sweat.

"They're not horrible. They're passable." I tell him while we walk over to where our refreshments lay.

"Passable means boring and boring is horrible in your case. Maybe you should let them fight a little." He says with a smile and I have to laugh when I think about Marrus with a sword.

"Maybe you could be their sparring partner, then they'd have a chance." He throws me a glare.

I had a small audience with Marrus this morning and showed him our music hall. I thought maybe we could sit at the piano for a bit. Play a melody together but after almost half an hour I couldn't stand it anymore. I tried to but he wouldn't stop talking and asking questions. About Aerwyna, our forces, our resources.

I'm glad he's interested in our kingdom's politics and tasks but my ears needed a break which is why I gave Marianna a small wave of my hand who was lingering behind us in case I needed her.

She made an excuse and reminded me of my training session with my brother so I could escape the talking plague. No offense. Maybe Marrus's skills could talk his victims to their death.

I take a sip from my water and put up my hair neatly again.

"If you put them in a ring they'll most likely start to talk to each other and not fight."

"That's because they're fancy princes."

My brother rolls his eyes as he takes a sip.

"Well, it is their title. They don't need to fight in a war."

He raises a brow.

"Then why are you training me?"

"Because I want you to be able to defend yourself. And not run away like a coward."

"Cas wouldn't," Henri says and I slightly tense up at the nickname. I hoped we could avoid this topic all along but I should've known better with the curiosity flooding through Henri's veins. It's the same that I carry with me at all times. He raises his brow and I narrow my eyes at him.

"I knew he'd be here anyway, I don't know why you're avoiding the topic."

Because you didn't get bullied by him when you were a kid, I did. I know Henri worships the ground underneath Cassian's feet.

He is the big brother he never had and the king is not making a good father figure these days. Well, any days to be exact.

But does it have to be Cassian? It always makes me uneasy how much Henri likes the Prince of Demeter.

I shrug my shoulders and drink again deciding to say nothing; it will just end up in a discussion anyways.

"He's a great fighter. He asked me to train with him this afternoon."

"What did you say?" I ask unsure of what to think of this.

"I said no, you're going easy on me, if I would fight against him I'd be dead the second he raised his sword." He pushes his darkened locks from his sweaty forehead.

"I'm sure I could beat him," I mumble making my little brother smile.

I know I can because I already did. Cassian is just making up excuses to deny that a woman defeated the big bad wolf.

"Of course, you could." He agrees, making me grin.

I'm just about to ask if he wants to go another round when Marianna steps into the door frame curtseying.

"Princess! I searched for you throughout the castle. I got what you ordered me. . .to bring." She says unsure her eyes flying over to my brother.

"Give me a minute," I tell Henri before I make my way over to her and notice the pressed look on her face. My muscles tense, alarmed by her behavior.

"I didn't know if I could write you a note, in case it got into the wrong hands." She says unsure and I nod with a smile.

"Everything is fine. Tell me, what did you learn?"

She shoots a look over my shoulder and when she feels like my brother is not listening she speaks up in a whisper.

"I talked to maid Angeles, she is the one who was assigned to Prince Cassian and she told me your father and he met in the gardens yesterday to talk to the captain."

"Yes I saw them both and they looked worried but I didn't know why," I say thinking back to yesterday.

"Well, apparently the king sent out an army with Lord Romanov three weeks ago because Protestants were edging too close to the borders of Aerwyna,"

I furrow my brows at her words grasping their content but not understanding.

I knew the protestant groups were growing every day but never once did my father say they were near the border. And I mean even if they were, wouldn't our guards be strong enough to hold them?

"Lord Romanov?" I speak the name in distaste. Another problem I have to worry about. Since he's been gone I almost forgot about him and his cruelty but the right hand of my father seems to have his fingers in every little thing in our kingdom.

He isn't even a lord accorded to the army, he is just a little royal adviser and one of my father's oldest friends.

"Is that why they're worried? Because the groups are growing?" I focus back on Marianna who shakes her head no.

"Lord Romanov is back and with him, not even a quarter of the army he left with."

My face drops at her words.

That can't be right. The usual groups of guards send out to keep Protestants under control were twenty to thirty but if they were at the border they must've sent forty to fifty plus a lord.

And he came back with so little. My blood runs cold at the thought of the repercussions. Fields tinted with blood and dead bodies.

Maybe the Protestants have been getting stronger than I thought. But my father always said it was just a useless group of farmers, bakers just little people. They could've never defeated trained soldiers.

"What has Cassian to do with that? I don't get why they're involving him?"

She grimaces at my question and I know I'm not going to like what she has to tell me.

"The prince offered help. His soldiers are arriving in three days at the castle and they're going to fight the Protestants at the border."

A second of silence.

"But we have enough soldiers. Why doesn't send my father more?" I ask her and it feels like she's sinking into herself even more.

"It's in the contract. The contract your father made with King Moreau includes that they help with armies at any point because you're going to marry Prince Cassian." The last words are whispered. Marianna fears my reaction and I don't blame her because her words are clear. She doesn't say I will probably marry Cassian if I don't find another candidate.

No matter how I spin it, the meaning stays the same.

Hot lava bubbles in my veins as I repeat the sentence over and over in my head.

The King of Demeter is rumored to be ruthless and cruel and while I never met him in my life during the visits I know he wouldn't send armies out just for a loose promise. He's calculating just like his son is.

He gave us the army because he knows I'm going to marry Cassian. After all, I was a fool to believe any word my father had said to me.

He lied.

My father let me invite the princes with a false promise, leading them on with the thought that a marriage with me could be possible. How could he risk angering the other kingdoms with something like that?

My father isn't stupid enough to start a war over something like this.

Unless. . .he's been holding Cassian close to his side, advising him, telling him things. Like my Night-crawlers.

My father was plotting against me, helping Cassian to make me willing to marry him.

The thought makes me sick and I have to hold my stomach for a second.

They wanted to make me believe it was Cassian's wish to marry me out of a stupid childhood crush. It would've meant I send the other princes away on my own accord.

Bile sits at the back of my throat.

For a moment I forget that I'm still being watched by my maid, my brother just a few feet away.

"Thank you, Marianna, if you hear anything else let me know." I press out while I hold my stomach lightly with my hand. She takes a step forward as if to reach for me.

"Princess, I don't think it's a good idea—"

I shut her up with a look and turn around nausea hitting me, to grab my things.

"What's wrong?" Henri asks as he sees the look on my face while I grab the big dress shirt and slip into it not caring if

I'm going to see the king in my training clothes. There is no need for me to dress up and play the obedient little princess he wants me to be because this is too much. I tried to please him, to stay in line as much as I could so I wouldn't go against the man my mother once married.

But it seems like there is nothing left of this man. Maybe he wasn't even there to begin with.

"Dear dad has been lying to me that is what's wrong. I'm sorry but we have to cut the training short, we'll proceed in a few days alright?" I am already halfway out the door but Henri follows me.

"What do you mean he lied? Do you need my help?"

His jaw is set tight, a determined look on his face and I love him for always having my back but I am the future queen, so I will handle this myself.

It is time for the king to realize that he is not the only one having plans behind someone's back.

"I need you to stay out of this. It's bad enough that I'm fighting with the king." I tell him and start to jog letting him behind me. There's no chance for him to catch up with my frantic steps. No chance for anyone to get out of this unscathed.

"The king is having an audience—"

"Quiet." I snap at the guard and walk past him through the doors that lead to the chambers of my father.

I don´t waste my time knocking.

To my surprise, the guards won't stop me physically. I don´t know if it´s the murderous look on my face or not, but I am not kidding when I say I will fight my way through this damn door.

The king looks up from the table he's standing at, a map displayed of what seems to be Adalon.

Cassian is standing beside him.

The gods must be testing me today because I have no nerve for the prince to disrupt this rage I´m in right now.

It´s a familiar state of burning anger and I welcome it like an old friend. It´s like I can taste the ashes on my tongue.

Cassian´s eyes move curiously over my raging state and I move my head towards the door.

"Out."

His brows raise. An impressed look moves in his dark green eyes but I ignore it lazily.

I don't have the time for his games now I want to speak to my father and no one is going to stop me. Not even a pretentious little prince who thought he could fool me into falling for him so he gets what he wants.

"I swear to Adales, Cassian if you don't get out now. . ." He raises his hands and starts to leave the room, a small smile on his lips when he walks past me, whispering low enough just so I can hear him.

"No need to threaten me, princess."

It takes all my willpower not to turn and strangle him on the spot. But he is not the snag in this, he is just a puppet controlled by my father.

I turn to the latter when Cassian leaves the room to see his raised brows as he watched the interaction between Cassian and me.

Dare I say he looks impressed?

"Seems like you've done a good job with Prince Cassian." His eyes turn back on the map lazily.

He doesn't seem bothered by my angered state.

He's not even going to approach me, ask me why I stormed into his chamber like a death angel and sent Cassian away with one sentence. No, the king doesn't feel the slightest bit threatened and it makes the skin melt from my bones in rage. My heart is thumping loudly and it feels like with every thump my breath is getting hotter and I'm ready to strangle someone to death.

I ignore the bitter taste and the tingling feeling in my fingers.

"Whatever. Aren't you curious why I'm here?"

My voice is cold and calculated as I try to hold the literal flames inside my body. I imagine setting this office on fire, an inferno destroying every ounce of arrogance this man holds in his body.

"I'm sure you're going to enlighten me in a few seconds."

I clench my hands into fists at his words hating that he can get a raise out of me so easily.

"I just found out that the Protestants have been attacking the border of my kingdom and no one felt like it was a matter of telling me about it," I say crossing my arms in front of my chest.

This seems to catch his attention as his head snaps up to look at me.

"Where did you hear that?"

"That's not important. Important is, that my father keeps secrets from me and instead is talking to a strange prince who ran along just a week ago. It's pathetic to watch him follow you everywhere, yearning for your approval." I say with an eye roll.

My father finally straightens and walks over.

"I am talking to Prince Cassian because without his army we would lose my kingdom to the Protestants. A princess shouldn't have to worry about those things and you should focus on keeping those idiots of princes some company."

"You mean the ones I called because I thought I could choose my partner? Because funny thing, you lied about that too. There is no chance for me to marry someone else than Cassian is there?" I snap again making his eyes narrow lightly. The same fire that is burning inside of me is now eating up the dark blue of his sapphire eyes.

I take a step forward not backing down. I´m no piece of clothing you can sell on the fucking market.

"It seems like my conversations are not as secret as I thought. Well, you know now, you can leave I have things to plan." He turns around and walks over to the map but I'm driven by fury and follow him and stop him by his arm. Big mistake.

"Do you think I'm just going to let this sit on me? I'm not marrying Cassian, no way in hell! If you would tell me things we could find a different way to deal with the Protestants, just because I'm not queen yet doesn't mean I can't deal with it. It's my birthright to know, I don't need a stupid prince to govern." I hiss at him and he turns around his face cold and empty.

I don't give him a second to breathe and attack again like a seething viper.

"Why did you even let me invite Prince Marrus and Hector if you expect me to marry Cassian? Did you think I would've been distracted enough by them to go on with your secret plans? Do you feel powerful just because you took the easy way and made a deal with his father? He is a cruel man and so is his son, both of them are the downfall of Aerwyna." Something swirls inside me, slumbering deeply hidden from curious eyes.

"You don't know what is good for the kingdom or not, Katarina, that is the difference. He has experience; Cassian has the will to make decisions that are good for the kingdom, even though they aren't always morally right. Aerwyna needs a strong king and not an effeminate boy who doesn't know when to stop talking or one, who can't get a word out." He starts walking toward me and I try to stand my ground not moving a bit.

He knows damn well Hector is governing his kingdom gracefully and yet here he is slandering again. As if pain and destruction are the only way to hold power in this world. "The difference is that you think a kingdom can be led by love and gentleness. You are a fool for thinking that. The second you get on the throne the Protestants will run you over in a heartbeat. What the kingdom needs are power and strategy; you don't have that dear daughter." He finishes his voice deep and his face blurs in front of me with the angry tears stinging my eyes. He is mocking me again, making me a fool for thinking that I could lead alone. And I hate him for it.

"If my only purpose is to marry a man I am oddly replaceable. You don´t need me to govern father. And I won´t bow to your, nor Cassian Moreau´s conditions. Even if it is the only thing I can do, I will protect my kingdom from a man like him."

I feel his anger before he even opens his mouth.

"But this is not YOUR KINGDOM! It is mine as long as I remain living. It is I who will govern Aerwyna, not an immature girl who can´t take orders and is fooled by gentleness."

His booming voice feels like it could echo through the whole castle.

Like the cold slash of a whip, tearing my insides open and revealing my darkest emotions. It´s ripping apart every layer I carefully build, hiding. I´ve been cowering under my title, hiding under my cloak as the Red Saint.

Revealed is a small girl. A small girl that had to grow up without her mother and father. A girl that once was full of light and gentleness.

A long time ago my father worshipped me for my gentleness; it was something I inherited from my mother he said. Sometimes I think he would like the Red Saint more as a daughter and it hurts.

I could govern various kingdoms and win every single war but he's just too narrow-minded and stubborn to see it.

I will not stop fighting and I will not give him the satisfaction of crying in front of him. I clench my fists, digging my nails deep into my skin to stop myself from crying, the pain clearing the ongoing fog inside of my mind.

The girl is long gone and the woman now will not cower or take any fucking order.

"You know, I always told myself that once I grew up you would see me as the person I am and not just a girl. I spent every lesson with my teachers, I learned to fight against the cruelest men, and I listen to every word you tell me. I love this kingdom and I would do anything for them to be safe." I tell him my throat is tight and uncomfortable but somehow my voice sounds steady.

My father's eyes are quiet and calculating.

"The problem is you think women are weak for their emotions but that is not true." I shake my head lightly, smiling. "It is our emotions that make us strong, that turn us into hurricanes of destruction or breezes filled with gentleness. It is what makes us rulers worth following. You can be unsure in many things, father, but never doubt my loyalty to this kingdom."

"So then where is the problem in marrying Prince Cassian?" His voice is smug, with no trace of the former anger.

"The problem is that Cassian will be the destruction of Aerwyna, not the savior," I tell him again and he stays quiet. I don't know if it's out of tiredness or if he ponders my words.

I know this war isn't over but this battle I won. Because I won't back down and he can try and do whatever he wants but once I am queen, I make the decisions until then I will watch his every step. I will plot while he schemes and I will not let him win anything because I am the regent of Aerwyna and it is my right to handle the throne if he wants it or not. It feels like the storm is still thundering and yet getting quieter inside of me. The clouds are retreating the taste of blood leaving my tongue.

He doesn´t speak anymore and I sense it is time to go.

Just before I step out of his room I stop and speak up the last time.

"You know mother would've never made me marry Cassian if it meant my unhappiness."

He swallows and his eyes meet mine.

"But your mother isn´t here anymore."

~ 15 ~

"I put out your nightgown for you, princess, are you sure you don't want me to help you?"

Marianna watches me carefully, her hands clasped together in front of her gown. The light blue dress is in stark contrast to her flushed cheeks from the heat which is radiating through my chamber.

"No thank you, Marianna, you can leave now," I tell her from my place on the bed, a book clasped tightly in my hands.

She watches me warily but after a few seconds of silence, she curtseys and leaves the room.

Finally.

I throw the book on my duvet and open up my bathrobe to reveal a tight black suit I put on after my bath. It was such a relief to get all the sticky sweat off my skin after the session with my brother and the heated discussion with the king.

I didn't attend dinner tonight not just because I felt utterly stupid and couldn't look Marrus or Hector in the eyes knowing that I can't give them a chance but because I didn't want to face Cassian. I am sure he knew of the plan, I can't think of any other reason for him acting so thoughtful around me and trying to get into my head.

He tried to lure me into his net of lies like a spider lures their victims.

Am I avoiding him because I'm too proud to admit that he did fool me? Maybe.

But if the title of the princess does sometimes good use to anything, it is with doing things that I want. And I don´t want to face Cassian.

I feel humiliated, and worse I feel like a child. A child who has been fooled by two men plotting against someone who is going to be the next regent.

It makes me look unworthy of my title and I know they´re bathing in satisfaction and confirmation of their former doubts.

I will face Cassian sooner or later but when I do, I will make sure he regrets ever going against me.

While the insides of the castles presume very loud and present, the capital has been weirdly quiet for the last week and the Red Saint hasn´t gotten any new orders which appears to be unusual.

Another reason to leave tonight is that I can't stand to be inside of these walls for another second. So I should use my time wisely and meet my contacts to collect some information about the Dark Prince. Or I'll start a bar fight to blow off some steam, who knows.

I let fate decide.

I open up the hidden space in the drawer of my nightstand and grab the few knives, adjusting them to the belt around my hips.

Another dagger is pushed into one of my boots, the other one strapped to my thigh.

My cloak is hidden behind the bookshelf, so no curious eyes find it when they snoop around my chambers.

Once I have everything strapped to me, I blow out every candle in the room. It takes my eyes a few seconds to adjust to the darkness but once they do I start to move toward the bookshelf.

I'm lucky enough that the guards don't check on me during the day or night so I can sneak out whenever I want.

It's laughable really. My father thinks he's so damn clever for limiting my life but he has no clue.

My eyes wander over the many bindings and spines of the books, stopping at a sapphire blue with gold details. I tip it back lightly and wait until I hear the familiar soft crack, a second of silence and the door jumps open.

I grab the side and give it a sharp pull, a small groan emitting from my lips. This must weigh what feels like a ton or maybe it was made for a once giant prince who had the power of forty horses. Okay, maybe not forty.

I shoot a determinative look into my room that lays in silence and darkness, then I pull the hood over my head and I'm just a flattering dot of dark blue in the shadows. No one is going to know I left and no one will notice when I come back, just the way I like it.

I'm engulfed by an eerie silence, my eyes unable to adjust to the deathly darkness but I don't risk taking a candle with me, I don't need the light to lead the way anyway. My mind is trained enough to know the way by heart and even though I never met anyone or anything in these dungeons I'm sure, fire and warmth would lure out disgusting creatures, no matter if human or not. I might be able to fight with various blades and swords but I don't look forward to meeting rats or other vermin.

It takes me a few minutes until I arrive in the kitchens quietly, stepping into the shadows when I hear the maids, who are still up.

"I heard he was here to strengthen his kingdom. Lucas caught him snooping around suspiciously a few days ago, I mean the princess is a dream, she's beautiful but I would not marry him if I were her."

A scoff rumbles.

"She must find a husband and king, Elaine. It was wise of her to invite the princes."

"But—"

"No buts. It is none of our business and you shouldn't talk bad about a soon-to-be king or else they're going to punish you for it."

The voice is harsh, filled with fear. Fear of being caught talking about treacherous things. I mean I don't care I bet the only thing that keeps one going in this castle of hell must be gossip.

I peek around the corner to see them working over the stove. Curiosity doesn't cover the unnerving feeling that travels through me, caused by their whispered words. Even they think Cassian wants to strengthen his kingdom? Unless they were not talking about him.

But they had to, I don't think Marrus is snooping around he's more like the type to get lost in the castle. They can't be speaking of Hector because he already is king but they said soon-to-be.

"What the hell are you doing?" A voice whispers so close to my ear that I whirl around, the knife already in my hands as I press the man against the wall, blade to the throat.

Whoever just snooped up on me in silence will be dead in mere seconds.

My eyes narrow when I look into endless green and I press the blade harder against his throat even though I recognize the face. A small trickle of blood runs down his perfect skin and I grin satisfied. Even though I know he is not a threat, the simmering anger inside me wants to prove a point.

"What the hell are you doing here?" I whisper trying not to gain the attention of the maids around the corner. My fingers tremble lightly with the pressure, his sudden appearance making me paranoid.

"That was my question but I don't mind you asking like this. This is like my wildest dreams coming true." He tells me with a gleam in his eyes and I tilt my head smiling. "Really? You have a weird preference for dreams." I step back and ram my elbow into his stomach. He grunts and topples over while I ram the knife into its place in the belt. He looks up at me still holding his stomach, I hope I broke a rib.

"I asked you a question."

He tilts his head to the side, amusement glimmering in his eyes.

"Did I not answer?"

I shake my head deciding to not deal with this and open the wooden door that leads to the backside of the castle. I can't stand to look into his face without feeling sick and I hate myself. I hate myself for the glimmer of betrayal that swims inside of me.

I know better than anyone else not to trust Cassian Moreau.

Or any man that thrives on power and destruction.

I hear his steps following me outside but ignore his presence as I make my way towards the barns so I can get to my horse. I have neither the time nor the patience for another confrontation with this man child.

"Judging by your clothes I'm taking a hot guess and say you're going to town, but to do what exactly?"

Even his voice is fucking annoying.

"To do something that's none of your business." I snap as I make my way through the dirt and the barns come into view. It's quiet outside, no birds are chirping, the sky starless, like the lull before the storm.

"You are awfully demanding today, first you throw me out of your father's office, and now you're just being plain rude."

I throw a glare over my shoulder and it encourages him to go on.

"I'm not saying that I'm complaining. It is exquisite to be bossed around by you. Especially in this damn suit."

My steps falter and I narrow my eyes gauging if he's being serious or not. His eyes give me an obvious once over not caring to hide it the slightest bit.

I chose to ignore it, diverting my eyes from him.

"I'm not being rude; I'm always like this, now would you do me the honor and leave me the hell alone? I repeat it's none of your business."

"Well, I would like it to be my business, care for a partner?" He asks and at that, I look up at him to see the amused look on his face.

I stop walking to stand in front of him, trying to not deck him in his stupid, handsome face. He grins and pushes his hands into the pockets of his trousers making me narrow my eyes lightly.

"Is all of this a fucking joke to you?"

"I think you need to specify 'all of this.'" He arches a dark brow at me. Why am I listening to him again? Oh yeah because I'm fucking stupid.

I know I shouldn't do it. I should walk away as I planned, forget about what happened, and get some steam off. Who knows if he'll answer honestly anyways? It's stupid and pathetic but I don't think I'll be able to fall asleep tonight if I don't ask.

"Did you know he was lying to me? That you and I. . ." I can't even finish the sentence without feeling like a fool.

The amusement drops instantly from his face.

My eyes fly up to the sky, the cool dark blue color a relief to me.

After Cassian gave me that stupid ring I should've known. His saying that he remembered about the Night-crawlers was just to mess with me and I didn't notice it. I did feel suspicious but not enough to investigate further.

As if his outer appearance was made to distract me from any rational thoughts. It's aggravating.

"Does it matter if I knew?"

"Of course it does, it determines if I will assassinate you or not. Tell me and don't you dare lie to me, Cassian." I order pulling myself together.

"I knew it. Even before Zayne abdicated the throne, I knew."

I have to take a step back when a humorless laugh escapes me. That's more than I wanted to know. He knew it when we were children—?

And he continued to tease and torture me every time he visited the Sebestyen court.

"Well, you made an awful job at winning me over." The words are bitter but I don't care.

It takes me a few seconds to organize my thoughts and when I have I turn and make my way into the barn. Which parent would tell their child they would marry someone in the future? I don't understand why Cassian continued to be so mean towards me, even though he knew sooner or later I would become his wife, that doesn't even make sense.

Either he is braindead—which I have to object dreadfully— or he just has no clue what a woman finds attractive in a man.

"You think so? I think I rather stayed in your mind with my behavior."

He's still following me.

"Yes, you did. In my fucking nightmares, Moreau."

A deep chuckle escapes him and I shiver due to the cold.

Nighttail neighs the second I step into the barn, her black mane shining in a dark blue color enhanced by moonlight.

"I thought the ring was clear enough for you to know of my affections now. The fact that I told you the other princes have no chance was a clear hint towards the deal. Maybe I overestimated your intelligence." Cassian speaks up again as I make my way over to my horse. Is he trying to look like the good guy? As if he intended to make hints that we were to be wed no matter my objections.

"Judging by your usual arrogance I thought it was you needing to feed your ego as if it isn´t big enough," I tell him while I open the wooden door and step inside, greeting Nighttail.

"Hello, beautiful. You care for a ride tonight?" I ask gently and pat her side. Her fur is shiny and soft; I'm already excited to shoot through the chilly night on her back.

It´s always a good feeling to ride with her like I can flee the world and its traps.

Nighttail neighs again at my touch and when I turn my head I see Cassian looking at me.

"What are you still doing here?"

I thought I dismissed him with my rather rude comment about his arrogant behavior.

"I'm coming with you. I know there's no way to stop you from going into town, but I'm not letting you go alone."

I have to laugh at his words and I watch him furrow his brows.

"I can take you down and you're supposed to be a great fighter. There's no need to worry and no need to fake interest. It seems like I can't do anything against the fact that I'm going to marry you. The game is over, Cas," I tell him. I can´t stop the bitter tone that drips from my voice. I rather focus on getting my satchel and eye the prince from the corner of my eye.

He opens his mouth but halters considering his words. "But you did know it had to come sooner or later. That you needed to marry a prince?"

"Hector's mother governed for over ten years before he was ready to take the throne."

"But she is a widow. You're not. It is your duty—," I scoff at his words.

"If someone mentions my duties, as if I don't know what they are again, heads are rolling."

His lips twitch.

How is he able to find this funny? I have heard enough of duties and rights and all that nonsense. It might seem like a joke to him but this is my reality.

I ignore him and gently put the satchel onto Nighttails back, securing it on her stomach.

"What would your take be?" He asks and my head snaps up looking at him.

"What do you mean?"

"What would you decide, if you were queen, about the Protestants?"

I take my time to order the reins of Nighttail while I ponder his question.

Her dark eyes watch me and I wish I would know what swims in those deep pools of the abyss. Her head does a small tilt as if to tell me to go on and reveal my thoughts to the Moreau Prince.

"I would talk, listen to their conditions and negotiate." I turn and look at him.

"Sometimes that doesn't work. What if there needs to be bloodshed."

I have to smile at his choice of words.

"All of you think just because I'm a woman I'm scared of blood. But that's not the point. The bigger the army doesn't mean it's stronger," I tell him and he looks at me, focused like he is listening to me. It takes me a second before I speak up again, avoiding his eyes.

I shift, uneasy by his gaze.

It feels like he can see right through me, peeling off every layer.

"Instead of attacking frontally I would spy on them, make out their strongest points, and weaken them. Fight from the within with nimble and quiet fighters. With you men it's all about being buff and strong but the Protestants are people from the street, they fight differently. They're cunning and they use their brain instead of their muscles. That's why Lord Romanov came back with so much loss. The Protestants know their grounds, they're familiar with the texture, the wind, the weather, they can probably tell an unfamiliar army from a mile away, which gives them enough time to prepare." I finish and move my eyes from him to my horse.

I don't want him to laugh at me or belittle me just like my father did. I'm surprised he did even listen to what I said. Still, I braze myself, locking my heart up. I know I'm not stupid my plan is good.

The first reaction I receive is a dark chuckle that splits his lips into a smile. My hands clench into fists and I'm ready to break his nose at any stupid comment.

"It's like a horde of galloping horses to them when you step onto their lands. You're sending an army who fights like bears and use iron to fight against people, who use nature and wisdom. Their instincts are their greatest power in my opinion. It's practically programmed that you lose."

I shrug my shoulders and watch his lips stretch into a big smile. His body shakes with kept laughter. I narrow my eyes at him.

"What? Why are you laughing?"

I know there's a stupid comment dancing on his tongue and soon it will escape those cruel lips.

His eyes sparkle in amusement and awe.

"It's just funny how your father so desperately wants a strong and powerful leader for his kingdom and can't see that he has one right in front of his eyes." He tilts his head to the side and a dark strand curls against his forehead. "Kind of ironic, isn't it?"

~ 16 ~

The night is just as I expected it to be.

The wind bites coldly into my face, making my eyes tear up by the speed of Naighttail. Something euphoric swirls in my chest and it takes all of my willpower to not disrupt the silence of the night with a cheerful yell.

Every time I'm outside with her it feels like I'm flying, we become one unit adjusting to each other's movements. It´s a primal feeling that I hold within and I know no one can take that from me, not the walls of the castle and especially not my father.

I turn to my side to see Cassian´s concentrated face, his body tense and yet elegant as he moves on his horse beside me. He looks like he´s been doing it his whole life, born to fly with the wind and melt with the night.

His hair flies behind him, the curls a mass of chaos in the wind, a weird glimmer is in his eyes and I'm scared to think of what is going on in his mind. Something is bothering me about this raw picture of him.

He looks like a dark warrior prince and the worst thing about it is that I find it highly attractive.

I try not to focus on long elegant fingers that clutch the rein or strong thighs that press against the side of his horse.

I´m not someone to ignore beautiful things but it is dangerous terrain if it involves the prince. Admitting that I do find him attractive would feel like a defeat.

Even if it's hopeless I can't just hold up a white flag. No, if I have to marry him, I'm going to make it as hard as possible for him, starting with tonight. Carina Sebestyen is never scared of fighting and won't back down. Whatever this physical attraction between us is—it's just that. Physical.

"Where exactly are you taking me?" His voice cuts through the howling wind, making a small evil smile spread on my lips.

"Wait and see."

It takes us almost half an hour to get into the capital even though our horses are trotting quickly.

Once we enter the border of town I decide to let our horses tied to the side of the Green Knight, an inn that is known for its deliciously greasy food on the afternoons and their seductive visitors at night.

They've got rooms upstairs for discretion but tonight I'm here for someone to meet that I haven't talked to in a long time.

Cassian's insistence to join me is not going to keep me from my plans tonight. I'd rather have him with me and know where he is, instead of wandering the castle halls and potentially telling my father that I'm leaving the palace.

Once the horses have their sandstone troughs filled with water I get inside the inn, Cassian behind me like a big wall, ready to jump into aid at any given danger.

It's weird how he behaves but I've heard of the Demeter men and their stupid desire to prove themselves.

"For our first date, you're taking me into a brothel? Is that a kind of fetish of yours?"

I can hear the smirk in his voice and turn around to narrow my eyes at him.

"This is neither a date nor a brothel. Behave yourself I don't want my reputation to suffer under your bad manners." I scold him and walk over to the counter, sitting down on a barstool.

"Suffer? Your reputation will be lifted in my presence, Sebestyen." I hear him grumbling as he sits on the chair beside me.

My legs swing lightly from the height of the stool and I catch Cassian throwing an amused look at them.

A middle-aged woman, dressed in a red, astonishingly beautiful gown, catches our arrival a smirk moving onto her painted lips. Her dark hair brushes the curves of her breasts, accentuating them sensually. She is a woman who knows what her customers want the second they step into the inn.

Gisella tries to hide her wise and cunning mind under all those layers. I once talked about how easily men can be fooled by a hollow shell. This shell of a darkly beautiful woman has a beautiful mind too, using it and her tempting curves to hide how powerful she is.

She is a fighter like every woman should be.

"Carina Sebestyen, holy Adales, I haven't seen you in months," She says and immediately fills two jugs with an amber liquid while I lean over the counter to press a kiss against her cheek.

She smells of spice and liquor, a scent I've grown familiar with.

Cassian stays quiet but his eyes are observing, taking in the familiarity Gisella and I share. While he assesses the situation his hand drops on the rest of my stool, his fingers grazing my neck.

"And you've brought a friend, a very handsome friend." She grins and leans on the counter, making her breasts push up provocatively and I roll my eyes.

"Don't flatter him, his ego is big enough."

"No, no keep going, she's doing a good job in deflating it, so there's plenty to go. I want her to realize what she has in me," Cassian says with a grin and I jab my elbow into his ribs making him narrow his eyes at me. The pressure of his fingers on my shoulder deepens. His leg bounces slightly and I raise a brow holding his stare—Cassian is nervous.

"I´m her date. It´s our first one." He masks his nerves with a cocky grin and I pull my lips in a straight line.

"This is not a date."

"Definitely is."

"Nope."

Gisella smiles at our interaction as she quickly attends to a different customer before reappearing.

I don't touch the glass but it seems like Cassian can't wait to finish it. "Just so you know, I won´t hurl you up on your horse when we leave later," I whisper and lean a bit closer. Cassian grins and shrugs his shoulders. "I bet you can´t even wait to get me drunk and have your ways with me." A small bubble of laughter bursts from my lips. "Not happening in a lifetime, Moreau."

His shoulders slacken lightly as he eyes me and relaxes.

"So what brings you into my beautiful house, Carina? It surely can't be just a small chat?" Gisella catches my attention and I nod before I shoot a small look at Cassian whose eyes are flying over the different people in the bar.

I follow his line of sight for a moment and watch the people.

Some are playing cards others talking to the masked courtesans, who are hoping for a score tonight. As popular as the Green Knight is, the people inside aren't. Thieves, liars, and murderers but here they come all together looking for peace and an evening or night to enjoy.

The worlds collide in the Green Knight and find a common ground to forget all the cruelty that happens during the day.

I nod my head toward the back and Gisella understands immediately.

"You think you can stay alive while I talk to Gisella quickly?" I lean in closer to Cassian, whispering and his head flies around to look at me. His gaze darkens for a moment catching me off guard.

"You dragged me here to leave me alone?"

"I didn't drag you here. You begged me to come—" I know I've said the wrong words, the second his green eyes light up.

"Oh, you're going to beg me—"

I hold up a hand to interrupt him, the dirty smile on his lips making me narrow my eyes again.

This man can't stay serious.

"That blonde girl over there is watching you since we came in, she can help you wait."

I'm already off the stool when he protests.

"I'm your date."

"This is not a date."

I hear him grumbling when I follow Gisella around the bar and into the back room that is supposed to be for staff only. I'm not assured to let Cassian stay on his own, who knows what that stupid boy could start inside here?

The room I step into smells sweet and fruity and when I catch the small black stick on the table I know where the smell originates from.

"You still smoke that stuff?" I ask waving a bit in front of my face to get rid of the fog that's going to make my head dizzy if I stay for too long.

She walks over to the couch and sits down picking up the pipe filled with opium.

She takes a long drag before answering me. "I don't have the luck to sit on a throne all day worrying about which dress to wear. This makes it easier." The scent doubles as it floods the room.

"Come on, you know that's not what I'm doing."

"I do, but others don't." She says and I sit down opposite her furrowing my brows.

The cushions on the chaise longue are hard and uncomfortable, digging into my spine.

"What is that supposed to mean?"

"It means the people in town are getting restless. They're tired of your father's government and they think you're not going to do any better."

What a surprise another group of people who think I'm useless on the throne.

"Are the people of Aerwyna contemplating joining the Protestants?" I ask her and she shrugs her shoulders.

"I just hear bits of the guests and they don't sound very happy."

Add it to the list of ongoing disasters I try to avoid. I worry all of this will blow up in my face in the end.

"That's not my fault, I'm trying to change things but you know how he is."

"I certainly do know that."

A humorless chuckle escapes her and I lean back in my seat sighing.

It feels like everything is just turning negative at once and I don't know how to stop it.

"The castle has been hell without you." I shoot her a small smile and her features darken. She leans over and squeezes my hand for a moment. "If I could I would be there with you."

"But you aren´t."

I´m trying to dig my way out of my grave but somehow there´s an endless amount of dirt. It´s trying to suffocate me choke me and force me to finally take my last breath in this world.

My father has nothing better to do than yell at me and sent out army after army, with that bastard of a lord. He doesn´t even notice that soon there is no kingdom he can rule over if everyone will protest against him and the crown.

"You´re worried."

It's a statement of Gisella that doesn´t need to be answered. She takes another drag and I watch her.

I´m trying to fit her frame into the background behind her. There is such a stark contrast between her beauty and the moldy walls that shimmer in light green, the floorboards with various holes and cracks. Or the paint chipped from every wooden piece of furniture.

She now lives a life where it isn´t important what you possess. Materials are what they are needed for. A chaise longue to sleep on, a floor to walk on, a roof to protect you from the rain.

There is no detail or luxury and yet she is more alive than I ever will be. She has the gift that I was robbed of since birth. Freedom.

But I don´t blame her for leaving the palace when she could. I would do it in a heartbeat if I would have the chance.

Sensing my dark thoughts shifting in the air around us Gisella speaks up again.

"So you're sympathizing with the eligible bachelor Prince of Demeter?" She says with a grin and I groan.

"Please don't make me start on that, it's not important. What´s important is that I heard that the Dark Prince is forming an army. An army to fight against the king and my kingdom," I say leaning forward, propping my elbows on my knees.

Gisella furrows her brows and she puts the pipe down when she looks at me.

"The Dark Prince? Isn't that some kind of myth parents put out to make their children behave."

"That is what I thought. But he is a threat; people say he is the rightful regent of all Adalon. Maybe he is real, maybe someone is pretending to be him I don´t know. What I do know is that I won't let him take my throne," I say and I just know by the look on her face all of this is new information to her.

Gods, we are all damned.

That's what's so strange about it, if the Dark Prince was forming an army, Gisella would be the one to know. She knows everything and everyone. And still, someone paid me to kill all these men and find Ellister. As if someone wanted me to know about the Dark Prince.

But why would the Red Saint care about the Dark Prince? The people know me as a money-hungry assassin. Information isn't valuable gold coins are.

The Red Saint wouldn't care about an army going against the throne, it is the girl under the mask who would.

But that would mean that someone knows of my identity and that's impossible.

"You're worried." She repeats.

"Of course I am! The Dark Prince wants my throne, the Protestants are winning more land with every day and now my father wants me to marry a man I despise," I let out frustrated, pushing my hair out of my face.

My fingertips tingle in familiarity when the feeling of despair floods my veins.

"I'm going to meet the right hand of the Dark Prince on the blood moon and if it's true that he's here in Aerwyna I don't even know what to do. I don't even know if he's destructible," I tell her honestly and a thoughtful look moves on her face.

"Here's what you're going to do. You will meet that man of the Dark Prince and I will try to gather as much information about him until that as I can. Your father is currently in charge of the problem with the Protestants so don't carry that onto your shoulders, Carina. There have been no requests for the Red Saint in some time. Focus on the most important task, that is to become the Queen of Aerwyna and I know you don't like the boy out there but maybe he could be exactly the key to what you want." She stands up and straightens her gown. I furrow my brows at her last words. "Believe me when I tell you that Cassian isn't the key to anything."

I watch her as she walks over with a sly smile. "Are you sure?"

"I know Cassian forever, he might seem powerful but he isn't. He's just a cruel boy who likes to hide behind his title."

I get up from my seat while Gisella eyes me, and tilts her head to the side. "There was a certain familiarity between you two."

"Of course there is. If you mean familiarity based on us two fighting all the time and wanting to kill each other. I put up with him because Cassian is not a threat. He works only for himself and his favors, so how dangerous can he be?"

Gisella takes my hand in hers and I can feel the rough callouses on her palm. "Maybe then you need to make him want something for himself, so you're at the advantage."

Her eyes sparkle dangerously.

"What do you mean by that?"

"I mean that Prince Cocky over there is a prince, yes, but underneath it all, he is a man. And what is so similar about every single man?" She asks looking at me impatiently as if I should know the answer.

And she is right I should know, I should've known earlier on but I didn't think from the right point of view. I had to look through her eyes to know. As the realization kicks, an evil smile forms on her red-painted lips. "They can be easily manipulated by a woman."

~ 17 ~

To my relief, Cassian is still sitting on the same chair, as I emerge out of the back room.

His arms are crossed in front of his chest and a sour look stains his features. I arch a brow at Gisella to let her see that this male species is not a man but rather a man-child.

We depart with a short hug before I pick up the prince from his spot and make him follow me. I ignore his mumbled questions he is not entitled to ask. Not after he hid his secrets.

Gisella likes to keep her identity hidden from the public. Being a consort of the king might seem like a good fortune in the beginning, until the moment he grows bored of you.

She was the first one of many. I made it hard for her to stay at that time and when I look back at it I feel horrible. She wasn't the one responsible, it was my father.

He was the one who brought a strange woman into the castle for his pleasure without explaining it to his children. I don't even think we were supposed to find out and Henri didn't, thank the gods, he was too young to understand but I did. I was always curious and I was raging when I met her for the first time. It is a memory I always keep in my heart because strangely the castle did feel less empty when she was around. Sometimes you think you despise people and their presence but once they're gone you realize how much you felt in their company.

Now she is one of my closest friends and the best information source one can get in Aerwyna. If you want to get some information without anyone noticing, Gisella is the right woman for you.

Not just that but she is caring, loyal, and strong. She might be everything I always wanted to be.

"That's it?" Cassian speaks up as he follows me out of the Green Knight, leaving the smell of liquor and a mixture of body scents behind.

The moment we step outside I take a breath of the crisp air and turn around to eye my companion.

"What did you expect?"

I put my hands on my hips as he stalks forward, the stones cracking under his boots.

"Ominous talking, revealing secrets, maybe being involved? Yes, I think that would've been nice."

I scoff at his words and turn, thundering down the steps that lead onto the streets.

I'm trying to avoid his gaze, still feeling uneasy with what Gisella told me to do.

"You don't want me to know." He states.

"What makes you think that, Your Highness?" I shoot back, the sarcasm dripping from my voice. As if I would tell him anything. We walk in silence for a moment, his boots dragging against the ground as if he's making noise on purpose.

"As alluring as secrets can be, sometimes they're not necessarily good for building common ground or a relationship."

I have to cackle at his words.

"Look who's talking."

"I already told you I tried to make it clear that it was a closed deal. Even if I did tell you, would you have believed me? And if you did you can't tell me you wouldn't have hated me even more."

My steps halter for a moment. I feel his body heat right behind me but I'm too stubborn to face him.

"That's not the point. You're talking about building a relationship on trust and honesty while you lied. And it's not as if I've been dying to build a—,"

A soft breath escapes my throat the second I turn to glower at him. Instead of glowering, I'm pressed between a brick wall and a hard body.

Fuck.

My eyes fly up, wide and surprised my mouth parting as I stare into the swirling forest that is Cassian's eyes.

"What the hell are you doing?" The moment I manage to breathe out the words, his arm presses softly against my throat, his thigh parting my legs as it shoves between them, blocking the kick I wanted to throw at him.

I instantly try to go for my knives but I don't get the chance to move a centimeter when his other arm flies out, pinning my wrist to the wall.

I hiss when his long fingers wrap around my soft flesh and turn a glare on him. "Is this how you try to earn my trust? By forcing yourself on me?" I arch a brow and a secretive smile turns up his lips. I start to struggle but he presses on further.

"I wouldn't do that, princess." His voice is barely a whisper as it runs down my spine. Not a second later, voices appear in the night and a group of soldiers pass the alley he pushed me into.

I freeze completely, even lean a bit into the prince to make his frame hide me from view. But luckily the soldiers don't even spare the alley a glance as they pass. The street light glints off the coat of arms that is engraved in their armor. What are they doing in the capital?

I turn my head again to look at the prince, whose eyes are already placed on my face. We wait in that position a little while longer until I can't hear the shouting of the soldiers anymore.

A small breath escapes me and my muscles relax for a moment. "What are they—oh."

My sentence ends in a breath when he moves his face, his lips grazing my jaw in the process. I am still again when my skin starts to buzz.

His fresh scent of mint and a winter breeze fill my nose, circling my thoughts, and entwining them into a chaotic dance. A faint buzzing starts deep inside me and spreads through my body like an inferno.

"Princess." He looks at me and his grip loosens, he offers me to move. Instead, I get even closer to him.

His lips graze my cheek and I shudder, unable to answer. The thoughts of the passing soldiers vanish.

"I like it when you're being secretive. It's hot to see you in charge."

The words travel along my cheekbone before his lips graze my neck.

"But I like it more when you trust me." He places a soft kiss against my throat and I feel my knees weaken. No one has ever touched me like this and I try not to bathe in the powerful feeling that floods my veins.

I bite my tongue until I feel blood and he raises his face to look me in the eyes.

"Do you even know what trust means?" I should move. Get his hands off of me. I know I could, but I don't feel like I'm in any danger, even though his arm is placed against my throat it doesn't exert any pressure.

His eyes blaze lightly and for a moment I think I see genuine regret.

"I mistreated the little trust you gifted me with. I can imagine how you feel. And believe me when I tell you that I regret it." His words seep into my skin with ease.

My blood blazes at the proximity and my eyes fly from his eyes to his lips.

Fear rushes through me so cold that it clears my hazy thoughts. His hold relaxes a bit and it takes just a flick of my wrist and a blade appears against his exposed throat.

His eyes widen for a second just like mine do. We both look down between us, my breath labored as if I've run for miles. The blade almost slices his collar open, making him chuckle.

"I didn't see that coming."

"Always expect the unexpected." I applaud myself for my steady voice. I exert a bit of pressure because it seems that I can't move on my own.

His hold loosens on me while he looks from the blade to me. I expect him to release a stupid comment but instead, he speaks the most ridiculous words I've ever heard.

"I apologize sincerely, princess, for breaking your trust."

And I don't find any words good enough to strike back.

"You can go to hell, Cassian."

~

"You look majestic when you ride her, do you know that?"
I shoot Cassian a glare when I put the satchel away making
him chuckle.
We didn´t speak one word on our way back to the palace but
it seems like he is not fazed by my obvious anger.
   "I didn't mean it in that way; you have such a dirty mind,
princess."
   "Shut up, would you? You can be happy that I took you
with me."
I had time to think about Gisella´s proposition of seducing
Cassian and taking advantage of him in my way and I
concluded that she is a crazy, lunatic for thinking I could
seduce someone. A top of it all the one I should seduce is this
idiotic moron. Besides that, I am never going to sink that
low. I want to beat him fair and square so I can laugh him in
the face at the end. Seducing him on a physical level would
be contra-productive. The way I seem to react to his touch
further enhances the fact, that I´m not the right one for a job
like that.
   "You're right I am so happy that you, mighty Princess
Katarina, took me to a brothel just to disappear and do
Adales knows what. And the fact I still haven´t heard
thanks."
I turn around and narrow my eyes. "Thanks?"
"Well, if the royal guards would've seen you, you´d be in a
lot of trouble now." I shut my mouth and clench my jaw
angrily. He did save me a lot of trouble but that is the least he

can do. "I take my thanks in a kiss, right here." He taps his cheek and grins, making that stupid dimple appear again.

"You haven't got enough? Because you looked cozy when that blonde was eye fucking you from across the room," I say fixing the satchel against the wall. My hands are cold and stiff, I'm tired and I still don't know one more bit about this stupid Dark Prince.

I can already feel Cassian when he's in my back before he speaks up.

"Jealous princess?"

I scoff at his words and turn around to tell him off but he's closer than I expected which makes me walk straight into his chest.

I take a confused step back and collide with the wall of the barn in an instant. I have the urge to close my eyes in embarrassment but instead, I narrow them and stare right up at him, tilting my chin.

This feels all too familiar.

His green eyes shine amused and I shake my head quickly.

"I'm rather pitying the girl who has such bad taste."

He can't come closer, please, not again.

He chuckles lightly and presses me against the wall making my breath hitch in my throat when his hand places itself on my waist. Gone is the childish play and it's replaced by something dark that tickles my curiosity. This time the touch is gentle, careful even. Still, the sense of déjà vu rushes through me.

"What are you doing?" I breathe out pathetically when his lips graze over my cheek and stop at my ear. My heart thunders so loud that I'm scared he might hear it when he moves closer just for an inch. My body shivers all over and my promise not to let him close again crumbles. It lasted twenty fucking minutes.

Pathetic, that's what I am.

"Proving that you have bad taste as well." He whispers and suddenly moves back.

"Asshole," I mumble while I follow him out of the barn. I curse myself internally because I´ve fallen for it again.

"So where do you know Gisella from?" He speaks up as we walk around the quiet castle.

He just goes back to normal like that. How am I supposed to manipulate someone that has been born to manipulate?

Hope leaves my body slowly but surely and I just want to crawl under the covers of my duvet and hide from the rest of the world.

His scent lingers around me for a moment. It´s like a warning that no amount of soap and scrubbing can get rid of the fact that I know how his touch feels against my skin.

"She is a former lover of my father, the closest thing I ever had of a mother figure, she's like an aunt," I tell him to satisfy his dangerous curiosity and he nods, his eyes set on the Royal Gardens we pass.

"And what did you talk about?"

"Nice try."

I watch his lips stretch into a cheeky grin.

"It's really rude to be this noisy, prince," I tell him making his jaw harden slightly.

"You don't want me to know?"

He repeats the question.

"Well, else I would've talked in front of you if I wanted you to know. Just make something up in your head; I talked to her about my unrequited crush on you. You think everyone is in love with you anyway," I offer and the sudden look of anger on his face confuses me. Maybe now is not the right time to joke. I thought I made it clear in that alley that I wouldn´t talk.

"I get it. You don't trust me. What do I need to do so you trust me again?" He suddenly asks while stopping his walk.

"Maybe be trustworthy?" I offer with a sarcastic smile but he just rolls his eyes, a muscle ticking in his jaw. How can he seriously be mad, if he was the one plotting with my father?

"Do you think that´s all you have to do? Throw an apology at me and then everything will be alright?"

"I´m not stupid." His teeth grind and I narrow my eyes.

"You are if you think you have any right to know about this. You´re not a very trustworthy person, Cassian."

His eyes blaze at me, urging my anger.

"Do you think I would've chosen to marry you if I had a choice?" He tells me angrily.

"Oh wow, that convinces me to like you, good one," I say before I walk past him, purposely ramming his arm against mine.

I´m sick of this back-and-forth game.

"That's not what I mean and you know that. You just see the enemy in me, even though I wasn't the one who made the deal."

He takes a step forward the anger dissipating in his eyes.

"I am in the same situation you are in, Carina."

I glare at him not believing that he just said that.

"Are you? Because I don't recognize everyone in your kingdom watching your every step, disrespectfully letting you know that they won't ever see you as their leader. Telling you that you can't do what a man can do. It doesn't matter if you marry me or not Cassian because you will govern over your kingdom anyway. They will respect you as their king, it doesn't matter if it's out of fear or not."

I take another step closer, my hands curling into fists.

"You just need a wife as a small accessory, something pretty to look at. If I marry you I become the queen but I will not make any decisions. You will. You will decide what happens to my kingdom and I can just hope that you don't hate me enough to make my life horrible because regent or not, you will decide." I have to take a deep breath before I speak up again while he stays quiet.

"I will be the one who decides what carpets we have in our rooms, which maids will clean up while you fight battles that are supposed to be mine. I will be bathed in jewels and gilded gowns, at your service. I will be carrying your heir. I can be just a queen if I have a king. You will be a king without any conditions. Just because you're a man and I am not."

I'm breathless after everything I said and if we wouldn't be outside I'm sure I would've run away at the look he's giving me. Pity glimmers in his eyes and I have to look away to not get angry at it. I don´t want his pity it just makes me look weak again. I want him to be angry with me, calculating and cold. It´s the only emotion I can handle from him.

"If I had a choice I would not marry you. But not for me, for you."

My eyes fly back to his in a second at his words.

They stand in such stark contrast to his dark, icy demeanor that I've grown used to.

"But you don't have a choice," I say with a sad smile and turn around to walk away. Before I leave the barns I turn to see him still standing at the same spot. "Thank you, for pulling me into that alley."

Luckily he doesn't follow me as I start to walk again and I slip back into the castle and my cold room.

My heart is still racing as if I've just run for days but it's neither from adrenaline nor from the ride from the capital to the castle. It's because of his words and while I know I shouldn't believe anything he says I somehow know he meant what he said. A lump rises in my throat as tears sting in my eyes.

I don't bother to take anything off as I dive directly under the safe covers of my bed and squeeze my eyes shut to ignore the upcoming tears.

It doesn't take long for sleep to wind me into its cold grip and when I fall, I dream of pine green eyes and choices that have to be made. I dream of a different life and who I would choose if I had a choice.

18

"Princess!"

I turn my head surprised, stopping my rushed steps to see Hector jogging towards me.

"Hector, good morning," I say with a smile and I let him kiss my cheek when he reaches me.

Even though I know about the contract I came to find a liking in Hector's silence and even though he still thinks he has a chance I don't dare to correct that. His presence is sometimes so calming it makes me shut off the racing thoughts I have in my head and that doesn't happen often these days.

I have to make it look like I chose Cassian over him and Marrus once I turn eighteen but it doesn't mean I can't enjoy his company until then. I try to ignore the slight flutter I feel every time his fingers graze my skin and the look he gives me with his honey eyes. It's so different than the one from Cassian. It's open and honest, he doesn't have anything to hide from me, he is strong and he shows me the most vulnerable parts of his soul.

"You weren't at breakfast this morning and I was wondering if you were alright." He says.

"Oh. That's kind of you, Hector. I'm alright, I had a meeting with the cook this morning and had to help my brother with homework, I'm sorry I would've liked to join breakfast." I tell him and his honey eyes glimmer at my words.

Pine green flashes in my mind and I have to think of this passing week since I was in town with Cassian and suddenly I get a tight feeling around my throat as if I would miss the dark look. Something about it is always so familiar. But is familiarity always good?

I never knew eyes could be that secretive like Cassian's while Hector's tell you the tiniest emotion wandering through him like an open book. I don't care to figure out which one I prefer because it should be obvious.

Cassian seems to be busy being the lapdog of my father and I didn't have the courage in me to talk to him after what he said.

If I had a choice I would not marry you. But not for me, for you.

It's like his voice is lingering around the walls I wander, clinging to my skin like a promise. Every time I try to push them away they come back louder and clearer, haunting me in my dreams, following me when I'm awake. It's like they edged their way into my bones, reminding me, sending waves and pulses through me. It's as if I can sense his presence, his scent lingering around certain areas, even though I can't see him.

What is that even supposed to mean? That he would want to marry me even if he had a choice? But he wouldn't because I don't want to?

These questions have been running in my mind for the whole week and every time I saw Cassian passing I tried to read his eyes but he was always closed off. I don't know if it's anger or if he finally understood that I don't want him close to me but now that he is at distance I don't know what I want anymore. My skin itches every time I think about it; a weird burning sensation inside of me like something is missing. I tried to shake it off but every time I see him it comes back, stronger than ever like it was never gone.

He didn't even make any stupid jokes or gave me ambiguous looks and I'm not saying I miss it. . .I'm just saying it's weird.

"Katarina?" Hector speaks up again and I try to focus on the man standing in front of me currently. Gods, I'm awful.

"Sorry, so much has been going on that my mind is spiraling all the time, what did you say?"

I feel bad, instead of appreciating the tingle I feel with Hector I spend my time thinking of a man that has done nothing more than manipulate me and use me.

"I was wondering if you wanted to ride out into the forest tonight. The flowers are in full bloom and the afternoon sun makes them appear in beautiful light, we could have a small picnic." He says and my lips stretch back into a smile. He's perfect.

It feels like I can't stop but smile when Hector is around it's great. It's just comfortable and safe with him I like it and I deserve to enjoy that for one time and give him my whole attention. I need to pull myself together and forget whatever I think happened that night with Cassian and me. Because there was nothing and there will be nothing besides an arranged marriage. An agreement nothing more, nothing less.

"I would love that. I have to change and wanted to talk to my maid first. Maybe we could meet in front of the gate in the afternoon if that's alright with you?"

"That would be perfect."

He presses another light kiss against my cheek and watches me make my way down the hall while I smile over my shoulder at him. Something small flutters in my stomach and I hope that it is enough. I don´t know for what but I do.

Once I'm around the corner I continue my way towards Edlyn´s chambers and shake off the dizzy feeling because I came here on a mission and

I´m confident in reaching my goal.

She's giving me the silent treatment for longer than I expected and I've had more than enough. I need my best friend now. I can´t believe that she´d be able to ignore me for this long and I have so much to talk about or else I will burn up into flames. Maybe that would be a way to fix my problems.

I need to talk to someone about this whole contract with my father and about how annoying Cassian is, how Marrus gets on my nerves with talking all the time and how sweet and caring Hector can be. Maybe I need to talk about the burning sensation I have when I think about the Prince of Demeter as well. It can´t be healthy how much my thoughts are spiraling around him and his stupid eyes. But most importantly I need to hear her snide remarks, her chuckle, or her scoff when she thinks I'm full of shit.

With these thoughts, I make my way to her chambers and knock against the door, softly, once I arrived.

"Miss Edlyn is currently in a briefing, Your Highness." The guard beside the door suddenly speaks up and I turn my head surprised.

Two blue, intelligent eyes stare right back at me and something feels familiar about him but I don't know what yet. Maybe he stood in front of my chambers sometime but that´s not what I should focus on right now.

"Oh, do you know when she is coming back?" I ask him and he shakes his head no. Something feels off. "Maybe the evenings but I'm not sure."

"Could you tell her I was here? And that I would like to see her in the evening or at night, it's important. " I tell the guard and he slips me a small smile, nodding his head. The weird feeling moves in my stomach at the smile as if I've seen it before but I'm not sure where. My skin buzzes as if sensing danger but nothing happens.

"Of course, Your Highness."

I turn and make my way to my chambers, disappointed that I couldn't talk to her like I wanted. A cold shiver runs down my spine and I turn slightly to see that the guard's eyes are still on me for a second I hold my breath before I snap my head back to the front and run straight into a chest.

"Princess Katarina, what a pleasure to meet you here." A deep voice speaks up and I try to shake off the weird feeling I had and look straight into the face of a familiar man. His green eyes are not comforting like others that I know. They're light and full of cruelty. The transparency in them tells me what he thinks of me. The color is washed out like old clothing does over the years.

I look into the face with a straight nose and high cheekbones, red, long hair swiped back on his head and he's dressed in what seems like expensive materials.

"Lord Romanov," I say, not sounding the slightest bit enthusiastic about his presence. I hoped I could avoid him for another week even if it was just meant to outrun the inevitable.

Many would call the advisor of my father a handsome man even if he was in his late forties but I could never see him that way with the three scars that start right on his left cheek and seem to drag their way over half his face. While it would make most people look courageous it makes him look just like the monster that he is deep inside of him.

I don't know where Lord Romanov came from and if he was here from the beginning, I'm not able to remember I was probably too young but I know he adds to misery in my life.

I try to give him a polite smile and move around him but he speaks up again making me stop and turn around.

"I heard you found a liking in the Prince of Demeter." An arrogant smirk sits on his lips and it looks like a horrific grimace due to the scars stretching his skin. I raise my brows unimpressed as I tilt my head lightly.

"Seems like you got your information a bit mixed up this time, Lord Romanov," I say with a sly smile my hands turning cold with sweat.

I know I can take him if I need to, I've been doing nothing else but wait, wait for him to finally make a move. He has done everything to hinder me from being happy, advising my father with the most horrible punishments when I stepped out of line, making it impossible to live under the same roof as him. It was a blessing when my father sent him away more times than I could count. I'm still waiting for the day he lays a hand on me so I can justify my beating him up because he took a wrong step. But he never did.

The older I got the more I spoke up and fought my stubbornness the fuel to my anger but to my dismay, he is too clever to lose his temper. Not enough at least for me to do something about it.

"Am I? Nightly adventures with the prince don't seem to tell me that

you're not interested, that he's visiting your chambers at night while no one is around as well?"

Fuck.

How does he even know that? He wasn't here during that time and still, he knows. I try to take a deep breath to clear my thoughts because the only way he could know is if Cassian or I told him.

The betrayal I felt last week makes its way back into my heart like a cold claw is gripping at the soft flesh. Romanov's eyes glimmer and he nods satisfied at whatever he thinks he sees in my face.

"Like I said. He did a good job, fighting your disgusting character which has the only desire to talk back and break rules."

I clench my hands into fists by my side and even though I know I should turn around and walk away I can't. He's right I have a bad temper and if no one is going to stop me right now I'm going to rip his ugly face apart. The dagger strapped to my thigh seems to turn colder at my anger and I know it would take me a second to grip it and slit his throat with it. Maybe I could elongate his scars a bit, torture him before I rip him apart. Something deep inside me hums at the thought.

"A good job?" I ask my hands trembling lightly while I understand. Of course, Romanov knows of the deal. I could imagine him knowing of my dislike for the prince when I was a child and marrying me off to him on purpose. Fucking bastard.

"To tame you, make you willing to marry him, seems like he's close enough. I have to congratulate him on that."

I take a step forward at his smug words, my skin feels like it's burning right off my bones.

"He didn't do anything and if you, my father, or he thinks I would marry him, even if it's just for a second you are all fools."

It takes all my willpower to turn around after that but instead of stalking away I feel an iron grip around my arm and a moment later I'm pressed against Lord Romanov's chest.

Acid moves up my throat when I notice the proximity to the man, making me want to throw up.

"Who are you calling a fool here, you little girl? I could marry you off to the prince in an instant and make your life the most miserable it could be. I would make sure it would be torture for you. Every. Single. Day." His voice is low and calculating and for a second I feel cold fear run down my body at his words.

My muscles tense at his proximity and I get ready to rip my arm out of his cold and connect my knuckles with his jaw any second.

"Lord Romanov."

A voice colder than ice cuts through the thin air making both our heads snap to the side to see a tall man approaching us. His dark curls are swiped back as if he just ran a thousand miles, his cheeks reddened and I hold my breath when I look into his eyes. They're of a pure black, so dark I've never seen something similar to it. I feel I'm looking straight into the Abyss.

His body is tall and lean, with no indication that he could feel threatened by anything. This is Cassian Moreau, the regent of the cruel brother that was once called Demetrus. There is no amused glimmer in his eyes, no relaxed posture or cocky smirk on his lips. He looks ready to kill.

The hard grip around my arm relaxes for a second before it appears even harder, making me wince and for a small second I see Cassian's eyes fly down to the grip Lord Romanov has on me.

"What a surprise, we just talked about you, Cassian." Romanov's voice speaks up, not the slightest bit threatened by Cassian's demeanor even though I respect him right now.

"The king wants to speak to us in his office and I remember Princess Katarina having an audience with Prince Hector, so I would advise you to take your hands off of her now." His voice dropped a few octaves and it moves right through my body and stops at my core. This time a shiver runs down my spine but it is not out of fear. Something stirs deep inside me at his command.

Lord Romanov laughs and finally, lets go of my arm. Bastard.

I start to rub the sensitive skin and watch Cassian narrow his eyes the slightest bit. It could be my imagination tricking me but it looks like his skin is vibrating as if he's holding himself back to take a step closer. To my horror, I'm encouraging him in my mind. Do it. Do it. Do it. I want him closer.

"I forgot how possessive you become of what is yours."

"She is not mine or anyone else's to be. Carina can look after herself."

I have to swallow again at Cassian's words and I wish I would say something, anything just to get my stupid mouth to use.

"I'm sure she is, still it is very convenient how. . .fond you are of her and the way you are willing to protect her," Romanov says his hands gesturing around us.

What is this old man even talking about? I feel like my head is going to explode at any second at the tension that shifts through the air while the prince stares the lord down. Challenges him to take another step so he can rip him apart.

"He doesn't need to protect me, are you deaf or just stupid?" I finally find my voice and drop my arms to my sides. I still feel Cassian's presence behind me and even though I would think his behavior is stupid I appreciate his trust in me. Or whatever convinces him that I can handle this.

Romanov gives another little laugh while his cold eyes place themselves on me.

"You are lucky to be on the side of a man like him it's the safest place you can be. Or maybe the most dangerous." With that, he curtseys mockingly and wanders down the hall to get to the office of my father. He just completely brushed over my words. My hands itch for a moment, wanting to grab a dagger and ram it into his back no matter how cowardly it would look.

My eyes fly towards the tall frame of the prince who stares at the Lord until he is out of our sight.

I take a step forward not knowing what I want to do but I stop when Cassian's eyes meet mine. There is a glint of the familiar green in them again but they still look creepy with the blackness lingering.

"You didn't have to do that," I say and his cold laugh rings in my ears.

"I didn't? You were close to pulling out your dagger, Carina, and if you'd done that I can't imagine what the Lord would have done. You can't play your games with him."

"I didn't want to, he came on to me!" I protest anger rising inside of me and I don't even know why. I wanted to thank him, thank him for stepping in and telling the Lord that I could take care of myself. And here I am again fighting with him. But deep down I know he is right. Grabbing my dagger and exposing myself would've been fatal and I'm lucky Cassian turned up conveniently.

"It doesn't matter, he's not going to hold his punches as I do when
you're fighting against him."

His eyes are dark again as he takes a step forward slightly ducking to look at me. Fire is blazing in them his features hard and unyielding. It is so different from his usual anger, so much rawer. He looks like an angel of death ready to get rid of anything that stands in his way.

"You held your punches?" I say surprised at the information. His hits were strong, they made me bruise for days and it wasn't even his whole strength.

"Are you even listening to what I'm saying, Carina? Lord Romanov is dangerous, stay out of his way, I know that is hard for your impulsive, childish behavior but next time I might not be around."

"You're calling me childish?"

My mouth opens perplexed at his words. They're tinted with anger and I can't stop but clench my fists again.

"I don't need you around. You're the one who is plotting with this man."

At that, he straightens up his jaw locking tightly.

"Right, I am."

His features freeze and I realize that he's hurt. I immediately feel bad for it and take a step forward my arm outstretched but he moves out of my way curtsying. Gods, this just went a completely different way than I wanted it to.

"I hope you have a great date with your prince, Your Highness." He says and rushes right out of my view, his words like burning coal right under my feet. I brush my hands through my hair sighing. How the fuck did this escalate into a fight when I wanted to thank him?

19

I almost cancel the audience with Prince Hector on my way back to my chambers, a heavy feeling settling in my stomach. I don't know if it is Lord Romanov's touch that makes me feel sick to my stomach, that I have to bend over the toilet for a few minutes, dry heaving.

My stomach burns and still feels queasy afterward.

I try to scrub my skin, wishing the feeling of his hard grip around my arm would disappear but sadly it doesn't. The ghost of his touch lingers like a warning, the nausea stays for another few minutes.

At least I get the sweet scent off of me but the image of Cassian and his black eyes stays in my mind. I feel many things about the prince, from hatred to anger, annoyance, and rage but I never feared him. Until this moment today. The way he looked at the lord made my skin crawl and my insides twist and even though the look in his eyes changed the slightest bit when he placed them on me I could still notice the burning rage. I could sense that I wasn't in any form of danger. Yes, most of the time my fists did itch with the desire to punch his face. His arrogance and superior behavior are unnerving and annoying. But not once did he put me into any danger, it's not as if he could anyway. It doesn't erase the fact that I never felt unsafe in his presence, despite our differences.

I almost forget about the fact why I ran straight into the lord and the sick feeling moves back into my stomach when I think about the guard and his eyes. Eyes that were familiar one moment and the next turned into a cold white. The iris and pupil vanished as if they were never there but it was so quick I wasn´t sure if I started to see things. He looked like the color of the ocean got swallowed by the white foam of crashing waves, leaving it empty and dull.

I´m sleep deprived of my nightly adventures so I don´t try to believe everything I see today. Still, I would like to be anywhere else than I am right now, stuffed into a lightweight dress, soft silk flowing around my legs as I stare out into the grass. Even the calm presence beside me goes mostly unnoticed.

"It's beautiful isn't it?"

I turn my head to look at Hector and muster up a smile.

"Yes, feels like it's almost summer," I say softly while I watch the sun bathe the kingdom in warm, orange light. The light hugs me in a secure grip making me forget the moment in the cold west wing of the castle and replacing it with the soft brush of the wind against my exposed skin. Birds are chirping not far from us, and the scent of blooming flowers lingers around us. It is mixed with an extraordinary smell, sweet and warm and it´s coming from the person who´s lying right beside me.

The last sun rays shine on Hector's high cheekbones, setting him in a soft tone and it feels like it's closing around his whole being. Like a big aura protecting him. He´s glowing from the inside out and for a moment it makes my stomach flutter in a comforting way. My fingers itch to brush the small strand of hair from his cheek but I´m sure it would be too inappropriate to do so which makes me settle on staring at this beautiful man.

He turns his head and catches me watching him, making my cheeks heat up in embarrassment.

I quickly divert my eyes and start to adjust my legs on the thin blanket we placed on the forest grounds. It's like I feel every blade of grass underneath me, every little stone and stick. It grounds me and I feel weirdly connected to the land as I've never felt before. He was right the flowers are beautiful in this light it looks like the forest is alive during the sunlight. Now that the sun is setting everything goes to sleep, a comfortable silence settling in.

Hector turns his head, his eyes on me as his body tips to the side and when I turn my head I can't help but take a small wavering breath in. His lashes are brushing his high cheeks and a warm feeling spreads from my fingertips through my body and stops deep in my belly. His arm brushes the side of mine as if on accident. The touch is hesitant; probing like he's scared of how I might react. So instead of pulling away like I probably would've done with anyone else, I subtly move my body closer showing him that it's a pleasant touch. Our thighs press against each other and I shiver lightly.

"Do you come here often?" I ask into the calm silence around us.

He nods and puts his chin on his hand, his eyes wandering over my face slowly. It feels like his eyes are caressing my skin with every movement. Roaming, memorizing as if he is going to paint my face after this time we spend together.

"Every time I needed to take a second to breathe or just think I came here. Your castle is beautiful but sometimes it's really. . ."

"Suffocating?" I offer and his lips stretch into a sad smile.

"Yeah, it kind of is. What do you do, to escape?" He asks me and it surprises me that he asks. More than it should. Instead of telling him I sit up on the blanket and offer him my hand to take. It's not just me wanting to show him the place I have called my haven for so long but I want to feel his touch against my skin. Will his finger be warm and trusting? Or cold and demanding, like a dangerous fire, burning me right to the ground.

"Where are we going?"

"To a place that doesn't shine during the day." My lips form a small smile.

He looks at me confused and my smile widens when he takes my hand and stands up. Warm and trusting.

My heart jumps lightly at the contact but I don't dare to let go of his hand as he intertwines our fingers. I don't think I have ever felt something so gentle compared to his touch. So soft and delicate and yet it makes my body feel grounded, and protected.

"You're not luring me into a trap to kill me are you?"

I shrug my shoulder nonchalantly.

"It's not my style to kill someone silently. I'm an open book about it."

"That is reassuring." I tug at his hand and watch his boyish grin that lights up his eyes. It somehow makes me feel like a girl. For the first time in my life, I don't weigh a crown sitting on my shoulders.

I'm glad to have chosen such a light dress it makes my steps in the grass almost dead silent and I feel that Hector enjoys silence. With him, I never feel the burning rage that always appears deep in my stomach when I talk to Cassian. I don't feel the slightest bit angry or aggressive against Hector, it's as if he can cure the fire that Cassian always fuels with his words.

I try to push the thought of the Prince of Demeter out of my head and focus on the prince walking beside me.

He's silent and while my father thinks it's a bad trait I would call him a fool for thinking that way. A man who can speak his mind without saying anything should be bathed in glory and appreciation. It's great to be comfortable enough to stay in silence sometimes. It says so much more than talking about nonsense and feigned manners.

I lead Hector out of the small forest and we step back into the Royal Gardens again, the guards straightening their spines at our arrival but turning their heads away discreetly.

"I'm going to show you a place that will always be some sort of haven for me. Nothing or no one could ever make this a negative place or ruin it with cruelty," I say softly while Hector squeezes my hand lightly. He's thanking me. Appreciating that I'm letting him see a part of me that I mostly keep guarded.

I feel his presence in my back when I lead him through hedges and flower grasslands, the cautious eyes of the guards following us when I stop in front of the black metal door.

Beautiful ornaments are engraved into it, making it look like a small secret garden due to the hedges that surround the small space. The sunlight reflects on the metal making it look magical to the eye. I don't hesitate to push down the handle and reveal a part of myself I don't let most people see. I've been trained my whole life, whether it is manners or language, fighting or feeling, a vulnerability was always bad. Something that could be the death of someone.

Hector and I slip inside and are submerged in dim lighting, surrounded by the gigantic hedges that tower over both of us. It is a small square space with a stone bench in the middle, the only source of light are specks of sunlight that reach through holes in the hedges.

I walk over to the bench Hector trailing behind me before I sit down motioning for him to do the same. A small breath escapes him.

"We have to wait until the sun goes down, then you'll see what I mean."

The small space is beautiful during the day, with specks of light shining through but to see its real beauty you have to be patient and brave enough to stay until there is no source of light beside the moon.

Hector takes the small space in for a moment before he nods and sits down beside me. His knee knocks against my leg for a moment and I inhale sharply at the touch.

"I can´t imagine how this could get any better."

"Believe me you will when you see it." His eyes jump back to my face and we share a small smile.

"Tell me something about you that no one knows," I say and turn towards him my hands placed in my lap. I wait for his words, trying to distract myself from his proximity. Who would´ve known that I fear nothing but the proximity of a man?

It takes him a second to think, his honey eyes unfocused into the distance.

"I know Oceanus is known for its beautiful beaches and their turquoise water. But there is this one place not far from the palace at home; it's a beach that leads into a small cave completely swallowed by darkness. But at a certain time at night, the moon shines high in the sky and places its light inside the cave.

The walls are made out of crystals and shine in the light so beautifully that it reflects on the water in thousands of ways. It always feels like magic when I sneak out at night to go there. You would like it."

I have to smile at his words wondering what Polyxena is like. I know he misses his home and while it is always enriching to see new kingdoms a true ruler's heart will always stay in his kingdom.

I can only imagine his people adore him, how could they not? Hector is elegant and has a quiet love that sits inside him, they must love him. Nonetheless, the Protestants are still growing and while I am sure he will be a good king, once he's officially crowned, people could get restless as well.

It's brave for him to take on this difficult task and I'm sure if I were in his place, the kingdom would be in chaos. I believe it is a fair difference to be prepared your whole life for a task and slowly ease into it. It's like he got thrown into cold water and everything changed in a matter of seconds.

"I wish I could see it sometime," I tell him and realize it's true.

I've never seen any other kingdom than my own and maybe if I don't do it now I never will.

"Maybe you can in the future." He tells me with a gentle smile.

I smile as well but it feels like it's rather sad than happy. I wish I could but I know I won't. Not if Cassian or his father call the deal off and I know they won't.

Hector's hand slips onto my cheek, pushing a small strand away, his fingers leaving a small tingle before they're back against my skin. His honey eyes glow lightly in the small space we're in and it makes me lean forward slightly, every inch of my skin aware of his proximity.

My heart rate speeds up quickly while his face inches closer to mine and I can't believe that I'm going to have my first kiss with a man I'm not going to marry, at my favorite place in the world. I should turn my head, speak up, and do something to stop this.

But instead of doing the smart thing, I let my eyes flutter closed while my hands fist the material of his dress shirt, waiting for his lips to meet mine. A moment of silence passes and when he doesn't move my eyes fly open.

"Woah." He breathes out as his hand slips from my cheek and his eyes move around us.

I follow them quickly and my lips stretch into a smile when I see the most magical thing that happens in the whole kingdom.

While we talked the sun set fully, diving the kingdom into darkness and that's when it happens.

The Night-crawlers bloom in every single hedge, dipping the small square space we sit in, into the purple light. It's almost as if we're sitting in a small cave chiseled out of a thousand amethysts. The light reflects on our skin, shining bright as if we were shining from within.

Their leaves are painted in a beautiful tone of purple and dark blue the center of the flower burning in a lighter blue. The light reflects around the whole space and I move my finger slightly enjoying the reflection on my skin. It always makes me feel like a child, playing with the little streaks of light as if they are alive. I look back at Hector whose eyes look almost blue in the lightening, a stunned look on his face.

"It's perfect." He says and looks back at me with a soft smile. I grin back happy that he likes it, that he cherishes this place as I do. I can see that it touches him deep within, leaving a mark. Telling me that the both of us won't ever forget this moment.

I don't know what comes over me if it's the soft glow of the flowers or the fact that Hector trusts me so much with his honest eyes but when I slightly lean forward and my hands wander around his neck, it's not Katarina Sebestyen regent of Aerwyna kissing the Prince of Polyxena.

It's just Carina pressing her lips against a boy she grew to like and is having her first kiss with.

~ 20 ~

The grin doesn't leave my face for a second on my way
through the halls of the castle, not feeling the slightest bit
threatened by the dark shadows wandering around, my steps
light and bouncy as I try to cherish the light feeling inside my
chest. Marianna waits for me in my chambers and gets me
ready for bed and I could swear I see a small smile on her
lips. My mood seems to be just contagious and it doesn't
waver until I get into bed and my eyes fly to the dark velvet
box, the lid opened.
Dark purple and blue tones reflect in the stone and they
indeed do remind me of the Night-crawlers which make my
throat close up lightly. Gone is the euphoria and the tingle I
felt on my lips after Hector and I parted only an hour ago.
I lean over and grab the box in my hands, the dark velvet a
stark contrast against my skin.
It feels like it's burning my skin while the ring glistens in the
candlelight, the amethyst shining in soft reflections. I can't
close one eye, sleep a stranger to me while my thoughts keep
spiraling thinking of the familiar burning of rage in me every
time I talk to Cassian. It feels like this small object weighs
tons and while I was excited an hour ago with the taste of
Hector's lips still on mine, I'm sure that that excitement is
gone now. I'm winding myself in a confusing net of more
problems with keeping such a close relationship with Hector
and I know it. I felt it the second before our lips met and still,
I didn't stop, it just felt too good to be a teenager for one
moment but I have plans to keep going with, I'm aware of
that. But maybe I don't need to go with them tonight, so I

shut the box right when a soft knock appears against the doors of my chamber.

"Come in," I call and the doors open just a slight bit before a slender body slips into my room.

"Oh. Were you going to bed?" Edlyn asks as she notices me sitting on the bed and I quickly get up, shaking my head.

"No, no. I was just ready but I'm not tired."

I make my way around the bed to walk toward her. Now that she's here I don't want her to leave so quickly.

She's dressed in a soft pink gown, flowers embroidered into the flowy fabric. Her hair is tucked up in a knot, a few stubborn strands peeking out and it makes my throat close up to see her, realizing how much I missed my best friend. Her soft scent engulfs me, so familiar and calming.

Her eyes drop to the velvet box that's still clutched in my fingers, a tight grip on it.

"I already heard about it." My friend says tensely while she nods at the box.

"Yes. . ." I say, unsure what to do.

Should I apologize? Maybe give her the drawings back, they're still hidden under the loose cardboard because I couldn't get rid of them. I would want to do nothing more than just fall into her comforting arms and never let go of her again.

"Do you. . .want to see it?" I ask her slowly, swallowing the thought and she nods making me open the box and place it in her hands.

"Huh." She breathes out when her eyes meet the sparkling crystals.

"He said he chose the color because of the Night-crawlers, that it would remind me of them," I tell her quietly while I admit that I couldn't stop thinking about what he said.

It's weird how he stays in my mind with just little sentences like that. I don't know if it's a mask he's wearing because he's so hard to read but can someone pretend this well? And who was he this afternoon I have never seen this side of him before and I hate that it somehow scares me? It's not him that scares me but the possibility that I don't know everything about him. Cassian might be annoying and cruel but he was never unpredictable, his familiarity is what never made me fear him. He has his dangerous secrets, protecting them behind sturdy walls. I didn't forget how easy it was for him to pretend but still, I wonder. . .

Wonder that the Cassian, who gifted me this ring with so much consideration, could be genuine. But who am I to judge? He is the only one who knows if it was just another illusion or if it was a real character.

"He certainly didn't use just a few coins for this." Edlyn pulls me out of my thoughts her eyes still on the ring.

"Practically it's not his gold he used for it."

"Still, the thought somehow counts, doesn't it?" She looks up and I shrug my shoulders.

"Well, the thing with the color is. . .very thoughtful of him. So you're going to marry Cassian?" She asks looking back up at me as she hands the box back.

Not if I can do anything about it. Even though the situation seems inevitable. Still, I nod and can't stop the next words that escape my mouth.

"I kissed Hector."

It needed to be said and even though it just happened a few hours ago it feels like a major weight has lifted from my shoulders, the consequences disappearing with it.

Edlyn′s jaw goes slack at my words but before she can say anything it bubbles all out of me, my impulsive self peaking through like always.

"This week has been hell without you Edlyn and I'm so sorry about what I said and what I did. Yes, I am your princess but I am also your friend and as your friend, I shouldn't have reacted that way. I still have the sketches you can take them and you can be forever angry at me if you want to be but please stop ignoring me. Because I feel like I'm drowning in this palace and while the kingdom is probably going to be defeated by Protestants, I'm out kissing a man who is sweet and gentle and I could actually see myself with but then there is Cassian who I'm promised to, who makes me feel weird things and now I haven't talked to him after this weird situation this afternoon. It feels like you′re the only person who believes me and is on my side. And I need you and I'm never going to decide for you again. You are your person and you can decide. I wasn′t any better than my father always is and it′s stupid of me that I didn′t notice it earlier on."

A deep breath follows after my speech but instead of answering me, Edlyn takes two steps forward and envelops me in a hug, answering my internal prayer. Her flowery scent tickles my nose immediately and all my muscles go slack.

"I am sorry. I know you just wanted to protect me." She whispers in my hair as I hug her with the same strength and love she gives me. For her being such a small person she carries a lot of strength in her. I don´t protest and bathe in the slight pain, of being crushed by her hug.

"I did want to protect you but I should've done it differently. I was a hypocrite." She shushes me and strokes my hair softly.

"It´s long forgotten. Take a deep breath and tell me what exactly is going on. Can't believe that I missed a week and you're already making out with a man and are engaged to a different one." She says once she lets me go and sits down on the edge of the bed. I groan at her words because it sounds even worse when she says them out loud.

"I'm not engaged and I didn't make out with Hector, it was just a kiss." I´m such a liar.

"Was it good?" She asks me with a smirk, making me chuckle lightly as my cheeks heat up. I stay quiet.

"Oh Adales, it was good!" She squeals and I quickly sit down beside her shushing her. The walls and doors have more ears in this castle than I can count.

"I didn't tell anyone about it and I'm sure if someone found out, there would be chaos everywhere. I don´t even think I´m allowed to kiss anyone but the moment was just perfect and beautiful." I tell her in a hushed tone so the guards' won´t hear us outside the door.

"This is so exciting I can´t believe you kissed him, what did he taste like? Did he taste good?"

The heat spreads from my cheeks down to my neck and I refuse to speak the words out loud. Of course, it was good. I might not have the experience like the women around town and the courtesans but by the trembling of my body and the lack of breath in my lungs after the kiss, it was pretty clear how it went. Hector tasted sweet and comfortable. It reminded me of the sweet delights, Mr. Rubain once sneaked into my room when he came back from Polyxena.

Edlyn's grin slowly fades as a thoughtful look moves in her eyes, her brows drawing together.

"But are you sure about what you're doing? I mean you have to marry Cassian in over a month."

"I know and I probably can't escape the contract. But is it so bad to have something real before I have to spend the rest of my life in what feels like a prison?"

My voice sounds pathetically foolish and I hate myself for even asking a stupid question like this.

Another thoughtful look moves on her face while she shrugs her shoulders.

"That's much of help, thank you," I tell her with a sarcastic chuckle and she grins, looking at me helplessly.

"Don't you need his man to fight against the Protestants? I mean the sooner you agree to the deal the sooner you'll get rid of them. I don't know if you can be selfish enough to abandon Aerwyna."

She's right and she knows me too well to pretend that I could have something real with Hector. How could it even be real when I'm leading him on, knowing that I won't— can't choose him in the end? It wouldn't be fair for any of us.

"And what about Cassian?"

I tense up when she mentions the prince's name.

"What about him?" I ask her defensively. She raises a brow and I sigh. I look away from her eyes because she'll see right through me and even though I need to talk about the prince, I don't know if I want to. It would mean analyzing his actions and words and my reactions to them. The way I feel about him is certainly split and I would like to ban all thoughts about him, even though I know it's impossible.

"If I recall correctly, you told me you felt. . .something in his presence a minute ago."

Damn her for listening to me so well. I already regretted the words the second they slipped from my lips.

"I feel anger and rage that's it." I try to sound as confident as I can.

I watch her raise a brow questioningly and I sigh running my hands through my hair. I quickly let go remembering that Marianna will scold me for ruffling up my hair in the morning.

"I don't know what I feel. It could be just physical and I'm just a deprived young girl that seeks closeness. My body's hormones are going crazy and Cassian is. . .attractive. But he is also so dark sometimes. It's like he has two sides and switches between those personalities. I don't know if I like that." I sigh.

"I don't even know who he is. One second he is flirty and annoying and I can handle that but then he switches and suddenly he's serious and closed off." I gnaw at my bottom lip, wondering if I should tell her about this afternoon. At her encouraging look, I go on.   "There was this moment today when Lord Romanov threatened me—"

"Lord Romanov? I thought you said you were avoiding that scumbag?" Edlyn interrupts me with furrowed brows and I nod. I can't tell her about the weird guard in front of her chambers. I don't want to worry her but I mentally make a task to let him be swapped just to be sure.

"I was unaware of his presence and he was being rude like always, he told me he knew of Cassian and that he approves of the marriage, he wants me to be miserable," I say and tell her quickly of the moment when he gripped my arm and how weirdly scary Cassian reacted when he saw both of us together.

"You know how he is, he just wants to get a raise out of me." I roll my eyes and she nods. "What did Cassian do?"

"I don't know what it was particularly but the way he spoke to the lord, it was clear he was threatening him. And his eyes were the purest black it was fucking scary."

"That is indeed creepy. You said his eyes were black?"

I nod and her eyes turn distant at the proposition. Before I can ask what she's thinking about she speaks up and beats me to it.

"But you said Lord Romanov approves of the marriage, then why did Cassian act like he was the plague?"

I shrug my shoulders at her question because I have gone over the moment a hundred times and still don't understand the dynamic.

"I don't know but it looked like he wanted to kill him."

Her eyes fly to my face and a sliver of emotion I can't put my finger on moves through them. My eyes narrow, uneasy at her behavior but I decide to let it slide. It's late and I'm tired.

"That should be a good thing, shouldn't it? You don't like Romanov and Cassian could be your alliance against him." I considered that as well.

"I know but after everything that he kept a secret I don't know if I can trust him and I can't decipher what that weird feeling is." I sigh and let myself fall back onto the bed, Edlyn following me. The soft covers envelop us comfortably. I stare up at the canopy for a moment, following the flowy fabric. The tight rope around my heart eases a bit.

"Okay, we need to categorize your feelings. You say maybe it's just physical what you feel for Cassian, which means it's based on his outer appearance."

That's the problem it's not just his outer appearance, sure the pine green eyes that shine in mischief and the crooked smile might be endearing and infuriating but that's not just it. It's the fact that he makes me feel like I'm burning alive with the things he says and the way he looks at me. His eyes are like hands diving deep into my body, making my blood boil and my insides twist. I never thought someone so aggravating could make the feeling of anger good. It's like he touches something deep inside me, unraveling me while he peels off every layer of my body. And mind.

Hector's eyes—his whole being—is such a contrast to the Prince of Demeter that this whole situation confuses me.

"I can practically hear the thoughts racing in your mind," Edlyn says with a soft smile and I give her a frustrated look.

"Maybe I'm crazy, maybe it's the fact that I know Cas since my childhood and saw him grow from this annoying kid into a very attractive but still annoying man." I turn my head to look at her.

"Things with Hector are different. Comfortable, I like him and his character and it's fun to spend time with him. I feel cared for, I know I can trust him, while Cassian held secrets and it just feels like he backstabbed me, he never shuts up and always feels superior to me, because he is big—"

"Big?" She raises her brows, making me roll my eyes at her suggestive tone.

"I don't know it's something about his being. Like when he walks into a room his character stretches out onto every wall. He confuses me with the things he says and I don't know if I should believe them or not," I say my eyes falling back on the velvet box that's still clutched in my hands.

"Fact is that the second he steps in the room I can't help myself and look at him. I hate him, so much. And I think it would be a deep satisfaction to ram a dagger straight into his heart but I know I couldn't. I couldn't."

Edlyn grabs my hand in hers and squeezes it comfortingly.

"You can't trust him if you don't give him a chance, Carina. If you have to spend the rest of your life with him wouldn't it be wise to try to get along with him? Even if it is just physical maybe that's the factor that's going to draw you close to him?" She asks and I let out a frustrated breath.

"It's just, that he always makes me feel so angry," I say thinking of the burning sensation every time I'm with him.

But instead of it feeling like I'm sick, it is a burning tingle that makes my stomach drop like I'm falling from high up.

"A good angry?" She asks me and my eyes fly up to her, mouth opened perplexed.

"What do you mean by that?" I ask and she chuckles lightly.

"Yes, Cassian makes you angry, he infuriates you and makes you burn but that can be a good thing. It's called passion, Carina, what do you want to do when he makes you this angry?" She asks and I try to think of every time I stood in front of him, chin held high holding his unwavering gaze.

"I wanted to stab him. . ." I repeat and she raises a brow.

"And?"

"I wanted him to kiss me as hard as he could, no place for air between our bodies," I say and close my eyes in horror. I swallow, trying to get rid of the burning shame that spreads through my body and into my cheeks. I want him to do so much more than that but I won't be able to tell her without flushing a deep scarlet.

"There you have it. He turns you on and that not just with his appearance but with his words, his teasing and whole being, and I'm sure you edge him on as well."

"But I hate him." I try to protest even though I know it's no use.

"Hate is a wide spectrum. It's such a strong feeling that invades your body, tearing your insides up, twisting your thoughts. Try to push it away as much as you want but it won't change a damn thing. You want him."

To hear the words she's speaking makes me press my hands over my eyes, trying to wish the realization go away. I sigh into my hands.

"Fuck me."

21

The next morning is cold and creepy which makes me wake up with stiff limbs and a layer of cold sweat lingering on my skin. I watch the grey clouds hover over Aerwyna, promising that rain will fall this afternoon. It's as if the weather knows that this day could only be cataclysmic. I need a few minutes of stretching my limbs and warming up the low temperature in the room before I get ready with Marianna's help.

The process is silent neither of us feeling the desire to speak up. It makes the whole process a lot quicker. But somehow I can't get rid of the goosebumps clinging to my skin, the small hairs standing on ends.

The castle seems to be asleep, slowly getting back to work the only thing heard in the halls is the echo of my heels clicking against the cold ground. I press my hands against the side of the periwinkle dress I'm wearing, the fabric flowy and soft with a slight pearlescent shimmer to it. I hope it will fulfill its purpose in taking off the hard edge that sits on my face. Yellow citrine crystals are dangling from my ears calming me down with the constant sound of them clicking against my skin.

Edlyn stayed with me last night talking and scheming the next steps I sadly had to go with and it felt like an eternity until we fell asleep late in the night.

Said steps are being currently dealt with as the velvet box sits in my hands tightly, the skin cold and unsure. I know there was no way out of it and that the things we planned weren't that bad. I just had to stop being a coward and hold my chin high, endure whatever has to come. It's probably my only way of surviving.

I use the whole way to the south wing of the castle spend in my thoughts, the temperature becoming hotter with every minute until the golden doors come into view. Two guards are positioned on either side.

"I want to have an audience with the prince," I say trying to sound as illiberal as possible while I push my shoulders back, my eyes cold and closed off. One of them moves their arm as if to offer me to knock for himself and I furrow my brows confused while the other speaks up.

"The Prince of Demeter ordered to never deny an audience for you, Your Highness." His words echo in my mind and I try not to show any emotion on my face when I raise my hand and throw a hard knock against the gigantic door. The vibration of the wood feels good against my knuckles, the feeling grounding me.

I bite my lip in anticipation, my heart beating in my throat but there is no answer so I knock again. Even harder. My knuckles throb in the same rhythm as my heartbeat does.

I get no answer.

He can't be already up and wandering the castle, can he?

I shoot a wary look towards the guard that spoke up but he doesn't look my way just when a grumble of an answer appears from behind the doors. I don't hesitate and push down the handle stepping inside the room to be hit with an aggressively sweet fragrance.

The chamber is bathed in dim lighting, the curtains are drawn closed, blocking the sunlight that tries to peek into the room and I roll my eyes while I walk over to the windows. The further I go into the room the stronger the sweet scent evolves, making my stomach curl in disgust.

My eyes fly over to the big king-sized bed to see Cassian squinting his eyes at me, grumbling something about sleep, and I notice a blonde girl lying beside him—topless might I add. My breath hitches in my throat when my eyes drop to his naked chest, the duvet slipped off to sit low on his hips. Two lean, straight lines wander from his hips downwards, dipping underneath the fabric but what catches my attention is the black ornaments that wander down his left side. Swirls and weird signs whirl and dance across his skin in the black color. It takes me a moment to understand that it's a foreign language I can't decipher. Something pulls at my heartstrings, the horrifically beautiful pattern looks like it's moving against his skin. It could be an incantation, a name, or maybe a story. A story that would be edged into his skin forever, branded into his soul.

I have heard of people prickling their bodies with dark ink, making all kinds of pictures appear on their skin, branding it forever but never once in my life have I seen it. It must've hurt like hell. My eyes wander from the prince back to the blonde girl and I try to make out if I recognize her as bile makes its way up my throat. I clench my fists, my nails digging into my skin but instead of turning my—very inappropriate—thoughts into reality I swallow the feeling and turn around. I grip the heavy material of the curtains and rip them open in one swift motion. Cassian protests loudly.

"Are you trying to kill me?"

"Why? Are you offering?" I raise a brow while I continue to walk over to the next window.

"Your friend can leave now, we have things to discuss," I say curtly, opening the next curtains. I'm afraid if she stays any longer I won't hold my temper and accidentally rip her heart out. That would make a big mess and I quite like these carpets. I have to take a moment to calm my breathing, hating this new feeling. This is not me.

"No need to be jealous." His taunt makes me turn my head and narrow my eyes.

"Jealous?" I arch my brows repeating the word slowly. His lazy grin stretches and fires up the anger inside me.

It seems like the prince doesn't pick up on my mood and stretches his body like a big cat.

"There's no need for it. You could happily join." This is the last straw.

I am going to kill him. I'm going to wrap my hands around his throat and watch his face go from red to blue, to purple. I can already feel his pulse pressing frantically against my squeezing hands and I do the only thing I can think of. I turn and walk away.

I rush through the doors and stop in the hall, my heartbeat pulsating in my ears. I grit my teeth and clench my hands before I let out a frustrated scream. I exhale, turn and catch the confused gazes of the guards. I straighten my spine, clean off my gown from nonexistent dust and walk back into Cassian's chamber.

He's still lying in his bed a brow raised and I tilt my head slightly, plastering a fake smile on my lips before I answer him. "Are you sure you're able to please two women at the same time"—the girl giggles and I shoot her a dark look—"Considering your big ego?" I use my hands to show him exactly how big I think he is. The distance between my hands is disappointing.

The girl giggles again and I narrow my eyes while I arch a brow.

"Well, why don't you come and find out? I believe the size will be to your liking." I give Cassian a bored once over before shaking my head.

"I don't think I can handle disappointment today. But it's cute how you think there's something to see." I turn and start to pick up the few scattered clothes before I throw them at the girl. She squeals lightly while I hear the prince scoff. I don't give him the satisfaction of looking at him.

"Make sure you get out of here before he webs you in. Believe me, you wouldn't want that."

The girl musters me for a moment before she quickly slips out of the room but not without throwing a lazy smile at the prince, who is still lying in bed. I throw her an irritated look and she leaves.

"That was not very nice, princess."

I meet pine green.

"What do you mean?"

"You know what I mean." His tone is harsh and I shrug a shoulder.

"Maybe you're overestimating my intelligence." A dark chuckle leaves his lips at my words. I watch him shift under the duvet, my cheeks growing hot.

"You know exactly what you're doing. Trying to embarrass me in front of my conquests."

I snort at the usage of the word.

"I'm sure she has no worries if her experience was satisfying. I wanted to talk." He moves again and I avert my eyes for a moment.

"If you wanted to talk, you could've waited until breakfast." He says and I watch him bury his face back into the pillows offering me a view of the tight muscles in his back. They ripple with his movement, dancing across his skin. Oh holy Adales, if anyone could hear my thoughts right now I would be dishonored in one swift motion.

Now that Edlyn has given my burning rage a name and put the idea of Cassian being someone desirable in my head, it feels weird to look at him.

I ignore the tingle deep in my core and divert my eyes from his skin and walk over, placing the velvet box on the nightstand and throwing the duvet off of him. And regret it immediately.

"Holy gods!" I squeal and turn my back to him, clutching my hands over my eyes in horror.

"Not a god but damn close." He mumbles and I flush a deep scarlet.

"You're not wearing any pants!" His deep chuckle echoes across the chamber.

"Good observation, I wasn't aware of that, princess." He mumbles lazily and the urge to deck him in the face resurfaces. Edlyn has to be wrong it's not passion for him that I feel but passion to hear his nose crack under my knuckles.

I hear some shuffling but don't dare to turn around.

"Are you decent?" I ask unsure and anxiously awaiting his answer.

"As decent as I can be." I turn around slowly, peeking through my hands, and indeed he turned on his back and pulled the duvet back up. Nonetheless, my eyes fly down to the two lines again and it takes me a lot to rip my eyes away from his upper body and force them to stay on his face. Gods, I didn't even know a man's body could be rippled with so much muscle. I mostly stay fit due to my nightly visits to the capital but there is too much tempting food in Aerwyna to be that ripped. I could never escape bites of salty cheese, freshly baked bread, and the berry-colored wine, that is sold on the streets. Maybe they don't have any food in Demeter. But that couldn't be possible no one is gifted with beautiful, lean muscle without being well nourished.

"I would've expected more of you, with these dirty drawings." He shoots me a suggestive smile and for a second I have to hold my breath when I meet the green of his eyes. His brow rises daringly and I swallow before narrowing my eyes.

"I already told you they weren't mine and this matter couldn't wait until breakfast which is why I came to see you now. How would I know you're indecent?"

"The fact that a naked woman was lying beside me didn't give you a hint?"

I decide to ignore him and cross my arms in front of my chest angrily making his eyes dip down for a second. My cheeks heat up again when I think of the low neckline of the dress but I quickly shake the thoughts away. Not important right now.

"I want to talk to you before you slip out of my hands and are back joined at the hip to my father."

"I'm not joined at the hip to him. And whatever it is it can wait." He says suddenly annoyed and when he starts to move, indicating that he is getting out of bed, I quickly turn my back to him. I feel him walk past me, his arm grazing mine softly before the touch is already gone and the door to the bathing chamber slams shut. I will the goosebumps away that cover my skin.

My jaw goes slack when I hear the water start to run and realize that he just completely ignored me because he wanted to shower. The audacity that this man has is unbelievable.

If he thinks I'm just going to ignore his behavior and leave like an impatient girl he is wrong. I shoot a quick look towards his bed but decide to go for the lounge chair which is placed in front of his fireplace. No way in hell will I touch these sheets after whatever he has done with that woman. A prickling feeling moves around my heart as it contracts painfully and I have to put my hand over it, taking a controlling breath.

Everything is fine, this is nothing.

I open my eyes again and stand up to take the matches sitting above the fireplace and turn on the fire to heat the room a bit. And get rid of the awful, sweet scent.

Goosebumps cover my arms due to the cold in the room and I hold my hands towards the fire. The pouring water disturbs the silence around me, a steady background noise. I have to shake my head at this stupid man who thinks he can do anything he wants while at the same time my mind wanders back to the ink sprawled on his skin. I don't know why the strange symbols bother me so much. The image is replaying in my head over and over as if to taunt me. I don't know if

I've seen it somewhere. Old letters I skipped over in my many classes of history. Or maybe an ancient language I wasn't interested enough in to listen to Professor Bernath's blabbering. I hate that it bothers me so much and that my curiosity gets the best of me, wanting to know what it means. Maybe if I tried to find a book in the castle's library, if there's someplace that harbors old languages that are long forgotten it is there. Probably sitting in a lone corner, covered under a layer of dust.

It takes Cassian exactly twenty minutes before he steps out of the bathing chamber and when I turn around my eyes widen and I quickly slap my hands over my eyes but it's too late. Instead of his backside, I got a perfect view of his front and while I hate myself for thinking that it was anything but disappointing, I don't dare to move my hands from my eyes. My skin grows burning hot at the inappropriate situation and yet I can't ignore the feeling bubbling inside of me. Curiosity tingles in my hands, telling me to peek between my fingers. I press my hands harder against my eyes.

"Oh, you're still here?" He says as if nothing's wrong, making me growl lightly.

"You know I was still here, you bastard did this on purpose!" I hiss and he chuckles.

"Don't flatter yourself, princess, I always walk around in my chambers naked." I take a deep breath to calm down, my hands still clutched over my eyes.

"Could you be serious for one damn minute, I came here because I wanted to talk to you and you just walked away," I say frustrated at his childish behavior.

"I told you I was busy." He says lazily and a chuckle follows afterward.

"I'm decent; you can take your hands off your eyes now, Carina." I hear his voice but I don't dare to move my hands.

"I don't trust you enough to open my eyes," I say with flushed cheeks while I listen to his soft steps. A fresh scent of soap and pines envelops me before I feel warm fingers wrapping around my wrists and pulling my hands from my eyes. I let out a small, shaky breath as my eyes stay closed. I feel his breath hitting my cheek and I don't dare to open my eyes when my heartbeat picks up its pace. My lips open the slightest bit, my wrists still in his secure hold. It doesn't feel the slightest bit threatening, I can barely feel his grip. It's a ghost of touch yet it makes everything inside me jump up to life.

"Carina," He says quietly and I finally open my eyes, meeting a glowing green. I gasp quietly as I move my head just a tad bit away but when I blink the green isn't glowing anymore, well not like before.

My eyes drop down to see that he indeed is dressed in dark pants and a dress shirt that is halfway buttoned before my eyes dart back to his face, his eyes hooded and placed low on my face, making my lips tingle lightly as if he was touching them.

My tummy flips at the look he's giving me while I turn my hands and grip his wrists as well but my fingers don't wrap around fully as his hands do. A moment of silence is shared between us when our eyes meet and I slightly lean forward. I don't know what for but I hope he follows my movement and hears my wishes. Instead, his eyes drop down and he shuts me off, taking a step back.

"What did you want to talk about?" He clears his throat after his question. I blink perplexed while I try to grasp what has happened right now. Did he just reject me? I get up and walk away from him, the distance giving me enough space to think like a sane person. Who cares if he rejected me? Did I want him to fucking kiss me?

I need to see a healer.

"I came here to offer you a deal. You have been ignoring me this past week and when I tried to talk to you after I met Lord Romanov. . ." I trail off when I see the dark look in his eyes and clear my throat lightly.

"Well, I couldn't just walk up to you and talk," I tell him while my eyes fly down to his stupid unbuttoned shirt. Isn´t he able to button his shirt correctly?

My fingers itch to button it for him but I grit my teeth together and turn my eyes to the ground.

"Princess, you can always walk up to me and talk. What happened didn´t have anything to do with you. It wasn't my intention to ignore you, even though I like it when you're so territorial." My eyes fly back to his, mischievously glinting at his words. I´m relieved that he doesn´t go back to his closed-off self when I mentioned Lord Romanov.

"I'm not territorial and stop calling me—whatever that's not what I'm here for," I say and follow him when his eyes drop down to his shirt where mine have been stuck to apparently.

"Will you help me?"

"What?" I ask perplexed and look at his face. He motions to his shirt and I sigh before I walk up, stopping in front of him. I try to ignore the shake in my fingers as I button his shirt and speak up again.

"Could you do me the favor and finally listen to me?"

"I'm all ears. Tell me, what did you come here for?"

I hear his voice and suddenly I'm very thankful for the distraction, my eyes stuck to the buttons on his shirt.

"I wanted to talk to you about. . .us. And the engagement and I wanted to offer you a deal." I repeat myself.

"I got that. What could you offer me that I'm not going to have?" He asks and I hear him inhale sharply afterward when my knuckles graze his chest slightly. I look up for a moment and speak up again, focusing on the green color of his eyes.

"You could have me. As your queen. Willingly. We combine our kingdoms and I will come with you to your castle. I will not make your life any harder for you and I'll listen," I tell him and finish closing his shirt.

I feel his eyes on me and hope he can't see the doubt that must be written all over my face.

"You would marry me without a word? For what?" His voice is quiet and almost gentle. For a moment a warm flush spreads through me. The gentle tone reminds me of the time we were in the capital together.

I dare to look back up and pull myself together, my gaze not wavering.

"I want you to tell my father what I told you about the Protestants. Tell him how to defeat them. If I marry you, my brother is out of the case, they can stop training him and he will go wherever he wants to. Edlyn comes with me until she doesn't want to anymore. If she decides to leave she will earn a title, a place of land, and a fortune." I hesitate for a moment before I speak up again.

"If she decides to marry she will. I want her to have a choice in who she chooses," I tell him breathless, not moving an inch as I await his answer. I can just hope that he'll have a decent bone in his body and let me have these things if I marry him.

I won't let my brother suffer the rest of his life when I can change that and if my father is too proud to take any advice from me for his war strategies, he'll maybe listen if Cassian offers him my plan. Just because I'll marry him doesn't mean I'm abandoning my kingdom. I know the ceremony of our marriage will be in his lands and that I probably need to live at his castle but still we're combining our lands which means both of the kingdoms are our responsibility.

I take a deep breath and the scent of pines and soap intensifies and pulls me into a soft cloud. Please say yes. Please, please, please.

"You're a masochist, princess. Sacrificing yourself and your happiness for everyone else so they can be happy." He mumbles and something close to appreciation moves in his eyes.

He suddenly places his hand at the place where my neck and shoulder meet, his fingers trailing upwards and stopping on my cheek. My body immediately answers to his touch, covering my skin in goosebumps. This touch is different from the moment he gripped my wrists. There is nothing possessive or demanding about this touch, he does it just because he. . .wants to. A shiver runs down my spine while I watch his eyes caress every inch of my skin. They curiously follow the trail of his fingers that caress my chin, my jaw, and up tracing my cheekbone.

"You would sacrifice yourself to be with a man that you think will make you unhappy. Even if you wouldn't agree to marry me, Carina, I would give you all of these things, everything you would ever wish for. You deserve every bit of it." His voice is so intense it feels like it's moving through the entirety of my body.

And there he goes again with saying things like this. This can't be the same Cassian that I remember from my childhood.

Before I even have the chance to form any kind of thoughts and compare him to my memories his hand drops and he walks over to the nightstand to grab the velvet box I placed down when I walked inside his room. My body throbs with an unfamiliar ache and I miss his touch the second I am robbed of it, yearning to feel his warm fingers back against my skin.

My mouth opens lightly as I watch him, unable to say a word as he pulls out the ring and takes my hand his eyes on mine.

"Katarina Sebestyen, would you do me the honor and agree willingly to my proposal? So you become my wife and I become your husband. From this day on and every other, we spend in this world." His eyes flare up and I don't know if it's the way he words his proposal or how my skin covers in goosebumps when he calls himself my husband, either way, I can't help but nod.

It's just a wobble, almost not there but he still catches on.

I'm agreeing to a pact with the devil and there's no way out after this. But I made my choice. It is the only right thing to do but before I do this before I marry him I need to do one more thing.

He slips the ring onto my cold fingers and he bends down to press a soft kiss against the back of it, making me swallow hard.

When he looks up from my hand I dare to ask another thing.

"Can you do me a last favor?" I whisper, not willing to disturb the silence. Cassian pulls me close by my hand, nodding.

His other arm winds around my waist and something feels weirdly comforting about it. It is stupid to think like that but now that the ring sits on my finger it feels like an invisible band has formed between us, connecting us ridiculously.

"Before we tell it to anyone I need some time."

His body grows rigid for a moment.

"How much?" He asks me and something shifts in his eyes.

"Until the blood moon ball."

He ponders over it, his thumb circling on my waist. It's as if he doesn't even notice his movement and it makes my heart hammer against my chest.

"All right, princess, you have until blood moon. Then we will announce our engagement before we leave for Demeter."

He presses a kiss against my knuckles.

22

When I leave Cassian's chamber something lifts from my shoulders. I don't know if it is relief that is flooding my veins. But it feels like I'm one step closer to ending all this wondering.

The rest of the day is fairly uneventful, I listen to Marrus at dinner, and try to ignore Hector's glances. We haven't spoken since the kiss in the royal gardens but now that I've decided, or more like accepted my fate I don't know what to tell him.

I excuse myself early from dinner and get up from the table. For a split moment, my eyes meet Casssian's over the table and he arches a brow teasingly. I ignore him and leave the hall.

"Katarina!" I wince when I hear Hector's voice calling from behind me. I turn with a soft smile and watch him jog over to me in the hall.

"I haven't gotten the chance to talk to you during dinner." He shoots me a soft smile and my heart clenches. "Marrus conversations are always time-consuming."

"I understand but I feel like we have to talk." I blink trying to calm down my erratic beating heart. "Of course, what do you want to talk about?"

He takes a step closer and takes my hand in his. "I can't help but feel you distancing yourself from me. If what we did in the gardens made you uncomfortable and you didn't enjoy it, that is completely fine. I would never want to impose on you." His hand is warm around mine and I have to look down to escape his amber gaze. A soft bitter chuckle escapes my lips. "I wasn't uncomfortable at all. I enjoyed it." When I look up I watch his eyes light up and a soft smile stretches across his lips. "I did too."

His thumb grazes my skin and I try not to compare it to the touch of Cassian's hand against my skin. "I wish we would have more time, I feel like all of this is a bit rushed," He says and I smile. "Our heritage doesn't gift us with time it seems." My hand gets sweaty in this, I don't know how much longer I can endure this. I need to go, now.

"That is the price we have to pay," He agrees and I nod before I inhale sharply. "You don't need to worry, I don't feel imposed by you in any way. But I do need to leave now because I have many things to plan."

"Of course, I don't want to hold you up any longer." He shoots a look around us and when he is sure we're alone he tugs me closer. I lean forward and meet his gentle kiss halfway. This time it feels like acid is burning on my tongue telling me that what I'm doing is wrong.

We part and I smile again. "Have a good night, princess." He departs and I can finally breathe again.

~

"You're packing."

I whirl around to notice Henri standing in the doorframe to my chamber, a disappointed look sitting on his face. I knew it was inevitable but somehow I hoped to drag out the meeting with my brother because I am seriously unable to lie to him.

I shoot Marianna a look and she lets go of the dress she held up seconds ago before she leaves the room quickly.

"I do. Who told you?" I ask confused because it seems like he knew exactly when to come as if he knew of the engagement.

"Cas did."

So much for sparing me some time.

"He talked to you?" I walk over to my dresser to pick out the rest of my clothes. I told him I needed time and the first thing he does is run to my brother and tell him that I'm leaving. Of all people, he could tell he told Henri.

I came straight to my chambers after Hector talked to me in the hall I was too scared to run into Marrus as well. Hector doesn't deserve to be in the unknown but I'm just too much of a coward to tell him now. My time is already ticking; the blood moon is coming closer with every passing hour.

I planned everything out and I know it's risky but before I leave Aerwyna I need to see the man Ellister told me about. I still haven't figured out anything about the Dark Prince while Gisella keeps sending me letters and tells me that she finds it unsettling. The lack of information should be a warning to us. It is getting weirder with every second and it makes my skin itch to meet the handyman of the Dark Prince. I regret not ordering Ellister to set a date that would've been sooner. But the blood moon ball is a perfect alibi and everyone will be too distracted by the different lords and royals to care about me going in and out of the castle.

My father is going to govern officially for as long as Cassian and I travel to Demeter and get married but I still need to do this.

I grew up here, these are still my people and I won't let them stay in the danger of a lunatic recruiting murderers. I focus back on my brother who speaks up again.

"He did. He said that you love him which made me laugh."
I hear him step into the chamber. Cassian should've known not to tell anyone that I loved him and I'm sure he did it on purpose, knowing it would get on my nerves.
I hear Henri's favorite boots click against the ground, his steps coming nearer by time while I figure out what to tell him. There is not enough time to come up with a good lie so I sigh and decide on the truth instead.

"Listen, I'm not going to lie to you Henri, you know me enough to not believe him. But the more people think I marry him because I love him the better. You can have what you wanted you will be able to leave the castle the second I'm married." I grab the next dress but he rips it out of my hands and throws it away. I turn my head, narrowing my eyes.

"Do you think that that's what I want? Of course, it was a dream of mine to see the world but I don't want to come back home every time and you're not here. Knowing that I'm away happy while you're married to a man you don't love, I could never let that happen," He says angrily and it warms my heart that he thinks that way but it's not his decision to make.

"I am happy if you are. I never expected anything else out of my life Henri and neither should you. I am a regent and I must create an heir and protect my kingdom."
He scoffs.

"Is it not possible to have both? Why do you need a husband to rule?"

Because that's the way it is. And people are scared of change so much that they cherish old habits. Old rules. The parliament would never agree to a queen ruling on her own.

"I accepted my fate and you should too."

I put my hand on his cheek; smiling while he gives me sad look. I watch his shoulders slump slightly.

"I need my big sister, Carina. I don't want you to leave, these whole rules are stupid and I swear we'll find a solution if you let me help you." His voice is desperate, the look in his eyes breaking my heart.

"There is no need for a solution, Henri, because there is no problem. I'm engaged to Cassian and it's good that way. He sent out another set of soldiers to negotiate with the Protestants at the border and I believe Aerwyna will be safe with his power," I tell him as I give him a small smile.

I already accepted my fate and while I was scared in the beginning the decision started to feel better with every second I continued breathing. I know this is the right thing to do and the prospection of Edlyn accompanying me to Demeter makes it less of a torture.

"You sound like dad and that's not a good thing. You can't let them take you away," He says again and I sigh before I let my hand drop and walk over to the books I want to take with me.

I don't want to leave the castle I grew up in and I thought if I didn't tell anyone it would be easier to leave. I will miss this but it's not like I can't visit, if I listen to Henri I will think too much about leaving and that's exactly what I don't want to do. It's not that I'm leaving now, I still have much over a week to make amends and enjoy the last moments here.

"You can visit me at the Moreau castle at any time, I'll make sure to organize private chambers for you that will be available. And if you need me at any time I will make sure to take the fastest horse and come here. I promise," I say and hear him laugh bitterly. He takes a step back, his hands clenching into fists.

"So you're just going to leave. No one knows about this and you planned to leave in silence without saying goodbye." I shake my head, grimacing.

"I would've said goodbye to you, Henri, you're my brother. But I still have some time and I need to sort everything out before I leave. Stop seeing it as a goodbye, you can write me and like I said I will see you at any time you want." He shakes his head with every word I say and I can see the rebellion shining in his eyes.

"If you could tell me that you like him genuinely, just a little bit, I will let you leave."

I have to smile at his words because sadly he has no say over me. Even if he would try to make me stay, he can't. But I can't stop the image from a few days ago flash in front of my eyes. I leaned forward into Cassian's touch. I wanted him to kiss me.

"It doesn't matter. You never understood the duties we have to carry, Henri." I know it's a low blow but he won't let this go if I don't play dirty.

His face moves into a cold mask when I walk towards him, grabbing his hand in mine.

"I will have to learn to like him. It could've been worse."

If Henri somehow finds good contributions to Cassian's character that made him like him, I will too. And it's not like

I realize that he has good sides. No one is just black or white; maybe Cassian is just right in the middle. Steely gray.

"You shouldn't even have to learn to love or like someone, Carina, that's wrong. Please stay." I give him a small smile and it seems like that reminds him of his former anger.

He slips his hand out of mine and takes a step back, fury seeping out of him. I sigh frustrated by his behavior, he makes it seem like I want to go even though it was the opposite for a long time. I tried to change this disaster for the good but I couldn't.

I sadly don't have a choice. "Okay, then leave. Just so you know I won't ever talk to you again if that's what you're going to do." His brows are drawn in, his voice stubborn.

"Henri, don't say things like that." I understand where his anger comes from but I accepted the situation and I just can't be selfish enough to escape it. This is not just for him but for all the people in Aerwyna, with Cassian I will be able to protect them as well as I can.

Henri just shakes his head and rushes out of my room and I try to stop him.

"Henri don't leave!" I call after him and he throws a glare over his shoulder.

"Why? You're doing it too!" He snaps angrily and slams the doors shut behind him. I sigh and let myself fall onto the mattress of my bed. I eye the dark blue canopy over me, glittering in the dim candlelight until the color starts to spin and my eyes fall shut.

23

I don't know what wakes me but I haven't been sleeping for a long time when I reopen my eyes. My skin feels itchy and when I continue to blink at the canopy I decide that I can't stay here for another moment.

Edlyn is planning our departure which means I can't talk to her and instead of moping around my chamber, waiting for sleep to come I slip back into my dress and leave to go fetch my father.

The itching turns stronger with every step I take and I find myself rather wanting to turn and hide under my duvet for the rest of the evening. For the rest of my life.

I didn't tell the king about Cassian and I's engagement and even though I know he will be delighted, I want to drag it out as long as I can. Maybe it is the childish side in me, wanting to disobey my father and his stupid plan.

But instead of doing that I should look him in the eye and tell him that I agreed to be Cassian's queen because I decided to do so.

Yes, it is because I can't outrun the stupid contract and yet I want to keep my last ounce of pride and tell him myself.

If I want to survive in a world full of people thriving in power, I need to adjust myself.

The Red Saint is not afraid of confrontation, she speaks her mind and doesn't let anyone take what's hers. So why should I, Carina, be any different?

The floors of the castle are bathed in silence, candles and torches light up to lead the way up the stairs and towards my father's office. I am sure he's not asleep yet and rather scheming in his office to take down another nonexistent enemy.

Once I round the corner that leads towards my father's office I halt my steps when I hear muffled voices. I curse my shoes for scraping against the floor, hoping that whoever is talking didn't hear it. The door towards the office is slightly ajar, with no guards in sight. Did he send them away?

I look around for a second before I hide in an alcove, not far from the office, making the shushed voices float toward me. My body tenses the second their words turn from muffled noise into clear words.

"Where was the body found?"

"The dungeons, a maid was on her way to wash sheets, the body wasn't hidden, no intention of covering up the act."

I recognize the first voice as the one of my father but I can't make out who he's talking to.

"This is the second incident this month and you tell me you still haven't found the one responsible for this?"

My father's voice sounds awfully cold, it always does shortly before he bursts. It makes goosebumps rise on my skin but I'm lucky that this time I'm not on the receiving end of his wrath.

They're talking about a body. And that it wasn't the first incident, what does that even mean?

"I'm sorry, Your Majesty, my men are looking all over the place, Cassian offered his help."

Cassian?

What the hell is going on and who is my father speaking to? I try to lean out of the alcove but they're still in his office, making it impossible for me to see anything. I take a few steps towards the door to hear them better.

Damn these shoes for being so fucking loud.

"Good, he will be able to find out whatever did that, I want the maid who found her questioned, no one needs to know about this."

"Understood. . .are you worried?"

"I'm not surprised. I waited long enough for my enemies to find their way into this castle. Nonetheless, I need this to be dealt with before Cassian and Carina leave for Demeter. The blood moon will be the only chance for this person to do anything but I'm sure the prince will be able to protect her. Make sure he knows that Lucien."

Protect me? What the fuck is going on?

My blood runs cold when I repeat his words in my head.

When Cassian and Carina leave for Demeter.

Is he saying that because he knows sooner or later we're leaving or does he already know of the engagement? I was careful not to wear the ring on my finger, not for his sake but for the other princes. Who would've told him? I hate the eerie suspicion that immediately rises under my skin, knowing that just one other person knows about it, besides me. My father's voice rings back towards me but if possible it got even quieter, making me take a step forward, so I'm almost standing at the door. I try to steady my breathing, my heartbeat hammering against my ribcage. Who is this Lucien person talking about and what has the death of a maiden to do with me? This is just another thing my father keeps a secret from me and I'm sure—

"Fuck!" I exhale once I hear the steps of the men coming closer and before I can hide something snags me at the waist and pulls me back into the darkness of the alcove. My body goes rigid in an instant while I feel a hard chest in my back, a rough hand clasping over my lips. My heartbeat goes to full speed as the alarm bells go off in my brain, raising the first instinct in me to scream.

Maybe my father will hear me; I am not that far from the office but instead of doing that I wriggle my hips and try to make my body weight as heavy as possible but I´m met with a dark chuckle and hips pressing closely against the curve of my back. I let out a muffled gasp at the closeness, the hand swallowing every sound I make. My body freezes as it dawns on me. I know that damn chuckle.

"No need to panic, princess, but you need to stay quiet because if someone sees you, you´re going to be in big trouble."

A shiver runs down my spine when his breath hits my neck from behind but I instantly relax knowing that I´m not in danger and don´t have to expose my location to my father.

I hear my father and the other man step into the hall, making Cassian pull me even closer into the shadows. I inhale as he slowly lets his hand wander from over my mouth and rest it on the place where my shoulder and neck connect. Goosebumps cover my skin again but this time not out of fear.

"There is no way this person will be able to strike again we have guards everywhere, Your Majesty."

Oh my gods.

Now that the voices are clearer I recognize the second as Lord Romanovs, making me go rigid again.

Cas´ arm is still around me and I try to push myself deeper into him and the shadows because if the lord indeed finds out I was eavesdropping, I am sure he will find a suitable punishment for an act like that. Instead of helping me, Cassian moves his other arm over my chest holding me completely still. I furrow my brows angrily and turn my head to the side just to stop midways, realizing why he is holding me still. I completely tune out the men´s voices as I feel his erection press into my back. Is this idiot aroused right now? While we are standing so close to danger?

My cheeks burn at the realization, my dress suddenly feels inappropriate, the material too sheer, too thin.

"I want no one disturbing me the rest of the night." My father´s voice tunes in again before I hear retreating steps. I let out a small breath, my cheeks still flushed, as my tummy coils deeply at the sensation in my back. The men are gone. Finally.

It is silent for a few seconds and I don´t dare to speak up too aware of my raised peaks, pressing against Cassian´s arm. The slight tightening of his arm tells me that he´s surely aware of my arousal.

"Are you alright?" Cassian´s voice is controlled as he speaks quietly, not moving.

I am too scared to speak; afraid my voice could sound weak, so I just nod. His arm over my breasts tightens for a moment, making me exhale and squeeze my eyes shut. A wave of pleasure ripples through my body before his hold on me disappears. I turn around, craning my neck so I can look into glowing green eyes, making my heart jump lightly. He swallows and my eyes jump to his bobbing throat for a silent moment.

"What are you doing here?" I question, making one dark brow of his quirk up.

"Trying to keep you from getting into trouble." He offers with a sly grin, making the tight feeling evaporate in a second. It´s like he´s pouring a bucket of ice-cold water over me, drowning the hot desire.

"Don´t lie to me. You know what they spoke about, right?" I ask quietly, not moving an inch from him. His body is oozing a comforting heat which stands in stark contrast to the conversation I just listened to. "Maybe we should talk somewhere else."

"No, we´re talking now, Cas." I snap making his eyes glow.
"That is the second time you called me that."

"I don´t want to hear any other lies—what?" I ask confused by his words.

"That´s the second time you called me Cas." His voice is a deep whisper and I have to bite my tongue to not say anything, as he gives me another one of his intense looks.

"What does it matter? Don´t try to distract me from the important things."
I try to stand my ground but when his hand wraps around my waist and pulls me in, my tummy coils again. Stupid, stupid body.
My heart flutters when I feel his cold breath and I try to somewhat look angry but can´t when his green eyes glow in their special way.

"You don't even know what it feels like when my name drops from your lips like that."

I swallow hard at his words, his grip tightening on me.

"What does it feel like?" I whisper lightly, my head dizzy from our proximity. My heart cramps up and a deep ache forms between my thighs. If possible his eyes glow even brighter as the color disappears behind his lowered lids. His black lashes are full and long as they brush against his high cheekbones, caressing his glowing skin.

"It feels like what I imagine heaven feels like." He murmurs and I grip the soft material of his shirt between my trembling fingers. Something charges in the air dark and dangerous and I know he can feel it too. My back arches, making me press into him and I try to remember why we're here.

I wanted to ask him something, something really important but right now I can't feel anything besides his hands on my body, his arousal that is now pressing against my stomach, and when he turns and presses me against the cold wall in the alcove I can't help but moan softly. I want— no I need some friction between us or else I might fear I explode. These past weeks of yelling, and fighting for the upper hand, has strung every nerve with boiling blood inside of me.

The air ripples around us, like the fire, crackling at the torches, bathing us in shadows and orange light.

"Cas," I murmur my eyes on his luscious lips, watching how they part as I speak his name. Gods, how I wish I would know what they taste like. It's a deep need that settles into my veins, urging me on, telling me to find out.

"Yes?"

"Do you want to kiss me?"

I don't look away when his tongue darts out over his lips, a deep groan eliciting from what I imagine lips that feel like a sin against mine.

"You don't know how much. I wanted to take those lips between mine, the night I met you on that roof. With your dark hair, spilling over your back like the night sky got spun into strands and those glowing sapphire eyes. You looked like a fierce-less warrior. A warrior princess."

My eyes fly up to his, surprised by his words, just to see that his eyes are trained on my lips.

It seems like he is just as affected by me as I am by him and when I feel the tension tighten in my core to the unbearable, I swallow, my mouth opening lightly.

"Then do it."

His eyes fly up in an instant at my words confused.

"What?"

"Kiss me, Cas."

I order and thankfully it doesn't take him even a second to understand and push his body against mine in one movement, his lips crashing against mine.

Holy gods.

A tremble moves through both of our bodies, lighting us up from the inside as if the tension from all those weeks bursts through us like a firework.

No matter what everyone told me about different kisses and pleasure and that feeling as if your insides explode, I never believed them. Cassian kisses me with so much force that my head would've collided with the wall behind me but thankfully his hand slips between, securing my head lightly. There is no escape as his sharp teeth graze my lips and a second later his tongue meets mine. A hot lazy stroke of his tongue makes my blood hum and I groan when he does it again. And again.

A fire deep inside me burns my whole body as I push my hips against his, swallowing every ounce of air between our dressed bodies.

A soft moan escapes me when he angles his head to deepen the kiss. Holy Adales, this man can kiss.

It feels like I've never been kissed before because truly I haven't.

Cassian conquers my lips like no one has, claiming them as his, burning his taste into my memory.

What Hector gave me was not a kiss. It was a slight peck. Fuck, Hector. It feels like a bucket of ice gets thrown over my head.

What am I even doing here? Letting the Prince of Demeter kiss me in the cold shadows, with no ounce of care for each other.

My body freezes and I push him away from me, staring up at him, breathlessly. His eyes are glowing, his lips swollen as his brows draw together. The fog dancing around my brain clears and I grip a normal thought again. My breathing is labored the taste of his tongue still on mine. The sweet taste consumes me and confuses my tongue.

I still haven't regained the power over my lips as they open slightly and the worst kind of words escape me in one hushed breath.

"Sorry to disappoint you, prince, but Hector kisses way better than you do."

24

"Carina."

The growl rumbles through the halls of the castle but I don't dare to turn around. If possible my steps pick up, even more, the material of my soft dress fluttering behind me. I can feel that he's close behind but the adrenaline pumps through my veins so hastily, that it urges me forward, in the direction of safety. Away from him.

Why did I have to say that after our lips parted?

I could practically see my words push through the fog of his arousal and made it disappear in a matter of seconds.

Sorry to disappoint you prince but Hector kisses way better than you do.

Who would've known one sentence could turn Cassian off in one second, making his eyes turn darker than the night sky, his features frozen and hard. It was panic that flooded my veins and drove me to say the words and I knew I was in trouble, the moment I saw the look on his hauntingly beautiful face.

There was nothing else to do but run.

"Stop running away! Fuck." Cassian's voice booms again and when I turn around the corner, I throw a look over my shoulder, my hair flying around me like a curtain.

The look on his face is ballistic, I know I hurt his pride with the things I said but I did it to save myself. Even angry his features look like they were carved by the gods, the dangerous glow in his eyes thrilling. Nonetheless, I don't want to feel his anger against me.

"It's late, I need to go to bed. I'll see you tomorrow." I tell him in a steady voice, knowing he can hear me from his proximity. But instead of turning into the right wing, which leads to my chambers, I rush down the steps that lead toward the Royal Gardens. I don't think I can handle an angry Cassian in my bedroom right now, my mind is still swept up by the kiss, making the most inappropriate images flash in front of my eyes.

"If you think you can leave, after dropping a comment like that, you're mistaken."

His dark chuckle dances behind me, his voice too close, I need—

Whatever I need to do halts when his hand wraps around my wrist and spins me around just when we step out onto the court.

The prince is lit up by the moonlight, making it reflect in his dangerously dark eyes as he glowers down at me. Oh, he's really angry.

"Take it back."

His tone is dark as he speaks, making a shiver run down my spine in anticipation, arousal pooling between my thighs. Something has to be wrong with me. I push the feeling away and rip my wrist out of his hold, glaring up at him with the same intensity.

"No can do, Your Highness, wouldn't want to tell any lies."

He growls at my response, making me raise a brow tauntingly. I build the walls around me, carefully, concealing what his anger does to me.

He doesn't deserve to know that my knees still feel wobbly from that stupid, earth-shattering kiss.

"Is your ego that fragile, that you can't take any critique?"

"My ego is perfectly fine, princess, I just don't like to be lied to."

He takes a step closer, keeping his eyes on my face and for a moment I feel like I'm his prey, falling right into his trap. This is a battle, a battle occurring in the war I have been fighting with him for weeks. But I don't let his trap get me because I'm about to win.

"Sorry to disappoint but I'm not lying." I hiss through my teeth before I turn to intend to leave but he latches onto my arm again, making my boiling blood finally explode.

I turn in one swift motion, swinging my arm with only one mission in mind.

The crack of his nose is so deliriously satisfying for one moment until it dawns on me what I did.

My eyes widen as I look at his surprised face, pain etched into his eyes as I watch the trickle of blood run from his nose and travel over his lips.

"Did you just. . . hit me? Again?"

His voice is breathless as his hands catch the glistening blood that doesn't stop running from his nose.

Horror strikes me at the look and suddenly I don't feel so satisfied anymore.

I killed various men in my life, I beat them up, and I was stained in their blood from head to toe but whatever it was about Cas' blood, it made me sick to my stomach. I try to push sudden nausea away as I straighten my spine.

"You provoked me. I just wanted to leave."

"Are you fucking kidding me? You broke my nose!" He sounds pissed as he tips his head back, robbing me of the emotions swirling in his eyes. I watch him try to stop the blood flow as the former irritation returns, knowing that he's fine.

"Stop being a baby," I grumble and earn myself another glare. The tension around us is weird, it's different. I grip the hem of my dress and decide to rip off some material, wincing at the sound before I offer it to him.

Cas takes it without a word and presses it against his bleeding nose, the lilac material now stained with his blood. It looks weird how such a pure and soft color can look violent the second the blood soaks into it.

"At least say thank you."

"For what? Breaking my nose? Fuck no." His words make me angry and somehow he brings the violent side in me to the surface.

"Do you want me to hit you again? Add a broken rib maybe? You were the one who didn't let me go."

"Because you were lying to my face!"

"I. Was. Not!"

We both glare at each other. The air thins between us as we both step closer, ready to shed blood. I can't believe I felt sorry for hitting his damn face, he deserved it.

Before the prince can protest a soft crack echoes around us and catches both of our attention. My head flies around when I hear heavy footsteps, passing by in the shadows, not aiming to move in silence. I don't waste a second before my body tenses in alarm, Cassian steps in front of me to shield my body with his.

Both of our eyes search the dark trees and bushes for the intruder creeping around in the shadows late at night.

Cassian starts to move and I do too, to follow him but he stops me with his arm.

"What are you doing?"

"What does it look like? Protecting you."

I scoff and slap his arm away, slipping from the court into the Royal Gardens to follow the ducked shadow.

"Carina! For fucks sake."

I hear Cas curse in the distance but I don't bother to turn back around to him as I unsheathe my dagger from my thigh. It looks like the suspicious figure vanishes into the maze of the rose hedges and I'm hot on their heels while I feel Cas's presence right in my back.

"You can't just follow a suspicious-looking figure into the shadows." He hisses and I turn my head, to look at him over my shoulder, his face closer than I thought.

"I obviously can." I bite back with a raised brow before I dip around the corner and come close to what obviously must be a hooded man.

He hasn't noticed my presence yet, too entranced in his pacing. What an idiot.

It takes me one swift step of my feet, a kick into the back of the man's knees, eliciting a grunt before he falls to the ground. His head turns as I already hold my dagger to his throat, ready to slit his skin when Cas finally appears too.

I ignore his pants and focus on the person, the blade digging slightly into the skin as I push the dark hood from his head, only for my heart to stop beating for a second before it drops right into my stomach.

"Henri?"

"What in Adales name are you doing here?" My voice is breathless as I pull back the cold blade from my brother's exposed throat. He's still on his knees, his eyes flying from me towards an approaching figure behind me. I detect from the soft steps that it must be the prince as he steps beside me but I ignore his presence completely, not able to deal with it right now.

"That's none of your business." Comes the rude snap from my brother as he gets up onto his feet, dusting off the nonexistent mud from his breeches.

"You bet it is my fucking business if my brother is wandering the Royal Gardens at night. Hooded. Don't you know how dangerous that is?" Henri looks away at my words, the fire burning in his eyes which makes me straighten my spine immediately.

"I'm inside the castle grounds it should be safe." I ignore his words.

"Tell me what you did out here."

"Why should I? I don't owe you anything, you weren't the one who told me about the engagement, you wanted to disappear like a coward!"

Not this again. I take a step forward, anger boiling in my veins because it won't go through his thick skull that this was dangerous. Bodies have been going missing, people were killed and out of a teenage rebellion he has been putting himself into immediate danger. I step close to my brother who's towering over me but I still make sure that he looks me in the eyes when I speak up.

"You can't just leave whenever you want, Henri. Hate me for what I did, yell at me, be angry I don't care. But never put your life at risk, I couldn´t live with the thought that you could get hurt because of something I did."

  "But you´re already doing it! You´re hurting me by leaving Carina, leaving me alone in this stupid castle!" His yell pierces right through my skin and scratches at my heart as I watch the tears pool in those soft brown eyes.

I open my mouth exhausted but Cas speaks up behind me.
  "Carina."

 I turn my head to look at him, I don´t have the time for discussions right now.

But the look in his eyes makes me freeze, liquid emerald is asking me a silent question. Let me talk. I furrow my brows, confused by his intentions when I give him a quick nod and he steps up to my side.

"My word may not be of any importance in this situation but believe me, Henri, when I tell you, that your sister would do anything just to stay here with you. You´re angry, you feel betrayed, Carina is no stranger to these feelings."

I flinch slightly at his words as I look at my brother who´s now eyeing the prince beside me.

  "She would´ve never left without saying goodbye, just like I wouldn´t have. Sadly the situation can´t be changed. Maybe it was written in the stars, or whispered by the wind but it was long decided that she would have to marry me. You´re entitled to be angry, I don´t blame you but imagine how your sister must feel like. Being ripped out of her own home, she will accompany me, a man who she despises and who is willing to be my wife to protect the people she loves. To gift you with freedom. Because she loves you, a gift not many of us are entitled to have."

I'm stunned into silence by the prince's words. I eye him curiously, trying to figure out if this is yet again a game or if it is nothing but the truth. His demeanor is closed off, it doesn't show the slightest bit of emotion which makes me turn my head to Henri.

"I don't want to leave. But I can't be selfish with this. I'm not trying to boss you around, I know better than to do that."

I watch as my brother angrily wipes at his cheeks to erase the tears that escape his eyes. It pains me to see the disappointment swirling in his eyes, it pains me to know that I have just another week left where I can see him any time I want. "Did you even try?" My brother's question makes me raise my brows.

"Try what?"

"To somehow change it, to not leave."

I sigh, my shoulders dropping, of course, I tried. Well I believe I think so, this whole chaotic story of me inviting the princes was my plan but I failed. I tried to change something that was once set in stone, out of my power.

"It's not her fault, it's mine. Be angry at me," Cas says and I shake my head at his words.

"It's not your fault just as it isn't mine," I say because that's the truth. Both he and I are bystanders whose future got decided without our consent. We serve the crown and no one else. No freedom, no choices.

I look back at my brother who looks far less angry, his jaw nonetheless clenched tightly.

I can see the thoughts swirling in his head, moving, working but it is no use. No matter how you put it the result stays the same, I tried.

"Don't leave your room late at night, Henri, I'm serious it's dangerous," I say exhausted.

This conversation needs to find an end so I can slip under my covers and forget everything that happened tonight. The killing, the kiss, and this.

I can't believe I kissed Cassian just minutes ago, it feels like an eternity.

"The palace is the safest place in the whole kingdom." My brother protests making me shake my head.

"You never know what wanders these halls at night."

"I would listen to her." Cassian ensures me, making Henri's eyes narrow slightly.

"Am I endangered to have my nose broken if I walk around at night?" He nods towards the dark man and my eyes fly back to Cas, to see that his nose bleeding has stopped but the trail of blood has dried on his skin, chipping off lightly. He looks like he was stabbed multiple times instead of getting his nose broken. A smirk moves on my lips, satisfied with my hit right now. Cas' eyes light up at my amusement.

"What's there to grin about, princess?"

"Nothing, you should wear red more often, it suits you." I bite back, making his gaze flare up. The air charges again and I swallow. Henri clears his throat, making my head turn back to him, my skin flushing in embarrassment.

"You should go back to your chambers, it's late," I repeat, making him raise a brow as he eyes us both. If possible I flush even more and thankfully the prince speaks up again.

"She's right."

"Do you agree with everything she's saying so she likes you more?" Henri questions, making a small chuckle leave my lips when I see the slightest blush on Cassian's cheeks. I have to memorize that look on his face.

"I think you two should go to bed. Separately." My brother says, straightening his spine so he's closer to Cassian's height, which makes me roll my eyes.

"We definitely will."

Cas turns his head at my words, raising a brow teasingly which makes me glare at him.

"I—"

An intense rumble shaking the ground stops my words as I raise my arms to hold my balance.

My head flies up meeting Cassian's surprised gaze as another rumble hits us, the earth vibrating as we try to hold our footing.

"What the hell is that?" Henri yells through the earthquake, rose petals raining down on us, the rumble not stopping as the earth cracks beneath my feet.

My heart rate picks up as a sudden deep carillon shakes through the Royal Gardens. My blood runs cold at the sound, the familiarity hidden deep down in my body, carved into my memories.

"Gods," I mumble as I turn my head confused as the carillon keeps going and I immediately unsheathe my dagger as soldiers storm outside and I turn to my brother.

"To your chambers now!"

"But—"

"NOW, HENRI!" I yell no place for questioning me and he glares before he starts to run towards some guards. Another carillon shakes the ground and dances with the earthquake as I watch one guard take Henri by his arm and lead him into the safety of the castle.

Goosebumps cover my skin as I turn around to Cassian.

"Do you have any weapons on—" I stop talking when I see that he already has two long knives placed in both of his hands.

"Would you tell me what the fuck is going on?" He yells over the carillon as we start to jog out of the maze, surrounded by guards with cold faces that draw their swords confidently.

"The carillon is a way of warning the castle! We're being attacked." I tell him as he runs beside me through the hard cobblestones, my steps unbalanced as another rumble hits the earth. Someone is attacking the walls of the border that surrounds the lands. I stumble slightly but Cas quickly grabs my elbow steadying me.

"Thanks."

"Don't mention it." He says as he continues to follow me. I try to stay as calm as possible as we follow the guards, my heartbeat up in my throat at the ear-piercing gong of the warning bell. This is way too familiar. I vaguely remember the sound from the night it changed. The day my mother was taken from these lands. From this world.

"THE PROTESTANTS!"

A yell moves from the guards and we all freeze as another shake rumbles through us my eyes widen when I look up into the night sky.

"Fuck." Cas curses beside me as he follows my line of sight, his eyes flaring up but this time they don't do it on their own. They're lit up by thousands of arrows, their tips burning with fire. The whole sky is lit up as the fire sizzles through the air, the goal set on us.

Holy Fuck.

25

We're going to die. Surely we are, there is no way to escape, nowhere to run. The second the arrows hit the grounds of the castle, Cas and I crouch into safety. The guards of the palace aren't harmed by the fire, their armor, makes the arrows collide with the metal and fall to the ground. While the armor survives, the flowers and bushes in the Royal Gardens don't, the ground lights up with fire, bathing everything into hot, dangerous flames as the Protestants burst through the highly guarded gates of the castle. Battle cries erupt in the air as throats are slashed, swords are swung and blood is shed.
It's so much chaos I can't even make out who is a friend and who's an enemy.

"I want you to get straight back to your chambers, Carina," Cassian says as he leans close to me, his eyes following the attackers and he doesn't notice the fall of my face.

"Are you crazy? I can fight better than most of these guards I won't go anywhere but out there," I say in a steady voice, the hold of the dagger heavy and familiar in my hands.

"Carina, I'm not about to discuss this with you right now."
"Good, then don't." I bite back and don't spare him a second to react as I roll out of the hiding place and let my eyes scan the crowd. On closer look it's easy to keep them apart, the guards of Aerwyna are the more skilled ones, and their armor is safer. I tighten my hold on the dagger before I step out and catch a guard struggling a few feet from me, making me jump through flames and arrows, and fallen soldiers until I'm right beside him and slit the throat of the man who's been trying to choke him.

Blood splashes and tints my skin as the Protestant grabs for his throat the guard's eyes flying to me, alarmed.

"Your Highness—"

"Not a word," I say coldly before I let the adrenaline consume me completely; let it sink into my veins, dropping a case around my body. There's no time to think or regret any actions. Either you kill or you get killed. For the next minutes I fight my way through fire and fallen people, slitting throats, and gutting men as I try to fight my way through the chaotic crowd but there is no end.

The number of Protestants can't be overseen, it feels like now that they've bombarded the walls, thousands of them usher through. Their faces are set in stone, their eyes cold and determined. Whatever happens tonight we can't let them get into the castle because that would be the final tipping point.

The world tints into hot flames as if someone threw a canister of liquor onto the grounds, making my skin slick with sweat, and my heartbeat thrum in my ears. Somehow in the middle of it, I lost sight of Cassian but I know he's fine on his own, there's no time to worry. Not that I would.

My head flies around as another man approaches me, a creepy grin stretched onto his big mouth. His hair is pulled back by a leather band, his dark eyes catching the light of the fire in them. He looks crazed as if he's starved of destruction and pain.

"What a pretty thing you are. What are you doing here on the battlefield, M'lady?" I raise my brows tauntingly as I play around with the dagger in my hand, making his eyes flicker to the blade for a second.

"I was just taking a stroll around the gardens, trying to get some piece. And you disturbed it." I tell him, my tone ice cold as I eye the sword in his hand. I won't be able to hurt him in any way if I don't get close but he chose the right weapon. A sword will keep me in distance and him in safety.

"I guess from your tone that you didn't like that?" The man says as his eyes wander over my body, violating me most disgustingly. I watch the sweat triple over his forehead and roll over his brows, the fire a relentless heat around us, caging us in.

"Seems like you have enough brain cells to realize that," I say and the second his eyes stop at the swell of my breasts I attack. Instead of stepping close, risking getting hurt, I throw the dagger straight into his chest. The air whooshes as I put all my strength into the throw hoping it will catch him off guard enough.

The blade slices the cheap material of his clothing as he takes a surprised step back. I won't spare him enough time to process and use the moment of surprise to let my foot fly straight into his stomach as I pull out the dagger, eliciting an ugly cry from the man.

"You bitch!"

"I was called worse," I say with an evil smile as my elbow flies out and rams against his chin. Blood is oozing out of the wound on his chest but he still walks forward and when I let my foot fly out again, he catches my ankle. My eyes widen, and his lips stretch into a smile.

A moment passes as my body flies through the air, and soars before I grimace as I land with a thud on the ground. My next inhale is sharp, it burns, and pain shoots through my ribs. I try to save my fall with my hands, making my skin scrape open against the stones. The man laughs.

My eyes fly to his boots as they approach me and I push myself up to my knees groaning at the pain in my side. Nonetheless, I stare up at him as he grabs my hair and yanks me up into a standing position. I clench my jaw at the sharp pain, the dagger lazily in my hands as the man raises his face close to mine.

"If you weren't so fucking impudent I'd take you right now." My stomach coils in disgust at his words and instead of speaking up I do the only thing I can think of.

I spit right into his face. His eyes shut close as I watch my spit mixed with blood running down his skin. My hand tightens around my only weapon and I gather as much strength as I can.

"You can try you bastard." I hiss while his eyes open angrily but there's no time for him to try anything as I ram

my dagger straight into the side of his neck. His hand lets go of my hair and I pull the dagger out of his throat. Then I ram it in again. Blood splashes onto my face, warm and dirty. The dagger is out and I push it in again. The man gurgles and falls to the ground as I stare him down panting.

"Oops—you can't because you're dead." I hiss as I stare down at him, his eyes open, unmoving, with no dirty glance in them. That's what you get for being a vile asshole.

"Fuck that was hot." My head turns and I see Cas standing a few feet away, his green eyes wide and burning.

"You're seriously sick if you're turned on right now," I say but can't help myself from smiling. His throat bobs with a hard swallow as his eyes wander over my ripped dressed, my skin drenched in strange men's blood.

He doesn't look any better, his clothes drenched and ripped open. The air reeks of burned flesh, sweat, and blood. But the only thing I can focus on is Cassian, walking through the burning flames, his eyes set on me. My body feels hot for a whole different reason as he looks at me as if I'm the one thing in this world that can make him beg on his knees.

Sudden relief flushes my veins I was so distracted by fighting that I didn't even realize how worried I was about him.

It's a weird picture to watch him walk towards me, his dark curls flying in the wind.

The world slows as I tune out the screams, and the scent of the air but instead of feeling relieved, the hairs on my arms stand and I look around to see that most of the protestants retreated. A few of them are still scattered around, trying to fight but they have no chance.

A shiver runs over me the next second and when Cassian calls my name I freeze.

"CARINA!" His voice is hoarse, filled with panic and I turn in horror to see a Protestant creeping out of the shadows and lunging straight toward me.

I raise my arms, trying to catch the blow but it's too late. The blade of the sword reflects the light of the fire as it swings down on me and the next moment I fall.

I get hit with such force and I cry out when my skull collides with the cobblestones and my spine bends uncomfortably. Air rushes out of my lips when something collides with my stomach and I try to prepare for the pain of the blade. But the burning sensation doesn't come. I blink my eyes open, and my vision blurred for a moment as I cough and stare right into Cassian´s face.

He coughs and blood runs down his lips as he hovers over me before dropping to the side.

My eyes flicker to the protestant who has a satisfied grin on his lips his sword dripping with the blood of the prince who threw himself over me to catch the blow.

~ 26 ~

The man looks down his full focus on Cassian as he crouches and whispers something into his ear that I can't make out. Anger bubbles inside of me, building up the cold fire that evades my skin.

It doesn't matter what he says, what does matter is that it will be the last words this man has spoken in his life. I get up as fast as I can and clutch my dagger. My stance is wobbly and I have to focus to stop seeing him twice before determination straightens my shoulders.

I fly out, dagger securely in my hand. There is no time to play any mind games as I ram the blade straight into the back of the man. A growl leaves his lips, his sword clutters to the ground as he turns and I duck down grabbing the blade.

The second his eyes meet mine they widen, I don't know if in horror or surprise but the expression doesn't stay long as I swing the sword and it slices right through skin, nerves, and bones.

His mouth opens but he doesn't even have time to speak up, my swing too fast and brutal.

The head flies off the body, both tumbling to the ground but I have no time to watch and drop the sword and fall to my knees. I ignore the burning pain when I scrape my knees against the ground. My eyes widen when I see Cassian's shirt which is drenched in his blood.

"You're so fucking fearless I could kiss and kill you for that." He mumbles making me look up into his face. Even though his voice is steady I can see the pain edging into his features as his hands commit pressure to the wound.

"How bad is it?" I ask brushing away his comment as I try to lift his shirt but he slaps my hands away making me glare up at him.

"I'm fine."

"You're not." I protest angrily, as worry seeps into me. Gods, a wound like that could be deathly and by the amount of blood, he has already lost he's close to it. His skin turns even paler than usual making me look around, panicked, searching for help.

"Relax, Carina, I'm fine."

"You're not fucking fine, you're bleeding to death!" I cry out as I search for the guards but the crowd has thinned. Most of the fires have died down but there is still some fighting going on. We're on our own.

I need to get him out of here. Now.

"Can you walk?" I ask as I look back at the prince to see his eyes glowing slightly as they widen to something behind me. I turn around alarmed, ready to fight anyone off who tries to hurt him again but the attacker is closer than I thought.

A burning sensation ripples through me as he slides out his arm, a small knife cutting through the material of my sleeve, slicing my skin in the process.

I reach out for my dagger but his booted foot stomps on my hand making me cry out as he breaks probably a few bones in my hand.

His knee flies out and collides with my jaw making Cassian growl behind me as the world spins lightly in front of my eyes. Before the prince can move the attacker suddenly drops to the ground, right in front of my blurred vision.

"What—" I whisper but stop when I see a lanky boy standing behind him. Did he just stab him?

A hood is perched over his face, hiding any real features but I can make out that he must be around my age range. The real important thing is the fact that a blood-stained dagger sits in his hand.

He saved our lives.

I start to blink to regain my normal eyesight and get rid of the blur in front of them while the kid rounds me. I try to stay in a defensive stance but my lungs are burning so hard that I need to topple over, coughing. Blood splatters from my mouth and stains the ground beneath my hands.

I try to get up and shove Cas behind me when the stranger takes a step forward.

"Relax. You need to leave, he's going to bleed out any minute if no one patches him up." The voice is deeper than I expected. I register his words slowly as my ears ring. Cassian eyes the stranger suspiciously but the boy scoffs and forcefully puts the prince's arm around his shoulders.

He freezes in position and looks at me with raised brows.

"Well, you need to help me. I might be strong but not strong enough to stabilize a six-four-man." He rumbles and I quickly scramble over to Cas' other side. To my better judgment, I decide to trust this strange boy. If he wanted to kill us he could've done so already, Cassian and I are in no condition to protect ourselves.

I clench my teeth at the stabbing pain in my arm or the way every breath hurts in my ribs, the pulsing pain on my chin. That's all not important, it's small things and we need to get Cassian out of here.

"I can walk on my own." Cas protests making me glare at him.

"Shut up."

After two tries, filled with grunting and complaining, we get him onto his feet and even though I see everything blurred I keep my spine straight as we walk through the small fires. I try not to look at the ground, at the dead bodies lying around us, and rather focus on the castle that comes closer with every step we take.

I can feel that Cas tries to stay quiet but the way his jaw clenches from time to time and his muscle tense tells me that he´s hurting.

"Who are you?" I ask the boy on Cas's other side as we slip through the shadows, our feet echoing on the stones in the court. I can already see the steps that lead inside and exhale relieved.

"I´m the guy that saved both your lives, you owe me." The prince growls at the words, making the boy chuckle lightly.

"We don´t owe you nothing. I could rip you apart in seconds."

"I would like to see you try." The boy gives Cassian a once over and I shiver in awareness. I don´t feel the slightest bit good about this but I know I won´t be able to get Cas up these steps on my own.

So I suck it up and stay quiet, leaving the cries behind us as we both help the prince up the steps. I grunt and clench my teeth, making Cas try to move on his own, to take some of the weight away but the sweat on his forehead tells me that he won´t be able to hold himself any longer. I gnaw on my bottom lip in panic, the cold skin of his is not a good sign.

The way to my chambers feels endless but after a few floors the saving double doors come into view, the guards positioned in front of my doors stiffening at our view.

Their eyes widen as they both look at each other as if they thought I was in my chambers all this time.

"What happened—"

"Someone needs to call Edlyn, now," I say with gritted teeth, and one guard leaves with no question as the other replaces the strange boy. The doors to my chambers fly open, the wood crashing against the walls with a loud thud but none of us care as we carry Cas towards my bed. He hisses sharply when he drops rather harshly onto the mattress and I wince as I stare at him worriedly. The bleeding hasn't stopped and soaked through every material, dropping onto the floor. The amount of blood he's losing isn't normal, how deep did the slice go?

The carpet taints in a deep red, making me wonder if we left a trail on our way.

I turn to look at the boy who's slowly backing away. He shows me with a nod of his head to follow him outside and I throw a glance at Cassian whose eyes are narrowed but glinting with pain.

"Stay with him," I tell the guard who nods and I turn to follow the cloaked boy into the hall, not far from my room. A hand wraps around my wrist and I halt, looking back at the prince.

The green in his eyes is pale, with no ounce of its usual glimmer inside.

"Where are you going?" Cassian's voice is rough and I know he should spare his energy.

"I'm just outside. I need to find out who he is." Cas shakes his head and amplifies the grip on my wrist.

"Hell no. That's stupid it could be a trap."

"Well, then we answered the question of my intelligence." His brows furrow in anger but it doesn't look scary at all with the way his body is crouching in pain.

"I'm going to be back in two minutes tops, Cas, lay back down. I know you're in pain."

His hold on me loosens as he grumbles incoherent words.

"What?"

"Nothing. If something happens, scream."

"Yeah, sure." I raise my brows and he finally lets me go.

I don't waste more time before he can change his mind and step outside the hall.

"If you don't tell me who the fuck you are right now, I won't hesitate to slit your throat, no matter if you helped or not." I hiss but the boy doesn't even look impressed.

He slips the hood off his head to reveal a head full of fluffy hazel hair. His eyes are like pools of swirling jade sprinkled with purple flecks, a color I have never seen before. His features are young, still not really in the hard lines of a man. Something about him oozes comfort and warmth.

"What's your name?"

"It doesn't matter what people call me. What matters is that I'm not your enemy, Katarina Sebestyen."

I try not to look shaken by his words even though I am, wondering who this boy is.

His shoulders are broad and skilled, he knows how to fight, if that wasn't confirmed before while he was saving my life. He is right, he wouldn't save my life if he was an enemy.

Unless he wants to be on my good side to slither his way in and attack at a time the least I expect it.

"What are you doing here?" I ask instead as his head snaps to the side, hearing a sound that my ears aren't able to pick up.

"I came here to warn you. The people closest to you are going behind your back. Betraying you." His words are suddenly rushed and I furrow my brows at the widening panic in his eyes.

"I wish there was enough time to explain but there isn't. You need to find the story of when everything began—"

"What's that even supposed to mean?" I ask but his head turns again and this time I hear it too. Approaching steps.

"I need to go."

"Hell no, tell me what you mean first." I snap and grab his sleeve—well I try to grab his sleeve but he slips right out of my hold.

"Try to be cautious, around every corner lingers another enemy. Find the story of the beginning, Carina." He's already retreating into the shadows and I see Edlyn rushing around the other corner the guard behind her but I follow the boy.

"Why should I trust you?"

"You shouldn't. But you can believe me because what I told you was the truth. Shailagh Sebestyen believed they were true." I freeze at the name and watch him run down the corridor as he adjusts the hood on his head. Instead of chasing after him and questioning how he exactly knows that name I turn and come face to face with Edlyn's beautiful face.

It is etched into a mask of worry and it doesn´t take one word of me before we both rush into the room of my chamber.

The sight that meets me makes me swallow hard.

Cas is lying on his back, his upper body void of his shirt exposing his pale skin, the tight muscles, and—oh gods. The cut looks even worse than I imagined.

"He passed out—it´s too much blood." The guard beside him says panicked and I have to close my eyes for a second to not get angry at his helplessness.

I speak up while Edlyn rushes over to the bed, dropping the contents of her small bag over the sheets.

"I want someone to guard the door, while one of you goes straight to the chambers of my brother. Make sure he is okay and guard his door, no matter if two guards are already positioned. No one disturbs us understood?" I say harshly, making both of the guards nod before one rushes down the hall and the other closes the door harshly. I dare to inhale the second the doors close and immediately turn around to see Edlyn hovering over Cas, holding a vial to his lips. It´s filled with a red liquid and she lets all of it run down his throat, making him swallow forcefully.

I quickly walk over to her, my knees wobbly as I eye the sliced skin on his stomach, making my head spin.

"I need your help, Carina," Edlyn speaks in a steady voice and I nod swallowing the bile that rises in my throat.

The mattress dips under my weight as I carefully sit down beside his unconscious form. Edlyn pushes a big chunk of wood into my hands.

"Make sure he stays awake." She tells me and I realize what the wood is for. My eyes fly to Cas´ face, his eyes fluttering open lazily, the green in his eyes pale. I grab his chin and open his mouth gently pushing the chunk of wood between his teeth so he won't bite his tongue out.

"Hey," I say softly as his eyes turn to me and something knocks against my knee. I look down to see his hand grasping for the material of my dress and I quickly take his hand, my heart thundering as I intertwine our fingers.

"He's going to be okay, isn't he?" I ask Edlyn as I swallow my eyes not meeting his.

"Gods, the man did good work. He sliced deep which means I'll have to use a few herbs to stop the internal bleeding, afterwards I need to clean the wound, stitch it—" She stops when she notices the look on my face.

"He'll be fine." She states and shares a silent look with the prince. I furrow my brows confused but soon I'm distracted by the squeezing of his hand as Edlyn starts to work on his stomach.

Luckily he's holding the hand that hasn't been hurt but it feels like he's going to crush the bones in this one as well.

His jaw clenches as he bites the wood and I squeeze my eyes shut trying to block out the sounds of wet blood, vials clinking, and the cursing of Edlyn. Instead of yelling or grunting, he stays quiet. His thumb draws calming circles onto my skin even though I should be the one to calm him down.

"Okay, it looks good. I'm going to stitch the skin now." Edlyn says with a steady voice and somehow I relax slightly, knowing that she has everything under control. The adrenaline leaves my body, making me more aware of my broken ribs, the slice in my arm, and the pulsing of my chin.

"You saved my life tonight," I speak up quietly as I look into Cassian's face. His eyes seem more alive now, the green less dull but they lower every few seconds as if he's close to falling asleep.

"You need to stay awake." I press and squeeze his hand making him open his eyes again. They glower lightly at me telling me what he thinks.

"I don't care if you're fucking tired. I swear if you die right now I will kill you."

His body shakes with laughter at my words but he quickly stops, wincing at the pain.

I smile lightly my hand dropping out of his I hesitate. . .and decide that I'm too tired to think of my actions right now. My hand wanders up into his dark curls and I start to brush them slightly out of his sweaty forehead.

Small drops of blood paint the skin on his face making me clean it with the tip of my fingers.

He stares at me while I brush through his strands of hair, my spine aching because it can't hold me up any longer but I stay by his side.

I stay by his side while I watch the color return to his skin, it's actually creepy how quickly the pain moves from his eyes. I stay until the wound is closed and he removes the wood from his lips. I stay when he speaks his first words.

"She's hurt. Slice in her arm, broken ribs, probably a few broken bones in her left hand, a bruise on her cheek." I narrow my eyes lightly at him. He just almost died and thinks my injuries are worth mentioning right now.

My hand moves out of his hair as Edlyn's eyes widen, guilt shining in them because she didn't notice that I was hurt too.

"It's no big deal, you were close to death, Cas," I say but don't protest when Edlyn pushes a vial against my lips.

I open my mouth obediently and wince at the bitter taste of the liquid before she binds my upper arm with gauze. "Gods, this tastes awful what is that?" I gag lightly.

"It's a mixture that naturally helps your blood building. Now hold still."

The slash isn't too deep so she doesn't need to stitch the wound.

There is nothing to do against the broken ribs but she wraps gauze around my hand and applies a cooling ointment to my jaw, where the knee of that bastard collided with the skin.

"Thank you." I breathe as she starts to pack her things away, making her look up at me. The brown of her eyes is warm and exhausted making me feel remorseful.

"Come on." She nods with her head towards the washing chamber and I furrow my brows confounded.

"Your hair is dried with blood and we need to clean you up." She elaborates and I shoot a look towards Cas.

"I'm fine."

I narrow my eyes in disbelief.

"He's not going anywhere. He'll be here when we're finished." My best friend says with a smug smile before she disappears into the bathing chamber.

I turn one last time towards the prince who's leaning his back against the headboard of the bed.

"I swear if you die while I'm gone—"

"I'm not going to die. Clean the blood off of you, princess."

I inhale slightly before I nod and turn. I hide the tears that well up in my eyes before he can realize what's happening. I quickly slip into the bathing chamber where Edlyn starts the procedure without a word. I stay quiet not knowing what to say while she helps me get my skin cleaned of the blood. She carefully takes off my ripped dress and I stare at the mirror. I stare at the blue color already blossoming at my jaw and stare at her skilled hands.

She starts to dip my hair into the tub that she filled with lukewarm water. I close my eyes and sigh when her hands weave through my scalp. The first tear drops on my cheek but I don't wipe it away. I endure my best friend cleaning me in silence and letting the tears flow. I'm thankful she doesn't say anything until she slips me into a night dress and my cheeks are finally dry from the tears. My hair is wet and heavy, soaking the back of my dress but I don't complain.

"Thank you," I tell her quietly my eyes meeting her hazel ones.

"No need to mention it. I'll stop by Henri's chambers on my way to mine just in case."

"You don't need to—"

"I do." Edlyn protests and I know by the look in her eyes that she won't back down. We both step back into my sleeping chamber and I nod. I'll feel more at ease if she stops by his chambers anyway. I shoot a glance at Cas who's leaning against the headboard of my bed, his eyes closed.

I walk Edlyn to the door, my voice dropping when we're far enough for him to not hear us.

"Thank you. I mean it, I don't know what I would've done if you weren't here."

Edlyn smiles at me before she pulls me in for a hug.

"I'm glad you're alright, I'm not surprised you got into this mess, still I'm relieved he was with you." She whispers and I squeeze her a bit tighter for a moment, somehow emotional by all of this chaos happening.

After a slow moment, we let go of each other and her eyes place themselves on Cas' sitting form. His eyes flip open as if he can sense our gaze.

"I'm glad you're alive." She tells him with a nod that he reciprocates before she leaves. The door closes behind her quietly. I take a second to inhale, my shoulders dropping with tension before I turn around and meet Cas's gaze.

"Come here." He speaks up softly and I decide not to fight anymore tonight. But instead of joining him immediately, I grab the brush on my dresser to brush out the knots in my hair. I know I'll regret it in the morning if I don't.

The prince doesn't comment on my sheer dress and I sense that we're both too tired to play any games right now.

He raises the duvet and I slip under, leaning my back against the headboard beside him. I start to brush my hair and wince slightly when I meet resistance. His green eyes fly over my face as if to search for another scratch, ready to hurt whoever put their hands on me. Before I can push the brush through my hair his hand lands on my wrist. I stop and look at him confused.

"Let me do it."

"You're hurt—"

"Let me do it, Carina."

His hands go around my waist and I yelp in surprise when he picks me up and sets me down between his thighs. I turn to look at him with wide eyes.

"Are you completely mental?" he quietly chuckles while he pries the brush out of my hands.

"If I'm willing to stay in a bed with you, yes."

"Asshole," I grumble when he gently pushes my face away from him.

I cross my arms stubbornly but relax the second he moves the brush through my hair. To my surprise, he doesn't meet any resistance, No knots, nothing.

"Are you alright?" The question is gentle, meant to ask me about my well-being physically and mentally. But weirdly it makes me chuckle. I sigh when the bristles scratch against my scalp.

"What?"

"I don't know, I just find it amusing that you're asking me if I'm alright, while you were almost stabbed to death."

Another soft stroke makes me shiver.

"I'm fine."

"Yeah, you already said that," I say with a small smile.

The brush disappears and I turn when I feel him move. I watch him put the brush on the nightstand and grab a small band laying scattered on the surface.

"What are you doing?" I ask confused.

"I'm going to braid your hair out of your face." He says with nonchalance and my mouth drops open for a moment.

"Did you just say what I think you said?"

"I don't know." His lips stretch into a small smile. How is he already this back to normal after he was deeply hurt? Am I always a baby about my bruises and broken ribs?

"What?" He asks now.

"I don't know. . ." I repeat his words. He chuckles and turns my head back. I don't know why but I still think he was joking until his hands gather my hair. He's awfully careful as his fingers dance through my hair softly, picking up strand after strand. He doesn't hesitate, doesn't protest or curse. We both stay silent as he braids my hair as if it was the most normal thing in the world. Goosebumps cover my skin every time his knuckles graze my skin. After a few minutes, I close my eyes and let go of the confusion letting him do his thing. I feel him inch his way down my back until he stops midway, binding the band around the end of the braid. Once he's finished we both lay down face to face.

I'm breathless and highly aware of my thumping heartbeat. I can't remember the last time someone did my hair for me just because they want to. Usually, it is one of the maids braiding or putting them up in the most beautiful styles. But no one did it just because they want to.

Cassian's eyes shine intensely in the dark at me and his fingers reach out, tracing the lines of my lips. My breath hitches slightly, a small wave of shock moving from his fingertips over my skin.

"Thank you," I whisper and he smiles.

"I should thank you."

"Why?"

"I recall you were the one saving my life." I try to search his eyes to see if he's honest. He is.

"And the fact that you trusted me enough to turn your back to me and let me braid your hair." I chuckle lightly and his eyes flare up.

"Is this a creepy kink of yours? Braiding girl's hair?"

"Just if it's yours. I love your hair."

My breath halters at his words.

"The way it moves and dances across your skin. The way it always smells of roses. I could bathe in the scent for eternity."

I close my eyes and swallow. I don't know what to say to his words so I say nothing. Instead, I relish the feeling of his fingers tracing my features, the touch soft and comforting after everything that happened tonight.

"You saved my life tonight, as much as I hate to admit it, I owe you." I look at him and meet his burning gaze. "You don't owe me anything. You could've left me out there to die and you could've gotten away with it. You would have an out of the deal."

I ponder over his words as his fingertips tickle my skin. I didn't even hesitate. I don't think I could've lived with the knowledge if I didn't help him and left him to die.

I look back at him. "Still, thank you."

"Anytime."

"Now go to sleep, I'll be here, princess." His voice is a whisper and I relax further.

My limbs grow heavy, sleep pulling at my body to get rid of the exhaustion that floods my veins. It doesn't take long before sleep captures my body, lulling me into its claws. I finally fall asleep to the sound of Cas's steady breathing.

~ 27 ~

I had many opportunities in my life to experience the sting or burning of cuts and bruises. After my trips to the capital, I get used to the fact, to clean small little wounds with some liquor, so they do not get infected.

I always numb the pain with some wine or give my body the time to heal on its own during sleep but the morning after the attack of the Protestants doesn't feel healing at all.

The first thing that I notice when I'm conscious is the weight of my limbs. Gods, it feels like they weigh a ton. Have I miraculously gained weight over the night?

I groan softly as I pull the duvet over my eyes, shielding them from the playful sun that pokes through the glass of my window. I don't dare to open my eyes to check the time, I know from the place of the sun that it must be far after breakfast. The second I'm back enveloped by the darkness I melt into the warm, soft—hard comforter.

Memories seem to flood my brain at an alarming speed and my body freezes in the next second. I try to inhale quietly, the scent of pine and a fresh breeze hitting me so intensely that I realize why my limbs felt this heavy.

My heart rate immediately picks up when I finally come to my senses and feel the thigh that has wedged its way between my legs, capturing them with dead weight, accompanied by a warm big hand that has snug under the short night dress and rests on my raising and falling stomach.

"Oh, my gods." I dare to whisper to myself as I completely panic when the large man behind me moves, pushing his nose into my hair, the arm around my stomach tightening for a moment. I stiffen further when Cas moves his hips and his hard length presses right into the low curve of my back.

Oh no, no, no.

My eyes widen at the feeling in my back, cursing myself for being too tired last night to calculate the outcome of this. I should've forced him to go to his room even though he was in pain. Well, now I am the one who has a prince pressed against the back of her body. Apparently, Cassian likes to cuddle.

I inhale sharply as I'm ridiculously aware of every place my skin touches his and every place that doesn't. The top of the duvet is clutched tightly in my hands, a lifeline that somehow grounds me, and makes me focus.

I slowly raise my top leg, squeezing my eyes shut at the loud rustling of the covers, to slide my bottom leg out of his hold. I wriggle my hips, pushing myself forward but the grip of his arm around me is so heavy that I can't move and stay where I am. A frustrated exhale tumbles from my lips before my heart plummets right into my toes. Cassian is moving his thumb in slow circles over the skin of my stomach, making the muscles tighten under the touch.

He's awake.

"What exactly are you trying to do, princess?" His voice is laced with sleep, his hot breath hitting the back of my neck, making goosebumps rise on my arms.

"I'm. . .I'm trying to stand up." I hate my voice for wavering, as I close my eyes, relishing in the feeling of his thumb that hasn't stopped drawing circles onto my skin. Holy gods, if anything comes close to the place where the dead rest in peace, it is this feeling.

"Mmh, I don't think I'd like that." He murmurs and before I can say something before I can even inhale, he presses a hot kiss against the back of my neck, lighting my body on fire.

This fire is so different from the one from last night that was made to destroy and kill. This fire burns from his lips against my skin, crawling through my body and ending in my toes, with the mission to make me writhe, and beg for more.

"Your skin feels a little hot, are you alright? Don't want any wounds giving you a fever?" His voice is taunting, I can practically hear the smirk sitting on his lips as he presses another, feather-light kiss against my shoulder. I shiver.

"Must be you who's hot, you're a hotbox," I complain as I try to wiggle out of his hold again, my head turning hazy with his proximity. His arm only tightens and pulls my back flush against his front and I inhale sharply.

Oh, this bastard is enjoying this.

"If you won't stop wiggling your hips, Carina, I won't be able to go on with my pure intentions." I freeze at his words, my stomach coiling, before I turn my head slightly, to finally look into his face. The view revealed to me makes my heart plummet, the obvious emotion in Cassian's face flaming up. His eyes glow in their familiar green, his lids hooded, awakening the wish in me to count every single one of his black lashes.

"You have good intentions?" I ask raising a brow at him.

"Right now, I don't." And as if to confirm his words he pushes his hips back against my back, making me gasp.

My cheeks flame up shyly as I try to clear my hoarse throat. I turn my body onto my back, giving me a better view of his undressed upper body, while his front presses into my side.

His palm lays flat on my stomach, making me shiver lightly, aware that if the duvet were off he would be getting a show of every naked part of my body. My inexperienced body.

"How's your stomach?"

"You're really bad at changing the topic, princess."

"I'm not changing the topic, I'm just concerned if you're going to pass out on me. Again." I say trying to look as unaffected by his proximity as possible.

"Well, why don't you look for yourself." With a glow in his eyes, he softly grabs my wrist, placing my palm on his chest.

My eyes drop down as he starts to drag my hand across his skin, making my fingertips graze every delicious peck, every dip, and rise of his muscle.

I swallow hard, squeezing my thighs together to somehow create some friction for my tightening core. I can't concentrate on anything besides the feeling of his body and my racing heartbeat that echoes in my ears.

"Cas. . ." I trail off unable to form any coherent words as my hand travels down, his grip cold and demanding around my wrist, making my throat burn, scream at me to move closer, to act, to do something.

"Yes?" Our hands stop moving and I look up to see his eyes glowering at me, his stare burning my skin deliciously.

"Should I continue?" He asks raising a brow but instead of answering him, I do the only thing that will cure this desire burning my soul, the only thing that will make me sigh relieved, make me cry out when the tension finally leaves my body.

I do the only thing that makes any sense and push my body against his, in one swift motion, my lips crash against his. He doesn't inhale surprised, with no second of hesitation as his lips meet mine in a cold kiss. My blood sings as we open our lips, Cas hungry and willing, mine hesitant and impatient. My lips burn, sharp pain erupting in my jaw but I don't back down as our hot tongues meet, making Cas release a low groan that travels from his throat and over my skin. The hairs on my arms stand, and my muscles tense as I want him closer, harder, faster.

His hand grips my waist pulling me flush against his body when his hot tongue strokes against mine.

I grip his dark locks making him moan and softly bite my bottom lip in answer. My hips move, shivers erupt, and multiple groans and fire bursts around us. A bubble of desire, hot sweaty, and real.

Another brush of my hips against his, makes the prince shudder under the impact, his lips leaving mine for a short breath. My eyes flutter open, my lips agape with short breaths erupting as my body is still clutched to his, making me feel every hard ridge of him. I have to stop myself from moaning at the beautiful feeling of his hands on my body, hard and secure, his eyes hooded.

"Is this a reaction to the events from last night?" He asks me his voice strained and unsure.

I know what he's asking me with these words, is this what you want?

Instead of pondering his words, analyzing my burning blood, our skin still tinted with the scent of fire and blood I push my lips against his, for a moment, a short breath.

"Does that matter?" I ask quietly against his lips, confidence flooding my veins with the way he´s looking at me. Admiring, worshipping.

I don´t want to analyze what I´m feeling, it´s hard enough to describe my reactions to him half the time. Putting a name to the feelings he evokes in me would feel too real, I am supposed to hate him, he is entrapping me in a marriage.

I watch a flicker in his eyes disappear, his jaw hardens, and his throat bobs.

No time to think and his lips are back on mine.

A soft sigh escapes me as I move against him, the sheets a tumbling mess, rustling around our moving bodies, soft groans leaving our lips as his lips travel down my throat, scraping, tasting. His tongue darts out and tastes my skin, a hot groan leaving his lips

My stomach coils, and my fingers tingle as I push my nails into the hard flesh of his back, trying to keep control but the way his teeth graze my skin, making it burn before he soothes the pain with his tongue, makes my body fall.

Fall into the deepest pit of desire as my skin burns, my fingers dig into his skin making a deep moan echo around my chamber. A sound so beautiful I have never heard it before.

"Fuck. You´re so beautiful." Cas groans, his hips pushing against me, his cock straining against the material of his breeches. I open my eyes that I somehow squeezed shut during his taunting.

I stare right into his dark eyes as his body hovers over mine, at his mercy, under his control.

The fog clears lightly in my head and my stomach coils again when my eyes drop to his lips, swollen, and red, inviting me to capture them again.

This time when he lowers himself our eyes stay locked, I can count the green specks in his irises, as my hands wander up his hard biceps. His face comes closer but his eyes stay open, daring me to close mine first, which I don't. Our lips meet, they open, our tongues lap over each other, lazily, hot in a dance, while I stare into an endless dream. It is the hottest moment I have ever lived in my life, making me clench my thighs together for relieving friction.

His teeth capture my bottom lip in a hot bite and I lose. I close my eyes, arch my back, and let out the lowest moan that has ever left my lips.

"That's the most beautiful sound in the world."

I open my eyes again to look at him before my eyes fly back down to his stomach, his breeches low, gifting me with a view of the two long, lean muscles running down the sides of his hips, disappearing under the material of the breeches. But what catches my attention is the stitches holding the skin together, low on his stomach.

The world tips and I quickly push at the prince's chest, making him exhale surprised as he falls back onto his back on the mattress and I lean half over him.

"Are you crazy? You shouldn't be hovering over me with that wound." I snap, the heavy fog disappearing from my brain, making me think properly.

A deep chuckle shakes his body which makes me look from the stitches up into his amused face.

"I'm fine. It's just a scratch."

"It's not just a fucking scratch, you almost bled to death last night."

Right, last night. The Protestants, fire, guards dying, Cassian getting hurt and the boy helping us. I exhale, closing my eyes for a moment before I look back at the prince lying in my bed.

My heart plummets at the realization and it seems like his features harden, the second he notices the look on my face.

"I'm fine." He repeats, his jaw tight and I nod. I move to leave the bed to get ready for the day but his voice stops me.

"What did I do?"

"What?" I ask surprised and turn my head to see his watchful eyes on me. His face is serious an unfamiliar look on him. Cassian is never serious, he's angry, raging, flirty or cocky but I don't think I've ever seen him serious. It almost makes him look older. More mature.

"You're closing off, I could see it happening right in front of me, why?"

"I'm not closing off. Everyone is probably wondering where we are and I guess you'll stay in bed today just to be sure that your stitches won't rip."

"I'm fine."

"You keep saying that," I state while I slide off the bed, the sheer dress dropping into place.

"Because you're not listening to me. What did I do?"

"You didn't do anything, Cassian."

I did. I kissed him. Even worse I made out with him and it felt good. It felt amazing. My cheeks heat up. I let my hair cover my face as I round the bed to get to my closet, the desire to leave my chambers burning stronger than ever. I want to get out of his presence, his scent that sticks to my skin like a curse. It was one thing to agree to the marriage, to go with him to Demeter but a whole other to kiss him and to enjoy it.

"You're lying. Is that how you deal with things when they get real? You run away? Like a coward." I turn at his words angry but a surprising breath leaves me when he's standing in front of me while I thought he stayed in bed. I didn't even hear him move. I tilt my head back to stare into his beautiful, angry face.

"I'm not a fucking coward. Yes, we kissed and? It isn't something new to you and—"

"I dare you to say that Hector kisses better again and I swear I'll rip out his throat and make sure that you won't ever want to taste anyone else on your lips beside me." He takes a step closer, his naked chest pressing against mine as I almost swallow my tongue at his words.

"You don't get to decide that. I might marry you but you don't have a say in who I want."

His lips stretch into an evil grin and he tips his head to the side. "You're right, I don't." His hand flutters over a strand fallen in my face and I let him brush it away suspicious at his unfinished words. He leans down and his lips graze my ear. "But I don't think I have to either. Your eyes are already begging me to fuck you every time they look at me.

And I gladly wait to the day that you can't hold it in anymore and beg me to do it. When that happens, remember this day." His voice drops during his speech, and my breathing turns unruly with unfamiliar desire. I want him to do it, even though I know it's wrong. It's wrong in a thousand ways to want him. So I do the only thing that my wobbly knees are capable of. I grab the first dress that comes into my hands as I forcefully move my body from his and speak up, my words tangled and unsure.

"You can stay in my chambers for the day to rest. I´ll talk to my father about the attack." I breathe the words, barely there before I slip into the bathing chamber and shut the door close with a loud bang. It echoes around me and taunts me as my knees slowly give out and I slide down the cold door that presses against my back.

The amount of time I spend pressed to the door and listening to Cassian move is laughable. His steps are heavy and vibrate against the door but even after I hear him leave I stay pressed to the door. I stay huddled against the door until my chest stops heaving and the door suddenly opens. A baffled Marianna stands in front of me, her young face a great surprise to me. The feeling that floods my body at the sight of the empty room is astronomical. Marianna's eyes widen when she notices my wounds and bruises and not a couple of minutes later I find myself hurried into the bath to clean up. I tell her to change the sheets on my bed, which are covered in blood, dirt, and sweat before I ensure her that I'm completely fine and taken care of. I couldn't exactly tell her that I wanted to change the sheets not just because of the dirt. I can handle the smell of iron the blood, the sweat, or the dirt but what I can't handle is the scent. His scent lingers around the whole room, as if it clung to the sheets like a lifeline, soaking into the material to drive me crazy. It makes my body aware of the feeling that infected my blood when he touched me and kissed me. A shiver still runs down my spine when I think of how his teeth grazed my skin, hot and dangerous. Some sort of anticipation has built up between us and now that I got the taste of it my body and mind crave more. I leave the bath early and let Marianna tend to her duties to leave the suffocating air of the chamber.

Now that I'm out of my chambers it seems like I'm able to breathe again, the air in my lungs no longer tinted with his scent that seems to be having the same effect on me as

Gisella´s opium pipe. Sweet and luring, ready to pounce at you the moment you breathe in the toxin.

"Gods, Carina!" Hector´s voice is the first thing that I notice when I step into the hall for dinner, his amber eyes wide and worried as his chair scrapes back when he stands up, making it almost lose its footing. He barely notices it as he rushes over to me.

I choose a light lilac dress today to somehow make the bruise on my jaw look less purple, the sleeves long and flowy, so they mostly hide the gauze around my arm and left hand. Seems like it wasn´t distracting enough because Hector looks at me as if I´ve revived.

"I´m fine, I swear it looks worse than it is." I try to calm everyone at the table when Hector puts his hands on my shoulders. I notice Marrus shooting me a worried glance no sound escapes him, Edlyn seated beside him. My father is sitting in his usual place at the head of the table, his eyes on me but I can´t decipher the emotion that´s swirling in them at that moment. To his left sits, to my dismay, Cassian, dressed in dark blue breeches and a dress shirt, his shoulders broad, chin high but his eyes look everywhere else than at me.

"Did they get into your room?" Hector speaks up again and I realize that I´ve been staring at Cas for a little while too long.

"No, I was in the Royal Gardens when they attacked. I´m fine though, Cas was with me."

"Cas?" Hector´s arms drop from my shoulders.

My father raises a brow as he focuses back on dinner and I feel my heart sink.

"I mean Prince Cassian. He escorted me to my chamber to stay safe." I clench my teeth when I say the words and

Hector seems less concerned now. I decide to ignore the look on his face and make my way over to the table to sit down, everyone's head now swiveling to the prince sitting beside my father.

"I'm glad I could aid you in a moment tinted in need of help." Cassian's tone is icy, making me narrow my eyes at him as I clench my fists under the table. Why is he angry?

"Yes, I don't know what else I would've done if it weren't for you." My voice is dripping with sarcasm as the room turns silent. No clutter of forks or knives echoes around us as we both stare each other down.

"That's the kind of person I am, princess."

"Dripping with kindness and selflessness?" I offer, raising a brow and by the clench of his jaw, I know that it won't be long until he explodes. Instead of edging him on I turn, dismissing him and his childish play to look at my father.

He may have saved my life but that doesn't entitle him to anything.

"Did anyone else get hurt? How far did they get?"

"Not far, the fight stayed on the lands, the Royal Gardens."

"How many did we lose?" My father looks up from his plate at me before he eyes everyone sitting at the table. Instead of dismissing me he stands making everyone go quiet.

"A word." He says in his usual commanding tone and I get up from the table, I haven't even touched my food, my stomach has turned into too many tight knots to make me swallow anything. I'll make sure to drop by the kitchens after I talked to my father. My body needs the energy to heal itself. The chair scrapes against the floor while my father already leaves the hall and this time I don´t bother to excuse myself from breakfast. I´m fed up with all this bullshit of pretending, it doesn´t matter in the end anyway. I follow my father but not without throwing Edlyn a look, to make sure she´s okay and ask her a silent question.

Is my brother alright?

A reassuring nod from her makes one knot in my stomach disappear before I rush out into the hall. My father waited surprisingly for me, turning his back to me when I step into the cold hall and I follow beside him, quietly.

I don´t speak up knowing that every wall could have eyes and ears and wait until we climb various steps and find ourselves in the west wing. The guards straighten their spines discreetly when we come into view but my father doesn´t spare them a glance when I nod as a greeting, following him through the opened doors. The room is eerie, filled to the brim with maps and books about foreign lands and people. I was always amazed by the amount of knowledge that could be stacked into one small room, the candles lit up, always giving the space some kind of secrecy. As if you belonged to an elite club, in which you had to endure some kind of test to be accepted. That was a disappointment for me when I realized they were not in a club and that my father hasn´t read half of these books and land maps. I move my eyes from the stacked books over to his standing form, the dark blue stole, glimmering slightly, ornaments sewn into it as if it were borders to different properties.

His back is to me, his eyes placed outside the window that overlooks the castle's court, his shoulders tense and stiff.

I can't stop and try to detect his emotions, to get a look inside of him before I speak up, not wanting to whirl myself into problems that I don't need right now. But after two minutes of standing in silence and playing with the gauze around my hand, I speak up.

"I know you bathe in the satisfaction of scolding me, telling me that Aerwyna is your kingdom. But please tell me what happened. How did the Protestants even get into the castle?" My voice is gentle, and unsure, something I usually scold myself for but I sense that my father is close to breaking and I don't know if it is out of anger or a different emotion. It turns out that I find out the second he faces me, his sapphire eyes shining brightly with. . . worry?

"Gods, Katarina." Goosebumps rise on my skin when he speaks my full name. Two steps. It costs him two steps before he is in front of me and my father pulls me flush against his body, enveloping me in a hug. A soft breath of surprise leaves my body as it goes stiff, caged inside the arms of the king. The usually cold king scolds me, telling me my place all the time but instead of yelling at me, that I was in the Royal Gardens during the attack, he just hugs me. Hugs me like a drowning man as he puts his cheek on the top of my head and a wave of his cologne hits me at our proximity. My arms finally move out of their stupor and wrap around his torso. I squeeze him tightly while I inhale his scent again. A scent that is filled with memories of my six-year-old self, jumping and running around the gardens, him hot on my tail. One day when we both sneaked into the kitchens to dip our fingers into the chocolate sauce that Orlah prepared for my mother's birthday cake.

His big hands were on my shoulders as we stood reverent at the foot of my mother's bed, Henri cradled in a thousand blankets, his hair just a small patch of blonde fluff on his head.

His scent mixed with sweat and blood, and I cradled into his side while the doctors told us she didn't survive.

A small sob escapes my lips, making my father squeeze me harder. My cheeks are wet, tainted with tears I didn't notice shedding.

"I was so worried about you. When there was no sign of you and Cassian I thought you two. . ." He trails off and I wonder if he's doing it so I won't hear his voice break. This is the first time in what feels like a century that he shows me his affection.

"I'm alright," I say, hating that I'm crying like a small child but I don't want to leave his comforting hug now or ever. After all, he's my father and whatever might tint his bad decisions, I yearn for the love of a parent. I always have and probably always will.

"What happened?" He speaks and makes me look up at him, his eyes warm and familiar.

"It was a surprise, Henri was with us but I made sure some guard brought him back to his chambers. But. . .Cas was with me. I was safe." I bite my tongue the words leaving a bitter aftertaste in my mouth. My father dries my cheeks with the rough pad of his thumb before we finally let go of each other and sit down. His undivided attention is on me without his gaze filled with anger or his body stiff with rage.

"Seems like the prince didn't do such a good job." He says and motions to the gauze around my hand, making me flinch.

I don't know if Cassian already talked to my father so the little detail I give, the better. We have to have the same story of the events from last night or someone will get suspicious. I can't have anyone know that I stayed because I fought alongside the guards.

"Didn't you talk to him?"

"Cassian was unusually quiet this morning, seems like he isn't as tough as I made him out to be." My brows furrow at his words as I play with the ring on my left hand, spinning it around the finger, and grazing it against the gauze.

"Cas wanted to bring me to my chambers as fast as possible and I tripped. Sprained my wrist." I try to muster up a small smile to convince him of my clumsiness. He takes the gauzed hand into his calloused hands, making it feel small and weak. He eyes the amethyst ring with interest before his eyes raise back up to me, my hand still cradled in his.

"Seems like you have big news to tell."

"It's not important. I would like to know about the attack." I say my eyes slightly narrowing. According to his talk with Romanov he already knows about the engagement, so why is he pretending not to know? Here I am yet again questioning the man in front of me, the man who let me cry into his shirt less than a minute ago.

"You're right, you deserve to know. I already sent Lord Romanov this morning to talk to the troops who are cornering the Protestant lands to find out what's wrong."

"How did they even get to Aerwyna without anyone noticing? It was a considerable amount of fighters. Someone must've noticed." I urge him to tell me because things are not adding up. They build bombs to blow up the wall, travel across Aerwyna with them and no one questions them?

"It's a sloppy mistake, which shouldn't have happened. We concentrated on the troops in the north with Moreau's added soldiers and didn't notice the ones that already slipped into our lands. It won't happen again and you will never be put into any danger like that again." If only he knew. Even though he answered my question somewhat I believe it's not the answer I hoped for. Protestants found their way into our lands and he doesn't look the slightest bit alarmed. Maybe it's the king in him, telling him to keep a straight face but the way he cracked and was so worried about me tells me differently.

"Did anyone survive? Did you capture a Protestant so you could question them? How they got here or what they wanted? They surely weren't hoping to invade the castle, they knew they wouldn't have a chance against so many guards with their untrained fighters." The words tumble from my lips making my father halt for a second. Something close to calculation shines in his eyes the movement is unsettling.

"Every last man of them was killed. They didn't want to risk anyone getting too close to the castle."

How convenient, if they would've captured one we would be enlightened with their intention, in case they would've opened their mouths.

"But it's not unsettling enough to worry about, Carina. Lord Romanov will handle the situation."

"Yes, because that seems to be his task lately. Keeping tabs on our soldiers?" I ask with a raised brow, letting him know that I don't buy any of this. A lord and especially the advisor of the king shouldn't be out of the castle and negotiate with the enemy.

"The thing that should be on your mind is what comes with the ring on your left hand. Cassian sure was prepared to propose. As beautiful as the ring is, I'm more surprised by your change of mind." He raises a brow, shooting back after my little nudge about Romanov.

He stands from his chair and paces the room, his hands on his back. I watch the light glitter and reflect on the embroidering of his clothing. It's a skill of him to change the topic so smoothly and usually, I wouldn't be distracted from it but I know it is inevitable to talk about the engagement.

"Of course, he was prepared. He knew of the contract just like you." Another small jab of mine before I straighten my spine and speak up again.

"I said yes because I decided he was the best option to go with right now."—A sentence to please him before I anger him—"He agreed to certain terms before I accepted the proposal."

His pacing stops as he turns around, raising both brows.

"His promised army was sent out to the Protestants, you're aware of that, Edlyn will accompany me on my way to Demeter after the red blood moon ball and Henri will be free." I stand up from the chair so I won't feel as small as he stares down at me.

"And you believe you're the one to decide over Henri?"

"Of course not. I do not decide, I offer. Let him go if he wants, you have no use when I become queen, and Demeter and Aerwyna will become one." He ponders my words, dragging them out even though I'm sure he already planned his decision. He looks at me, with a hard face, before he relaxes and a small smile moves onto his lips.

"This kingdom will be in good hands the day you turn queen. Henri is free to go wherever and whenever he pleases, the second you'll be crowned. But I have a small suggestion?" He is asking me to speak. He is offering me a suggestion. As if he never trampled over me as if he suddenly realizes that I am a regent. I try to compose myself, offering him a wave of my hand to go on. Something brews inside me as if my subconscious tells me that it was too easy to convince him. Maybe the attack of the Protestants left us all shaking.

"The red blood moon is a holy tradition and even though I believe you desire to leave the castle in silence with just a small announcement it would be an insult to the gods not to use this event to announce your and the prince's engagement." I furrow my brows not knowing where he wants to go with this. His lips stretch into a small smile.

"A strong union like this should be celebrated and announced at the ball, sealing the news with a blood oath."

The air around me is filled with anxiety and a whole lot of doubt the second I leave my father's office. I know it was a risk, to speak so openly about my points which led to accepting Cassian's proposal, I knew it could've angered my father. I shouldn't be surprised that he was able to come up with a whole different plan while I was distracted with my lips attached to Cas's.

But accepting my father's suggestion is the ticket to my brother's freedom and who am I to deny that? The red blood moon ball will be the perfect time to announce our engagement, it will honor the gods and it would be a gift to them. A gift that two regents would unite their kingdoms and their bodies. The blood oath is an old tradition rarely used by any engagements in Aerwyna I don't know much about it. Maybe if I listened to Professor Bernath's speeches during my training I would know more than the fact that a blood oath binds people to each other. Their life strings intertwine on whatever level. But mostly it is just symbolic, nothing happens. If I didn't know that we would have to spend the rest of our lives together any way I wouldn't have accepted. It felt wrong, to spill our blood, and taint the earth with something so sacred to the gods while I wasn't in love with him. But it would be a statement, not only to the gods but to the rest of the world. The two strongest forces together until the day they die.

It's just another deceiving tactic to ensure the loyalty of the kingdom to the crown. Give them a big show and they will follow you everywhere.

I agree and allow my father to have that one win because I know it would be the right thing to do. And while the planning for the blood moon ball is already happening I know I could use the time to inform Hector or Prince Marrus of the news.

To give them a soft blow before it is announced to the whole kingdom that I am to be married to Prince Cassian. But instead, I'm doing the complete opposite and rather use the late hours of the day to go see Gisella.

"I don't feel good, I have this gut feeling, Carina." Edlyn expresses her thoughts as her dainty hands analyze my unwrapped hand. I called for her the second I stepped through the threshold of my chamber so she could evaluate the broken bones before I leave for the capital.

I roll my eyes when she looks up at me, her eyes wandering over my usual uniform, the velvet blue cloak draped over the chaise longue that sits in front of the crackling fireplace.

"Your hand isn't strong enough, your arm could get infected with the graze of a blade and your chin looks like you've been beaten up a couple of times." I narrow my eyes at her statement; rubbing at the purple mark on my jaw that bastard gave me.

"I called you so you wouldn't worry if I'm gone, I don't need my left hand to slash a throat Edlyn. I'm going to the Green Knight, not hunting in the woods."

"Yes, and how do you know there aren't any Protestants lingering in the safety of the inn? What if one recognizes you?"

"They won't." I protest, making her glare at me and I go on,

"If someone recognizes me—"

"You mean when someone recognizes you." She interrupts me with a raised brow, making my features harden.

"If someone recognizes me, they won't find their way out of the Green Knight alive." She shakes her head again as she applies a cooling ointment to the skin. My aching bones sigh at the feeling. I settle slightly as I watch her adjust the gauze around my hand before changing to the graze on my upper arm. It's not that bad it doesn't even hurt anymore, thanks to her skills.

"At least take Cas with you, I would feel much less worried if he was with you."

"Yes, because he is so trustworthy." I raise a brow and she grins.

"He proved to be regarding your life. You could use him as bait if you get cornered."

"I didn't help him get patched up by you to let him be the bait if I get in trouble. It doesn't matter anyway I didn't talk to him today besides dinner." I say while I trail my eyes across the room. I am too exhausted to see his face yet again, the feelings swirling inside me, scaring me to death.

Maybe it was just the adrenaline of the fight; I was worried about him getting hurt and that's why I let my guard down. Sure I can't stand the man and he drives me insane in more than one way but I would never want to be the cause of his death. I don't know what that says about me, especially when I spend all of my life despising him.

"I talked to him." My head snaps towards my best friend in question.

"Well, I assumed you wanted me to check on his stitches, just for your information they're alright no infection visible."

"Great," I say stiffly while she finishes up the gauze around my arm.

"You don't need to feign you don't worry about him."

"I do but probably not in the way you think," I say and get up from the place on my bed, closing the buttons on my uniform, to escape her watchful eyes.

"Oh, I think it's exactly the way that I think. It's not a bad thing to care, Carina, he surely cares about you." My fingers freeze for a moment before I continue buttoning the shirt.

"He was worried about you. About your hand, the graze. Isn't it time to let go of the past?" I surely let go of the past when I kissed him but somehow I'm afraid to tell her. I need some more time to evaluate the feeling that twists my stomach before I can even handle uttering the words.

"Cas is an arrogant, cold, indecisive idiot. I don't want to spend more time with him than I have to."

"You're such a bad lair. Cassian might be these things but he seems to also be passionate, strong, and fearless. He doesn't back away, he doesn't let you win and it's bothering you."

"It's not bothering me because I am the one who wins," I tell her, narrowing my eyes. She raises a brow at me, crossing her arms in front of her pale blue dress. She sees right through me.

"Why are you on his side?" I ask suspiciously making her sigh frustrated.

"I'm not on his side. I'm on the side that wants to keep you safe and Cas supports that. Don't go tonight."

"I can't stay. Maybe someone knows about their intentions or how they got into the castle. Thanks to my father every Protestant is dead and maybe I'll find the boy who helped us." I tell her urgently making her bite her full bottom lip in thought. I told her about the young boy who we probably owe our life, if it wasn't for him helping me get Cas into my chambers we would be dead. He told me to find the story where everything began, whatever that's supposed to mean. And it feels like Gisella would be the best source of information when it comes to stories from the past.

"What if it's a trap, a Protestant who wants to lure you out and kill you?" I understand her concern, and I thought about that too. I considered every way this could be a trap to capture me but there was one thing that didn't let me go.

"He knew my mother's name, Edlyn. That has to mean something."

"Anyone interested in the Sebestyen family knows your mom's name. It might be a long time since the people talked about her but it's not secret information."

"But her full name? He must've done some serious graveling to find out that Queen Sheigh is Shailagh Sebestyen. Do you think I should just leave it at that? I can't do that." I say shaking my head and the sigh she meets me with is aggravating. I walk over to the cloak and wrap it around my shoulders, watching the—almost—full moon inch higher in the sky, currently hiding behind a crowd of clouds. The clasp closes easily around me before I grab the mask and walk over to my most trusted friend.

"It might be a trap; it might be someone trying to kill me. But it could also be the answer to everything, from the Protestants to the weird behavior of my father. I am willing to take that risk." I tell her before I open my palm the black mask staring back at us. Edlyn takes it hesitantly before telling me to turn around.

"If anything happens, don´t make a show out of it. I know you, Carina, but this time don´t show off. If there´s any type of danger you turn and run." I stay silent while she puts the mask over my eyes, binding it at the back of my head.

"I didn´t hear you?" She presses and I clench my jaw before speaking up.

"I promise to not make a show. I just want to talk to Gisella, find out if maybe a few of the Protestants stopped by the inn to talk about their plans, nothing more nothing less."
I turn when she´s done and look at her hazel eyes, glimmering with a foreign emotion.

"I swear if you´ll get hurt, I will kill you."
I grin at her words amused by her threat. Edlyn is like a small fairy, she´s elegant and it always seems like she´s floating. She couldn´t even hurt a fly if she wanted to. Edlyn is a healer, not a killer.

"With what? Your herbs?" I ask with a grin as I walk backward to the faux bookshelf.

"Maybe I´ll just beat you to death with the forbidden sketchbook." She says putting her hands on her hips.

"So violent," I say with a grin before the shelf pops open. The angry look on her face leaves and my smile turns lenient. "Don´t be so worried, I´ll send a messenger to your chambers when I come back."

She nods, her hands fiddling, I never saw her this uneasy.

"Be safe."

"I always am."

~ 30 ~

It seems like I hit the jackpot when I first step through the threshold of the Green Knight. The inn is filled to the brim, the scent of cheap liquor, sweat, and excitement swirling into one displeasing cloud. The tables are occupied until some of the men had to squeeze in their large frames, the bar is packed with drunken slurs and waving hands, triggering the panicked look onto the waitresses, who usually seem composed.

The noise level can be compared to a horde of soldiers riding into war, the clinking glasses high-pitched while the voices of the men are gruff and deep. The risk of getting stumbled into is higher than usual and I set my focus on the small booth in the back, unoccupied by any men because it is hidden in the dark.

I walk over, my stride confident, and slip onto the bench. Not many people chose it due to its location, hiding their presence. The people who come here want to be seen, if not by friends, they want to be seen by the courtesans who linger around the scenery, their eyes watchful, their hands elegant.

I catch sight of Gisella at the bar and she greets me with a small nod but her hands are occupied with filling enormous glasses, amber-colored liquid splashing over the brim sometimes. So I sit down and wait. Wait, while the voices grow louder and the desire to leave becomes more urgent. Until I focus my ears on the conversation of the booth in my back.

"They had it coming. Old sack of royal blood sitting up in the safe walls of the castle while we have to work."

My brows shoot up at the words and I push my back against the rest of the booth to listen more closely.

"You're just jealous you couldn't fight them yourself. You're too much of a coward, James."

"I'm not a fucking coward! If someone told me they would attack I'd happily slit the throat of that motherfucker, or maybe his sacred princess. Imagine the look on her face when I spilled her blood onto her dress." The table erupts into booming laughter and I clench my jaw to stay put. They are drunk. You can hear it in the drag of their voices, the laziness to pronounce the words correctly.

"I heard she must be a real beauty. Like her mother once was, pity she got murdered, seemed like she was the only one with something in her head." My hands clench into fists at the mention of her and the sizzle of my blood tells me to end the conversation, to get up and punch all of them into oblivion, so they will see how little I care about any kind of blood spilling.

"Patience boys. It isn't long until the kingdom will be swept over with darkness and you will wish for the old sack of royal blood to come back." The new voice makes me straighten up again, the cold shimmer circling the tone like a warning to me.

"What do you mean?"

"He means that the little princess has found her suitor, to rule beside her in no other than Prince Moreau." My blood freezes at the revealing information and I turn my head to get a better view of the group. They're leveled into darkness, making me catch a head of red hair but nothing more. Who could've already known about the engagement? The fact that it has traveled into town makes me press my feet to the dirty ground of the inn, the feeling of cold terror spreading through my veins.

"There is no way!"

"You suggest I'm lying?" It's the cold voice again and this time I can't stop my body as it moves on its own accord, out of the booth to destroy whoever spread that information. I don't make it out of the booth except for one step before I am pushed to sit back on the hard surface, eliciting a surprised gasp from my lips.

"What in Adales name are you trying to do?" The voice hisses lowly but it doesn't take my head to snap up and recognize the person crouched into the booth with me, his face hidden behind the shadows the dark curls create on his skin. The tone of his voice is so familiar, we could've been in the dark and I would recognize it.

His luring scent of pines and fresh wind captures the booth in a moment but I don't let my body fool my brain and glare right up at the prince in anger. What the hell is he doing here?

"What does it look like?" I hiss back and want to make my way past him and beat up whoever gets on my nerves tonight. I already climb my way half over his rigid body but hesitate when a thought occurs to me. I stop and sit back down to look him in his cold eyes.

"How did you know I was here?" My voice is cold as ice, and my muscles tense up ready to put up any fight. Edlyn is the only one who knows of my location and I was extra cautious tonight, not taking Nighttail with me, so no one would notice her and me missing.

"Call it intuition."

"I rather call it bullshit," I say, narrowing my eyes while he eyes my body suggestively. My blood sings immediately at the look he's giving me, flashes of this morning dancing in front of my eyes.

"Don't play games with me tonight, Cas."

"I'm not playing any games but I would be up to play a few. There's this one I—" I immediately get up at his words because I know this will end in some dirty joke and I'm not interested in that at all. Well, maybe I am, a little bit but he doesn't need to know that.

Instead of moving so, I can leave, his fingers wrap around my wrist and gently pull me back down to sit beside him, the playful look vanishes, replaced by a hard clench of his jaw.

"A day hasn't even passed since the Protestants evaded the walls of your castle and the first thing you think is wise to do, is traveling to the capital? I know you're impulsive and that it often leads you to ridiculously stupid decisions but are you completely mental, Carina?" His voice is a low hiss and I try not to concentrate on the flushed color on his cheeks.

"I am not fucking mental. What did you expect me to do? Just sit around and wait for something to happen again? I was not safer in the castle than I am currently in the Green Knight." His eyes flare at my words and the grip around my wrist hardens which makes me circle his with my fingers, even though they don't wrap around entirely.

"It doesn't matter what happened at the castle, you're not fucking invincible and to hear from Edlyn that you left. . .can you imagine my worry?" His voice loses its hard edge and we both let go of each other. I try to understand his words, try to believe him, and trust him. Maybe he was worried.

"I don´t think I´m invincible but I know my skills. Do I need to remind you that I killed your attacker?"

"Do I need to remind you that you had help with it?" He´s back to being angry as he pulls me closer, enveloping me into a cloud of his scent. I try to stay angry but a girl can only resist so much and the blazing fire in his eyes combined with his hard lines makes my resolve falter for a moment.

"If you are not able to tame whatever possessiveness or honor to protect your fiancée you have, we will be in a loft of fights. I can handle myself, stop making me look weaker than I am." The blazing look leaves his eyes completely and his fingers drop from my skin as he looks at me surprised.

"You think, I think that you´re weak?"

If he would trust me and my strength he wouldn´t always hold me back. He´s defending me in front of Lord Romanov and others bragging about how I can handle myself but every time it comes down to it, he gets angry at me for doing things that he redeems dangerous.

"It doesn´t matter what I think, your actions speak for themselves, Cas. But you should know better than to think that I will sit around and do nothing while you almost died last night and I was lucky to get away with a few scratches. I will not sit down and let any man handle this just because he is a man." I raise my chin slightly not scared to meet his gaze.

His head tilts dangerously to the side, watching me with new anticipation.

"I'm not telling you to stay out of dangerous situations because you're a woman, Carina." He says in a steady voice. Something shifts in the air around us and some kind of realization dawns on his features.

I'm baffled by his words, confused even.

"Then why are you doing it?" My voice trembles and my breath hitches when his arm wraps around me and pulls me close to him in the booth. My resolve finally crumbles when his eyes travel between my lips and eyes before his chin trails along my jaw, so his lips graze my ears carefully. It is as if he wants me to listen to every word closely, branding it into my skin, and marking my heart.

"You can protect yourself perfectly on your own, I don't doubt any of it. You're the strongest person I know and might I add you're really hot while doing it. But the moment you met my lips willingly, edging me on, telling me with your delightful little sighs that you were mine to take, the world tipped. You became mine and I will make sure that you will never need someone else besides me, no hands will touch you any way again in hurt or desire because you are mine to take. You belong to me as much as I belong to you and I will protect you with my life. For this life and every other." A shiver runs down my spine at his possessive tone, shooting a hot wave through my body, which makes my toes curl and my stomach coil in anticipation.

"You're not the one who decides who I belong to," I tell him and his gaze turns dark when I feel his thumb move on my waist.

"You're right. You are. So tell me no." His voice sounds dangerous and anticipation builds inside of me. I felt on edge the whole day, wanting to finish whatever dangerous game we started this morning until I needed to rub my thighs against each other, hidden underneath my dress, to somehow release the tension that has built up in my body.

But with one look out of his emerald eyes, noticing the way my back arches and my nipples press against the suit he lights the tension back up. I see the desire swirling in his eyes, his grip on my back tightening, inviting me to move closer and I'm close to accepting the offer. I am one second away from giving into my desires, to let him do whatever he wants, with those possessive hands and soul-searching eyes.

"Tell me." He speaks up again and I furrow my brows. "Tell you what?"

"That you don't want me. That you can't stand my touch. If you do I'll back off. I won't ever take your choice away, Carina, ever."

I stay silent after his request. I know the right thing to do would reject him and stay neutral towards him. We're going to spend our lives together and if we want this to work it would be better if we stay unbiased with each other.

But something inside me holds me back, maybe I'm a masochist for it. Most of the time I can't stand him but there is a sliver of moments that I crave, that make me curious and want to know more.

"If you look at me like that I might lose any self-control I have left right now." He mumbles while I fixate on his face, tension rippling through both our bodies. This is mutual, the weird feeling of familiarity, the desire to run our hands onto every inch of skin we can get, to engrave each other so no one else ever will.

"Maybe that's what I want." My words are bold, bolder than I usually am but the noticeable rise in his groin tells me he is affected by my intimacy as much as I am by his.

So I dare to move even closer, my eyes staying on his stronghold as my hand places itself on his thigh. The muscles in his leg tense immediately at my touch and I enjoy every second as I move it upwards, Cassian's eyes turning darker with every inch that disappears between my hand and his cock.

"Carina." It's a warning growl but he doesn't make any moves to remove my hand so I palm him with my hand. Oh fuck.

"Yes?" I ask tauntingly when his eyes fall shut, his lashes fluttering against his beautifully high cheekbones.

Gods I barely palm half of his cock with my hand, the size makes me swallow hard.

One stroke of my hand. His body jerks unexpectedly, making me grin. It's all it takes and his eyes fly open, his hand wrapping around my wrist delicately as he stops my movement.

"I don't like it when someone plays." He says his eyes pitch black.

"I'm not playing," I say innocently, my hand squeezing lightly, his hips buck in answer. His gaze is dripping with desire, reminding me of the feeling between my thighs. Cas leans closer his teeth capturing my bottom lip, drawing hard, and my body jerks at the sensation. He draws blood; his eyes flutter close when he leans back and a guttural groan leaves his glistening lips. Holy gods, the lazy look he shoots me with his eyes makes me clench my thighs.

"If you don't stop I'll have to taint my honor and bend you over this table right now. Everyone will watch how I fuck you and you're going to enjoy it." I shiver visibly at his words, my eyes focusing on his lips. They're tinted slightly by my blood, turning me on even more.

"Fuck your honor." Is this me speaking? It can't be. His face looks surprised for a moment but his arms encircle my waist fully and he pulls me to sit on his lap, making me inhale sharply. I grip his shoulders for support, as he nestles his hard erection right at my center. Oh, gods. It would just take one roll of my hips to get rid of the aching inside of me.

"You don't know what you're asking for." He whispers, his lips grazing mine. The tension inside my body almost explodes but the second I look up to tell him to do whatever he wants I stiffen in profound horror.

The door to the Green Knight bangs open and crashes against the walls inside. The sound echoes for a moment when I focus on the people in the inn. Some have turned around to look at the rude intruder that steps through the threshold.

His face is vicious and calculating, a mask he wears often to defeat his enemies and win his followers. He's joined by a group of soldiers and I don't need the crest of Aerwyna etched into the soldier's armor to know who they are. One look at the man's face and my reaction to it makes Cas's head spin to take in the picture in front of us. Lord Romanov has stepped foot inside the Green Knight, a group of royal guards following him like little ducks. It doesn't need the tension rippling through Cassian's body underneath me, to tell me what he's thinking and neither do his words.

"Oh, fuck no."

"Carina, look at me."

I always thought it was just a metaphor when people told you their heart stopped. That they would use dramatics, to lure you into their stories, to make them more convincible or compelling. Seems like it wasn't just a saying because I experience the stutter of my heart the second Lord Romanov steps into the inn.

"Hey." Cas grabs my chin to move my eyes from the man towards him when he moves both of us into the shadows of the booth.

"Are you having a stroke?" I furrow my brows at his words before I notice that I haven't spoken yet.

"I'm fine. Well, not for long if he notices us." I hiss out panicked as I duck my head slightly, getting out of the lord's view. My upper body is pressed flush against Cassian's and in any other situation it would make me flush, heat grazing at my veins but the irritation is keeping my head in a cool state.

"He won't notice us, just stay crouched." He says quietly while he carefully slides my hood over my head and tucks my hair inside. Oh gods if Lord Romanov sees me, even worse, in the company of Cas, I don't know what consequences I'll have to bear.

I peek over his shoulder to watch the disgusting man shoo off a booth filled with men, to sit down with the soldiers, his shoulders straight and proud. What is he even doing here? If he wanted a drunken night, to spend with courtesans and the most unspoken things he could just call them into the castle as every other lord did. I feel my erratic heart thumb against

Cassian's chest as his hand travels up and down my spine, trying to soothe me.

"We're not going to get out of here, without him noticing," I state the obvious because his booth is located on the way we have to pass to leave the Green Knight.

"We'll find a way." He says and turns his head to look at me for a moment, the promise written in his eyes. Somehow the soft strokes of his fingers along my spine and the relaxed look on his face makes me clear my head. He's right, if we don't get out of here, we'll wait until he leaves. I throw another look at their booth, shifting my hips which makes Cas groan. My eyes pass back to him surprised.

"If you keep on wiggling on my lap, we'll have to stay the whole night, princess."

"You have such a perverted mind."

"Don't act like you don't like it." His grin distracts me for a second as he nestles his hardened cock into my back, making my core clench in answer.

"Are you seriously turned on right now? We have better things to do." I tell him as I wind my arms around his neck just because it feels right. He tightens his grip on me and presses a soft kiss against the side of my throat. My blood boils at the sensation of his cool lips against my heated skin and when I feel his lips travel, his teeth grazing my skin, my core clenches again. Gods, it's embarrassing how easy it is for him to distract me. It's like his lips were made to place themselves onto my body, fitting against every hollow and every rise.

"Cas," I mumble while my eyes flutter close, the prospect that we're out in public, with Lord Romanov a few feet away, doesn't bother the prince. He hums against my skin and for another second I get distracted but I finally get out the words.

"You need to call a waitress."

"What?" His head snaps up surprised and I nearly moan at the loss of his lips against my skin but I stop myself at the last second. Instead, I focus on his hazy state as I slowly climb off his lap.

"What are you doing?" His voice sounds wary, his hands pushing against my back so I stay close.

"Call a waitress Cas," I order him again and his green eyes seem to find something in my face as he turns his back to me and calls a waitress with a wave of two fingers. The gesture is so small it's too inconspicuous for anyone to notice besides a woman behind the bar. I nestle with my hood as she scurries over to us, her red dress swirling around her calves.

"What can I do for you, sir?" She asks the prince before noticing my presence beside him.

"We need the services of Madame Gisella." I offer the young woman our proposition, making worry edge into her beautiful features.

"I'm sorry to disappoint but the madam is busy tonight—" The movement of my hand shuts her up as I pull out a purple sack and let it hit the table. The gold coins make enough noise for her to widen her innocent eyes.

"I'll fetch her for you." She curtseys and scurries off while Cas turns to me brows raised.

"She's the only one who can get us out of here without anyone noticing."

"You could've let me fetch her instead of wasting your gold." He says disapprovingly. I raise a brow while I shoot a look over his shoulder to see the lord engrossed with a young girl sitting in his lap, a scandalous dress sitting tightly against her body.

"And risk the devil notice you, hell no."

"You think I'm scared of him?" He arches a dark brow tauntingly and I sigh annoyed by his behavior.

"No but you have a fresh wound and I'm too tired to save your ass." He chuckles darkly at my words and the glimmer in his eyes tells me he's about to comment on something inappropriate, which is why I speak up first.

"I'm not interested in any type of comment from you right now." His dangerous lips pucker lightly at my words and I can't help mine from spreading into a small grin. His eyes spark in an intense green at my smile, stretching his lips into a crooked grin. Something weird shifts between us but it is gone as fast as it came, making me straighten my shoulders again.

"Gods Carina, you need to get out of here." The new voice makes Cas and I turn our heads to see Gisella approaching our booth. I'm immediately calmer when I see her, knowing she will help us get out of here. Even though I would like to stay and find out what the lord is doing here I know we need to leave. By the look of it, he just wants to get laid.

"Well, I didn't think about that. Do you still have the tunnel in your office? Cas and I could use it right now."

I feel the prince tense beside me as he eyes the beautiful woman in front of us. I can feel that he mistrusts her but there is no need to be wary, Gisella would never betray me.

"Of course, follow me." She gives me a weird look but the second she turns, Cas gets up from the booth, offering me his hand, and even though I would want nothing more but to slap it away, I think the better of it and take it. The skin of his palm is rough against mine, so different from my silky skin and yet they fit perfectly together. His fingers wrap around my hand, swallowing it completely with its size.

"I just have the best room for you two, freshly bedded." Gisella turns her head to look at us while she says the words loud enough for the people to hear, that sit in the booths we pass. I try to stay mostly hidden behind my cloak, Cas squeezing my hand as he leans down while walking, to talk to me.

"I don't feel so good about this. Can we trust her?"

"With our lives," I speak with no hesitation and I feel his eyes searching for something in my face that seems to be hidden by my dark hood. He turns and decides to follow Gisella past the booths, my body slightly stiffening when we pass Lord Romanovs table but the red-headed girl on his lap preoccupies him enough to not even detect someone passing him. I'm starting to wonder if Gisella send the girl purposefully, so Cas and I have a safe escape. Once we escape the main hall and dive into the shadows of the inn, I relax a little but don't let go of the prince's hand. It keeps my head cool, the swirling sensation in my chest unsettling me. Gisella leads us down the hall until she stops in front of an inconspicuous-looking door. I watch her fish out the key out of her cleavage before she leads us both inside. The office lies in secret shadows, the sweet scent of opium lingering in the walls just like I remember. There was a time I spend most nights inside here, bathing in the company of my friend.

The walls are still painted in an eerie yellow, the wallpaper chipping off at its edges.

There is no window in the room and the only source of light is the oil lamp placed onto the dark wooden desk filled with various papers. The armchair behind it is in a faded red and its stuffing is showing at the edges.

"You´re crazy for coming here tonight, Carina," Gisella says when the door closes behind us. I take off my hood to look at her properly.

"You know me better than to think I wouldn't come after an attack of the Protestants occurs."

"Well, I thought he would keep you at bay and in safety." She nods her head at Cas who places his sharp eyes immediately on her.

"The princess has her ways of. . .persuasion," Cas says as he shoots me a look while I lift a brow.

"You mean my skill to do what I want and beat you?" I taunt him with a smirk which he mirrors as his hand lets go of mine and wander around my waist to pull me close.

"All this talk of beating me is you want me to feel what exactly, princess? Because it doesn´t turn me off in the slightest bit. Men who feel threatened by a woman's power are nothing but bland and small."

I shoot him an incredulous look and watch the crooked grin on his lips as he crouches down his lips grazing my ear with his next words.

"And I can promise you I´m the farthest bit from small . . .in many departments." Goosebumps cover my skin as he moves away, satisfied with the obvious reaction his words have on me. And gods I hate that he´s right, I know what I felt under his breeches in the booth and there was nothing small about it. I flush lightly but I am not aversed to the idea of finding out.

"Great. Now that you´re finished eye-fucking each other we should get you out of here." Gisella says with a raised brow, making Cas chuckle while I flush even more. I watch my friend round the wooden desk to reveal a trap door hidden under a red and gold woven carpet.

"These underground tunnels lead you right to a side alley at the Green Knight, make sure to only go the right way," Gisella says before she pulls open the trap door. Cas and I share a look before I turn to my friend.

"What is the left way?" Cas wants to know and the brunette woman arches a brow at him. "You don´t want to know." Then she turns to look at me.

"You shouldn´t come here for the next week, Carina, seriously. Listen to the handsome prince for one damn time. The capital is full of hidden Protestants and soldiers."

"Did you hear anything worth mentioning?" I press as I grab her hand in mine, feeling like all of this can´t be coincidental. The Dark Prince turning up, the Protestants going crazy so close to the blood moon. Lord Romanov visiting the inn? It reeks of treachery and foulness and I´m not ready to let go of this.

"What I hear is not made for the ears of a princess. Don´t come back, I mean it." I´m surprised by the urgency of Gisella, gritting my teeth when her nails dig into my skin.

"We should go before it gets too late and people start leaving the inn," Cas suggest and I nod slightly before letting go of my friend.

"Promise to be careful," I tell Gisella who shoots me a small smile. "It's not me who I'm worried about." Her concern touches me and while Cas climbs through the trapdoor first I rush back to the woman and envelop her in my arms. Her body stiffens, she's not used to genuine skin-to-skin contact but everything that happened these last hours tells me that our living hours are delicate. Destroyed easily.

The hug is over as quick as it came but I dare to press a light kiss to her cheek before I climb after the prince into complete darkness. The soft click appears when Gisella closes the door behind us. I stop once my booted feet hit the ground with a small thud, the silence swallowing the sound. For a moment everything is still, the only thing heard are my steady breaths.

"Cas?"

"I'm right here." I flinch, his voice closer than I thought. My hand moves on its own, knocking against his knuckles before he intertwines our hands.

"She couldn't have left us with a small gas lamp? A torch would've been fine." The prince speaks into the darkness making me smile lightly.

"Luckily you have a kick-ass assassin with you who knows the way with closed eyes," I tell him and maneuver my body past his body heat, tucking him after me.

"Gods, princess, if you keep on surprising me with all your skills, I might wrap you up into a bag and keep you hidden from the world's eyes." The tone in his voice makes a shiver run down my spine but I keep my voice steady once I speak up.

"You have a weird imagination; did you let a healer check your head some time?" I ask with a small smile on my lips, listening to our steps. My left-hand travels along the stone walls, leading us through the familiar tunnels that run under the capital. I'm sure this isn't the only one in the capital, it was probably once made for the servants of lords and ladies who lived in the capital but they're long abandoned, probably as old as the stories of our ancestors.

"My head is fine, thank you very much for your worries. I bet you'll be delighted by all the imaginations dancing around there. Care to hear one?"

"Pass." I bite back, knowing he'll turn it into something dangerously inappropriate, messing with my mind. I fear I'm not in the state to deny his advances and right now is not the right time.

"Your loss, princess."

"Stop calling me princess."

"Your right I should get used to calling you my queen, better sooner than later." My heart thunders at his words as I tug hard at his hand to urge him on.

"Please don't call me that."

"Why? You like it, don't you?" My cheeks flame up at his suggestive tone and I have to admit I do like it. Not because I like the title of it but because he is speaking it in a way that makes my core clench and my thighs squeeze.

"Who would've known little Carina is into dirty talk? Gods if I would have known earlier I—"

"Will you shut up?" I'm thankful for the darkness enveloping us right now, knowing that with some light he could see how much it turns me on. Surprisingly he shuts up but I can practically feel the smug look on his face.

"Be careful there are some small stairs next. Maybe six." I warn as I climb them, exhaling relieved when I feel the cold handle of the door in front of me. Sounds are echoing from outside into the tunnel. Drunken slurs and crashing glass, are the saving sound for me right now.

The second I push through the trap door, I let go of Cas's hand and crawl outside, my trousers getting dirty from the streets of the capital. A soft breeze envelops us as we both appear in the side alley like thieves in the night. I clean my trousers with a few slaps on my thighs, watching Cas close the door beside him.

"I'm never going back inside there." He says with a small shudder causing the raise of my brows.

"Is the little prince scared of the dark?" I mock and he throws me a narrowed glance, and I shoot him a smile. Before he can bite back some comment, I dismiss him, drawing up my hood. The street is mostly vacant, the houses laying in silence but the sounds of the inn beside us are still prominent, it seems like even music started playing. That were probably the sounds we heard inside the tunnel.

"It's probably a thirty-minute walk to the castle but I know a few shortcuts," I tell him with a look over my shoulder just to catch a small smile on his lips.

"Who said we would walk?"

~ 32 ~

When Cassian tells me we won't walk back to the castle I expect him to pull out a few gold coins and rent two horses to take us back to the palace. But when he orders me to follow him into a dark side alley I halt immediately. "No. No way."

He turns to look at me half a smirk splitting his lips. "Is that fear I see in your eyes?"

"Falling off a horse does more damage than one thinks," I say and cross my arms in front of me eyeing the horse bound to a lone railing. It neighs softly when it senses our presence and Cassian pats him on the side as a greeting. "Oh come on, you're not going to fall."

"I rather lend a horse." I start to turn because the prospection of riding on one horse with Cassian strikes deep-rooted horror inside of me. He's making me nervous enough as it is but with that kind of proximity I might lose my mind.

Cassian steps away from the horse and catches my wrist in his grip. I turn and look up at him ready to fight. "It's just a horse, Carina, at this time of the night there will be no stables open."

"It doesn't hurt to try." I insist and he tilts his head to the side arching a brow. My eyes fly to the horse and asses the space we will have. My feet are hurting and it is getting late, I don't want anything more than to get back to the palace. I look back at the prince whose eyes are scanning my face deep in thought. "I swear, Cas if your hand slips just for one second or wanders off you're going to live without it." I hiss and his eyes narrow. "Is that what you hold me for? Someone who forces himself on others?" His voice sounds almost offended. "I think you proved that on many occasions." I tilt my chin up and he chuckles. He turns his back and starts walking toward the horse. "Don't turn this around to be something that just I feel, Carina, we both know you enjoy my touch very well," I grumble under my breath and he turns around when he reaches the horse.

"Are you coming?"

With a huff, I stalk past him and get on the horse. He follows my actions quietly but I can practically feel his smile. "You'll have to hold on to me, or you'll fall." He says over his shoulder and I make sure to glower at him before I wind my arms around his narrow torso.

"Just get us back to the damn palace."

  "Your wish is my command."

~

I was a fool for actually thinking that I could somehow create some space between the prince and me. With every movement of the horse, my body slides forward leading to my thighs pressing against his. I try to have a steady hold on his torso, my spine straight as a rod as I refrain my chest from touching his back.

I can't help but think that he is enjoying this very much and for a moment I squeeze his stomach hard making him clench the muscles beneath my hold.

His scent seems to cling to his skin, seriously does he bathe in it? It floods my airways and burns itself into my lungs. I force myself to focus on our surroundings my lips sealed shut as I try to ignore the synchronous movement of our hips. It takes us almost twenty minutes to get back to the palace before Cassian speaks up again.

"Carina?"

My eyes snap open and I'm met with Cassian looking over his shoulder at me. "What?"

"I said you can let go of me now." As if my hands got seared by his words they retract to my sides and he hops to the ground. I realize I'm still sitting on his horse, my legs clenching against the flanks of the big body as if it would somehow save me from my thoughts. My lips part as I look down at the prince, tracing his hard features that call my name, and beg me to touch the silky skin.

His curls are wind-swept and his cheeks have a slight flush tainting them.

Somehow his scent lingers around me luring me in, pushing me to want him. Fire tingles in my fingertips as I try to regain myself.

It appears Cassian is tired of my stalling and his arms reach around me, just to pull me off the horse. A small gasp leaves my parted lips as hard ground hits the sole of my feet, the prince now back to towering over me.

"A coin for your thoughts, princess?"

The words are murmured, his hands not leaving my waist as he stares down at my lips. His gaze is hot and so intense it feels like it's tracing my skin, burning through the flesh like a never-ending fire. Indestructible and relentless just like him.

"Hold my thoughts that little value to you?" I raise a brow, hoping to somewhat change the subject and ignore the aching between my thighs.

"You know I would give up a kingdom for your thoughts." His eyes glow at his words, his lips forming that stupid little smirk that makes my skin grow hot. Instead of answering him, I turn and make my way over to the door that leads into the kitchens, escaping his presence with a small breath.

"Where are you going?" He calls after me but I don't dare to turn, fearing I might do stupid things when I linger in his presence. "To bed."

He'll be caught up bringing the horse back into the barns which means I have enough time to flee like the coward I am. Well more like I thought I did because the second I step into the warm safety of the kitchens, I'm pushed against the cold, stone wall without a warning. The scent of a fresh breeze surrounds me. I don't make a move to fight as I glare up at Cas's face, knowing it was him the second his hands touched me.

"I dislike it when you just walk away from me, princess." His voice is deep, sending a shiver down my spine.

"I don't give a fuck what you like and dislike, Cas." My voice is harsh, even though my limbs feel like jelly, yearning for his touch. I even catch my body slightly leaning in, the touch of his hands right at the top of my ribcage, searing through the material of my suit. The green in his eyes darkens at my words, his hand grasping my chin while his thumb grazes my bottom lip.

"Careful with that mouth, Carina, it might get you into trouble."

"Empty words. You have a knack for threatening me, telling me what you would do with me, and then leaving." My words are valiant, spoken by someone I don't know. His eyes narrow at my words and I raise my chin in his hand, daring him to move closer, to touch me, kiss me, do fucking anything. I'm tired of this constant state of tension, I feel restless and unsatisfied all the time.

"Either you do something about it or you let me be." I hiss, offering him my body on a silver platter. Instead of—finally—crashing his lips against mine, putting both of us out of our misery, Cassian surprises me. He clenches his jaw and lets go of me, completely. Disappointment floods my veins as I exhale a small breath.

"Go to bed, Carina." He doesn't dare to look at me, his body is tense and still. He's right I should go. I should go to bed and fall into a peaceful sleep; the gods know I deserve it. So I take a step to rush past him but instead, I freeze and peek up at him but he won't meet my eyes.

"You're a coward you know?" I hiss, somehow hurt by his denial of my offer.

"I better be a coward than a dishonorable man."

"You think you're an honorable man right now, Cassian?" I scoff at him, jabbing my index finger into his chest. His sudden lack of interest in me, or whatever this is right now, makes me rage.

"You're way past that point when you kissed me this morning and claimed me with your mouth as no one else did." He finally looks at me and snarls.

"I thought Hector kissed better than me? Why so hell-bent on my services now, princess?" He challenges me and now it's my turn to clench my jaw. I take a step back from him, loathing the fact that he's always towering over me.

"Instead of whining about him all the time, prove me wrong." My voice is hoarse when he steps forward, his body edging me forward until I feel the cold wall dig into my back. His hand positions itself on the wall behind me, his eyes glowering at me.

"I'm giving you a chance to back out, princess."

"Don't." I bite back, my blood sings in the back of my ears when he presses his body against mine. I need to close my eyes for a second at the feeling of him.

"Take what you want. It's yours to take anyway." I know it's the weakest I've been with him but if he doesn't put his hands on me in the next minute I might pass out. His eyes fly between mine as if to search for a flicker of doubt, a spark of reluctance but I know he won't find any. His tongue darts out to wet his lips, making my core clench at the sight, imagining it on my skin, exploring every rise and every fall. When I look back into his eyes I see the dangerous black color, making the hairs on my arms raise in anticipation for him to move.

"Take what you want, Cas." My voice is a whisper, hunger burning in his eyes and when I grip his shirt in my hands it doesn't even take a second. There is no slight hesitance, or a last look in my eyes to confirm that I want this. There's just a growled 'Fuck' and that's it. His lips crash against mine so hard that he needs to slip his hand behind the back of my head to hinder collusion with the cold stone behind me. I barely notice it as I release a hot moan, relief flushing my veins as his lips meet mine. His kiss is hard and seductive just like I like, my peaks standing immediately at attention, begging to be touched. The second I moan Cassian uses the invitation to roll his tongue over mine, causing my core to pulse at his sweet taste.

My blood boils as he pushes his body harder against me, making me feel the hard ridge of him strain against his trousers. My hands reach up to tug at his hair, making him hiss and a satisfied smile splits my lips.

"You're really on a mission to piss me off tonight, aren't you?" He says in between kisses, while I trace his hard jaw with my lips.

"Always," I murmur when his hands wander over my body, taking in every curve while I taste his sweet skin with my tongue before he claims my mouth again. When Cassian kisses me there is no denying he does so. He claims me from head to toe, making my blood sing and my heart sigh. He etches himself into my mind like fire, intending to leave burnt traces. He lets go of my lips to trail along my jaw and throat, to bite lightly into the skin and I moan again. If I wouldn't be so turned on I might be embarrassed by the primal sound but the chuckle that escapes his lips is worth it.

"You like that?" I nod as I rock my hips against his erection making both of us shudder.

"Fuck, don't do that again." He mutters and instead of listening I buck my hips again, my center brushing against his. My hands tug at his hair and when he hisses I feel a spark of triumph burn inside me.

"Oh, gods," I whisper at the rippling wave passing through me, tightening the knot in my core. Before I can move my hips again the prince gets a hold of them and stops me. My eyes flutter open to stare at him, soft breaths escaping my lips.

"As much as I like you rocking against my cock, I might remind you that we're in the kitchens of the palace and there will be no returning once we start."

Once we start? I thought we already fucking started this.

"There's no one here beside us," I say and put some pressure on his neck so he claims my lips again.

"But there could be at any second." He tries to stay away but the way his eyes focus on my lips tells me that he's just as on edge as I am.

"Less talking and more kissing, Prince Moreau," I tell him with a small smirk and I push my lips back against his. Our teeth clash and our tongues dance as I push my breasts against him, releasing some tension as the rough material of my suit grazes against my nipples.

"Gods, the sounds you make. . ." He trails off as his tongue trails the side of my throat, running along my aorta like he can feel the heavy thumping of my blood beneath my skin.

"What's with them?" I ask breathlessly as my hands wander over the hard muscles of his stomach.

"I wish I could bottle them up and listen to them whenever I want." His words make me groan and before he can press my body back against his I go for the buttons on the front of my suit.

"What are you doing?"

"Too many clothes between us." I breathe and hastily open the buttons, revealing the fact that I have nothing underneath the suit.

"Holy gods, I'll be damned." Cassian curses as he stares down at my lush chest, the rosy peaks hard and sensitive. They rise and fall quickly with my labored breaths and I can't help but moan lightly when I watch Cassian watch them.

"They're perfect." It's the only thing that escapes him before his head lowers and I wait in cheerful anticipation before he finally closes his hot mouth over one nipple.

"Fuck." I curse and Cassian hums his tongue leaping over the soft flesh, as his hand grabs my other breast, barely fitting into his palm at the size. His thumb grazes over the peak, flicking, twisting and I buck my hips in answer.

My hands wander into his hair, as he pushes his thigh between my clenched legs, making me brush against his hard muscle. He switches the nipple when my panting gets unruly. His teeth graze my other nipple and I rock my core against his thigh.

"Fuck, you don't know what you're doing to me, princess." Cassian groans and I continue to rock against his thigh, sweet agony rushing through me at the tension that builds in my core.

"This is what I imagined for a long time."

I moan at his words before he bites into my soft flesh, making the tension grow unbearable inside of me.

"It's not enough," I whine at the slow pace and hear him chuckle before his hands fly to the rest of the buttons. I watch his skillful fingers unbutton them at an inhumanly fast pace.

"Who would've thought you'd be such a greedy little thing."

"Shut up." I bite back; my cheeks heating up which makes him kiss my lips softly. This time his tongue is gentle, soothing my embarrassment with every stroke of it.

"No need to be embarrassed. Ask me, princess. Ask me who I think of at night, in the morning when I'm fisting my cock?"

I swallow for a moment, staring into the black pits of his eyes.

"Who. . .who do you think of?"

"You. It is always you; it will never be someone else." His eyes glow and I feel like I melt into a small puddle at his hot stare, my insides imploding at his words. I don't notice the fact that he opened the suit enough for his hand to slip right to my center, making me cry out when his fingers brush against me.

"Holy—" I don't get the chance to finish my words when Cas makes our lips collide again, so hard it makes me worry they might bruise. Cas's fingers slide right through my arousal, making him part our lips as he stares at me in surprise.

"You're dripping down your thighs, Carina." He whispers and I flutter my eyes closed in embarrassment.

"Look at me."

I open my eyes again, aware that his fingers are still inside my suit.

"Never. Never be embarrassed about what you want. There is no denying how much I want you." He takes my hand and places it right against his erection, making him clench his jaw in restraint as a small breath escapes him. The fact that I can feel the size of him, and the heat oozing from him makes even more arousal drip from me, which I'm sure he can feel.

"Gods Carina, if you look at my cock like that I might come right in my pants, then I'll be the one who's embarrassed." My eyes fly back up to his face, to see the hunger igniting in his eyes. My mouth opens lightly but I don't know what to say so I grab his shirt and pull him close again to kiss him. Slow and gentle. It's a kiss filled with emotion, defining me. Defining him.

Cas shudders at the kiss before his fingers move again, making me exhale harshly when he pushes one finger inside of me. Knuckle deep inside.

"You okay?" It takes me a moment to answer and I need to grip his shoulder to steady myself.

"Yes. Move." I edge him on, moving my hips slightly to gauge the feeling of his finger inside me.

"Fuck." I curse and stare right into his eyes when I move on his finger. His lips glisten, swollen and red from our kisses and the look of them makes me want to capture them again.

"You're so fucking—" Cas doesn't get to finish as we both freeze at the piercing sound erupting in the shadows.

We both turn our heads listening for another crash but nothing. My eyes focus on the dark, the pans scattered on the counters, the aprons hanging against the walls. We wait for someone to appear, to catch us in this improper act but nothing happens. The only thing heard is our labored breath, mingling in the air around us.

"Maybe you're right. This isn't a safe place." I whisper and I almost groan when his finger slips out of me in one slick movement. I quickly close my suit before I notice Cas stare right into the shadows. I try to see what he does but there seems to be nothing. The tension and heat from our bodies disappear. Fear crawls in from the edges, startling me.

"Maybe it was just a rat." I offer quietly but he doesn't move, his muscles tense. It seems like he senses some danger but I'm sure it's nothing. No one is awake at this time of the night. And if they were they would already show themselves.

"Cas," I repeat and tug at his sleeve, causing him to look down at me. His jaw clenches and the black in his eyes churns dangerously.

"You're right. I'll accompany you to your room, just in case." He says stiffly and I nod, both of us remaining still on our spots.

Gone are the heated gazes and mumbled words. It takes me a moment to finally move after he stares past me, his gaze hard.

Whatever just happened changed his whole mood and I'm afraid to ask why. But I'm more afraid of the fact that it wasn't a rat running into plates or glasses and someone saw the prince and me in an inappropriate situation.

Because that would be the end of me.

~ 33 ~

I had weird dreams that night.

Hot and steamy, filled with soft skin and searing kisses, that could capture the purest soul and lead it towards the darkest places in the world. I would lie when I say that I wasn't disappointed, Cas and I couldn't finish, whatever we started in the kitchens last night.

To my dismay he escorted me to my chambers, to keep his promise but he left with not much more than a somber goodnight. Whatever haunted his thoughts after our fiasco, made his usual cocky self evaporate into thin air. His obvious dismissal and cold behavior did nothing to my burning thoughts, which kept on wandering, images flashing in my mind as if someone had cursed it. So instead of doing the right thing and going to sleep, to somehow keep my pure soul out of the depths of Gehenna, I did the complete opposite. The goosebumps on my skin itched at my mind, scratching at the weak surface. The arousal dripping down my thighs was undeniable, urging me on, luring me to do the one thing forbidden. And I did. I caved as if I have no ounce of self-control.

I knew it is the only thing that would finally help me fall asleep so I slipped my cold hand down the hills of my breasts, over the ridge of my stomach, and in between my burning, hot thighs.

My cheeks burned in embarrassment when I slipped my fingers through my slick arousal, my eyes closing on their own as I imagined my hands to be someone else's. Stronger, with long fingers. Skilled movements. A face moved into my mind, with beautiful hard features, with glowing green eyes. Desire was dripping off his features as the imagination watched me arch my back in pleasure. I imagined the fingers inside of me bigger, stretching me and giving me just the right amount of pleasure. I was frustrated by my small short fingers, not filling me entirely but with the image of him hovering over me I came so hard, Cas's name a forbidden sin on my lips as the tension released itself in my body. Sleep found me immediately afterward.

Even though I have to plan the blood moon ball this morning, I dismiss my duties and head for the library, one mission in my mind.

Edlyn offers to spend the morning with Orlah to go over the menu and the guests and I grant her with a relieved smile and a big hug. Now I´m on my way to the library and exhaling a relieved breath when I see that no guards are positioned outside of the library doors. I´m sure that if there are books still existing with the myths and secrets of Adalon they have to be hidden in the deep ends. Where no light makes its way through and no man dares to wander to. Good thing that I am a woman. My steps echo across the gigantic shelves in the room, the early morning lighting kissing the spines. The light allows me to see the small particles of dust dance across the air.

The story of the beginning. . . the words of the stranger somehow etched their way into my skin and while I ponder over them for hours I just got to think of one story.

Adales and his four children, the descendants of this world, reign passed over for centuries.

The temperature drops a certain amount in the dark area and I need to take a candle with me, despite the sun shining outside, to find what I am searching for. I try to look for old bindings, used more than one time. I remember the blue binding of the book, gilded ornaments edged into the cover. I know the story by heart, had to learn it my whole life, which is why I can´t imagine something has slipped my watchful eyes.

But with the course of recent events, I may have a different view on the words, things that I wasn´t looking for may have slipped my eyes.

It doesn´t take me long to find the book about the story of this kingdom but after I skimmed over the familiar words it seems like these were the stories I learned about in class my whole life.

There is nothing new, nothing that could somehow explain a dead body being found or why I should be careful who to trust. Maybe the boy was talking about the Dark Prince and that he wants to take my throne? But wouldn´t that be too much of a coincidence if he knew?

By the sounds that echo around the halls of the castle, I assume the inhabitants finally find their awakening and while I thought I wouldn´t be bothered in the deep ends, I still hear footsteps circling.

I shut the book, blowing out the candle on my way. My body moves quietly as I wind my way around the table not a single step heard. My heartbeat thrums lightly and I wonder which pour soul found their way into the library. A shadow dances between a bookshelf not far from me and my body tenses as my heartbeat stumbles before it quickens. The erratic beating accompanies me as I approach the bookshelf slowly, and cautiously. The hidden slit in my gown gives me access to unsheathe my dagger in one swift movement. The heavy weight of the weapon immediately makes me feel more calm and safe. My body slips into the role of the assassin in a second, no steps are heard as I follow the figure behind the shelf. The person doesn't even notice me following, making me internally shake my head in disappointment. Before they can move another step I make sure to kick my leg into the back of the knees, pushing the tall form against the shelf, dagger pressing against the exposed throat.

"We have to stop meeting like this, princess."

"Oh Adales, it's you."

A relieved breath leaves my lips once I recognize Cassian's voice. Still, I don't move the dagger an inch as I stare up into his eyes angrily. A thought crosses my mind like a sharp arrow. He was spying on me.

"How wonderful it feels to see you express the lack of excitement when meeting me."

A small smirk accompanies the prince's words, making a shudder of awareness flood my veins. To cover up my awareness of him, I jab him in the ribs with my elbow. A soft groan escapes his lips and I smile satisfied before I sheath my dagger back into place.

"That was not friendly."

"Who said I'm friendly?"

"You were yesterday when your nipples were in my mouth and my finger knuckles deep inside your sweet little cunt."

I almost choke on my next breath when I hear his words, causing a satisfied grin to move back onto his lips. My fingers tingle with tension, telling me to somehow get rid of the embarrassment that floods my skin. I´m sure if I had a mirror right now, I´d see myself flushing from head to toe. The image fuels my anger even more. It was my choice to touch myself; it was my mind that conjured up the image of him doing it for me. Still, my embarrassment overweighs the voice of reason inside my head. A soft brush of air is the only thing felt and a soft groan meets my pulsing knuckles.

I shake my hand lightly hissing at the burning pain when I meet the guttural growl of Cassian, who holds his nose yet again. It is not broken, I know because there was no satisfying crack meeting my ears but I wish it was when I see the look he´s giving me.

A cold shiver runs down my spine and I´m too slow to escape him as he moves his tall body over me. My back collides with the bookshelf behind me, rattling the books but my mind can´t focus on the fact of them dropping to the ground.

I rather focus on the fact that Cas´s hand wraps around my throat with a slight squeeze, his eyes as dark as the night sky. A dark shadow envelops his body and for the first time, I am scared.

"I don´t know who put the idea in your mind to solve every problem with violence, princess, but let me tell you it´s not nice to hit your fiancé." His words are a dangerous murmur, making my breath hitch when his lips graze my neck softly.

"If the so-called fiancé would stop spying on his fiancée, she wouldn´t feel the need to hit him."

My voice is barely a whisper, his hand tightening around my delicate throat. I know he's not choking me but the soft squeeze makes something tighten inside me. I shudder when his thumb swipes over my larynx, the rough pad eliciting goosebumps on my skin.

To my dismay, I feel my body leaning into his touch, anticipation making my stomach coil. I swallow and watch Cassian trace my throat with his eyes, narrowing them slightly at the movement. Heat pools in the pit of my stomach as I try to clench my thighs together to get some friction going. His jaw clenches for a moment before his hand releases my throat, making me exhale in disappointment.

"What are you doing here?" I demand again as he still hasn't spoken a word after his outburst. My body is still hot, searing in the places he touched me and I try to put some distance between our bodies. His arm stops me from doing so and wraps softly around my waist to pull me flush against him. I will seriously suffer from whiplash at this man's mood swings.

His fingers skid over my waist as I try to breathe normally but the second our bodies hit I feel it. He's just as aroused by my presence as I am by his. I can feel the hard ridge of his erection pressing into my stomach, making my core clench delightfully at the feeling.

"I saw you ominously sneaking around the halls and followed you inside."

"That's a lie," I state, making him grin lazily. His eyes are back to their normal green color and I know that whatever he felt seconds ago is back under control now. I try not to move too much, my breasts coming close to press against him with every breath I take. I can already feel my nipples hardening, my body screaming at me to let him touch me. To beg for his touch.

"I wanted to check on you, after last night. But then I saw you sneaking around and I wanted to know where you'd go." He admits, his eyes glowing softly. Both his arms are wound delicately around me now. His thumbs draw circles onto the fabric of the gown and it feels like his touch is burning right through it, yearning for my skin. The next breath gets slightly stuck in my throat as I divert my eyes to his chest.

"Has someone ever told you that you're lousy at sneaking around?"

Yes, good. Distract yourself from his burning touch, Carina.

"Am I? Because I remember myself sneaking up on you on that roof." He says with a satisfied smile making me roll my eyes. My eyes get stuck on his lips as if they're calling to me, pulling me closer with every breath. No, no, no. Not good.

"That was beginner's luck," I say before I wind myself out of his grip, scared of what I might do if I stay too close to him. I wander back to my hidden corner, listening to his elegant footsteps behind me. It is weird how such a tall person can be this quiet. Sometimes I wonder if he's being loud on purpose because it seems like he can be quiet and invisible if he wants to.

"Try to convince yourself of that, Carina."

The way he speaks my name makes a shiver run down my spine, goosebumps rising on my skin. The effect he has on me is pathetic. The fact I can't deny it, even more.

His hand grasps my arm to turn me around; making me protest but the look on his face is tense. I stop my movements and offer him my attention, curious about what's plaguing his mind.

"Seriously how are you holding up?"

His question surprises me more than it should. The genuine tone makes me take a step back, frightened that he lures me back in easily. I don't make it far when I feel a table behind me, pressing into the back of my knees. I bite my lip in thought staring at the shelf behind him. How am I holding up? I don't know. I fought against Protestants, who almost killed him. Then I sneaked out of the castle because of a stranger's cryptic words just to almost get caught by a lord. On top of all of that my feelings are going crazy every time I see him. It's as if he's making me question everything I ever dreamed of, yearning for something different. Dark and danger were never involved in my plans. I have enough of that when I am the Red Saint but I never believed I wanted more of it as Carina too. I have to laugh at my thoughts, which makes him probably think that I'm a lunatic.

So I settle on a lazy shrug of my shoulder, not knowing what else to say. Cassian moves closer, the grip on my arm easing slightly as he stops, towering over me.

"Nothing will happen to you, I promised you that."

"I'm not worried about myself but the people who can't protect their selves," I admit, trying to avoid his burning gaze. It makes my tummy coil every time and I hate that he makes me feel this way.

"And I don't understand how certain things can be." I try to make sense of my knotted thoughts and take a deep breath.

He leans down, his knuckles grazing my arm softly. Happy goosebumps greet his touch like an old friend, longing for its feeling.

"I can help you with everything, Carina; you just need to ask me." He tells me in a small whisper. Instead of listening to his words, I find myself falling into the deep ends of green, the fire inside my body burning right up.

"The boy said something before he left after the attack of the Protestants," I whisper and his eyes narrow. "What did he say?"

"He said to find the story of the beginning."

He crosses his arms in front of his chest nodding. "So the story of Adales and our ancestors."

"I thought that too but I skimmed through the book there's nothing out of the ordinary." I scratch my arm unsure how all of this sounds. Is it a waste of time to consider some stranger's words?

"Is that the only thing he said?" I nod and he starts to pace. "And you believe that the information he's going to give with whatever the story of the beginning is would be vital for you?" I nod again. He stops pacing his features set when he nods. "Alright, then let's start scouring."

~ 34 ~

Cassian and I are surrounded by mountains of books, some spines are broken some shining with their gold impregnation. Dust particles dance in the afternoon light and for a moment they remind me of snowflakes descending to the ground. A dull ache has made its way into the back of my head and the words are starting to blur in front of my eyes creating a mess of letters.

"Have you got anything?" I ask as I lean back in my chair, my spine popping when I stretch it. Cassian grumbles incoherent words from his place opposite me. His face is hidden behind the red cover of a book just the tops of his furrowed brows are visible.

I muster him for a second, how the light bounces in his curls, making them look as if they have a blue tint to them. His company is surprisingly calm in the confidence of the library. We scour for hours but I do not come to any kind of conclusion. I stumble across the story of the Dark Prince in one of the older books but my suspicions that he is just a horror story for children get confirmed.

Someone seems to be using his name to inflict fear on people like Ellister.

"What?" I flinch at the question and realize that I've been staring at Cassian for the past few minutes.

His gaze musters me curiously and I shrug my shoulders. "Nothing."

He shuts the book he's currently reading and runs his hands along the back of his neck to massage the tense muscles.

I lean forward in my seat chewing my bottom lip. "Be honest, do you think I'm crazy? For trusting a stranger?"

His lips spread into a grin. "Not crazier than I am."

I huff out a small laugh and focus on the amethyst ring on my finger. I spin in making the light dance across the stone. "Seriously, Cas. What if all of this is just a distraction? Maybe the boy is a Protestant and wants to waste our time."

"I'd hardly call this wasting our time." I look back up at him his eyes glowing. "I just feel like we're missing something. If he does mean the four siblings and their story I don't understand how it is related to me besides the obvious ways."

Cas leans back in his chair and looks at me. "What do we know about our ancestors exactly?"

"Besides the obvious characteristics? Technically they were just all lunatics, especially Demetrus, no offense."

His lips spread into a grin. "None taken."

My fingers trace a random wood pattern on the table as I search my brain. "It just seems like the prospection of peace was never close by. Maybe if Oceanus wouldn't have married Demetrus soon to be, the kingdoms would've never gone to war. His mental stability was already on edge and then his sister dies. But that is the past our kingdoms are in good spirits now." Cassian arches a brow and he gets up. I watch him stalk over his steps elegant and quiet before he leans against the table right beside me.

"I wouldn't say you and I were in good spirits." I scoff. "And who's fault is that?"

"Not mine." I have to laugh humorlessly. "You men are all the same never seeing your flaws."

"You are judging me on the faults I had as a child, Carina. I don´t think that's fair at all."

I look up at him and grimace. "You´ve cut the hair of my favorite doll and threw it in the fireplace."

"That was my brother I just stood beside him,"

I get up as well or else I will get neck problems. "Zayne and you manipulated the arrows on the midsummer fest. So I couldn´t hit the targets."

"That was Zayne," He tells me and I narrow my eyes. "But I caught you sneaking around my room that day, where the arrows were stashed away." His lips stretch into an embarrassed grin and his cheeks flush. I´m surprised by the look of it it almost makes him look like the nineteen-year-old boy he is.

"I sneaked into your room after I found out what Zayne did. To switch out the manipulated arrows." My lips part surprised. "You´re joking right?"

The prince releases a small chuckle and shakes his head. "As serious as I can be, princess."

I ponder his words for a moment. It does seem convenient that he´s telling me this now when he is forced to marry me to get what he wants.

"What is going on in that scheming head of yours?" he taunts when his arms wrap around me and pull me between his legs. Goosebumps cover my skin when I look up at him. "I´m contemplating if I should hit you again."

Booming laughter travels through the library and echoes against the walls. I look at the prince surprised as our bodies shake with his laughter. A small smile splits my lips because something about his laughs sounds so free and clear that it tugs at my insides.

His laugh turns into a chuckle when he looks back at me. It feels like he sees something in my eyes and leans closer our lips grazing. "I'd be your punching back any day."

He presses a featherlight kiss against my lips surprising me with his gentleness.

When we part I look at him. "I didn't expect you to be like this."

"You mean charming and handsome?" He runs a hand through his curls and I hit his chest lightly.

"No, you big idiot. I mean that you're so humane."

A serious look adorns his face at that. He seems to fight with himself before he speaks up again. "Not every monster is inhumane, most of them became monsters because they had to."

"I don't think you're a monster. Not anymore." I speak the words and feel that they're true. Cassian grimaces lightly, squeezing me assuringly. He seems to be fighting for words I can practically see his thoughts racing through his brain.

"I wanted to talk—"

Something in the back of the library crashes and interrupts the prince's words.

My head swivels around and my muscles bunch as I scan the shelves. "What was that?" I whisper when I scan the place in front of me but I see nothing but empty tables and bookshelves filled to the brim. I narrow my eyes when I feel the air shift around us.

"Probably just a rat." I turn back to look at Cassian. "There have been many rats scouring the palace lately." He considers my words before we both start to walk towards the direction the crash sounded from. Both of our steps are soundless when I draw the dagger from my thigh.

Cassian and I both share a look and decide that we round the bookshelf one of us on each side to trap whoever sneaked behind us.

My heart pounds in my chest and my hands get clammy around the hilt of the dagger but I focus on keeping quiet as I jump around the shelf.

My arm is raised ready to attack but I freeze when I see what´s before me.

Cassian´s brows are furrowed as he watches the scene. He squats down to examine the tumble of books on the ground and an abandoned oil lamp, its glass broken and scattered.

"Someone probably left it here last night and the wind knocked it over." He ponders and I sheathe in my dagger and squat down. There is no gust of wind in the library all windows are closed.

I grab the handle of the oil lamp to feel that it´s still hot.

"You think someone was stupid enough to leave an oil lamp in a room full of books and it burned through the whole night?" I look at him and he shrugs his shoulders not convinced.

"Maybe."

"Or maybe someone was spying on us just now." I offer and he shakes his head as we both get up. "We would´ve seen the person, or heard their steps."

I eye him worriedly not feeling good at all with this. Something bizarre is going on.

"Princess!" I flinch and turn surprised to see Marianna rushing into the room her cheeks flush. Her dress bunches around her ankles and her hair sits in a mess atop her head.

"Holy gods, you scared me, Marianna." I hold my chest and the maid's eyes widen at the boy behind me. She curtseys quickly. "I'm sorry to interrupt but I wanted to make sure that you were ready for the gown fitting."

I hit my forehead in horror. "Right, that was today, shit." I turn to look at Cassian who shoots me a small smile. "I'll clean this up."

"Thanks." I turn to scurry after Marianna but turn as I walk to call at the prince. "Sorry for wasting your time but thanks for the help." He shrugs his shoulders as he starts picking up the shards. "It wasn't wasted time." My steps falter as he winks. "I spend it with you."

In the evening I find my way into the bathtub, the warm water calming my tense muscles while Edlyn babbles excitedly about the oncoming journey to Demeter. It is like her to see the best in the change of scenery and I won't complain either.

I'm tired of everyone keeping secrets and if I'm being honest the palace doesn't feel like the safe space it once did.

I'm frustrated, I feel fooled, believing a strange boy to search for a story I've read a hundred times about. I wasted hours in the library just to come up with nothing. Even if he is telling the truth, what does the story have to do with me, any other than that Aerwyn is my ancestor? They died a million years ago; yes Cas and I are the current regents. We're carrying their legacy but it's not like we're kept in the dark about it. I'm sure every regent feels the weight of the situation every day.

It nags at me, not knowing what the boy means because I somehow know he isn't lying. Logically it wouldn't make sense to lie because he helped us. There is no motive.

"I hope the men of Demeter are how they are told." Edlyn disrupts my wandering thoughts.

"How are they told?" I ask while I twirl the hot water with my hand. I prop my chin up on the edge of the bathtub to look at her. The soft rose scent is floating around the chamber, bathing us in its energy and dizzying our minds.

"Their skin is to be told like gleaming gold. I've had enough of your pale ass," she chuckles lightly as she holds her arm up the candlelight reflecting on her darker skin. She goes on before I have the chance to interrupt. "Fearless is what they called them and handsome like the gods carved their faces themselves, I mean you've seen Cassian, he's gorgeous."

At the mention of the prince, my muscles tense up even more. The afternoon flashes in front of my eyes, the way the sun beamed upon his head creating some kind of halo. I still wonder what part of Cassian is the real one and if the things he tells me are still calculated by him. I wouldn't call our current relationship a friendship. We are both attracted to each other a blind man could see it.

There is no denying the way my body is hyperaware, my eyes searching for him every time I step into a room. My fingers itch to touch him every time he is near.

"He's. . .viewable."

I´m cautious with my words, scared to admit what I think. Edlyn rolls her eyes at my words. "He's handsome admit it. Your babies are going to be gorgeous."

She says it carelessly but I feel my chest tighten at her words, the bad feeling of this afternoon bubbling to the surface again. I swallow the upcoming panic in an instant.

"Don't say things like that."

I don't know what it is that she hears in my voice but it triggers a sad look from her.

"I'm sorry. Are you unhappy to leave?"

She scoots over to the bathtub, placing her chin down beside mine. Her brown eyes sparkle lightly in the light of the candles surrounding us. I take a second to watch how the light reflects the color as it does with amber. Entranced is the best word to describe the way it feels to look into the color. She always had those trusting eyes.

"Not necessarily sad. Yes, this is the castle I grew up in but nothing is holding me back. Henri will leave to see the world, you are coming with me to Demeter and Hector. . .Hector will go back and govern perfectly as he did for the last months." I tell her with a sorrowful smile.

I will tell him that I've chosen Cassian. Before the ceremony, in two days I will look for him and tell him. I tried to look for Marrus today but he was nowhere found, which means I have to tell both of them tomorrow; it is the last chance for me to do so.

"You liked him, I'm sorry it had to happen that way. Maybe if the two of you had a little more time. . ." She trails off and worries her bottom lip.

I pull my hand out of the water and grip hers in mine while I shake my head.

"But we don't have more time and I'm not sad. At least I had the chance to catch a glimpse of what it feels like to care for someone in a pure way. I'm thankful for the time with him and I'm thankful that my first kiss was with someone as gentle and understanding as Hector."

And yet it's not his lips I miss, our touch I crave. I am fucking pathetic. I yearn for a man who is unable to give you something different besides possessive touch and fiery heat.

"Well, maybe you needed someone like that for a short time. I know you don't want to talk about him but I'm sure Cassian is an excellent lover if you will let him be." I know he will be that's not the problem.

I'm almost excited. Almost. To let my anger out at him, to fight and scream. The rippling tension in the air always fills me with excitement, hoping for it all to finally explode. To release the pent-up anger and collide in hot pleasure.

Gods I am as sick as he is. It´s like he´s infecting my mind, placing all of the bad thoughts inside. I grimace at her words and flick my fingers to spray her face with small drops of water, so she doesn´t notice the heat spreading on my cheeks.

"Hey!" She protests, chuckling while her lips stretch into a smile on her face.

"I'm not interested in any kind of relationship like that. Especially not with someone as aggravating as Cassian." I get a smug smile in return.

"Yeah? Is that why you kept the dirty sketchbook?" She asks and my cheeks flush an instant red color—again—at her question.

The defensive answer is already on my tongue but my friend is quicker.

"How was it?"

She eagerly leans forward but I shake my head instantly, it's embarrassing enough that she knows I looked at it. If she digs deep enough I might cave and tell her about the alcove or the night in the kitchens. Cassian doesn't seem to want to continue whatever we did but I don't know why.

After all, he is the one with the flirty comments and the heated gazes.

"You can have them back. But I don´t advise for you to continue in such. . .vulgar sketching." I say nonchalantly playing with the warm water around my body while I watch her grin.

"Not dirty enough for, Your Highness."

"Ha-ha. Why would I ever find pleasure in those vulgar paintings, primal feelings, and all that?"

I wave my hand through the air, trying to appear unfazed but she can see right through me.

"Which did you like the most?" She says secretively. Her eyes sparkle lightly, her cheeks flushed. My eyes widen at her, caught off guard by her lack of restraint. I lower my lids to hide whatever she can see in my eyes, my thoughts wandering to the sketches. It's not like I've found a liking in a certain one but I was wondering about a few things. No one prepared me for anything like this once I became a queen.

The lack of a mother figure seems to be the most prominent in these kinds of things. It's not like I can't ask Gisella but I fear she will traumatize me with her stories.

And I'm sure Cassian is much more experienced than I am— he already proved that—and I know of the ritual after a royal wedding.

It makes my skin crawl to think of it. It doesn't matter how many years you get prepared with the ritual it is best if the information stays locked in the back of your mind. I can handle being an assassin and killing people but when it comes to intimate things I become a stumbling mess.

"You look all green in the face, did something disturb you?"

"That's not it, I was wondering about a certain thing, that you sketched. How do you even know these things?"

She casually shrugs a shoulder and grins. Something ancient glitters in her eyes.

"People talk and there are books that can educate you very well. If you're interested?" My eyes widen and I scoff. We bathe in silence for a moment and I decide to drop my morals for a moment.

"There was something that I was wondering about."

"Tell me."

My friend leans forward again.

"I was wondering—just out of curiosity—there was one sketch where the woman did something for the man." Her eyes widen in understanding and my cheeks flush.

It is not like I am going to do anything but the time Cassian and I were in the kitchens I was so clumsy and unsure of where to put my hands on how to elicit pleasure from him.

Somehow I feel a little dirty, with curiosity itching at my skin. I would love to be the cause of his deep groans, to have so much power over him.

"You mean when she kissed his unmentionables?"

I almost laugh at her wording but bite my tongue and nod.

"I never thought things like that could go beyond the act of love."

I obviously know of the courtesans in town I'm not stupid but I know these men are paying for pleasure but never really think of what that pleasure looks like.

"Have you thought about doing it?"

"What? Of course not!" I protest at her words and it seems like that was the wrong thing to say. Her eyes widen as she seems to realize something and my hands grab the edge of the bathtub, my knuckles turning white.

"You did think about it. Have you already done something? That explains the weird glow I´ve seen around you these past days." She seems to murmur the last words to herself, making me frown.

"I haven't thought about doing anything." I did. Multiple times. Every night, if I'm being completely honest.

"You're such a bad liar. Instead of letting the knights train you in combat, they should've shown you how to lie. I want a name now. What did he do? It's not Hector, is it? Wait—is it Marrus? Is there someone in the capital? Oh my—"

I clasp my hand over her mouth so she stops ranting. I get a heated glare in return.

"I promise to tell you if you stop guessing. No, it's not Hector." I sigh, making her speak up but her words are muffled due to my hand that still sits over her lips. I let go of them and she raises a brow.

"Thank you—I wouldn't have thought it to be Hector anyway, he seems too. . ."

"Gentle?" I offer but she shakes her head no.

"Boring."

"He is not boring."

"He so is."

She says it with so much conviction in her voice that I don't protest. Hector isn't boring, he is just quiet and reserved. Yes, he doesn't make me feel like my body is on fire every time he touches me. But he doesn't have to because I appreciate his presence otherwise very much. I don't favor sparks and passion over someone you genuinely like. Well, I thought I didn't. Now I'm a bit undecided.

"You look like you're trying to solve a puzzle. I'm almost bursting from curiosity, tell me!"

She jumps lightly, her balance on the back of her thighs and I clench my jaw before I relax again.

I lean forward so she can hear me better, I know no one is around us but having to say the words makes my body heat up in embarrassment in an instant.

"Somehtingmighthavehappenedwiththeprinceofdemeter."

She furrows her brows at my murmur and blinks.

"A bit louder and maybe slower, Your Highness?" She mocks me and I sigh.

"Something might have happened with. . .the Prince of Demeter," I whisper and what I receive is a dramatic gasp. Edlyn leans backward, her hands clasped over her mouth.

"That bastard!" She curses and I furrow my brows. Before I can help it, it bubbles right out of me.

"I don't know how it happened, he just kissed me in the alcove and I felt things I have never felt before, the attack of the Protestants caught me off guard, then he surprised me in the kitchens that after we went to the capital and his fingers—Adales—the way they curled.

"When his hands are on my body, it feels like he's claiming every part of me And now I'm all confused."

My words are barely a whisper and Edlyn's eyes widen with every word I tell her.

"Holy gods."

I can hear the confusion in her voice and chuckle lightly. I take a deep breath and instead of keeping anything a secret I tell her about the evening I eavesdropped on my father's and Lord Romanov's conversation, her face visibly tightens at the mention of them but relaxes when I tell her how Cassian appeared out of nowhere. I reluctantly tell her about the kitchens, spearing her details and how amazing it felt, and lastly how he helped me in the library for hours and kissed me gently and slowly as if we have a secret that no one is in on.

I hold back on the morning we woke up together in my bed. Somehow I want it to keep as my memory, untainted by anyone's opinion. The worry that I felt that day was new and somehow raw, desperate. It felt too real. Whatever it meant, I'm not ready to talk about it.

"That is so hot. How does it happen that I always miss these kinds of things?"

"That's what you have to say about all of that?"

I raise a brow while she grins apologetically. It feels good to tell her about this, some weight lifts from my shoulders, but still, the fear is nagging at my heart.

"Well, I knew he cared about you. I saw it after the attack."

I quickly shake my head at her words.

"It's not like that. We still hate each other."

At least I think we do.

Edlyn raises a brow unconvinced but she drops the topic as if she could sense my discomfort.

"I can't believe you let him fuck you with his fingers— Adales you're not the saint you told me you'd be."

"Don't act like I've planned all of this mess. It was an accident."

"You trying to tell me you somehow fell and his fingers slipped inside you?" I blush and she arches a brow.

"And now you're asking me about pleasuring a man?"

I cradle my face in my hands. I hear her soft chuckle before she brushes my wet hair from my face. I look up completely frustrated with my situation.

"It's okay to want things, Carina, who tells us what is forbidden and what is not? You're going to be a queen for Gehenna's sake. You can do what you want, with whoever you want."

"I won't once we perform the blood oath at the ball. After that, I'm bound to him and it scares me to death." I confess gnawing at my bottom lip.

"But if he's the source that can make you feel this way it won't be that bad right?"

She offers but I shake my head no. She doesn't understand, it's bad enough that I desire Cassian in a physical way but with the things he always says and does I'm afraid I can't keep hating him as I do.

"Hey you don't have to go through this alone, I will be at your side at all times."

She grabs my hand in hers, making me smile sadly.

"I know you will but you're not going to shed blood, binding yourself to a man in front of the gods. I will have to face the dark King of Demeter and from what I remember he is not a kind man. I don't even want to think of what has become of Zayne."

I refer to Cassian's older brother who refused to step onto the throne. A shiver runs down my back at the thought of the cruel boy.

"Don't make yourself smaller than you are, Carina, you're a badass assassin who kicked Cassian's ass the first night you met him. You are strong and beautiful and you are a rightful queen. If anyone should be scared it's them. They have the honor of serving and spending their time with you."

Her eyes glow intensely with her words and for a moment something sparks in my chest, a small glimmer of hope at her words. I squeeze her hand and nod.

She is right, I will manage the blood oath and marriage with Cassian, I have handled much worse things.

"I like that look in your eyes." She tells me with a grin and I tilt my head slightly.

"What look?"

"The one where you plot and settle on a plan, that is going to destruct every enemy who dares step into your way."

~ 36 ~

Being scared of the blood moon ball is justified, much is at stake. But the sweaty hands, a thumping heart, and hot skin in front of a prince's chamber, which I talked to a hundred times, is pathetic. I've been pacing in front of the dark wooden door for what seems like hours but it could've been barely minutes.

The two guards ignore me completely, facing the other way as if they sense that I need some privacy. I was in a similar position minutes ago, in front of the doors of Marrus chambers, and after minutes of pacing—and finally having the courage to knock—the only answer I got was an eerie silence.

I start to wonder when the last time was that I saw the prince. I am slightly alarmed at first but then I remember dinner last evening, I talked to him and everything seemed fine.

Maybe he is taking a stroll around the Royal Gardens. The irrational fear of someone finding out about Cas and I's engagement, before I tell them, have drawn me up this morning in my bed. I made it my mission to search for the princes before I have to head to breakfast.

Now that I have to face Hector, to stare into his open amber eyes and tell him that I fell in love with Cassian and chose him? I can't seem to handle it gracefully.

Not just because it is a blatant lie but I don't think I can handle the disappointment on his face. But it's a needed step and I have to face it, preferably now.

I try to calm myself, cleaning the sweat off my hands on my dress. Not lady-like. I raise my fist, my heart pounding so loud it might echo through the whole palace.

But when I move my hand to knock, my knuckles meet air instead of hardwood.

The door opens in one swift motion and those honey eyes come into view, open and honest. Damn it.

"Carina?"

His question waves through the air, and his face looks caught off guard before it settles into a small smile.

"Hey." I internally slap myself for the lighthearted tone that escapes me.

"Hey. What brings you to my chambers this early?"

"I wanted to have a short talk, in your chambers?"

My voice trembles lightly and he nods, moving to the side so I can enter first. Warmth hits me once I step into the room, the curtains drawn open, letting every bit of sunlight touch the furniture. A soft scent of coal and fire lingers as if he just put down the fireplace.

I can't help but let my eyes wander to notice that Hector is neat. But not in a purposeful way, it almost looks as if he doesn't spend any time in these chambers. The bed is neatly made—it seems like no one even slept inside it—the nightstand dustless and clattered with no belongings like mine usually is. No clothes are lying around, no books or any indicator that someone has spent the past weeks in this room.

It should be an unsettling view but I brush it off. It's none of my business and I have more important things to worry about. I gather myself and stop snooping, turning around to see Hector's watchful eyes on me.

"Something is bothering you."

Damn him and his skill to pick up on everything I feel. I try to ignore his words—and eyes—while I make my way over to the big windows. His windows give one a perfect view of the Royal Gardens.

A column juts out right beside his window, usually a place where the stone gargoyles sit but this one is empty.

"I'm sorry for bothering you this early on, it seems like the upcoming event tomorrow is certainly keeping me on edge."

I turn around, readying myself to look into his eyes. The look on his face is unreadable yet, I am glad that he is giving me time to organize my thoughts.

"Do you want to talk about it?"

"Not really. The more I ignore it, the less I fear fainting once I step into the ballroom tomorrow."

I shoot him a small grin, making a soft laugh slip from his lips.

"I'm sure even then you would look majestic like you always do."

He leans against the windowsill I'm standing at, a soft smile adorning his lips. Can't he be less charming and understanding? It would make this task a lot easier.

"Don't say things like that."

My voice sounds desperate as I move my eyes back to the gardens. My breath halters for a second when I see a tall frame wandering around the maze, dark curls sitting on top of the head.

As if his name was called, Cassian turns around and I swear my heart stops for a moment when he looks up, right to where I stand at Hector's window. He can't see me, that's impossible. I blink and notice that his face is already turned away and focus my attention on Hector. My heart beats even faster now and I fear that I might break a rib with how hard it's thumping. I can hear my blood rushing and adrenaline pumping through my veins. One could think I was facing an enemy with how nervous I am.

"Why shouldn't I say things like that?" He asks and something washes over his face which makes me think he knows. He knows what I came here for.

"Because it makes me like you even more and what I'm about to do is the complete opposite one should do to someone you like."

I look down to the floor, not ready to face him while I have to speak the words. I register him taking a step forward; a second later his fingers are at my chin. The grip is soft but still demanding enough to tilt my head up. I meet his eyes and instead of disappointment, I see understanding.

"You're afraid to tell me but you shouldn't be. Whatever you will say won't change my opinion about you."

He offers me a sliver of a smile and it seems like the question lies in my eyes, open for him to see.

"You are the most courageous and intelligent woman I've met in my life, Carina. How you handle things is more than captivating, the elegance with which you move, the obvious beauty you hold, not just on the outside but on the inside.

"You're afraid to tell me because you don't want to hurt my feelings and yet you are courageous enough to tell me beforehand. You do it honorably, easing the shock you think I would've felt if you waited until the ritual."

"How do you know?"

The question escapes me in a small breath when he lets go of my chin, his eyes wandering to the gardens.

"I assumed your father would use the blood moon ball to act in favor of the gods. I felt honored to spend every minute in your presence, Carina, and I ensure you I don't regret a single moment."

I have to take a deep breath at his words, appeasing myself. I should've known Hector's ego wasn't small enough to not handle this like he handles everything. With certainty and gentleness.

"So tell me, do you love him?"

His words echo around the room, the one forbidden question I shouldn't be asked. He doesn't need to clarify who he is talking about and it scares me how much he knows. I thought I was keeping everything a secret and yet it seems like he knows of everything anyway.

His question scares me more than it should.

The answer should be easy. A quick no would suffice, that's what I would've told everyone a week ago. I fear that now if I try to answer the question, everything would change.

"I love you."

I say instead and a small smile cracks on his lips as he tilts his head.

"I know you do. You feel as comfortable around me as I do around you. Maybe it is the way our ancestors felt around each other and it's resurfacing now that we are joined again. I do love you too, Carina, I am in awe of you but I also do know that what you feel for Cassian is something different, it is uncertain and you're scared of what to think of it."

I let out a surprised breath, staring into his eyes. It feels like he's grasping right inside of me, bubbling up the emotions that I felt these past weeks.

I wish I could tell him it's not like that, that I'd probably never be able to love a man like Cassian but it wouldn't be the use of anything. It doesn't change the situation. And sadly it would be just another lie, piled onto every lie I carry around with me.

Instead of speaking, I grab his hand in mine, squeezing it comfortingly. He pulls me in for a hug and it surprises me so much that my body stiffens for a moment before it goes slack. His chin finds its way atop my head as his fingers stroke my back. A weird feeling surrounds me, it's not the same as I feel with Cas but it is familiar.

"He is destined to be with you, Carina, and maybe what you feel now for him is just the tip of what he will make you feel in the future."

How can he say things like that and not be hurt by it? What I said was true I do love him but I know it's not enough, it is an iridescent bond between us. It feels like we're at peace.

There's no heat, no desire, not the wish to strangle him like I often want with Cas. Whatever that might say about me, I don't want to know. I squeeze my eyes shut and take a deep breath, his honey scent engulfing me comfortingly.

"Thank you for being my first kiss, Hector."

I tell him before I move away and look up at him.

"Thank you for letting me be your first kiss."

I have to smile slightly at his words. I don't know why but I feel better. Who would've known something I dreaded so much could end in such a good outcome? It feels like I've found a genuine friend in him, a friend I can learn from and rely on, in the future.

"Have you talked to Marrus?"

I shake my head at his question.

"I wanted to but didn't find him, did you see him after dinner last night?"

When he shakes his head my stomach moves into uncertain knots. Where could he be? Hector notices immediately and offers me his arm.

"Will you accompany me to breakfast? I am sure he will be there waiting and you can tell him."

I nod and take a deep breath while I hook my arm around his. Instead of leading us out of the chamber, Hector stops and looks back down at me.

"Whatever might happen, Carina, I want us to continue being allies. There is not a single day the doors to Polyxena won't be accessible for you. It doesn't matter if you are in aid, or just need a friend's shoulder to cry on. Nothing will change that."

His words are like the last straw and tears form in my eyes. I never genuinely had a friend who just wanted to be my friend for me. I love Edlyn, I certainly do but it was always her duty to keep me company. I still count her as my family but it feels good to hear Hector say the words.

They mirror exactly what I think of him.

Instead of breaking into a wailing woman I push the tears away and smile.

"The same goes for you."

The Royal palace is supposed to be the most guarded place in the whole of Aerwyna. No one gets in or out without being noticed by someone. Guards are placed in front of every door, and every entrance protecting the walls from outside. The problem is when your enemy is already inside those walls, he can move easily and slip through everyone's fingers as he wants.

The body that was found is not the reason why I know this. I knew since I turned eight and found the secret passages residing inside the old walls of the castle. I loved to hide in those whenever I was bored, scaring my parents to death. They never knew how I escaped out of my room and they never found out. I was clever enough to make the guards seem like the careless ones and now that I think back on it I feel really bad about it. I knew many of the guards were probably standing in the wrath of my father every time they thought I somehow escaped the castle.

Once I got lost in the passages for hours, I found a way that lead to the highest tower in the castle. The view was breathtaking, it overlooked the whole kingdom. At night you could count the stars, they were so close it felt like you could reach out and grab one of them. Stealing one from brightening the dark sky. That day I never got into the passages again.

I didn't have a feeling for the time yet and when I returned to my chambers at night, I found my mother crying. It was the most heartbreaking sound I've ever witnessed. Knowing that I was the cause of her pain, that she was worried sick because of me made me feel like the most abhorrent being. I never stepped foot into those passages again until the day she died.

Tonight something is pulling at my heartstrings, making me slip from under the duvet and grab my dark blue cloak. I don't bother to change from my white night dress and throw the cloak over me, disappearing into the familiar passages.

My nerves have been hanging on a loose end the whole day; my corset was almost killing me and I was close to suffocation multiple times. I didn't see Marrus, nor Cas the whole day, the worry sitting tightly in my shoulders. When I tried to ask my father about Cas' location, he brushed me off with a rude comment. Not much help.

I tried to stay focused, talking with Edlyn about the altering of the dress, and heading to the kitchens to help Orlah with some of the organization. The second I was in my chambers and Marianna got me ready to head to bed I couldn't stop my mind from wandering. After my mother died this castle barely felt like home. Yet it still makes my heart ache, knowing that I will leave in two days. Leaving behind not a place but the memories attached to it is hard. I feel terrible for barely remembering what my mother looked like. I try to keep her in mind but the more often you rewind a memory the hazier it gets. No matter how hard you try to claw your nails into it, grasping onto it for dear life, it slips right through your fingers.

So instead of torturing myself for the night, bathing in self-pity, I decide to visit the place that offers you the stars.

It doesn't take me long before I push through the trapdoor, revealing a cold breeze biting against my skin.

Strands of hair fly in my eyes but I ignore them too entranced by the scenery.

I climb up hastily, my hands itching to grab the round railing. Once the cold metal is under my fingers and the stars glisten above me, the tight feeling in my throat dissipates. Like I imagined the sky is tinted in its darkest blue, looking as if it is dipping its toes into black. The small round blips are the only source of light, bathing me in the shadows of secrecy. Knowing that I´m alone is the only thing that makes me let go for the first time.

I don´t swallow the sorrow away and stop ignoring the sting in my eyes. I watch my hands around the railing, my knuckles turning white as I finally let the pain inside. Years of pretending and ignoring crumble inside of me, like a card house dusted by the wind. Acid burns in my throat as I look away from my hands, the shadow dancing around them makes me imagine that they´re tainted in red blood.

"I´m sorry."

I don´t dare to speak more as the stars blur in front of my teary eyes, a small sob escaping me.

"I´m sorry that I never became the daughter you wanted me to be."

The words make me crumble completely as I sit down on the cold floor, hugging my knees to my chest. All these years of pent-up emotions get to me now that I need to leave the safe walls of this palace that I always used as my emotional wall. I drench my nightgown in tears as I allow myself to conjure the image of my mother one last time.

My mother was kind and gentle no matter who she was speaking to. She was wild and prickly like roses but she was protective and passionate as well.

She was a beautiful woman.

A cold claw winds itself around my heart as the image of her face is blurry, the contours the only thing I can remember, accompanied by the fresh scent of the Night-crawlers. It´s the only thing I have left of her.

"I should´ve tried harder. It doesn´t feel like I´m stepping in your footsteps." I whisper to myself, knowing that my mother can´t hear me. The only thing that I can confess to is the night sky that has no mercy or hope. There is no one to blame for everything that I´ve done than myself.

I murdered so carelessly, thinking that it was justified. But who am I to justify which person lives and which does not? Am I not becoming the same monster I accused these men to be?

I didn´t know what motives they had or if they had families. I spared Ellister´s life, not daring to take a father's life but who knows if the other ones didn´t have daughters? It may be the cause a girl or boy has to grow up without their father, the cause a woman turned into a widow.

"Fuck." The curse leaves my lips in a breath as I tug at my hair, the burning of my scalp not punishing enough for what I´ve done. It doesn´t gift me any satisfaction to sit here and feel sorry for myself. I move to get up but freeze the moment my eyes land on the shadow lurking at the very edge of the tower.

I´m not alone.

A shuddering breath escapes me as I stare into the unmoving darkness, my body frozen in fear. I didn't take a weapon with me. For the first time in my life, I let my emotions get the better of me and leave my chambers unarmed. I'm such an idiot.

What if this is the murderer of the maiden? If it is, I'm not going to get out of this without a weapon. Adrenaline is already pumping through my veins and I don't dare to move.

"You get off on listening to strangers in private? I dare you to step out of the shadows and show yourself."

My voice is hard, even though I feel like I could lose my dinner right now, fearing for my life.

"Usually I like to hear myself talking more but I seem to always make exceptions for you."

~ 38 ~

How is it possible that one cocky answer can make my whole body relax in one second? The breath that escapes me the second Cas steps out of the shadows is filled with relief. I quickly turn my back on him and clean my cheeks of the dried tears.

"I´m sorry I scared you but I didn´t want to disturb you."

"Then why didn´t you leave?

My voice is hard, despite the blooming feeling that erupts in my chest at his presence.

"Good question."

He sits down beside me, his long legs dangling through the railing. I tense when his thigh presses against mine, his intoxicating scent engulfing us in its cloud.

"Usually when someone sits by their selves they want to be alone."

"Do you want me to go?"

I turn my head at his question, to see his eyes already placed on my face. The green shines in comforting swirls making me sigh. I shake my head as my shoulders drop slightly.

He doesn´t say anything afterward and I don´t dare to as well. I watch the stars sparkling in the sky while I slightly lean into his side, my shoulder brushing his. What I´m doing is probably wrong and I will regret it the next morning but my eyes feel puffy, my heart is hurting and I need some company right now.

That Cassian is just the right company for me is a fact I try to ignore. This is probably the first time Cas and I are bathed in silence with neither of us ready to break it. I dare to say it's almost peaceful.

But as much as I like the silence, my body is covered in tingles aware of his presence so much that I need to be vocal. "How did you find this tower?" My voice is slightly hoarse but Cassian doesn't comment on it in case he notices it.

"How did you?"

His question makes me breathe out irritated but he knocks his shoulder against mine lightly, making me look up at him. The smile that meets me is so open and gentle that it makes my knees wobble. I'm grateful that I'm sitting down.

"What's more important is why you're up here in the cold, instead of in your bed. Don't you need to be well and rested for tomorrow?"

He raises a dark brow and I roll my eyes.

"I needed some time to think."

"About?"

"Nothing of your concern."

The words come out harsher than I intend, making me grimace. Somehow I'm not able to hold a conversation with him, without turning defensive.

When I go to apologize he speaks up, interrupting me.

"We have this lake in Demeter. Not far from the castle. I spend most of my nights sitting at the shore and watching how the stars reflect in the unmoving water. It reminds me of this place."

A small breath escapes me at his whispered words. Somehow his pain shines through them, revealing his emotions so openly.

"Do you miss it?"

"More than you can imagine. It feels like I haven't been home for ages."

His head turns to look at me with hooded lids, making a shiver run down my spine.

"Are you up here because you're scared of tomorrow?"

Somehow in this light, Cas looks much younger which takes away the hard edge on his face. I know he's older than me by two years but sometimes it feels like his soul is much older.

"I am afraid of tomorrow. But that's not why I'm here."

He doesn't press for me to elaborate. Maybe that's why I cross my legs and turn towards him, my knee pressing against his thigh.

"Can someone miss a place that they haven't even left yet?"

My question sounds even more foolish spoken out loud but Cassian looks at me as if he's thinking about it.

"Of course. One can miss everything they possess even though it's right in front of them."

I don't dare interpret the look he shoots me.

I avert my gaze to escape his burning eyes and want to turn away. I stop when his hand lands on my knee, making me look back up at him.

"The question is will you miss this place because you love it? Or because you never knew something different to call home?"

His question makes me swallow hard.

"I don't know. I will leave nothing to miss besides my brother. But it should feel like I'm missing this, should it not?"

"You decide to miss a place or not, Carina. No one tells you how to feel besides yourself."

A humorless laugh escapes me at his words.

"That's the biggest lie I've heard today."

"How is that a lie?" His brows furrow lightly, creating a cute look on his face. Gods, will you shut up Carina?

"Is this contract we're in, not ordering me to have certain feelings for you?"

My question makes his face go blank, his hand leaving my knee.

"The contract binds us to marry, Carina, it doesn't matter how you feel about me."

His voice is hard when a shadow passes over his face.

"But I automatically have to pretend that I like you in front of everyone."

"You don't have to pretend anything. Everyone knows you hate me, the marriage won't need the change of your behavior."

"Bullshit."

I freeze when he snaps his head towards me at the curse. Oh, he's really angry.

"I tried to make everything right. I tried to do everything to your liking. And still, you treat me like I am the villain."

"Because you are the villain, Cas! Do you think your words are somehow easing my anger because of this? You think a few stolen kisses and mumbled words are somehow changing my mind and making me like you?" I chuckle, exasperated by his stupid reasoning.

"I am just entrapped in this as you are! Still, I try. . .I try to handle this like an adult."

I scoff at his words and stand up, rage flooding my body.

I don't even try to remember what caused this explosion.

"Like an adult? Gods, Cassian, you've been nothing but a cocky, overconfident boy who needs to prove to everyone what is his. Do you think that makes me feel any better?"

He stands up as well, stepping close to me. His eyes are blazing with burning fire but I don't dare to take a step back, my rage urging me to stay persistent.

"Because you are mine. You were from the moment we were born and you don't need to deny that."

The rumble in his voice makes goosebumps rise on my skin.

"I am not fucking yours! This is exactly what I mean. How am I supposed to like you when we have nothing in common?"

He takes another step closer his chest pressing against mine.

"Why is it such a pressing matter? You didn't need to do like me when you practically begged my fingers to be inside you."

"Gods you can't always say these things while we're fighting. Physical attraction is not the solution." I hiss and try to step away from him but he stops me when his arm winds around me, holding me in place.

"Why?"

The question is a dark murmur on his lips, making me focus on them for a moment. Oh no. No my traitor of a body can't be turned on by this. Not right now.

"Because we're fighting right now."

"Multitasking."

He gives me a lazy shrug of his shoulder while his fingers skid my thin nightdress but I shake my head. I push him off me with enough force making his brows arch.

"I'm not letting you touch me when I'm angry at you."

"Angry sex is the best sex, princess."

My core clenches at his words, my peaks rising interested by his offer. His eyes drop to my breasts and I quickly cross my arms in front of them, hiding the rosy color that shines through the white of the dress.

"You know we can't do that."

"We can do other things."

His offer makes me so angry that I turn to leave the tower but his hand latches onto my arm stopping me.

"Let me go." I press, trying to rip my arm from his grasp but it's too tight.

"No, we're not finished."

"We certainly are. Yet again you managed to ruin another day of mine."

My voice is desperate as I try to leave again but he pulls me straight against his chest.

"I'm sorry." His voice makes me freeze, the anger leaving my veins as desperation settles in.

"Sorry doesn't cut it, Cas. I'm tired of all these fights. I can't do it anymore."

"I know. I don't want to fight with you."

His genuine tone makes me look up at him, to see the sadness etched into his features. My heart squeezes at the look, my skin hot when his fingers gently travel up my arm. I hate this. Feeling like this every time he is near.

It's like I'm burning alive, not able to stop once our skin makes contact. His eyes widen suddenly in horror as his thumb swipes at my cheek.

"Please don't cry, princess. I'm so sorry."

Cold realization settles in when I notice the tears dropping from my eyes. I have to laugh lightly; the situation is just too absurd. Cassian looks at me eyes widened in panic, clearly overwhelmed by my tears as he tries to clean my cheeks with both his thumbs. The tears won´t stop and I suddenly feel pathetic.

"Sorry. I didn´t think I would cry."

I try to smile but a small sob escapes me which makes the prince flinch.

"Never apologize for showing emotion, Carina. Never."

He shakes his head and before I can react his lips catch a tear. My heart stutters when he kisses my cheek lightly, his lips elicit sparks deep in my soul. My hands fist the fabric of his shirt as he pulls me into his chest, his lips wandering over my cheeks, every tear accompanied by a small mumble of an apology.

My heart flares up at his words as my body molds right into his. Every kiss mends a small piece inside of me and when his lips graze the corners of mine I let out a small sigh. Tension builds up inside me with every kiss. Cas freezes before I grab his face with my hands and finally make our lips collide.

A soft sigh escapes me as I finally feel his lips on me, sweet and soft, satisfying the yearning inside me. His hands grip my hips gently as if he needs to control himself from moving. After a moment I realize what he´s doing. He´s offering me to take control, offering me to somehow overcome the pain and confusion inside of me.

I gladly do as my hands wander into his hair, tugging at the soft curls.

His deep groan makes my stomach coil as I bite into his bottom lip, asking for entrance. Once he opens his mouth it feels like I completely melt, the contact of our tongues sending a wave of pleasure through me. The sweet kiss turns into a hot, burning fight.

The prince moans again when I roll my hips against his our tongues fighting the war our lips always speak. Another tear escapes me when I realize he tastes like the stars and the moon, he tastes like hope. The strings in my heart sing desperately to be closer to him.

Our breathing is uncontrolled when he detaches our lips, our noses grazing lightly.

"I hate you so much," I whisper as my lips hover over his.

"You don't."

His voice rumbles between us, his nose touching mine. I watch his eyes close, as he grazes his lips against mine, our shallow breathing competing with the loud thumping of our hearts.

"No, I don't. It seems like I don't hate you at all."

My throat closes up as I realize what I've been trying to hide for so long.

"I—"

"Don't say it."

His interruption makes me freeze and I slide my hands out of his hair. His eyes snap open, revealing the black color as if he realizes his mistake.

"No, that's not what I meant."

I try to step away, the pain of his rejection blooming in my chest like wildfire. Instead of letting me he growls and pushes me back against his chest, his erection pressing into my stomach.

"It's not like I don't want to hear the words. But I might fear that once you tell me you have to repeat them. Every day, every hour, and every minute. I won't ever be able to let you go."

My body shudders in response and I tilt my chin up, staring straight into his dark eyes.

"Then don't. I permit you to, Cas."

His eyes close at my words, a groan leaving his lips.

I dare to go even further as I speak the words that scare me the most.

"I do hate you. Every day I try to but somehow you made my walls crumble—"

"Carina."

My name is a warning but I don't listen to him and go on.

"I hate you. I hate you so much that I want to kiss you hard that your lips bruise. I hate you and your stupid hands when they wrap around me, I want to fight them off. But mostly I hate you so much that I want to wrap my hands around your throat and squeeze until you can't breathe. And the moment you take your last breath I want to pull back, I want you to live so I can hate you even more." My eyes flicker between his the intensity in the green touching me from head to toe. I inhale for the last words, barely a whisper on my lips.

"I hate you so much I'm not able to live in a world where you don't exist. A world that I'm not able to hate you in."

A moment of silence passes.

"Fuck."

His curse sounds so desperate that I don't question it a second before his lips crash hungrily against mine. We both moan in synch as our teeth clash and our tongues claim each other's mouth in a hot white kiss.

He rolls his hips right into mine, eliciting a gasp when his lips trail my jaw, nipping at my skin as if to memorize my taste in his mind.

I shudder when his hot tongue licks the path right over my pulse, making him chuckle darkly against my skin. I whine when he takes his lips from my skin to look at me. My core pulses when I look into the storm of lust residing in his eyes, a clear sign of his arousal.

"I think I'm going to get you into bed now."

It takes me a few seconds before I realize what he said, making my brows furrow.

"What—"

My sentence ends in a yell when his hands wander to the back of my thighs and lift me with ease.

I quickly wind my arms around his neck, my eyes widening when his erection nestles right at my core.

"What are you doing?"

The question slips from my lips in a small whisper, and he grins before dropping a short kiss on the tip of my nose.

"Getting you into bed like a good little prince. We both have a big day tomorrow."

He starts to walk towards the trap door, engulfing us both in the darkness. I tighten my arms around his neck, my cheek pressing against his while he doesn't struggle the slightest bit with me in his arms.

"You know I can walk right?"

"But this is so much more fun."

He shifts me slightly and I exhale raggedly when I brush against his hard cock.

"Don't do that." I breathe, tugging at the short curls on his neck.

"What? This?"

He brushes me back against his hardened length while he walks, making a soft wave of pleasure roll through me. His breath, even and controlled, is such a contrast to my panting even though I'm the one who is being carried.

Usually, I would've insisted on walking on my own but the exhaustion of every emotion I felt tonight makes me compliant. So I rather focus on the soft rock of every step he takes, my lips grazing his thumping pulse. Cassian slips through the darkness like a shadow as if he knows the way to my chambers by heart. A few weeks ago the proposition might've concerned me but now I'm happy he knows a way to my chambers where no one will see us together.

I press a light kiss against his pulse, making him groan.

"I don't know why I'm doing this to myself."

"Seems like the Prince of Demeter is a little masochist." I tease before I press a kiss against his cheek.

"You missed."

He teases and I chuckle before I press a soft kiss against his lips. His steps halter as he pushes me against a wall, his tongue rolling over mine in sweet pleasure. If we go on like this we will never reach my chambers but I can't see where that could influence me in a bad way. It is Cas who parts our lips after a moment and starts to walk again.

"If we keep on doing this I might do things I promised myself not to do."

I shiver at his words, daring to tell him that he can do whatever he wants. We break through the wall to my chambers, engulfed in the light of a few candles.

He drops me onto my mattress and when I look up at him I notice that his eyes are back to their green color, glinting mischievously. There's a moment of silence between us, neither of us knows what to say. It feels like something has shifted with me revealing my feelings. I'm aware that he didn't exactly reciprocate my unspoken words but either way it's too late. I'm way too deep to back out and I fear that I don't even want to. When he moves to leave the bed I grasp onto his arm, making him freeze.

"Stay."

"That's not a good idea, princess."

I quickly drop the cloak on the ground and pull the duvet over my body.

"I'll behave I promise."

I draw a small cross over my heart before I pat the space beside me.

"I hope I can." His lips drop a heavy sigh before he motions for me to scoot over. My heart is back in my throat when I make him some space, my head hitting the pillow beside his.

His big body settles beside me, our knees knocking together, and somehow it reminds me of the morning after the attack.

"Stop staring at me and go to sleep, Carina. I don't think I can handle your grumpy sleep-deprived self."

Cas has a soft smile on his face as he adjusts the duvet around my shoulders. His hand goes to stroke through my long strands before he slightly scratches my scalp. My eyes flutter close for a moment; goosebumps cover my skin as I melt into the soft covers of my bed. He continues his journey through my long strands and when I open my eyes again I'm surprised by the view I get.

I don't think I've ever seen him this relaxed and open. It's practically a sin to not use the moment of peace between us.

"Do you. . .remember her?"

His fingers hesitate for a moment before they continue their strokes.

"Who are you talking about?"

"Doesn't matter," I mumble, backing out.

"It does if it's something that bothers you."

His tone drops as he tugs at my hair lightly, making me look at him.

"I was just wondering because you're a little older than me. . .if you remember my mother. From your visits with Zayne."

My voice is quiet, unsure of his answer. I fear that he'll tell me he doesn't remember her but I'm even more scared that he can. A stranger who knows my mother better than I do.

"Shailagh Sebestyen. I think it would be an insult not to remember her."

My eyes widen lightly at his words as I watch the small smile on his lips.

"I didn't know her that well as you know I was focused more on getting on your nerves."

"Successfully," I add and he tugs my hair again, making both of us smile.

"She is the one responsible for your obsession with the plants isn't she?"

"They're not plants. They're flowers, Night-crawlers." I correct him and he grins, flashing me his adoring dimple.

"That's what I said. I remember that she was kind and gentle. Your father seemed much more relaxed back then."

"He was." I agree before I scoot closer to his body heat. He pulls me flush against his chest. I dare to inhale his fresh scent again.

"Sometimes I don't even remember what she looked like."

"That's not a problem, you just need to look into the mirror."

Something warm floods my chest at his words. I know she had the same long dark hair as me but I always thought she looked more elegant, wiser than I could ever look.

Cas bends his face and pushes his nose against the side of my neck, placing a small kiss on my skin.

"I know it's scary. Living with limited memory of a person you feel obligated to know. Memories might fade but the feeling you connect to that person never does, Carina."

His whisper is the softest caress between us, lingering on my skin like a soft blanket.

"Sometimes I think everything would've been better if she was still here, things might've turned out differently."

"Maybe they would. But what tells you things would've been better? It is our choices that make us, who we are, not the circumstances around us."

"Huh."

I don't find another answer to his words.

"What?"

"You might be wiser than I thought you'd be."

He growls and I chuckle lightly as he squeezes me against him. I sneak one leg between his, loving the weight of his over mine.

"You can learn much from me. Especially right now, sleep is the most precious thing one regent needs to survive the day."

I roll my eyes at him even though he can't see.

"I get it we need to sleep."

"Damn right. Now close your eyes and listen to your fiancé or he might need to punish you for not listening."

A shudder shakes me at his words, anticipation bubbling low in my stomach.

"Somehow it seems like you're not averted to the idea, huh." His dark whisper makes my cheeks flush instantly.

"Shut up. I'm trying to sleep." I mumble before I close my eyes. His chest rumbles with laughter, making a small smile sneak on my lips as I openly invite sleep to take me over.

~ 39 ~

Waking up to an empty bed is nothing unusual to me. I wake up alone in my bed for seventeen years now and hell I always expected that another person would rob me of my sleeping space.

But somehow my body knows subconsciously that during sleep it is entangled with long limbs, hard muscles pressing under my fingertips and soft breath caressing my cheek. So to find the other side of the bed unoccupied, the mattress already cold shoots a small stab of pain through my chest.

That's the bad thing about sharing some sleeping space. Your body becomes accustomed to the added weight, yearning for the source of warmth beside you.

Cas gets unbelievably hot during the night and I remember waking up, to throw his searing hot arm from around my waist.

I haven't got much luck because it just squeezed tighter, a low rumble escaping his lips. After a moment I decided I liked the heat, the weight that tells me he was with me. Big mistake. Huge.

The prince certainly doesn't find it in his honor to stay until the morning hours and I am tempted to mope in bed all day and ignore every duty until the preparations tonight.

But I don't.

I decide to spend the day with Hector and try to find Marrus but after a small walk, I get swiped away by Marianna who tells me she needs to prepare me for the ball tonight. My nerves are far from calm, the uncertainty that comes with tonight feasting from my uneasiness.

I ask Edlyn to look out for either Marrus or Cassian and that once she finds one of the both, to send them to my chambers. Usually, I would ignore Cassian. Given how I so irrationally offered my feelings but sooner or later I have to face him. I don't want to avoid this feeling anymore, the unknown a torture to my judgment.

Carriages are arriving every hour, guests dressed in only black gowns, crystals dangling from their ears, shining in the sinking sun like the amethyst on my ring finger. The ring feels like it's weighing tons and I have to put it down for the routine Marianna puts me through.

My finger feels naked without the added weight and I absently rub circles over the new space.

Marianna soaks and washes my hair in rose water, the scent lingering around me. She scrubs my skin harder than usual, before removing every hair from my skin in the most painful way. My nails get trimmed and dipped into berry juice, making a soft rosy stain linger on them.

Once Marianna is finished with the base layer—as she calls it—my skin feels raw and red even though a lotion is applied to my skin. The soft lilac smell will linger on my skin all evening. . .It was a scent never used on me and it makes me sick to my stomach when Marianna says it was an order from Lord Romanov as a present for Prince Cassian—it seems to be his favorite scent.

My hands turn sweaty the second my skin is dried sticking to the material of the short silk dress that goes under my gown. My hair is wet and heavy, the strands twisted and attached to my head with pins so they'll dry in beautiful waves.

Marianna circles me, a frown edged to her features when she eyes the strap on my thigh, where my dagger will sit tonight.

Guards will be positioned at every entrance and a suspicious feeling inside me tells me it's not just to ensure the guests but the person who is out murdering people, who still haven't been caught.

A small problem that should've been dealt with long ago. If it is revealed that a king can't even protect his castle from intruders, how can he protect a whole kingdom?

"No one will see it, Marianna." I tell her because I can feel the disapproval of the sheath around my thigh.

"I know but it ruins the aesthetic."

I roll my eyes before I walk over to my bed and grab the dagger from under my pillow to sheathe it in. It is not just for my safety at the ball but for my little date tonight that I haven't forgotten about. My skin-tight suit is hidden behind a statue sitting in an alcove in the west wing.

It's the closest to the banquet hall and I know I just have a little spare time before someone notices I am gone. That is why I wrote a letter to Gisella two nights ago, gifting her with a beautiful red gown.

It cascades elegantly around her curves and turns darker until it ends in an endless black color. The cleavage is riskier than my usual dresses, lined with beautiful gold leaves at the bust and the small straps that fall over the shoulder. The dress is accompanied by two long black silk gloves that will come in handy because once I shed my blood with Cassian; the wound will be hidden under the glove, so when Gisella steps in and pretends to be me for a while, no one will notice the difference.

My heart pounds when I think of the possibility that someone might notice my absence. But the possibility should be small, by the time I'm gone everyone will be drunk on red wine and the lulling music that surrounds the evening.

It seems like after everything that happened, the meeting with the handyman of the Dark Prince is the only thing that keeps me going, grounding me in my panic.

"Marianna?" I ask once she steps behind me and lets down my almost dry hair. I feel her pull a few locks up, pinning them in place and braiding a few small roses inside them. The red is going to be a stark contrast to my dark hair it is tradition for every royal to dress in the color of the moon that night, honoring the gods and the gift of life they ensured us with.

"Yes?"

"I will not require your help after the ball; you can enjoy yourself after you're finished with my preparation," I tell her swallowing when I think of the promise I made to Cassian. I will spend the night at his chambers for whatever reason.

My body hums at the anticipation to continue such a close space between us, even though I know it shouldn't. But my heart seems to be long gone; it ran away with any sense of rationality. It's like it's sprinted right into the hands of the prince, slowly creeping into his touch, branding himself inside my soul.

It is foolish to ever think that I can outrun him. No one can outrun someone like Cassian Moreau. He's the embodiment of a hunter. And while I always thought I stood in the place of the hunter I was mistaken. The second Cas put his eyes on me was the one that I became the hunted. The prey.

"Are you sure? What if you need my help?"
Marianna eyes me concerned.

"I won´t. I´ll spend the night at Prince Cassian´s chambers."
I say breathlessly, making her hands halter on my hair for a second.

"Alright." She says before she ushers me to the dresser and starts on my face. We agree to let my skin breathe tonight, besides a little flushed tint on the cheeks. I´m sure it wasn´t even needed because my body feels like it is burning up with every passing second.

I would feel much calmer if I knew where Marrus or Cassian are. Isn´t it somehow suspicious how both of them are missing? What if Cassian couldn´t stop being an ass and tell him about our engagement? He wouldn't. Would he?

The anxiety jitters that flood my body are relentless not leaving my body a moment of peace. Marianna finishes my face by the time the sky is already dark, the moon a soft orange as it rises on the dark canvas, making my heart thump even louder. I try to hold myself together, clenching and unclenching my fists every few seconds while Marianna gets the dress out of the closet. It is a complete replica of the one I send to Gisella, glistening magically in the light of the candle.

Marianna stops right in front of me with a surprised look on her face and I blink confusedly. I check in the mirror if I smudged anything or if a strand fell from its place. When I don´t find anything I look back at her.
"What?"

"Someone knocked."

Really? I didn't even hear a knock—oh. There it is again. It seems like the pounding of my heart overpowered the knock the first time.

I look around for something to throw over my silk dress and grab a shirt slipping my arms into the sleeves. It still doesn't justify the inappropriate length of the dress but at least you can't see my nipples shimmering through the see-through material.

"Come in!" I call and my muscles tense but release the second when I see who steps in. I immediately turn to Marianna to ask her for a few minutes of privacy but she already curtseys and puts the gown on my bed, disappearing through the doors.

Her steps increase as she passes the prince, a nervous tremor in her hands. I take a small breath before I turn around and face the prince whose jaw is set, his features hard and cold and so like him. His eyes land on the sheath with my dagger inside.

I haven't seen him since last night and somehow I just notice now how much it affected me. A wave of awareness tickles my skin, making me clench my thighs subconsciously.

"Are you expecting to fight tonight, princess?"

I can't help but release a slow breath as relief settles in. My body moves on its own accord as I rush towards the prince and throw myself against his hard chest. My arms find their way around his narrow waist, squeezing him shortly. I enjoy the familiar scent of a fresh breeze mixed tonight with his musky soap.

"Woah if I knew you'd greet me like this I'd come prepared." He says and I take a step back and ram my fist into his stomach. Hard.

"Oof." He breathes out and topples over, making me raise my chin high.

"I was worried to the gods, you idiot! I thought you and Marrus were at each other's throats because you couldn't keep your arrogant mouth shut." I hiss and his brows raise confused. After a moment he straightens up again, towering over me.

"You were. . .worried?"

His voice sounds incredulous and I turn around groaning frustrated.

"Of course, you can't just disappear the day of the blood moon and leave me alone with all this stress, while my father is ignoring my existence, a murderer is wandering through the halls and I have yet another corset I have to squeeze myself into!"

I try to ignore my embarrassment and keep the real words from slipping from my lips. Why did you leave this morning? I wanted you to stay. When I turn around I find an amused look on his face. I clench my jaw, my hands balling into fists as rage floods my body.

He seems to notice the fire in my eyes and the smile drops as he raises his hands.

"I'm sorry, I didn't know you needed me present. I wanted to give you time to think about all the recent. . events."

His eyes glint and I know he's not talking about the murderer. My eyes fly down to his body and I notice for the first time that he's not dressed properly.

His breeches are black and sit snugly against his thighs. The blood-red dress shirt is half untucked, a stark contrast to his marble skin. It seems like he headed straight for my chambers while he got dressed for the ball.

"I didn't need time," I state, swallowing when I focus from the sliver of skin to his face. My cheeks flush when I notice my inappropriate wardrobe and I hug the shirt tighter around me.

"I'm sorry to misinterpret your anger but you surely must've known I was never far away. I left your chambers this morning to escape any suggestions one might make if they see us together. In bed."

Oh. Gods I'm so stupid. He's right. I may think I can trust Marianna but who knows which ears linger around the walls? We didn't have the excuse of him being hurt like the other night he stayed over.

Cas and I aren't officially married and it would be a scandal to know we shared a bed even though nothing happened.

"You could've left a note," I tell him with a tight throat. He takes a step closer, raising a dark brow.

"You think so? It seems like you had a great walk with Prince Hector."

I avert my eyes uneasy by his gaze. He is questioning me yet again as if the words from last night were nothing.

"Hector is aware of who my choice fell on, despite my dislike." I hiss, clenching my teeth.

"I'm sure he does. Is that why your maid interrupted me getting ready for the ball and coming here?"

So Edlyn did find him and he came here, the second she told him I needed to see him. And I'm here snapping at him.

"I just wanted to make sure my fiancé's throat was still intact," I say and his eyes darken when I call him that. He takes a nonchalant step forward, making my body tense with anticipation. My body is nervous all over again but there is not a trace of panic felt at the upcoming event. Rather the desire that has been haunting me all day finally bursts through, clouding my judgment.

"It seems like you have too little faith in your fiancé if you think he can't handle a man like him." He says as he stops right in front of me, his fingers catching a small curl from my hair, twisting it around his finger. His eyes shine lightly as they watch the curl. He looks almost. . . fascinated.

"Your ass was kicked by a woman. I think you can't handle anyone." My voice is almost a whisper when his eyes wander from the curl to my face. His fingers are so close to my skin, yet not close enough to touch it.

"Maybe I'll have to remedy your wavers. Convince you of my skills."

I swallow at his words, clenching my thighs together in anticipation but he lets go of the curl and the green color moves back into his eyes.

"You say Marrus is missing?" He asks nonchalantly. I hate him.

I hate him, hate him, hate him.

"He is. No one has seen him since last night's dinner. Hector is optimistic but he doesn't know of the things happening." I say and at the mention of Hector's name his head turns to the side as he raises a brow. I ignore it, not having the time for childish games right now.

"Should I be worried?" I press when he doesn't answer. He stops in front of my nightstand where the amethyst ring sits securely in the velvet box.

"You shouldn't. Marrus is a prince, he can protect himself, you should concentrate on our task tonight."

His voice is hollow and he turns around, his lips stretched in a small smile. "Nervous?"

"Yes," I admit and something close to surprise flashes in his eyes. The thought of Marrus missing doesn't let me go but the proposition of the ritual makes me so sick to my stomach that I forget about him for a moment.

It doesn't take two steps for him to stand back in front of me, his hands grasping my shoulders. The second our skin comes in contact a small shock zaps through me.

"There is no need to be nervous, you won't be doing any of it alone, I'll be right beside you, following every step you take." His voice drops and I know he's telling the truth.

"Why do you think that's a comforting thought?" I jab just because I'm nervous and his lips turn into a crooked smile. I exhale relieved that he didn't take it personally.

"Maybe it's not comforting but you know you can trust me in one thing and that is keeping you safe."

The pressure on my shoulders tightens for a second before one of his cold hands wanders over my neck and up to my cheek.

He is right, it is weirdly comforting that the eyes of everyone won't be just on me but on him too.

We will both have to cut into our flesh, dripping blood.

"How can you be this calm?" I ask genuinely curious as I allow myself to push my cheek into his hand, making his eyes follow the movement a certain wonder in them. A soft red hue resides on his cheeks.

"I am not." He says but I don't believe him.

"I told you I am nervous, share your feelings with me, Cas. What I said last night wasn't in the spur of the moment. It was the truth."

My voice sounds almost desperate. I want him to have a stupid weakness just this one time. This is something new to him just as it is to me. His eyes flare up when I mention the moment of last night and realization settles in. He is unsure. He didn't believe my words to be true and that is why he fled this morning. After everything, he thought I was the one tricking him and it is obvious in his eyes that he feared I was playing, toying with him.

"I'm scared."

I let out a trembling breath at his confession. His thumb swipes over my lower lip his eyes following the movement, making my stomach flip tightly.

"I'm not scared of sharing my blood, combining it with yours in front of the gods. I am not afraid of marrying you and having you as my queen. I am scared I had my chance with you and threw it away so quickly, so you'll never grant me the chance to try and make you look at me with something different than mistrust glaring in your beautiful eyes. I am afraid that you will never feel as comfortable with me as you felt with Hector. Mostly I am afraid of you."

"Of me?" I ask breathlessly, my stomach coiling as I grab the material of his red shirt to pull him closer to me. This is probably the first time Cassian tells me what he thinks and it is nothing that I expected. I was blind. I was completely blind, misjudging him all the time. I believed him to be a cold-hearted idiot. I didn´t think his interest would go beyond the desire that we both so clearly share for each other.

He is not just capable of feeling anger, he can be gentle and I misjudged him, didn't I? My eyes are stuck on his lips, listening to every word he gifts me with so easily, admitting what he is afraid of.

"You, who stepped into my life like a warrior princess, challenging me with every look out of those sapphire eyes. Your ability to be as stubborn as I am and still be selfless and caring. Fuck, you go out every night, risking your life to make sure your kingdom is safe. I was never scared of anything but the things you make me feel, Carina, scare me to death."

His words hang in the air around us for a short second.

My eyes flutter shut for a moment, my body bathing in the tension that flies around us.

Even as I´m robbed of my sight I can feel him. Feel the pull that my body has towards him.

"Nothing has changed; I still hate you with everything in me," I say and open my eyes again to see he is trained on my lips.

"There is a thin line between love and hate." He murmurs and I swallow nodding.

"Not thin enough."

I can´t stand any distance between us for another moment as our noses brush against each other, daring the other to do the first step. My stomach coils when I feel his breath on my lips, the tension unbearable. My body burns alive and I don´t hesitate when I pull him against me, our lips crashing together.

He releases a deep groan when I push my stomach against his hardened length, my nails scratching over the exposed skin of his chest.

How can he say these things and yet always act as if he despises me? I don't know the answer to that but what I do know is that once his mouth opens and his sweet taste greets me with his tongue, something deep inside me hums contently. It is something ancient and yet I don't question the rightness I feel spreading through my body, making my stomach coil and flip at the same time.

I feel every hard peck of his muscle under my hands as he nudges me backward, the back of my knees hitting the bed. In one breath he puts his hands on my thighs and throws me on the bed, his body disconnecting from mine for a second.

I whine at the loss of contact, making a crooked grin adorn his sinful lips. I welcome the familiar darkness of his eyes as he crawls over me like a predator over his prey, loving every second of it.

"You don't know how often I have dreamed of you in this position." He murmurs before his lips are back on mine, his sharp teeth grazing my lips until he draws blood, making me moan in ecstasy as I arch my back. My hips arch against his, searching for some friction. The red gown rustles underneath me but I don't give a single fuck. Cas gets the shirt off me in no time, leaving me in just a sheer dress, the peaks of my breasts pressing against the silky material. They tighten even more at the look he's giving them.

He slides the material off exposing the rosy peaks, making goosebumps rise on my skin. I watch his lips linger over one nipple as he looks up through his dark lashes. Fuck he is beautiful.

The skin on his cheeks is flushed with heat, his hands dig into my squirming hips and his stare doesn't waver when he takes my nipple into his mouth. I bite my lip so hard at the sensation and throw my head back against the sheets, my eyes closing of their own accord.

"Cas."

His name comes out half a moan and his response is a hum against my other peak, making it ripple through my body. He bites and flicks his tongue, shooting waves of pleasure right to my core.

"We are going to be late." I struggle out, when one of his hands wanders under the sheer dress, grazing the skin of my inner thigh.

My skin burns everywhere he touches me, lighting up. He leans up and presses his lips back against mine shooting another wave of pleasure through me.

"Fuck them. They can wait."

I have to chuckle at his words and his movements freeze as he stares at my face shocked.

"What?" I ask confused and he shakes his head before he presses his lips back against mine for a short moment. This time the touch is gentle and sweet and it makes my heart pound with a completely different emotion.

"Cas?" I whisper when his lips trace my jaw, my nails digging into his back.

"Yes."

His murmur is a soft vibration against my throat, making my hips buck in response. I somehow lost my train of thought when he finds just the right spot on my neck. A moan escapes my lips as he nips at the skin. Teasing and biting until the flesh is tender. His tongue licks a path up my pulse and I roll my hips against him, brushing against his hardened cock.

We both groan as a shudder trembles through our bodies, feeling the connection. It seems like we´re designed to fit each other perfectly. His hard chest against my soft breasts, my nails made to dig into his skin, eliciting a deep groan.

"I want you to fuck me."

The words escape me in a soft breath, making his whole body freeze. He moves to stare down at me, his eyes blazing, his lips opened slightly. It´s a gorgeous view. The way the hunger swirls in his eyes makes me feel confident, desirable by someone with—what I guess—much experience.

"I will. I´ll fuck you wherever you want. Bend over a desk, against a wall, hiding between bookshelves. I´ll do whatever you want, the second you become my queen, Carina." His voice is raw and full of emotion, a sliver of green shining in his eyes. My breathing is uncontrolled caused by the desire that flames up at the things he says.

His hands grip the short dress as I´m incapable of forming any words. The material pools around my hips, revealing my soaked underwear.

Cas's hands grip my thighs, his fingers digging into the flesh so hard I´m sure it will bruise but I don´t care as he plants a soft kiss against my inner thigh. I want him to mark me, to have a reminder of what we did, even though I know it's going to be edged into my mind forever.

"Even though your wish is my command,"—he shoots me a look between his dark lashes—"my tongue will have to suffice for today."

My eyes shoot towards him confused by his words.

"What do you—Oh."

My words end in a deep moan when he pushes the soaked fabric aside and a long finger wanders through my slick arousal. Holy fuck.

"Gods you´re so wet already. Tell me you want this, Carina." He hesitates and waits for me to answer. "I want this, Cas. I want you."

He doesn't hesitate when one finger plunges into me easily, making me cry out.

"Yes!"

He chuckles satisfied as he pulls out his finger slowly, letting me feel every inch that stretches me.

I squeeze my eyes shut at the sensation, my hands fisting the sheets underneath me as hot pleasure clouds my judgment yet again. He pushes his finger back inside and I buck my hips making him chuckle.

"No moving." He orders as his other hand grips my hip, pushing me against the sheets so I won´t move. His finger settles on a slow taunting rhythm while his tongue makes sure to lick up a way between my breasts, making me whine that he doesn´t touch them. His lips stop at my ears, his finger continuing to fuck me slowly.

"How many do you want, princess?"

"What?"

My answer is breathless as I open my eyes to meet his. I try to move my hips again, speeding up the rhythm but his fingers dig hard into my cheekbone, challenging me with the look in his eyes.

"How many fingers do you want? One, two. . .three?"

He raises a brow and just when I open my mouth to answer he pushes his finger deeper inside, harder. A moan escapes me and I have to close my eyes for a second, the tension low in my stomach twisting beautifully.

"Two." I breathe out and the next second I feel him add another finger.

He pushes both knuckles deep inside before he stops, giving me time to adjust to the new size. Our short breathing is the only thing heard in the chamber around us. I open my eyes to look at him, his gaze half-lidded. Hot desire flashes through his eyes, making me roll my hips against his fingers that still linger inside me.

He takes it as his invitation to finally pull them all the way out before he slams them back inside, making me moan.

"Oh, those sweet little sounds are going to be the death of me." His voice rumbles straight through me.

His fingers finally pick up a fast rhythm as his lips tug at the skin on my shoulder, my core tightening at the feeling. He trails his lips downwards, the sounds of his fingers sliding in and out of me loud and clear. He misses my breasts again and I whine, my hands tugging at the dark curls.

"You want me to touch your tits? To take those perfect rosy nipples in my mouth?"

Another hard slam of his fingers inside me.

"Yes." I moan and arch my back, offering my breasts to him. His chuckle makes goosebumps rise on my skin, his thumb flicking against my most sensitive area and I swear I almost come apart at the motion.

"Touch them yourself."

My eyes fly open at his words, my brows furrowing. The challenge in his eyes makes my cheeks flush.

"What?"

"I want you to touch those perfect tits. Twirl the nipples between your fingers, Carina."

His demand makes me shudder but when he lowers his face, forcing me to let go of his neck, his lips settle above where his fingers disappear inside of me and I swallow the embarrassment.

He watches me as he places a soft kiss low on my stomach, his fingers continuing to fuck me steadily. I don´t break eye contact when my hands wander down my breasts and stop at the tightening peaks. Goosebumps rise on my skin right before I take the peaks between my fingers and roll them.

"Fuck." Cas and I moan in unison and my hips buck again.

With my fingers teasing my nipples and his fingers fucking me, I´m at the edge of falling over, my body writhes with tremors, my core clenching around his fingers every time they drive back into me. The filthy sounds around me make me moan and arch my back.

I chase my high like a starved woman, my hips rolling, and meeting Cas´ finger halfway.

"Fuck, fuck, fuck." I moan knowing it´s going to take a few more pushes of his fingers for me to come as if Cas can sense my thoughts he rids me off his fingers. My eyes fly open, my brows furrowing when I watch the satisfied smile on his lips.

"Why did you stop?"

I shift my weight onto my elbows to have a better view.

The prince smiles dubiously as he adjusts his body, his knees on the ground while he slings one leg of mine over his shoulders.

"You told me to fuck you. I already did with my fingers." He says and my eyes widen, his hand grips my thigh and pulls my center right in front of him.

"Now I'm going to fuck you with my tongue."

My heart skips a beat at his words and I try to protest.

"Cas—holy fuck."

I throw my head back when he slides his hot tongue right through my slick folds, my body shuddering at the new sensation.

My hips roll as his tongue laps again, his fingers digging into my thigh. The sharp pain from his grip mixed with his tongue makes me sigh.

When his thumb joins his play of devotion and draws circles on me I fall onto my back again fisting the sheets underneath me.

"Fuck yes." I moan earning an approving hum from Cas before his tongue and fingers switch and I'm gone. His fingers curl inside of me, fucking me hard and fast until my back arches and my head clears. His tongue flicks against my sensitive bud and I lose it.

"Oh gods, Cas." It seems like these are the only words that escape me when I reach my high, my hips bucking, his fingers plunging, his teeth grazing my clit.

He hits something so deep inside me that my vision blurs, my head spins, and the world tips over.

I clench around his fingers hard, my body finally exploding with the relief I chased. Hot waves flash through me, liquefying my body until it's just a hot mess.

There is nothing anymore besides deep satisfaction.

Cas continues his taunts through every wave that hits me until the trust of my hips gets lazy and my breathing calms down. I don't even remember closing my eyes until I open them to stare at the canopy above me. I feel Cas ease his fingers out of me, my limbs feel heavy as if they don't belong to my body. The most beautiful face moves into my vision, features carved by the gods and blessed by fate. I don't dare to move anything, my body in a weird state before I cradle his beautiful face in my hands. I inch my face forward and he meets me halfway, our lips connecting.

It's not a kiss like the others, there is no haste, no burn. There is fire and ice, controlled, dancing around each other. I can taste myself on his lips, loving the way it is branded on him.

A deep groan leaves his lips when I move back a bit to look at him. Different darkness is swirling in his eyes, a color that makes me uneasy but the words he speaks next distract me from the uncertain emotion.

"Do you remember your promise?" He asks as his hand makes its way out of under my dress and I nod when he helps me sit up. My cheeks heat up when he pulls the straps of the dress back up my shoulders, my breasts back under the material. I won't comment on the way his erection is straining against his breeches not knowing what to do. But it doesn't seem like he cares.

"I´ll stay with you tonight," I tell him, somehow feeling shy.
"I think I should go."

His face is closed off again a sudden silence settling between us. As if we could sense the change.

"You should." I agree but he doesn't move out from between my thighs his length pressed against my skin. I shiver at the wonder of what it would feel like without any clothes between us.

Something in my eyes seems to refocus him and he slides back taking me with him, an arm around my waist. My heart jumps when he places my bare feet back on the ground and I wonder about the new feeling inside me. Cassian bends to grab the velvet box pulling the ring out. He turns to me, a determined look on his face as he waits for me to offer him my hand. I do without a question.

The silver of the ring is cold against my finger as he slips it on and bends down pressing a kiss against the purple stone before pressing one against my knuckles. His body shudders as if it triggers a deep satisfaction in him. His face raises lightly, his lips still grazing my knuckles as he stares at me, the green in his eyes shining intensely.

"I promise you tonight will pass with you not feeling an ounce of pain. And after that, you´re going to be free."

40

I don't say anything when Cassian leaves my chambers. I don't say anything when Edlyn steps in and helps me into my gown, the question of where Marianna went sitting on the tip of my tongue but I am not able to speak verbally.

I feel Edlyn's worried glances and every comforting brush of her fingers against my skin but I can't stop thinking about what Cas said.

How could he think I would be free when I'm about to be bound to him for life and beyond that? I feel sick to my stomach and bile is sitting right at my throat when Edlyn hooks her arm around me leading me out of the chambers. I feel sick when we step into the banquette hall, already filled with over a thousand people excited over my arrival. The forms of their gowns are grotesque, the high-pitched voices loud. I can already feel the dull ache forming behind my eyes. I am greeted with curtseys, and praises, I endure it. I greet lords and their wives and check in on their children. I even manage to spit a few jokes even though I feel nothing through the conversations. It's as if my body goes into auto-pilot, moving on its own, charming its way through the crowd. I am merely a bystander, visiting encounters of a hollow shell and all these people. I endure dinner without touching the food, while Edlyn sits beside me, conversing happily with everyone, her hand clasped with mine under the table.

It somehow gives me comfort. Somehow it doesn't. My thoughts are spiraling, I am shocked by myself. The very thing I asked of Cassian in my chamber is nothing that should've ever left my lips. I know the rules.

A woman is to be married to enjoy certain parts of love. But that never stopped the prince before, so instead of taking what I offered him, he declined. Not completely but it seems like I owe the prince for restraining both of our desire. Everything he says continues to swirl through my thoughts in a slow dance. I realize that I've never been this vulnerable, the way I am with him.

I can't appreciate the light of the red candles lit around the enormous room, how the ceiling is accessorized with red rubies all over, making it look like everyone is bathed in red light, the reflection wavering in the clean marble beneath our feet.

If I didn't know any better I would say it looks like we're all under water, water that is tinged with the color of blood. I don't recognize my father at first, sitting on one of the thrones at the top, his blood-red breeches filled with golden ornaments. Lord Romanov is in similar clothing, standing right beside him. The only sense of security is the mask draped over my face, it is a tradition to do so which is a blessing this evening. It means no one notices the pale skin on my face or the relief I feel when I see Marrus mingling around, completely healthy and happy.

I was seeing ghosts where weren't any and cursed myself for being so fragile.

"You look like you're about to be sick."

A voice speaks up beside me and I flinch lightly, scared that my small hidden corner is exposed. I relax when I look up into Hector's face, granting me a small grin.

"Is it that obvious?"

"I'm sorry to disappoint you but it is, what is it that's clouding your mind?"

That's the problem, I don't know. Something feels off and the ticking of the hour tinting the moon redder with every second doesn't calm me in the slightest. It's like everyone is waiting for this one moment and I don't even know if it is the ritual scaring me or something different.

"I don't know." I sigh and my eyes wander over to Cas who looks gorgeous tonight. The black mask sits perfectly on his face, allowing him to gift everyone with his crooked smile as he converses with a small group of women.

Somehow the shadow of the edges highlights those hard cheekbones that I felt between my thighs tonight. I thought he looked gorgeous when he was in my chambers which makes his appearance indescribable right now. It looks like he is glowing from the inside, oozing charm to draw in every woman at this ball. Like a moth is drawn to the light. Sadly I can't say that I feel any otherwise.

My hands itch to run through his dark curls, wanting to tug at them until he groans in pleasure. I want to take those sinful lips back against mine, bite at them until they're tinged red and I can taste the ironic taste of his blood.

The red of his tunic reflects beautifully with his pine green eyes, and the dark curls framing his face make him look like the most beautiful man in this room tonight. A glass with red liquor sits tightly in his hands, his long fingers wrapped around it securely. Fingers that were inside me, mere hours ago, gifting me with a kind of pleasure I only feel with him. He throws a small glance at where Hector and I are standing, hidden from the crowd. As if on instinct my fingers graze over the purple stone in the ring, calming my senses lightly.

"At least he is enjoying himself." I sigh wishing I could seem as relaxed as him.

"That's just a façade he hasn't kept his eyes from you for more than two seconds," Hector says with a small smile on his lips, making me frown.

"Eyes speak a language that lips can't grasp."

"What is that supposed to mean?"

I place my eyes back on Hector to see he is still trained on Cassian.

"It means that your choice was right."

I wish I could say the same.

"If you say so."

The hesitant words slip from my lips and I bite my tongue in anger. I'm not supposed to let people know how I feel about Cassian. Even though I'm not averted to his latest efforts it doesn't mean I'm a love-struck idiot like I'm supposed to be.

"Sounds like you don't believe it."

"It's not like I don't believe it. But I know that affection can go as fast as it came. Many royals are an example of that."

He places his honey eyes back on me.

"Not with him."

"What makes you say that?"

Curiosity floods through me, the girl in me wanting to earn satisfaction. The knowledge that Cassian is as disrupted by my presence as I am by his. I know what he said hours ago. But he never actually said the words I wanted to hear.

"It's not something that people can explain. I'm certain I can't if you can't. What I know is that this man won't let anything happen to you ever. He will make sure with his life."

Hector's words make a shudder run over my spine. I itch to walk over to Cassian and prove that statement but instead, my brother approaches Hector and me. Henri curtseys as well as Hector before the latter parts with a small smile. My eyes turn to my brother who seems to have protested against anything red and is dressed in dark green breeches matched with a white tunic. A smile tickles my lips at his rebellion.

"Hey." He says quietly, his eyes searching mine. My heart aches at the look he is giving me and I do the only thing I know will save him from this situation.

"I'm glad to see that you're fine. Care for a dance?" I offer and his lips twitch lightly before he nods and we walk over to the dancing crowd, the soft tunes of the piano reaching us. It is accompanied by a swift tune of two violins, the bass of the cello making the piece somehow ominous. It plays into the red lighting of the hall, the music enrapturing every guest. I put my hands on Henri's shoulders as he steadies me with his on my back.

"I feel terrible." He starts once our bodies move out of rhythm. Henri was never a great dancer and yet it was the most fun to dance with him. It was his charm.

"I know you are and there is no need to apologize. I think we said everything in the maze that we had to say."

"But there is a need to apologize. You're my sister and I was being biased. I want to see you and I wish you would stay but I accepted you can't."

His eyes are filled with worry and the tension eases slightly out of me at his presence.

"Exactly. I am your sister and no matter where I am or who I'm with, nothing will change that fact Henri. I am not angry with you I promise." I say and he frowns before his foot slips and steps onto mine for a second. I wince but chuckle afterward.

"Sorry."

"You better be, I think I can't feel my toe anymore."

I give him a small fake glare and he relaxes. The most beautiful look on my brother is when he smiles. It always lights up his whole features, making him look his actual age. I wish I could see it every day, bottle it up like my own little sun.

"Toes are overrated." He says with a small grin and I raise a brow.

"Yeah? Are they overrated when I use my foot to kick your ass?"

"Solving a problem with violence is never a good idea." He says it in his best snobby voice, pinching his eyebrows, his lips turned downwards. We both break out into laughter simultaneously, the impression of Professor Bernath so spot on. After a moment we both need to stop to get some air into our lungs.

"I wish I could stay for the oath." He tells me and I look at him smiling. He's too young to be witnessing the blood bond even though nothing serious happens. But it plays right in my cards, avoiding another person who won't notice me missing after midnight.

"It's alright. You shouldn't be worried about me, Cas is not an enemy to me, not anymore." I say and realize that what I'm saying is the truth. I am not fighting against him. Sure the thought of Demeter still scares me but I have faced much scarier things. The dark notes of the cello fade; the piano picks up a higher note and slips into another song. I hug Henri tighter, putting my head onto his chest, his lavender scent enveloping me.

"How am I supposed to believe that?"

He sounds doubtful and I chuckle.

"Well, I tried to stab him a month ago, I don't have the urge to do that now."

"That's good to hear." A voice speaks up, making Henri and me step apart to see Cassian standing behind us. I raise a brow while he grins at us.

"Do you care to spare me a dance with your sister?"

"Of course."

Henri lets go of me and I promise to visit him in the morning for the last goodbye before he steps to the side but not with last words.

"Be careful."

"I can handle him," I say but my brother smiles lightly.

"I meant Cas." He says before weaving through the crowd, leaving me with a satisfied grin. It vanishes the second Cassian pulls me flush against his body overstepping every kind of appropriate boundary. Cocky bastard. My lips twitch dangerously.

"What are you doing?" I ask when one of his hands comes to a stop low on my back, the other at my ribs, right under my breast. His hand on my back tugs at the locks cascading down my back, making me narrow my eyes. As if on accident his thumb brushes the side of my boob and I quickly look around to see that the crowd around us is too thick and everyone is—like I predicted—high on the liquid to notice us.

"Dancing," Cassian tells me, wedging his thigh between my legs before he sways my body elegantly.

It´s a stark contrast to Henri and I´s stumbling. His strides are confident, his spine straight and chest open. I dare say it looks good on him, to dance.

"It seems like you´re spending an awful lot of time with anyone else than me." He says quietly, his lips grazing my ear. My hands wander from his chest up to his shoulders, gripping them to find some balance. Soft goosebumps cover my skin when I take a quick inhale of his scent.

"It seems like you have a terrible memory because I remember you being in my chambers hours ago. You promised me to have your cock inside me next time." The daring words leave my lips as a sin, flushing my cheeks. He´s already spoiling me. And I fear that I love every second of it.

An agreeing sound erupts in his throat, making me look up at him. He spins me quietly before pulling me back against his chest.

"Yes, I recall and if that is your wish we will spend as much time with me buried inside you as you want." I try to swallow and breathe at the same time and I end up coughing lightly, eliciting a small laugh from his lips.

"Was that too much for you, princess?" He asks as he gently pats my back, easing the cough. As if to make it even worse, his hand is warm, almost hot. The touch burns right through the material of the corset, and I wish it would come into contact with my skin.

"Maybe," I admit staring at the guests around us. For a moment we both stay quiet, our thoughts lingering while I let him engulf me like a safe space. My eyes fly over to the throne to meet dark eyes belonging to Lord Romanov. How long has he been watching us?

A satisfied smile moves on his lips, I narrow my eyes at the movement. His fingers twitch as if he has been waiting for something. My attention gets snagged when Cas brushes his lips against my ear.

"Did I tell you that you look like a goddess tonight?"

His words are a deep rumble making my head spin.

"No, but I´m always open for compliments."

Soft laughter rumbles through him.

"I´m sure you are. But there is no way denying it, the second you stepped through the doors I was lost. If I could I would take you with me and spend every second tasting your skin."

My breath hitches lightly, making him smile against my neck.

"I offered you to fuck me."

I can´t believe I´m saying the words. Cas stiffens for a moment before he raises his face, his nose bumping against mine softly.

"We both know that we can´t. I would never taint your honor like that."

"My honor will be just fine." He smiles and places a soft kiss on my cheek. It's as if he's apologizing for these stupid rules.

My father gets up from his throne and a loud gong sounds through the hall. Cas and I's steps halter and I look up into his eyes, panic washing through my veins because I know what's about the happen. The music halters while everyone turns around to look at the king, anticipating his words.

"It is time. The blood moon has risen to its highest point and like every time we are honored to celebrate this at the Sebestyen court. I thank everyone who followed the invitation to our humble castle, showcasing their devotion to the gods. Not only will blood be shed tonight from one royal but two. It is made to be a bounding ritual for life as two royals will become one soul and one heart. And I am more than proud to announce that we will honor the gods with a blood oath of my daughter Katarina Sebestyen rightful regent of Aerwyna who is about to step into the sacred covenant of marriage with Cassian Moreau, Prince, and regent of Demeter!"

41

There are days in your life when you realize that a certain event that you avoided out of fear, isn't so bad in the end. The fear is so much worse sometimes.

Well, today is not that day.

I don't know if I'm able to make my way up the small steps that lead to the throne on my own. I just know that I'm suddenly standing in front of the glimmering thing. The small metal bowl shines on the pedestal and it feels like it's reflecting its ugly color straight at me. The weird-looking dagger laying beside it doesn't do anything to calm my nerves.

Edlyn is already standing beside it. I chose her to be my witness while Cassian had no other choice but to let Lord Romanov do the job. My pulse is pounding in my ears, and my throat's going dry. I don't dare to search for Marrus's eyes in the crowd as Cassian leads me up and stops in front of the vessel.

I didn't get a chance to tell the Prince of Oceanus about the engagement. Well, if I'm being completely honest I don't necessarily need to see the look on his face, rejection isn't a good look on anyone.

Our backs are turned to the crowd while my father goes on about honor and how this is the first marriage between a regent heir, blah, blah, blah. Who fucking cares let's get this over with before I vomit right into this vessel. The warm hand of Cas on my back is the only thing grounding me, comforting me as if his touch is crawling through my skin and protecting my heart. I turn my head to search for his eyes, to make him tell me that everything is going to be fine. I catch him already looking at me. The green is intense and spends me some familiarity.

I wish he would say something, even though I doubt anything could calm me right now. My eyes fly back to the dagger, which has a weird black blade that shimmers purple in certain lights. A sudden picture flashes in front of my eyes, the blade of the Protestant a vivid image. The way the light reflected on it when he sliced it through Cas's stomach, is the same. Whatever it means, it makes a creepy shudder run down my spine.

I guess it's only used for this ritual, like the vessel standing beside it. It's just in the right place for the red moonlight to shine on, through the window, liquid already swimming inside with various herbs.

It's just a symbolic gesture it could be parsley swimming around the water the people wouldn't be able to tell the difference. My lips twitch at the thought, Cassian raises a brow and looks like he would do anything to know what's going on in my mind at the moment. It seems like my father finishes his boring speech and moves back in front of us, his face lit up creepily by the moon. I never realized how many lines he already has, the red color reflecting on his skin like fresh blood. It makes him look evil.

"The gods once gifted us with the power of life, lending us their grounds to live on, tonight we're going to repay that favor."

You already said that.

"The blood oath will bind Princess Katarina and Prince Cassian for life and everything that comes after, hurting their selves for the first and last time in their restless being."

What? No one told me I would need to cut Cassian; I thought the lord would do that. My eyes widen slightly when Edlyn stalks over to me and softly removes the glove from my left arm. My hand shakes, anxiety rushing through spreading like a virus.

"Why do I need to cut him?" I whisper alarmed as my father's booming voice goes on, drowning our whispers.

"I don't know, it's usually not done that way." She hisses before she steps away, her words alarm me even more.

"They will ensure both kingdoms with the most powerful heir, fulfilling their duty." My father ends and I get sick. He walks over to the dagger and picks it up, his eyes meeting mine for the first time in weeks.

"Katarina Sebestyen, do you obey the gods and their will and draw blood from your heartmate for the first and last time?" He asks loudly, making a creepy shiver run down my spine, my skin covered in goosebumps. This is not the man who I once called my father. His sapphire eyes are cold and calculating.

"I do."

My voice sounds steadier than I feel when I grab the dagger and turn around to the prince. All the tension seems to leave my body when I see the soft smile on his lips as he offers me his forearm. The green in his eyes is soft and gentle. His control and ease make my tense muscles relax. The sleeve of his red tunic is rolled up, revealing his clean skin. I can see his veins running under it, a million little lines that are all connected to his heart.

"I'm sorry," I whisper unsure as I step towards him and he chuckles lightly as his right arm wanders around my waist securely, steadying me.

I let out a shuddering breath, swallowing. His hand feels good wrapped around me; everything is going to be fine.

I know this is voluntary, I'm barely going to hurt him but it still makes me sick.

"Now you're sorry to cut me? You won't disappoint to surprise me, princess."

His words ease me, even more, when I press the tip of the black-purple blade against his skin. My hand freezes and I don't dare to move the blade.

"It's alright, I wouldn't want anyone else doing it."

His voice is a comforting whisper, just for my ears to be heard.

"If that's a dirty joke again I'm going to stab you," I say with an unsteady chuckle.

"That's my girl."

My breath hitches and warmth blooms in my chest at his words. For a moment my eyes fly up and I meet their green of his, something glimmers inside them. It allows me to take a real breath.

I drag the blade down his arm not meeting any kind of resistance. I flinch when he hisses before I stop and he lets his dark blood drop into the vessel. The liquid starts to bubble and hiss quietly. I'm frozen on the spot for a second, the dagger still in my hand.

"Do you, Cassian Moreau, obey the gods and their will and draw blood from your heartmate for the first and last time?" My father now asks, even though the blood in Cas' arm doesn't stop flowing, dropping onto the ground. My eyes follow their path, the expensive marble tainted in his blood. The scent of iron hits the air, overpowering his calming scent. Nausea hits me at the look of it and I try to focus on his face instead. All of this will be over in a few minutes.

"I do." His voice is steady and powerful, booming into every corner of the room. He gently pries the dagger out of my hands, cleans the blade from the blood on his breeches, and grabs my arm. Lord Romanov makes a small sound and my eyes fly over to him. His eyes are narrowed but he doesn't say anything. Cassian earns my attention back when he speaks up.

"This will sting a little, princess."

"I can handle it." I shoot back, even though I don't know if I can. His eyes lighten as he puts the blade against my skin and I bite my lip until I taste blood. I don't even get to raise my arm over the vessel, Cassian does it for me. The second my blood drops into the liquid the world seems to stop.

I register myself inhaling for a second. Before the world caves into two.

A simultaneous gasp moves through the crowd as the vessel breaks, spilling the liquid, and making it run onto the ground before it rumbles and ripples with power.

Cas lets go of the dagger to pull me close, ripping a piece from his tunic to tie it around my bleeding arm. But that seems to be my least concern as a powerful earthquake shakes through our castle, knocking off every glass and ruby hanging from the ceiling, showering us in deathful shards of glass.

We're bathed in a rain of blood-red crystals, slicing into the soft skin, tearing it apart with no effort.

"Carina!" Cas calls my name and I just realize that I slipped away from him in the rumble, my ears unfocused as if I am underwater. He somehow makes his way over to me as I shield my face from the falling rubies. Once he reaches me he cradles me to his chest to shield me from the shards but it's too late.

Most of the damage has been done, the slices on my arms not deep, nonetheless stinging with soft burns.

"What the hell is going on?" I try to yell over the shouts and endless thunders of the earth while my hands dig into the material of the shirt, trying to make out where Edlyn went. I can't find her gown under all the sea of black, panic starts to flood my veins.

"I don't know."

"Is this normal for a blood oath?" I ask and he raises a brow as he pulls us to the side of the room, telling me that it is not normal. Did our blood do this? The answer is certainly clear and right in front of our eyes. The second the binding of the oath was done, due to our blood mixing, the quakes started.

"This shouldn't have happened," Cas says over the next clap of thunder and I almost lose my grip on him, placing my eyes on his and the ground beneath us suddenly stops shaking. I hold my breath, staring into his eyes as we both seem to wait for the next shake of the earth which doesn't appear, luckily. Silence envelops us as if everyone is holding their breath, waiting for the next attack to come. We slowly step up, straightening our spines before my eyes wander through the crowd to see Edyln come up behind the throne, completely unharmed. Thank Adales.

A few people have scratches on their faces and exposed arms but mostly it seems like everyone is unscathed. My father steps back up, his cloak flying behind him as he raises both his arms in a majestic gesture with a satisfied look on his face. He is the only one looking calm, daring to break the silence. As if he knew what was going to happen.

"The gods have listened to our prayers and gifted us once again, showing gratitude for the bond!" His voice booms through the hall and I furrow my brows at his words.

What does he mean? Seems like I´m not the only one confused because the crowd stays silent. Some of them look at the man as if he is a lunatic. I can´t blame them. It doesn´t take long for my question to be answered as the king steps to the side and reveals the cracked vessel. The liquid has spilled a dark red mixture trickling down the column it´s sitting on and I hold my breath when I notice it. The surface of the cold stone broke right underneath the trickle of the blood and ended into a small puddle, the earth breaking at that point.

Purple and blue leaves cover the red stones that grew right out of the solid ground. A murmur wanders through the crowd before everyone erupts into cheers and the music starts playing.

The next thump of my heart ends in a stutter, the music too loud, the euphoria of the crowd smelling too sweet.

A woman dressed in a red gown steps into the hall, I catch the sign while my eyes stay on the flower that seems to be grown out of Cas´ and I´s blood.

Our blood made the castle shake and a Night-crawler bloomed right in the banquette hall, covered in small splatters of rubies.

~ 42 ~

It seems like the earthquake didn't just affect the castle but it moved through the whole Aerwyna. It is colder tonight, the wind bites in my face as Nighttail gallops through the forest. The blood moon is still up in the sky but this time when I look at it it doesn't spike fear inside me. It's like a warning that whatever I'm about to do is going to be dangerous.

My father said it was the gods listening to us and gifting us with Night-crawlers as it is a legend that the petals of the flower are supposed to be a talisman against dark magic. The rubies scattered around it are from the shower rain we endured from the ceiling and I think it was just an accident. something must've triggered this earthquake and maybe it was just a big coincidence that Cassian and I shared blood tonight.

Well, that's what I'm trying to convince myself of. With all the commission I almost missed the start signal but the moment Gisella stepped into the hall, Edlyn rushed toward me and used the chaos as an excuse to go clean up my arm. Cassian didn't want to let me go at first but once Edlyn gave him a silent glare he let go of me, a stern look in his eyes. I didn't want to go, I wanted to aid the people who got cuts and bruises on their arms and faces but I knew it was the only chance to leave this evening. I have the suspicion that the person I'm meeting will know something about the earthquake. All of this couldn't be just a coincidence.

Everything seems to be tied together, it's as if my subconscious is screaming at me, trying to tell me the truth. I hope Gisella will be fine with pretending to be me, I told her she should just linger a bit after the blood oath and then tell someone she is dizzy and lie down in her chambers. No one will question her due to the wound I have on my left arm.

So while everyone else is celebrating—what they think to be a—godly sign, I'm on my way through the dark forest which borders the coast of the lost. The forest rushes quietly and dark past me as if the animals are too scared to come out of hiding after whatever made the earth rumble with so much force. A dull ache has formed, pulsing from my arm, even though Cas bound his piece of clothing around it. I'm sure if more pressure would've been exerted, it would've slid straight through the bone without resistance. A clearing comes into view, Nighttail slows down and I take a deep breath, slipping on a mental mask. I try to leave behind whatever happened minutes ago and become the Red Saint again. A dagger is sheathed at my thigh and boot, various small knives are up my sleeves, and this time I also have a sword strapped to my back.

I'm prepared for war because I don't know if this person was stupid and arrogant enough to come alone or not. It would've been smarter of me to tell someone besides Gisella and Edlyn but I didn't want to take any risks. My hands softly grip the main of Nighttail and tug lightly, making her neigh.

"Shh, it's alright. We have to stop here." I tell her quietly, even though we didn't break through the curtain of trees yet. I'll leave her in the woods just to make sure she won't get hurt. She stops quietly near a fir and I jump off of her, my feet silent. I take her reins and bind them around the blunt.

It all happens mechanically, my body preparing for my upcoming task. It takes a bit of time to calm her down and I pet her side lightly, concentrating my senses on my surroundings. It's so quiet, it almost seems too quiet. With a last look at the horse, I slip over my hood, even though I left the mask on from the ball, and leave the forest. Once I step through the opening I'm met with the force of the merciless wind slapping against my face. It reeks of salt and wet sand, which I leave footsteps in as my eyes scan the coast. But no one is here.

The sound of the crashing waves is usually a big comfort to me but today it seems like an unnecessary sound clouding my ears distractingly. I don't dare to light up a fire to see better who knows which animal could be drawn out from the depths of the forest. Instead, I pace the sand quietly waiting for something to happen.

I roll my shoulders trying to relax as the sting in my arm turns noticeable and I pull up my sleeve to see that the cloth around the wound is soaked in my blood. It looks like it hasn't stopped bleeding at all. I push the material away and release the nasty wound making me groan disgusted. The skin is raised and red and the sight makes me slightly dizzy. I still make my way over to the water and dip my arm inside, hissing.

"Fuck, you sting like a bitch." I curse as the salt disinfects the wound and I use my other hand to throw handfuls of water over it.

"It also looks like a bitch."

I whirl around at the voice, unsheathing my dagger in the same moment to stare at a man standing a few feet away from me. Forgotten is the slit in my arm and I'm squatting down ready to pounce at this strange man. How did he make it this close without me noticing?

He is almost two times as big as me, with wide shoulders and strong arms. But size isn't everything. His hair is long and red, a thick braid falling onto his wide back. Some strands escaped the braid, framing a strong jaw and hard dark eyes. I can't tell which color they are due to the lack of light but what I do see swirling in them is not good.

I estimate his age to be between thirty and forty, he doesn't look immature with the deep lines running down his face and yet his muscles look as hard as stone.

His lips are in a straight grim line, his cheekbones sitting high. I have never seen this man before what is he doing in my capital, recruiting men? I scan the area behind him. At least he seems to have come alone. Good, he's underestimating me.

"I must say when I met Ellister one night, after a small inconvenience of all my recruited men being murdered, I expected anything. That bastard was scared shitless when he talked to me, telling me who killed these men. The Red Saint, another legend in this godforsaken kingdom that somehow seems to be true but who would've known a lady was behind the name?" His voice makes my skin crawl and I step slowly away from the water.

"That's alright I didn't expect the Dark Prince to not be a legend as well, you should've seen my face when that idiot told me about you and your master so willingly." I try to sound nonchalant while I push the sleeve over the cut, hiding the pain with a clench of my jaw.

"A woman, who can fight and has humor, seems to be my lucky day."

"I wouldn't say that too soon who knows if you outlive this day," I say circling him, the cold grip of my dagger seeping through the material of my gloves. I tilt my head watching his movements closely. We both try to edge away from the water, our eyes taking the other in. Calculating, guessing what it takes to take one another down.

His steps are light and quick, not a sound made even though he must weigh almost over 195 lbs. 195 lbs. full of muscle but I try to ignore that fact.

"I think I like you." The man says but despite his words, he tilts his head and frowns.

"But what's it with the hood and mask, don't understand that point, none of your victims stay alive to tell anyone of your identity."

"Ellister did."

He makes a mock grimace and another cold shiver runs down my back as I realize.

"You killed him."

"I mean what did you expect me to do? Telling just everyone about—how did you call him—my master? I couldn't let him live and tell another soul about my plans." He says lazily but I notice that he is trying to get closer with every step he takes. He's trying to distract me with his words but I know how this will go tonight. Just one of us will survive and it's not going to be him.

"So let me guess you came here to kill me? So I won't tell on your daddy? Isn't it a bit cowardly that he isn't here himself?" I ask with a smirk, making him growl and take a misstep. I take that as my chance and pounce first.

My arm swings out at an inhuman pace and the dagger slices through the material of his abdomen. I don't provide him a chance to recover and let the blade slice through his arm.

I don't get a third chance when his fist comes flying out and knocks me right in the stomach, breaking at least two ribs. I release a breath and stumble backward. We're back to the game of circling each other.

"I like that you already know of your destiny it makes this a lot easier."

How can he still talk? He only got me once and my breath is already rattling in my throat.

"Well, would it be in your kind body to at least tell me what the Dark Prince wants in my kingdom because as far as I remember we haven't done anything to enrage him?"

I try to play cool again, making the man chuckle deeply; my hairs stand at the sound. Something familiar rings in it, the way he laughs.

"Ellister was easy to fool with that kind of statement. You should've seen the fear in his eyes when I told him about the Dark Prince."

"I can imagine." I agree and he nods as if we are two old friends. My ribs hurt with every breath and I try to stabilize myself, my head dizzy but the cause of it seems to be my stupid arm. I should've told Marianna to stitch the wound before I left the castle.

"Superstitious pack that lives here in Aerwyna."

My eyes narrow.

"Wait. You mean to tell me it is not the Dark Prince who sent you?" My steps falter, so someone is using the name of a horror story to hide his true motives.

"So astute, it is almost a shame that I have to kill you." And it seems like the talking is done for him as he pounces at me, catching me off guard. His fist collides with my right wrist making the blade drop out of my hold as I duck from his second hit, whirling my legs under me. I knock hardly into his knees causing him to stumble.

He tries to balance himself but I don't let him rest and kick him again. He drops to his knees like a wet sack, the growl that escapes his lips makes him look ridiculous. With one turn he knocks me off my feet and I land hard on the sand, the back of my head colliding with a stone.

"Fuck." I curse at the blinding pain, my vision going black for a second. The next time I open my eyes the man is over me, his fist colliding with my cheek with so much force, that I bite my tongue in the process, tasting blood. Fire erupts from the spot he hit me, blazing through my veins.

I pull up my knee trying to get him off me but he blocks the attack, sitting down on my crushed ribs, eliciting a groan from me. He weighs more than 195 lbs. Holy fuck.

It feels like he's crushing me with his weight.

"You bastard." I hiss and he chuckles lightly as his hands wrap around my throat.

"You were arrogant enough to think he would send someone who couldn't deal with a woman? The men that I recruited were nothing but useless idiots. It was never his intention to recruit them but just to draw you out. He knew you would try to protect the people in your capital."

My brows furrow at his words as my hands claw at his face, anywhere I can reach him but my energy is leaving me with the little air I get from his chokehold. My hands go slack and I let him talk while I slowly try to get at the dagger, sheathed in my boot.

"You are arrogant and young. You don´t know half of what is going on in your kingdom, you were going to sleep in one bed with your enemy—oh you didn´t know? Your little prince? He is not who you think he is but sadly you won´t find out about that."

I freeze for a second but don´t believe a word he says as I finally reach the dagger and ram it straight into his back.

"Bitch!" He hisses and falls off me, allowing me to inhale a deep breath. My chest heaves, my lungs cry out and my ribs feel like they´re on fire still I stand up. I spit some blood out of my mouth while I stare at the man on the ground, the dagger still stuck in his back.

"How do you know who I am?" I ask, my voice hoarse as I draw a small knife out of my sleeve. My head is pounding from the lack of oxygen and the fact that I rammed the back of it onto a stone. The man rolls on his side laughing dirtily.

I need to get out of here quickly or I might get seriously hurt. This man is not an inexperienced thief. Whoever sent him knows what they´re doing. And they know who I am and what I am doing.

"Princess, that is why you´re here. Because of him."

My breath halters at his words. Anger flushes my veins and I kick his side with my boot, making him groan. I raise my fist and deck him in the face, cracking his nose but I don´t stop with that. I pin him on the ground with my knee in his stomach and he growls when the movement makes the dagger in his back move and I start to hit his face over and over and over.

Nothing can stop me as a hollow feeling slips its way into my heart, ridding me of remorse or guilt. When my knuckles are bloody and bruised I stop and the man laughs again, blood mixed with saliva running down his chin. My breath is labored as the thumping of my heart seems to overpower every sound around me. It urges the adrenaline inside me to travel through my veins at a fast pace.

"Who ordered you to kill me, tell me, or I will continue with this," I say not recognizing my icy voice. I can´t believe what he´s saying, Cassian is not a traitor. How could he be? He told me about my father, he kissed me and told me he was afraid of his feelings for me. I opened up, Adales I let him touch me like no one ever touched me. I am bound to him by life and death which is a measure of time that can´t be grasped.

"You can keep on going, I won´t tell you. Seems like I struck a nerve, have you found a liking in Cassian, princess?" An inhuman growl leaves my mouth and I lean down, ramming the knife right under his left chest barely grazing his heart. His mouth opens in pain and I stare right into the hollow of his eyes. Something dangerous flickers inside him, revealing his rotten soul.

"Don´t you dare put his name in your mouth. Why should I believe anything you´re saying?"

"You don´t need to but there is a traitor in your castle, walking right in front of your eyes without you noticing and it is not only the Prince of Demeter that I´m talking about.

What do you think did he do when you met him that night, dressed like a thief?"

The mask on my face slips and he shoots me a small grin.

"The prince easily wrapped you around his finger, I wonder if he needed to fuck you for it. Did he? I'm curious, princess—ahh." He groans when I twist the knife angrily and an icy feeling moves around my heart. Cassian never told me what he was doing in Aerwyna that night, even though I asked him.

He kept so many things a secret that didn't make me trust him and somehow in the end I still do. I let him wind himself into my heart distracting me with his words and lips. I am a fool yet again.

That moment of hesitation seems to cost me my life when the man knocks me off of him, grabs the knife I rammed into his ribs, and slices it right through my stomach, making me groan.

His arm swings out and stops right over my heart when I raise my hands with the last ounce of strength I have in me. My eyes flick down to the tip of the knife which is already slicing through my suit. My hands tremble with his force and I look back up into his eyes to see the triumphant look in them.

"Your emotions would've been the cause of your death sooner or later. Give up, Carina, you have no one who loves you, no one to return to, if you would survive this. It is okay to give up it is useless anyway. He is too powerful to be stopped."

Despite his words I don't let go of his wrists, even though the blade is already piercing my skin, shooting a new wave of pain through me.

"If you think I care about anyone else than myself you're wrong," I whisper, making him lean down and with a last groan and grit of my teeth, I raise my head and knock my forehead right against his. His grip falters as he blinks disoriented and I spin the knife into my hands and ram it straight into his chest. It slides through the clothes effortlessly, his skin, and lastly his bones straight into the cold hollow thing of his chest.

The man drops to the side, his mouth opened in shock and I slowly get on all fours, my head spinning as I pull the knife out of his chest, my lips close to his ear as I mumble my last words.

"You should know I hate it when someone uses my title as an insult." I hiss and even though he is already dying, I move my arm and slit his throat, making him gurgle with his next breath. I let myself fall back onto my bottom and put my head between my knees, listening to every breath the man takes.

I don't know when it stops but I stay put a long time after he is dead. My temples are pounding heavily and it takes me many tries to stand up and roll his corpse into the ocean, not without pulling out the dagger that is still sheathed in his back.

Once his body is swallowed by the water I put back my knives and daggers before I clean my bloody hands and face in the water and make my way back to Nighttail. I don't try to think of anything the man said about a traitor in the halls of the castle or about Cassian. I need to talk to him myself even though I am sure he didn't lie. Why would he, he had no reason because he didn't believe I would survive this night.

But who was he talking about when he said him?

I take a deep breath and look up into the sky, my eyes stinging with tears. The stars shine down at me, mocking my weakness. It seems like Cassian made his way deeper into my heart than I admit to myself and now it feels like a literal knife is stuck in my chest, slicing it with every breath I take. If it is true what the man said then I don't know what to feel. What to do. It feels like his cold hand is still grasping my throat, making it unbearable to breathe, the pain of my ribs reminding me every time how injured I am.

But the pain of the broken ribs, the sting of the slice in my arm, or the bruising in my face isn't the worst. No, the worst is the feeling of being stabbed in the back by someone I fell in love with.

~ 43 ~

Every breath burns, every step blazes, and every blink stabs at me. Pain pierces my body from the inside out, burning my flesh and my heart, with every step I take through the dark halls. Somewhere on the way through them, I hear the ball carrying on, despite the late hours of the night. By now everyone must be drunk from the expensive wine, their minds twisted and hazed with the opium my father probably drew out. How I wished to be a part of it. To drink and dance carelessly.

The ride back to the castle seems endless, the wind tugging at my unkempt hair, the moon making its way down on the sky, almost kissing the sea.

Nighttail is neighing restless, sensing my swirling thoughts while I sit on her back, trying to blame the cold wind for the liquid pouring out of my eyes. I wish I would be a coward tonight. To go back to my chambers and hide underneath my duvet, call for Edlyn to keep me company so I can bathe in my sorrow.

Instead, I'm dragging my half-stabbed body through the dark halls, my hands shaking in front of me. There is not much time to think about my actions before Cassian's door comes into view, the lack of guards tells me that he's inside. He must've sent them away when he left the ball. I know he is not stupid, he must know by now that I'm not at the palace. But that is not what makes me hesitate in front of the doors.

I can handle his rage. Gods I would prefer to handle his rage right now. But to face him after the things the man revealed scares me to death.

A small inner voice tells me to leave, to somehow prolong the naïve bliss that I'm in right now. Sadly that's not possible. Even if the man lied I promised Cas to stay with him tonight and if I don't speak to him if I don't hear him telling me that the man fooled me, I won't be able to sleep anyway.

The knock against his door is hard and steady. A stark contrast to my jumbling nerves. Silence is the only thing meeting me. I knock again. My throat closes slightly at the lack of his presence and I don't bother to knock a third time and push down the handle. A burning wave of heat meets my cold face when I step inside, the room filled with tension.

It doesn't take me long to find him, it's like my eyes are drawn to his presence. He is hunched over on a chaise longue, placed in front of the fireplace. His face in his hands, the dark curls hiding any emotion that I could pick up on.

"What a picture. And I thought you would be out there drinking your—" I don't get to finish my stupid sentence when his head flies up and the next second he is in front of me.

"I am going to kill you."

The words are a deep growl, mixing with my hitched breath at his threat. Instead of keeping true to his words, his strong arms wrap around me and his face nuzzles my neck.

"For fucks sake, Carina, I was worried sick."

My heart finally breaks at his words. It seems like it has been barely holding on, dangling on a loose thread. But to hear his voice break, genuine worry etched into it gives me the rest. His arms squeeze me tighter but I don't dare to move as I hear him breathe in my scent.

"I noticed you leaving immediately, Edlyn wouldn't tell me where you went and I almost went ballistic—gods you are hurt."

His words make me flinch and he finally lets go of me. How does he know I am hurt? His cold hands cradle my face while his eyes scan my body for injuries.

"Why did you leave? And where the fuck did you go to? You should've told me."

"Should I?"

I finally find my voice but it sounds weird. Restrained and scratchy. His body freezes and he finally looks me in the eyes.

"What did you do?"

"What did I do? What did I do?" I can't help the small scoff from leaving my lips. His hands finally let go of my cheeks and I straighten my spine.

"It is none of your business where I went."

"Hell, it is. Especially when you come back with wounds and bruises, smelling like death!"

I take a step back from his body, the proximity too close. I need air. I can't breathe when he's standing this close.

"That's nothing unusual. You know that I leave at night."

"You went to the capital?"

His brows furrow, his eyes narrowing.

"Tonight I didn't, no."

I can feel that he's getting impatient but I can't speak the words. I'm waiting for the anger to roll over me, to make a case of fury slip around me. I need it for my courage. I divert my eyes from his face, finding it easier to speak when I don't see the look in his eyes. The honest affection that reflects in them.

It´s a lie.

"But it´s funny that you mention it. I´ve been wondering about my visits to the capital, especially the one when I met you."

His whole body freezes.

"What is this?" His voice is hoarse, his mind finally catching up on the mood that I´m in.

"You never told me what you were doing that night. Dressed like a thief so no one would recognize you."

"I was taking a stroll."

A cold mask slips onto his face and my hands clench into fists. I welcome the pain of my nails digging into my skin, grounding me in my decision. I know the crescent marks on my skin will remain for a long time after today.

"What were you doing in my kingdom, Prince of Demeter?" I hiss at him and he shakes his head, slowly taking a step forward. I take one back.

"Don´t do this."

"What is this supposed to mean? Answer the question."

He takes another step forward and I mirror him taking one back. He raises his hands defensively.

"I'll tell you everything you want to know but you need to listen."

"What do you think I´m doing right now?" I say with a raised brow. He shakes his head, his curls flying around for a moment.

"You need to listen and stop looking at me like that."

"Like what?

"Like I´m your enemy."

I take a small breath.

"Is that not who you are?"

"No. I was never your enemy."

How I wish I could believe those bittersweet words.

"Yeah? Does that mean that you can look me in the face and tell me the truth? Tell me that you weren´t lying from the beginning, that you were an alliance, and that you´re not a goddamn traitor!" My voice gets louder over the words and I finally feel the burning fury inside of me.

"I´m not a traitor. I promise you will understand everything I did was to keep you safe!"

He takes another step forward, desperately grabbing my shoulders.

"Keep me safe? Look at me Cas! I am aching, burning not just from wounds but from the fact that I fell in love with my enemy!"

We both freeze at my words. No, no, no.

"You what?" His words are barely a whisper, a dark glimmer moving in his eyes.

I start to move my shoulders, wanting to throw his hands off me.

"Let go of me!"

"Fuck no. Repeat what you said."

"Fuck you." I hiss and knee him right in his groin, making him topple over. A breath of air escapes his lips as he looks up at me.

"I swear I´m going to kill you I´m not bluffing." I hiss and already unsheathe my dagger, red hot fury burning in front of my eyes. His eyes widen.

"Carina!"

I furrow my brows and realize too late that he is no longer staring at me but something behind me. His body lunges forward but it´s too late.

"No!"

His scream is earth-shattering, crawling through my skin and against my bones. A hit against the back of my head and everything goes black.

~ 44 ~

Dying feels weird. There is no light feeling, where your soul seems to part ways with your body. I never knew if there was something afterlife if once you're dead, your soul floats upon the endless skies and joins the gods in Empyrean. Or buries underneath the rotten earth, forever stuck in the deep pits of Gehenna. But hell I didn't think it would be this painful and cold.

I didn't think your thoughts keep on going like mine do. Maybe it was my fate to die the second I started to take the lives of these men. I started to justify their deaths, using an excuse of protection but who am I to judge who lives or dies? Who am I to doom certain families, robbing them of a person who could be their most beloved? I am in no way better than them, no matter what they did. And now there is a traitor at my court, while people who are important to me are unprotected. Well, two traitors. One still disguised and the other. . .

I hope Edlyn is fine, Henri and even Marianna. I wish they would leave and escape this life I was too afraid to leave behind. Adales, death hurts like a bitch.

My head is still hammering, my body shaking violently and some viscous substance is sticking to what feels like my cheek, it spreads a sickening scent like iron. My fingers twitch. My eyes feel heavy and unable to peel open but when a groan leaves my lips, they snap open in one swift motion. I'm not dead. And the world is upside down.

A wave of nausea hits me so hard that I dry heave and almost vomit right on the cold hard surface I'm lying on. My vision is doubled; my ears are ringing as I try to put the world back into its place. I blink until the spots in front of my eyes disappear. It's cold wherever I am and it smells of mold and that awful iron scent.

"Fuck."

I groan as I put all my weight onto my elbows and get up into a crouching position. Another wave of nausea hits me and I squeeze my eyes shut, breathing through the wave of sickness until it is gone. The ringing subsides and when my eyes open, they focus on the white gauze wrapped around my left arm. Someone must've cleaned the cut because the pulsing pain disappeared. Still, I feel the bruise on my cheekbone, my swollen lip, and the broken ribs which make it hard to breathe.

The throbbing pain at the back of my head makes it hard for me to form a proper thought and guess who did this. A cold shudder rocks my body as I push the imagery of the prince out of my mind.

I do what I always did best; locking the walls back into place, guarding my heart. Where the hell am I? And why would someone first kidnap me, clean my wound, and then leave me in some kind of dungeons? I sit up again under a groan my eyes wandering around before my heart stops. I find the source of the iron scent lying a few feet away from me, soulless eyes staring straight into mine.

A short cry leaves my lips as my heart pounds against my broken ribcage and I rob forward to where the young girl is lying. Marianna's skin is of an unusual pale color, her eyes wide open but even if they weren't I knew she'd be dead.

"No, no, no," I whisper as my hand wanders over her arms, her hair trying to grasp anything.

No matter what I touch I don't find the smallest ember of life that could've been circling her veins.

"Marianna!" I call her name desperately shaking her shoulders but she doesn't budge, she doesn't blink. A cold feeling rushes over my spine when the hollow existence of death lingers around me the young girl is gone. My hands are soaked in her blood and the stench is unbearable but I won't refuse her an honorable death. I slowly close her eyelids and press a soft kiss against her forehead. She couldn't have been older than sixteen and she will never become older than that. An innocent life was robbed. Whoever might've killed her, her soul won't live another day in peace. Another cold shudder creeps through me my fists tightening. I am going to kill him.

"May your soul rest and find peace in Empyrean."

"Oh, I don't think that is where she went to."

My head whirls around at the voice that echoes through the darkness of the dungeons, my eyes narrowing. The voice came straight out of the shadows, where a dark figure crouches expectantly as if it has waited for me to notice its presence.

How could I be so careless and overlook that another presence is with me?

"How do you know that?" I snap back, my voice hoarse as I try to stand up but I stop when I notice that my ankles are tied together. I'm going to kill this bastard.

"Because I was with her when she took her last breath to make sure her soul wouldn't go anywhere. A curious little thing, snooping around the halls of this castle, I mean I had to kill her or else she would've warned you."

I bite my tongue angrily trying to tame the anger inside of me at his careless words. He just revealed that we're in the castle, which is good; I will find my way towards Edlyn and Henri once I killed this man. If they're both still alive.

And afterward, I will hunt down the Prince of Demeter and will drive a dagger into his cold, dark heart. No joking, this time I mean it. I get sick again and topple over dry heaving.

"Huh, I already thought the toxin was out of your body, seems like it's still inside trying to get rid of it."

"Who the hell are you? Stop being a fucking coward and step into the light you wanker." I groan and a deep, inhuman growl meets me making me turn around surprised. This can't be a human I'm talking to. Hard footsteps appear out of the shadows and I hold my breath when he steps into the only place with light, his white eyes appearing creepily. Oh, my gods.

He is dressed in the deepest colors of the ocean but his skin shines weirdly as if it's almost iridescent. His fingernails are long and more of some sort of claws that can rip through skin effortlessly; small scales are dotting his skin above his muscles. His hair is a deep red and long, cascading down his shoulders. A stark contrast to the whites of his eyes. It seems to be a bonus to see in the dark with them and I almost vomit when I recognize him as the guard that once stood in front of Edlyn's chamber. I did not see things; his eyes did turn completely white for a moment. But that is completely beside the point because under all these monstrous differences I recognize Marrus Guithier standing in front of me.

"Woah, seems like the people have to redeem their words and call you one of the handsome men in Adalon."

He raises a brow at my sarcastic words and steps closer to me, making me rob back. I don't want his claws anywhere near my skin. The shock is sitting so deep in my bones that I'm sure too distracted to fight him off now.

He's the traitor Cassian is working with? It doesn't even make sense. And where the hell is the other prince? Something feels off in this setting. How am I fucking worrying about anything right now besides the fact that he is not human? That he turned into a fucking monster that looks like it's been conjured out of the Abyss.

"And yet you are here completely broken, chained and still you can't seem to keep your mouth shut."

His voice cuts straight through me like ice but I act nonchalant and shrug my shoulders.

"What can I say that's my natural charm."

"We'll see how much of your charm will be left once we're finished with you."

I freeze for a moment.

"So the prince is going to join us? I would say I miss him but that would be a lie."

I try my best to sound aloof but the wolfish grin on his lips tells me that he sees right through my act.

"Oh, it is not only the prince who will join us. But you might call him our guest of honor."

It takes everything in me not to pounce at this horrific monster in front of me.

"I prefer the term bastard but to each their own."

Seems like it's not smart to provoke him because the next thing I feel is his fist colliding with the soft skin of my cheek making my head fly around. The pain is so sharp that my ears start to ring again and I have to spit out some blood because I bit my tongue in the process.

The iron taste invades my mouth in no time, making my stomach coil in disgust.

"Not so much of a talker got it," I say and sit up again even though my body is screaming at me not to.

It burns on my tongue to ask why he's doing this but it seems like he is nervous. He is not the mastermind of this plan he is just another handyman in the game.

"The man who tried to appear as the handyman of the Dark Prince was he yours?" I ask instead of trying to piece the puzzle together.

The red hair both of the men seemed to inherit makes them somewhat look alike.

His cold, white eyes lay themselves back on me a soft grin on his lips. He reveals a series of murderous-looking sharp teeth. I might get sick again.

"No that was the idea of Lucien, clever isn't it? Luring you out of your little secret hideaway, I always wondered how did you get past the guards?"

He tilts his head to the side squatting down. Of course, Lord Romanov is a traitor too, that's not surprising to me. Still anger flares up in my veins. I can't believe I was stupid enough to not see the signs.

"I can show you if you get rid of these awful ankle chains," I say with a sweet smile moving my ankles, so the chain rattles. He grins and for a moment I see the smile that Marrus always sent me during meals. I can't believe he would go against me.

No matter how convincing Lord Romanov's arguments were, Marrus didn't like the man to be bribed with something. He always seemed so normal and trusting.

"You know I have to kill you. I invited you to my home and you stepped onto my kindness, spitting at my honor." I hiss at him. He stands up again pacing and I try to reach for the hidden dagger sheathed in my boot but halter when he speaks up again.

"I wouldn't do that. I got rid of every weapon on you. So now if you behave I'll tell you."

Instead of giving him an answer, I stay silent.

"First of all we should start from the beginning; you might have mistaken me for Prince Marrus Guithier, well that's wrong. He's dead."

A sharp intake of air makes my ribs press hurtfully against my skin. The whites of his eyes turn to me, his nostrils blaring lightly as if he was taking in my scent. Gross.

Still, I can't help a shiver from running down my spine.

I need to keep him talking whatever it takes. He was able to kill Marianna so he might be stronger than he looks. I can't forget the fact that lord Romanov and Cassian are still wandering the halls of the castle as well.

"You may call me Orkiathan."

"You killed a regent prince?" I ask even though I know the answer to that. He is a complete lunatic, whatever creature he is, he will die tonight.

"He was a pain, with all his babbling and when your invite came it was perfect timing for his life to end, no one in

Aerwyna knows what he looked like aside from the basic facts so I pretended to be him and slipped into your castle. There were a few incidents with maidens and I tried to keep it a secret but young blood tastes even better if they struggle against it."

Bile rises in my throat at his words, I don´t dare to turn around and look at Marianna´s body. He was the one feeding off of blood.

"Jamari, the man you so skillfully killed tonight, was a friend of mine but he is impulsive. Usually, he doesn´t listen to orders and it was his fate to die tonight because his task was to bring you here unharmed. It was bizarre how you stayed awake for so long after the blade of the bloodstone sliced your skin, you know we dropped a little toxin onto it because believe me I don´t underestimate your skills."

"Oh was that a compliment? Feels like we´re bonding." I spit out while I listen to his words intently. That´s why the wound on my arm didn´t stop burning and with a bloodstone, he refers to the weird-looking dagger, I knew something was up when I saw it. An image flashes in front of me for a second. Cassian cleaned the blade on his breeches, wiping off his blood. The small noise Lord Romanov made when he noticed. Does that mean that there wasn´t any toxin left on the blade? Either Cas didn´t know about it or he did it on purpose. I try to ignore the other possibility and swallow it down.

"Well, I did find out how you stayed so unharmed." His claws disappear into a pocket on his chest pulling out a shiny silver ring. The purple stone glimmers in the light and I inhale when I feel the emptiness of my ring finger.

"What a clever little boy Cassian is, isn't he? And yet he couldn't protect you what a shame."

My heart stings when he mentions the prince and I turn my head to the side to hide the emotions on my face.

"Oh struck a nerve? Wait, is that a tear I see? Poor girl."

I hear his footsteps nearing and a second later a hard grip latches onto my chin, turning my head to the horrific-looking creature.

A tear slips out of my eye and he catches it with his thumb, tasting it when he puts it in his mouth. My face turns into a grimace of disgust when he lets go of it and starts to laugh. But instead of distancing himself he grabs my arms and whirls me up onto my feet making me cry out in pain when his claws find their way into my skin.

That's it I am going to die. I'm going to die quietly and without a fight like a coward. Oh my gods I'm going to die like Ellister. But instead of killing me Marrus—Orkiathan or whatever his name is—holds me still as if he is listening to sounds my human ears can't catch. And after a beat of silence, I hear it too, footsteps that are coming closer. But they're not alone it sounds like the person is dragging something behind him. Something heavy.

My muscles tense in anticipation, and my stomach churns in horror. Oh please, Adales don't let it be another dead body, I'm not sure if I can hold in my condiments if I smell the horrific scent of death again.

"Seems like you will be reunited with your love sooner than you thought." He hisses in my ear and I curse myself for flinching before another person steps into the cold dungeons, his face no surprise to me.

Lord Romanov's eyes fly from the creature to me and the talons that are digging into my skin. His hand lets go of the heavy thing—which is another person—making him crash to his knees with a groan.

My heart stops and squeezes tightly before it goes on pounding loudly in my ears. Cassian is on his knees, his wrists and ankles chained up but instead of usual chains, his glimmer darkly with a hint of purple in them. Bloodstone.

Whatever the material is, it's burning the pale flesh on his wrists.

Why the hell would they chain him up?

"What are you doing, Orkiathan? I told you to not draw blood, she lost enough thanks to your stupid, idiot of a friend!"

Lord Romanov's voice is a hiss and I feel myself being tossed around to another person but my eyes don't move from the prince, whose eyes are fluttering up towards me. Their green irises are glowing the most intense color ever, making my stomach coil tightly.

"Princess."

It's just one word from his busted lips, it almost sounds like a breath but it makes a shiver run down my spine, clawing around my heart. It feels like I stop breathing for a second when I notice his bruised cheek, the claw-like gashes over his skin. There is a dark patch on his stomach, which grows larger with every second and it seems like it's giving me the rest.

Suddenly everything is forgotten, every little stab of betrayal or flare of anger that resides in my body. Flashes of hot kisses, gentle touches, us two fighting against the Protestants together, staring up at the night sky, telling him that I fell in love with him.

Something ticks inside me and I don't care how hurt I am or what bruises I have, I throw my head back in one movement, hearing the satisfying sound of a nose crack. I whirl around my muscles tense. My knee rams straight into Romanov's groin making him hiss but I don't stop as a deep sound emits from my throat and I force him against the wall. Concrete crumbles from the impact and my eyes blaze.

My hands wrap around his throat easily and I squeeze as hard as I can, my vision tinted red with rage. I feel someone behind me and kick out my leg with all the force I have left and spit on the ground in front of the creature which topples over surprised by the force of my kick.

The next time I have no such luck as its claws clash into my shoulder and throw me onto the ground. My back hits the cold marble and I swear I hear something crack. A soft groan leaves my lips. A deep guttural growl answers me and my head snaps to the side to see Cassian straining against the chains, which are glowing in purple light, and—oh gods, fangs are showing behind his curled lip. His eyes are glowing as his voice speaks up.

"Don't. Touch. Her."

I have never heard a voice like that before. It is a warning and even though he is chained up a shiver runs over my skin, making the hair stand alarmed.

His voice calls to something deep inside, flaring up a primal feeling.

The creature doesn't listen to him and squats down, his hands squeezing around my throat. I try to claw at his skin but he doesn't budge one bit. Blood is forming under my nails but it's my own. My vision blurs from the lack of oxygen and I almost think I imagine the voice booming faintly in the background.

"ENOUGH!"

The grip around my throat eases immediately and I turn to the side, gasping for air, coughing up blood.

"You idiots are not supposed to kill her!"

"She attacked first!"

"What are you five?" I hiss at the voice of Lord Romanov and I turn to see a third man has joined us. And nothing could've prepared me for what I see.

The deep lines that dance along his tan skin are so familiar. Hair the same color as mine, the same shine in them.

A face I once turned to seek help in the past. A face I once trusted even though I felt the change. That this was no longer my father was clearer as crystal. My squeezing heart crushes right under the cold stare he acknowledges me with and my eyes wander from him over to Cassian, whose eyes are glowing darkly, fangs still visible. I should've known he isn't human when I saw his green eyes turn so dark every time he got angered. I was naïve enough to trust him.

"Seems like you did a good job with her, Prince Cassian." My father says and I don't move my eyes from Cas who clenches his jaw and turns his head to escape my gaze. Fucking coward.

Can't even admit that he was a traitor and tricked me once again. My father steps over to me and offers his hand to help me up but I ignore him and get up on my own which takes a lot of energy from me. The pained groan that escapes me is inevitable.

"Three men against one woman, isn't that kind of pathetic?" I ask them making the lord glare at me while the creature stands behind him, is that fear on his face?

He fears the King of Aerwyna. . .What could scare a creature like him?

"From your little show right now it seems like it is necessary." My father says and I can't help but let my gaze slip to Cassian who still doesn't dare to look at me and it makes me almost crumble.

"Don't look at him, he's not going to help you. He is the one who got you into this position."

"That's a lie." Cas hisses making my father raise a brow and look at him.

"Is it? I remember you working against her. It was your idea, wasn't it? To make her fall in love with you and make her feel safe so we could conduct her and come right here to this moment."

A sharp inhale slips past my lips and Cassian's eyes go back to the ground. So Jamari was not lying. The realization hits me harder than I thought even though I already knew. My palms hit the cold wall behind me grounding me but somehow it feels like every ounce of hope has been squeezed out of my body.

I can manage to fight against one man unarmed, but a magical creature and two armed men? Even I wouldn't be able to win. I will die. I will die because I opened my heart and let Cassian slip past my walls.

People say that their heart breaks but that's a lie. It doesn't splinter into broken shards, which you can fix later with effort. Whatever happens in my chest is cold and hollow, something beyond repair.

"Don't look so surprised, honey, look at him." My father grips my chin and I try to escape his hands but they tighten and he turns my head to look at the blurred vision of Cassian kneeling in front of us.

Even though I try to stop them, the tears roll over my cheeks anyway.

"He couldn't do it. He fell in love with you, just like Demetrus. He asked you to stay with him this night so he could bring you safely to Demeter. Luckily once again you weren't obedient and left him to meet with Jamari, that was your mistake. Do you think I wouldn't recognize Gisella? I recognized her the second she stepped into the hall, dressed the way you were, you can't fool me, Carina. And even though it is a shame that Prince Cassian couldn't escape the lure of Sebestyen woman he is dispensable."

With every word, he reveals it feels like he's digging a deeper grave for my body.

"You're wrong." I snap through my tears, closing my eyes because I can't stand to look at the prince.

"Cassian is not able to feel anything besides greed and anger, he doesn't even know what love feels like," I say before I open my eyes again to stare hatefully at the face of the man I once called my father.

The man quirks a brow and holds out his palm towards Orkiathan who drops the purple stoned ring into his hand.

"Do you even know what this is? How rare this stone is?" He holds the ring up and my eyes narrow lightly, what is it about this ring that they all act up about it?

Instead of answering him, I let him talk because I don't have the strength in me to say anything.

"It is a stone made out of the petals of your favorite flower, ground with the blood of an Upyr and carved into a bloodstone. It is used to protect anyone from dark magic, or any kind of magic, that is why you didn't drop the second you left the banquette hall."

My eyes snap up to him confused. He grins satisfied that he made sure to own my attention. I have no idea what he is talking about.

"That and the fact he cleaned the damn blade on his breeches. He tried to save you from any kind of manipulation or toxin."

He throws a glare over to the prince who dares to grin in satisfaction.

"You'd think I actually would go with your plan?" Cas hisses and my skin crawls when his canines appear again.

"A pathetic attempt at fooling me. Well in the end it was her love for you that drove her back anyway. So it was all in vain."

Cassian tenses at his smirk.

My mind races and I can't stop myself from pushing around him, making the lord take a step towards me but my father raises a hand making him freeze.

"Is that true?" I ask my voice cold as ice as I stare down at Cassian. He doesn't answer which makes me swallow.

"Look me in the face and tell me if it's true or not," I repeat my eyes flying over the dark curls, the beautifully carved cheekbones, and the long lashes that hide my favorite color. Pine green meets my eyes as he stares up at me.

"It is. I wanted you to have it so you could be safe, if you'd listened to me we would be gone by now on our way home."

"Home? Do you think your kingdom is my home after you repeatedly betrayed me? After I let you creep inside my heart and foolishly use that to your advantage—"

"—that's not why—"

"Don't interrupt me!" I hiss at him and he clamps his mouth shut, his eyes shining up at me. He looks so vulnerable right now that it is hard to believe he plotted against me. But it is a mask, it always was from the moment I met him that night.

"Carina, what I told you before the ball, I meant every single word of it. It wasn't played I promise it was true." He tells me desperately but I still feel the chill spreading in my heart. Someone steps up to my back and a cold blade is placed in my hand.

"Do it, he is a traitor, he deserves death, Carina."

My father murmurs and I swallow hard as green eyes move over my face.

"Kill me, it won't change a thing. It won't change what you felt when we touched. I was sent to protect you—"

"Well congratulations, you royally fucked up in that department." I interrupt him.

He moves a bit forward on his knees even though it hurts him.

"No one could fake the things that we felt, Carina. I know you're angry—"

"Angry? You think I'm angry?" I scoff as I close my eyes for a second.

I open them when I can't push the images of the past weeks away.

"I'm not fucking angry. I am raging."

"And I don't blame you. Be angry at me; take it out all on me. I am happy to spend the rest of my life earning your forgiveness. If I have to I would turn the world by its hinges for you."

I hate what he says. I hate it with every cell in my body because it feels too fucking real.

"Empty words like always." The king murmurs behind me. I shudder for a moment before I make my decision, the weight of the dagger cold in my hand.

Instead of using the dagger I whirl around and go for the man standing behind me.

He has moved so quickly that I didn't even see him as he grips the dagger out of my hand, my hands on my back, pressed against his chest as the blade is held up against my throat.

"That was a big mistake."

"Was it? Don't you think I know I have no chance against you? Just kill me I don't care anymore." I hiss but I just get a chuckle in return. I don't have the strength in me to fight anymore. Everyone I cared for is dead. I don't know what is right or wrong and I'm too tired to figure it out.

"You don't even want to know why you're here?"

"I'm sure it's a stupid testosterone reason of greed and power." I hiss making lord Romanov chuckle.

"Shut your mouth you're just the king's little bitch." I hiss at him making him growl but my father stops him.

I don't dare to move with the blade against my throat and hear Cassian groan as he tries to fight against the chains.

It seems like they glow harder every time he moves and I realize that the bloodstone must be the only thing holding him down. It seems to affect whatever magic floods through his veins.

"Glorious thing isn't it? A weapon made out of his kind of blood. You should know the blood of an Upyr is a powerful thing, not just can it create weapons used as death on their own but it can flare up ancient magic." At his words, Cassian's head snaps up his eyes wide as if he didn't realize what this was about.

"You can't know," Cassian murmurs unbelievingly making me frown.

"What the fuck are you even talking about?" I snarl, my limbs aching in this uncomfortable position.

"It is so little you know, Princess Katarina, it seems like we have to dive into a whole history lesson, why don't you get comfortable."

He lets go of me and throws me onto my knees right beside Cassian. His arms grip my waist under a groan of pain to soften my fall but I quickly brush them off of me staring up at the king.

I try to ignore the spark of his touch and the weird feeling that erupts every time. The feeling that we belong to each other.

"I had enough history lessons in this life, I have a date with death and I would like to be punctual."

"Oh believe me this story will capture you completely." My father says twirling the dagger around in his hands. I glare at him not wanting to drag this out but it seems like he doesn't care at all. I ignore Cassian's warmth at my side and sigh defeated

"What is the story about?"

The king grins dubiously.

"It is the story of Katarina Sebestyen."

45

"There was once the first god, some would call him the father of gods and creation, born behind the gates of Empyrean. It was a place where gods and goddesses found their home, and could spend their time watching over the humans. The god who watched over all of them was called Adales—"

"Not that again." I groan but shut up when all three of the men narrow their eyes lightly. Touchy subject, I see. Maybe I´ll die out of boredom when he tells me the story everyone knows again.

"Once the humans started to become greedy and hungry for power, they stopped honoring the gods and became careless. Adales was enraged and sent four gods, four children of his, down from Empyrean, to remind the humans that the gods were still present under them."

I stiffen at his words, confused by the new prosperity, the siblings were gods? That certainly is new information.

A ghastly feeling flushes me, a tickle at the back of my head. Alarm bells ring in my ears and the image of the boy that helped Cas and me during the Protestant attack flashes in my mind.

Find the story of the beginning. Did he possibly mean the story of Adalon and the four siblings? But not the one written in the books.

"They were grateful to have the task; they would still live an immortal life watching over the humans and making sure the balance of life continued as it was. Polyxenus the god of the skies and protection was gifted with a form to turn into, keeping his wings. His skin would turn hot, once he changed; he was made out of indestructible stone, claws long and sharp to defend any treasure, horns growing out of his head, and fangs out of his mouth. His blood turned into hot lava, making it poisonous for anyone who touched it. They were the protectors of the sky and called the Custos."

My breath hitches at his words and I shift uncomfortably. This is a whole different story from what I know and it seems like everyone knew besides me.

And even though I was not interested in the beginning a sharp tingle that runs down my spine, tells me that I need to pay attention.

"Oceanus, the god of the seas was gifted with lungs that could breathe on the coasts and under the deepest waters, eyes as white as you've seen, able to see in the dark. I think you already made the acquaintance with a Tengeri." The king motions over to Orkiathan and I swallow hard, remembering the time when he posed as a guard, his eyes turned the same white as today.

"While the Tengeri were gifted with immortal life they needed to have a flaw and could only live as long as they fed on the blood of living souls, while the Custos were gifted with a life for just over a thousand years," Orkiathan growls at that fact and I roll my eyes, that little bitch kills people to live forever as if thousands of years wasn't good enough.

"Demetrus. . .he was a special god, he ruled over the lands of Gehenna, where all the sinners resided after they paid with their life. He was the god of death and gifted with the most wicked green eyes, able to see straight through souls and judge if they were worthy of Empyrean or not. His species was called the Upyr, they have deathly fangs, skin thin as ice but hard as stone.

Unfortunately, they have to feed just like the Tengeri but it seems like they have more strength to stop before it's too late."

My eyes fly to Cas beside me whose jaw is clenched hard.

He isn't listening to this story for the first time.

Deep horror crawls into my veins, of course, he's not, he is the regent of a god of death. I try to keep my emotions intact but that sliver of information makes me sick to my stomach. The fact that he could hide his true nature, that deep down he is a monster from one's wildest nightmares.

"Yes, your little prince is one of them. They can be quite possessive of what they claim to protect, it must be driving him crazy to be this near beside you when your fresh blood is oozing out of every cut."

The king grins when the prince lets out a low snarl at his words.

A sound that makes my spine bend and my skin crawl. I let a dangerous creature touch me, make me feel things. So many times I felt like he looked at me like I was his prey. I couldn't be more accurate.

"I could almost taste his hunger when he cut into your arm this night it was delirious. Tell me, Cassian, how much time has passed since you fed on someone?"

The king squats down in front of us making the prince's body grow rigid. I hold my breath, scared of what happens next but instead of pouncing, Cassian settles on a snarky remark.

"Why? Are you offering? I bet you taste as foul as your soul smells."

He can smell souls? I might throw up.

The king doesn't feel the slightest bit threatened as he stands up and puts his eyes on me.

"Once an Upyr finds his partner they refuse to feed from anyone else than them which means Cassian over here hasn´t fed in a long time. You know that is why you´re in this position, your weak with emotions and didn´t have enough blood in you to fight the blade and the toxin."

"Get me out of these chains and we´ll see how weak I am."

The prince growls back making me tense up. Whatever the king initiates with those words is something that should bounce off of my mental wall and yet it makes my heart clench once again.

The king notices with a slight raise of his brow before his cold eyes turn back on me.

"Not so perfect anymore your little prince is he? I´m sure he can smell the utter disgust you have for him now. What does she smell like, Cassian?"

The prince refuses to answer, making the king growl and take a step forward dagger in his hands but I push Cassian behind me glaring at the king.

If Cassian is as powerful as they say he is my only way out. I need to get the chains from his wrists and ankles so he can stand, I´m sure he would fight the men and I could slip away. I don´t know where to go but as far away from this castle as I can, sounds like a good plan.

The king is wrong, I´m not disgusted by the prince of Demeter. Neither am I angry. There is just nothing. A big black hole replaced the space under my left breast where once was a steady beating. The dagger stops right at my throat making the lord chuckle. My eyes fly to him almost forgetting his presence.

"Even now she can't but protect him, what a pathetic pair you are." He says and I narrow my eyes at him.

"The only thing standing between you and your death is the king, I wouldn't be so arrogant and think you'd have a chance against me." I hiss making Orkiathan speak up.

"She sure has fire."

"Shut it." The king shuts them both up and I am slightly amused when the lord glares at me.

If they think I will go down quietly they're wrong.

Maybe I can take one last life before I leave because my soul is lost anyway.

Taking Lord Romanov with me is my last will.

"Finish the story father, I am getting bored with, you lot," I tell him lazily when he retreats.

"That's a good way to start. You certainly know of your ancestor, Aerwyn. The most beautiful woman in the whole Empyrean. The Goddess of health and love, she was the most beautiful creature out there and yet so weak. She had eyes glowing like the moon, hair spun out of moonlight and she was loved by many. Adales loved her the most of his children, granting her immortal life without the need to take blood from another. She trampled that gift egoistically. There was one rule the gods needed to follow. It was allowed to not feel lonely, to have lovers but to never birth a child with someone else than a god."

"Let me guess that is what she did," I say lazily because it is so obvious.

The king ignores me and goes on pacing.

"The goddess fell in love with a magical creature that once lived called the Faye's. Descendants of the fairies; were shy creatures, untrusting of any living being besides themselves because their blood was pure magic. They were mortal creatures which didn´t mean they were easy to be killed. People still tried. Many of them were Faye warriors, able to defeat their enemy with their strength and wit, their wings were some of the most beautiful views in this world. A gift from the goddess Enya before she left to rest.

She gifted them with wings as light as the sky of Empyrean, a storm of purple-blue tones and white, the color of bloodstone. But it is not the only thing they were gifted with. You see, the magic in their veins gifted them with one thing no one could create: life."

"Where are they now?" I ask curiosity flooding me, I can´t hold back the shiver when he talks about the Faye. Their wings the color of bloodstone, the color of my flowers; the Night-crawlers.

This feels too much of a coincidence.

"Dead. Adales made sure to kill them all in his wrath and he started with Kaycen, the love of Aerwyn. She did the only thing she wasn´t allowed to and birthed a child with the Faye, ensuring the spark of life in the child´s body. Adales was outrageous and fuming. He wanted to see the child and make sure it wouldn´t have stronger powers than himself. Aerwyn wouldn´t let him and with the help of Demetrus she hid the child, it took a lot of magic and power to hide something from the father of the gods and it took, Polyxenus and Oceanus to help keep it a secret. Adales made sure to kill his beloved daughter with his own hands and take the immortal life from both Demetrus and Oceanus. Still, they wouldn´t give up the secret and Demetrus went as far as to mark every regent of his with the task to protect the child."

"What the hell has that to do with me? This child is dead anyway, I´m not responsible for Aerwyn´s mistake." I say and stand up confused. Forgotten is a way out once I realize these men are just lunatics on a revenge trip for something I didn´t do. Even if her child got to live and carry on my bloodline, it is long gone and I don´t carry any magic inside me. That´s for sure.

"You think a whole continent broke when an immortal child was born? Demetrus and Aerwyn combined their powers and hid the child for over a million centuries. This child grew up and into a woman until she died. And reawakened. She must have lived over a thousand lives hidden, thanks to the Demetrus line who were sworn to protect her, the child who had not just a goddess of health and love as her mother but the magic of life in her veins. She is the last of the regent of the Faye´s."

I stop breathing at his words, the answer written in his eyes.

"What you are saying is. . ." I trail off not able to speak the words. No, no, no. This is just another trick of his. Whatever his motives are he must be completely mad. Twenty minutes ago I didn´t even know magic existed and now he thinks I´m her daughter?

"That I am not a Sebestyen man and so wasn´t your mother. The Kingdom of Aerwyn broke when she died; the only regent left was her child that was nowhere to be found. Since then a line of humans ruled on the throne of the Fallen Kingdom until now. Because now I finally found you, Carina, the daughter of Kaycen and Aerwyn. The rightful regent of this fallen kingdom."

46

No.

He must be joking. It can't be true, I must be over a thousand years old to be her daughter and I can't remember one life besides the one I have now. I don't have any magic in my blood nor am I some kind of magic creature. He is my father, he has the same sapphire eyes as I do, I lived with him my whole life, yes he was not a good father after my mother passed but I never could imagine that we didn't share the same blood. It can't be true that Henri isn't my brother, that beautiful whirlwind of a boy, a soul I protected my whole life, ensuring he could experience the dreams that I never had.

"You're lying."

My voice doesn't sound like mine.

"Do you think I would make all this fuss and lie about something as important as this?" The king hisses and it seems like the world stops at this moment.

Chains break and Cassian towers in front of me like a dark shadow. My body seems to be stuck in a rigid state, not able to move, comprehend or even breathe. How the fuck did he get free?

I watch the prince move in seconds, how he is in front of me and then he's not. I see a whirl of nothing as Lord Romanov drops to the ground, his throat ripped open making me inhale horrified. Orkiathan pounces at the prince who elegantly ducks away from his claws, his fist colliding with the creature's cheek. His head flies and he spits blood but he doesn't have time to recover when Cassian's head moves and his canines slice right through the throat of the monster. A wailing sound erupts from his mouth, making a shiver of fear run down my spine. There is no doubt that it hurt like hell. Like it wasn't slicing through muscles and bone rather than through silk. I hold my breath, fear sitting deep in my bones for the first time in my life. Cassian's head turns and he looks at me, blood dripping from his lips, his eyes glowing. His eyes widen when he looks behind me and he tries to move but freezes the second I feel something cold against my throat.

A shuddering breath escapes me when I feel the presence of the king in my back, his blade against my throat.

Cassian takes a step forward, away from Orkiathan who's clutching his neck.

"I wouldn't do that if I were you." The king drawls and exerts more pressure against my throat. A small nip of pain washes through me when I feel my blood dripping down my throat. Cassian tenses but doesn't move again.

"Let her go. Let her go or I swear I'm going to rip off your balls and shove them up your ass so you're going to choke—"

I gasp when the king digs his knee into my back causing me to crush to my knees on the floor.

"If you're finished with your little fantasy now, I would ask you to get to your knees." The voice of the king is lazy as if he knew Cassian would listen to him. Dark shadows swirl in the prince's eyes and I'm sure he's about to pounce again but a soft breath escape at his next movement. He. Drops. To. His. Knees. The pressure in my back eases slightly and I watch in horror as Orkiathan steps to Cassian a wild look in his eyes.

He grabs the curls of the prince and tugs his head back painfully, making my fingers spasm. Orkiathan bares his canines and cold hard panic flashes through me when I realize what he's about to do.

"No!"

I trash against the king's hold when Orkiathan snarls.

"I swear to the gods if you touch him, I'm going to rip you apart," I growl not even recognizing my voice.

The creature chuckles darkly before coming close to the prince's throat, who doesn't fucking move. Why is he not getting out of here? I trash again, scraping my knees against the ground as something tugs deep at my soul.

"Enough." The king's voice makes the Tengeri hesitate before he looks back at us.

"You can get your revenge later, we still need him."

"But I—"

"I said enough."

He lets go of the prince's hair reluctantly, keeping his distance. I try to hold eye contact with Cassian to make him explain what the fuck he thinks he's doing.

"This will go one way and one way only." The king says and finally releases the blade from my throat. I immediately wind my fingers around the small gash to see how deep it is. Seems like he just grazed my skin slightly to scare Cassian off.

"How hard is this for you right now? The scent of her blood after so many days without feeding?" The king walks toward the prince who doesn't dare to look up. I only now notice his taut muscles, his stiff body remaining on his knees as if he is waiting for his death blow.

"I heard it is bearable when it´s someone strange but almost explosive for someone you claim. Is that what you did prince? Did you already taint her soul and claim Carina?"

My stomach hurls at his words when I see it gets a reaction out of the prince.

"It must cost you all your life´s years to hold yourself back. To not pierce your fangs through her skin and taste the burning—"

"Stop." I interrupt him rudely.

Those sapphire eyes place themselves on me, a dark brow raised.

"Whatever it is that you want just do it already. There is no reason in torturing him."

The king straightens, something glistening in his eyes.

"How can you after all hold affection for him?"

"It´s not affection, it's a fucking death wish. I can´t listen to your voice anymore." I hiss and finally get the reaction I want. The king's eyes narrow and it appears that his string of patience has finally snapped.

Oh, how I wish I could´ve held back my stupid mouth.

The king walks behind the prince and unbuckles the manacles, making my jaw almost unhinge itself.

"What are you—NO!" My sentence ends in a scream when the king steps forward again, slashing his blade right through Cassian´s throat. Dark blood oozes out of the cut but the prince doesn´t let a sound.

"He will heal no place for distress here." The king says it as if he didn´t just slash someone´s throat.

I don´t care what happens next as I crawl over to Cassian still sitting on his knees. My hands cover his gushing blood as my eyes met his asking him a silent question.

Are you okay?

He raises a brow in return.

My fucking throat got sliced open.

It is beyond me how he doesn´t feel any ounce of pain right now. His blood floods right over my arms, my skin humming weirdly at the contact.

"If you´re finished with your panic concert we may continue." I turn my head at the king's voice, narrowing my eyes.

"You´re a fucking monster."

"I´m well aware honey, thanks."

Something pulses inside me, the desire to wrap my hands around his throat and squeeze until he chokes, most prominent.

"It´s alright it´s going to heal." Cassian´s gentle voice makes me turn my head. His eyes gesture down to his manacle-free wrists as realization dawns on me. This is our chance; the king stands far enough for me to run. I could if I wanted to. If I can risk Cassian´s life for it.

"He´s right it´s going to heal. That's why you need to listen, Carina."

"I´m not going to listen to you for a minute longer you bastard."

The king scoffs at my tone his eyes focusing on the dagger in his hands.

"Feed off of him."

My body freezes at his words.

"The fuck she's going to do." The prince snaps and I feel his muscles tighten under my poor attempt to stop the blood flow.

"You're a lunatic."

I tell the pacing king who suddenly looks smug.

"Feed. Off. Of. Him."

Anger ripples through my body hot and strong.

"I'm not going to fucking feed on him."

Even the thought makes me nauseous, the iron stench churning my insides. The king sighs almost satisfied. Cassian and I both watch him, our bodies frozen. Anticipating his next move.

"Oh, I hoped you would say that." It's just a low rumble and maybe I should've seen it coming. My senses should go on high alert when he drops Cassian's manacles. The king might be a monster but he is not stupid. But I never thought that he would be the cause of my death.

I don't even have time to anticipate his move as the world tips, and freezes like a goddamn cubicle.

The times I stabbed people I thought the second the blade pierced their skin it would feel like an endless fire. A fire that's so destructive it makes any capacity to move dissolve. But when the king rams his blade right through my heart it is cold and hollow. I don't feel the impact at first. I don't even realize what happens until I meet those damned green eyes.

Trace how they drop from my face to my chest.

It is the trigger for me to follow his gaze to see that the black blade of the king has been pushed right through my skin and into my heart.

Cold seeps from the dark blade, and stretches through my blood and skin, sticking, tugging at me. Just now I realize what happened and before I can take my next breath I fall to my knees. The breaking of bones moves like an earthquake through the dungeons. The soaring pain comes a second later and I grasp the blade between my fingers not knowing what to do. A blur of dark curls washes in front of me before I realize that Cassian caught me.

I feel the blood ooze out of the wound and my mouth, coughing to get it out of my screaming lungs. I almost choke on the liquid as I stare into the most beautiful eyes I have seen in my life.

"Carina! Hey, hey everything is going to be fine." His voice is smooth and warm as his hands cradle my face but I can´t hear him as my head grows dizzy, gurgling sounds moving around me as if I am underwater. I must´ve already lost a lot of blood because I already smell the scent of death.

Maybe it´s coming from the lord who is lying on the ground.

"You. . .bitch." I say looking at the king who looks quite pleased with the prince cradling me to his chest. I grip the material of his soft shirt sighing. The pain moves out of my chest and it feels like I´m being lifted, every breath comes out shallow, shorter than the last. Finally.

It feels like it took ages for me to die and I´m thankful that it finally happens. It might be in the arms of a traitor yet I feel content. I try to imagine how things would´ve changed if Cas was a good man. An honest man.

If every tainted darkness inside him and me wouldn´t exist. If we still would´ve found each other in the way that we did.

Flashes of a girl and a boy, barely in their teenage years appear in spots in front of my eyes.

The boy with curly hair grins charmingly at the girl with sapphire eyes. They're both human, growing up together.

Friendship blossoms into love, so deep and light it makes them both feel alive in every kind of way.

I see myself in white material, a glow that looks almost magical on my face.

Cas appears behind me, winding his arms around my torso his lips pressing a lovingly kiss against my cheek.

"You can save her, Cassian, you know how." The voice of the king pulls me out of the possible future I would've wished for.

"That is what you wanted all along to let her feed from me and reawaken the magic inside her veins."

I hear Cassian hiss at the man towering over us.

What the hell are they talking about?

They should stop screaming and be quiet for a goddamn minute. I feel cheerfully light and try to ignore their harsh words.

"I can't even die in peace," I say—well it is what I try to say but I think my words weirdly gurgle due to the blood pooling in my mouth.

"Shut up. You don't deserve to die. I did all of this so you could live and now you're dying but I'll make sure you won't, I'm sorry to not give you the chance, Carina." The prince whispers and my eyes widen as I shake my head. Whatever he thinks he is going to do I will not let that happen. I don't want to feed from anyone and become whatever the hell he is. What would be life as a creature with a cold heart? It would be nothing but death for an endless time.

"Don't, please don't. "

I try to shake my head but it is too heavy to move. I focus on his face trying to stay awake but my eyes flutter every damn second before I drop into the unconscious. Please let me die.

~ 47 ~

Wake up. Wake up. Wake up.

A groan startles me and I flinch before I realize it left my lips. Wait, wasn't I dead? I sure as hell don't feel dead. It feels like my body moves to the pits of the ground, the Abyss pulling at my skin as if it is meant to be that I resume in Gehenna. Time for me to pay my debts.

I wonder if Cassian's father sent me here, searching for a good soul inside of me but he didn't find anything.

And I don't blame him. I lost, I lost the battle I tried to fight but it seems like I was trying to go against all odds. The gods only know if Cassian survived. What little time I have left in this weird state, floating between Empyrean and Gehenna, I use to pray.

For the first time in my life—or death—I pray.

I pray that the fondness Cassian had for my brother wasn't played and if he survived that he will make sure Henri stays safe. I pray Edlyn somehow sensed the danger and took my dresses, swords, or anything valuable and fled for the capital so she will be in no danger. Maybe she can get some gold coins out of the things and flee the kingdom.

I pray for my subjects, that whatever happens, they will get the regent they deserve who can protect them and fight for them, defeat the Protestants and stabilize the kingdom again.

Because I was not able to and I never will be able.

But I pray that my death wasn't for nothing and that somehow even if it is just a small stir, it will make the people fight. Fight for their freedom and their lives, fight like I didn't. It is their only chance and I pray that they should use it wisely.

I also pray for the mother who raised me and that even if my body doesn't find Empyrean that hers did. To raise someone else's child, knowing it was not of your blood must be hard. She still did it and received nothing but the end of her life. I pray for the real mother I never had an encounter with, who went against every odd so bravely out of love. Out of love for Kaycen and their child.

For me.

If it is true that Demetrus helped her and the rest of his brothers I pray for them too, I apologize for the trouble I've caused, to be the reason so many people left their life, just for me to turn out as a pathetic human who couldn't even protect herself. You're far from pathetic.

The words pulse straight through my body, making my fingers spasm. Wait my fingers? Oh my gods I can feel my fingers!

It's just a small tingling sensation but it starts at the tips and wanders up my palms over the skin where. . .where my pulse is beating. I am not dead. I try to grasp onto something, listening for the voice, as the tingle floods over my arms and stops at my shoulders. It feels like I'm lying down on a boat, crashing waves making my body roll and toss, nausea swirling in my stomach.

The amounts of times that I felt sick these last past hours is ridiculous as if my stomach still hasn't adjusted to this horrible feeling. The waves crush even harder, claws pulling at my skin, and soaring pain erupts from inside of me. A mute scream escapes my sealed lips as I claw at myself, my skin trying to choke the fire that resides inside of me, burning me alive. This is it.

This is my punishment, I took the right in my hands and killed humans, humans with souls and now I would pay for it in ten thousand ways worse.

I feel the skin tear under my sharp nails, hot liquid oozing out of the burns, cooling my skin down. My jaw clenches hard and stabbing pain itches at the soft flesh of my mouth. My hair feels like it is being ripped from my scalp.

I can´t take this much longer, it feels like it has been days or years.

If this is what every soul endures during their transition to Gehenna I am sorry for every lost life. Another pulse of pain moves through me but this time it feels warmer and it comes along with a whisper. Wake up. Wake up. Wake up. How can I wake up? I fear being drenched in blood once I squeeze my eyes open, soaring pain in my veins.

"I can´t!"

The words leave my lips in a cry as my body spasms, exhausted to fight the pain inside.

"You can. It´s not hurting, Carina, it is your mind. You need to let go."

I barely grasp the whispered words as my nails scratch at my scalp; my breath comes quick and shallow as I try to move the lids of my eyes. It´s impossible, the pain is too much.

"Let go, Carina."

The voice presses again and for a moment it feels like all the oxygen squeezes out of my lungs, giving me the ability to properly think again.

The voice is right; there is no pain, no burning, or clawing. My body is fine, it is just my head. The next breath I take is filled with nothing but relief.

I don't waste a second before my lids fly open and I feel the lengths of my lashes brush the bottom of my brows.

The moment I open my eyes I squeeze them at the blinding light in front of me.

"Good gods, I wouldn't have thought it would be this bad."

My head snaps to the side as the light disappears into a soft glow that enhances a figure. My eyes zero in on my surroundings noticing that I'm still in the dungeons of the castle. The torches are lit on the walls but there is no sight of Cassian or the king. How is this possible?

"They didn't overstep the line of life and death they're not with us."

My head snaps back to the voice and I watch a woman step out of the glowing light. I inhale sharply as the figure comes into focus, the skin not stopping to glow. It is of the palest blue, the veins a soft purple under the thin skin, swirling, moving endlessly.

Hair like spun moonlight envelopes the unearthly woman in long strands, falling down her dainty shoulders like a waterfall. It swivels around her soft hips, flowing like the material of her white dress that drapes around her body like she was born in it.

Two silver bands wrap around the soft flesh of her upper arms the flowy material attached to them, circling her arms. It's almost impossible to move my eyes from her beautiful body but I compel them to move from her astonishing gown up over her tight stomach and her round breasts, wander the lengths of her throat, over luscious, soft lips. The cupid's bow is swung in a heart shape and leads up to a straight nose and eyes. . .gods, eyes that look like two pools of the moon.

The white swirls dangerously, the soft grey ring around them like a barrier. Slightly elongated ears poke out of the almost white hair, making her look like a fairy. The goddess of health and love doesn't even come close to what I imagined.

Her skin glows with the prospect of health, and small ornaments are etched into the highs of her cheeks.

"Aerwyn," I speak without even thinking and try to get up on my feet but don't make it far as my head spins and I drop onto all fours, inhaling sharply at the dizziness.

The dark ground of the dungeons is in front of me calming my senses slightly. A warm tingly feeling erupts on my shoulder, spreading through my whole body as I look up and right into the pools of the moon.

Aerwyn's hand is pressed to my shoulder and to no doubt she is using her powers to make sure my body doesn't collapse right in front of her. What a pathetic picture I make.

"This meeting is long overdue but as disappointing as it might be, we don't have enough time for formalities."

Her voice rings softly, powerful and lucid. The most beautiful voice I have ever heard, it wraps itself around you like a viper.

My body is warm all over again and when she feels like I won't vomit in front of her—which would be embarrassing—she lets go of me and takes a step back. I don't have the strength to stand up so I stay put and sit on the cold ground.

It somehow cools my mind and I'm able to think around this ripple of power that oozes off of the goddess.

"What do you mean we don't have enough time? Why am I here?"

"You are here because Prince Cassian Moreau saved you." She says her eyes wandering over my face and somehow I feel little under her gaze. This is my mother, the woman who birthed me and did everything in her power so I could be kept safe. This must be a hallucination maybe I'm currently lying on these dungeon grounds on the verge of death and my pathetic mind is making this up.

"It's not your mind making this up. You died of the blade of the false king and usually Demetrus would've sent you up so your soul could rest in Empyrean with me but his regent stepped in."

"We should've seen it coming."

A dark voice speaks up and I topple back when I notice a second person hiding in the shadows. I inhale so deeply that my lungs burn and my heart stutters when the handsome man steps into the soft glow of the goddess.

I thought she was looking threatening but now that the tall frame of the man stands in contrast to hers she looks like a child. His broad shoulders stretch under his dark garments, two swords strapped to his sides. He looks like a warrior with his stance b it is obvious that he is by her side to protect her even though I know she would be able to handle herself.

It doesn't take the dark, long curls touching his shoulders, the high cheekbones, or the mischievous smile on his rosy lips. All it takes are those green eyes, swirling with dark shadows and a cocky glint in them.

Holy shit I might pass out. I don´t have just a goddess standing in front of me but two gods and one of them looks exactly like Cassian. Demetrus Moreau.

"Holy fuck, you look just like him. I´m sorry—" I start eyes wide when I notice my curse but the god interrupts me with a dark rumble of laughter.

"Well, as far as I know, he looks like me."

His voice sounds like honey and fire, with a deep timbre. Holy fuck this man—god—is oozing charm from bottom to top.

"You probably know my brother, Carina, Demetrus. He came with me because he´s got the opinion it would be safer for me." I raise a brow at her words and let my eyes wander over to him.

"I think she´s pretty able to defend herself, she´s a kick-ass goddess."

The words slip from my mouth without thinking and when I anticipate his anger I see nothing but a grin on his lips and a spark of familiarity in his eyes.

"I know she is. Maybe it was a tactic so she could take me with her, for me to get to know my niece."

"In that case, I would pick out my most gorgeous gown and offer you a stroll in the gardens but unfortunately I´m dead."

He chuckles at my joke and something moves in the air. A feeling of home skittles along my spine. . . like I belong.

It floods my veins, warming me from the inside. My blood sings and my mind clears up, healing the physical wounds. The feeling gets snatched away when Aerwyn speaks up again.

"As much as I would like to enjoy this moment, our time is limited as I said. Cassian injected you his blood which made you trespass the line of death and now you´re in what we call Purgatorium, it is where all the souls await their fate, to be sent to Empyrean or Gehenna."

"That would be my task." Demetrus throws in but shuts up quickly when Aerwyn shoots him a look. I observe their interactions and can´t push down the shock I feel. He was told to be as cold as death, the people fearing him while she was his opposite, soft and flirty but it seems like they switched the roles. Demetrus is the light one, joking, grinning like a small child while Aerwyn acted as if she was responsible for him. It´s an exciting observation.

"Where are you going to send me?" I ask my uncle unsure.

"I´m going to send you nowhere, Cas made sure the second you leave Purgatorium your body will be as it was in the human realm. His blood has saved you from death." His words make me shiver as I stare at the ground.

Cassian saved me?

"Your soul won´t be spending too much time in Purgatorium that´s why we need to cut to the chase. I am so sorry for all of this to happen to you, Carina, I wish there was a different way to tell you all of this. The second you wake up again, you need to make sure to run, to run as fast and as far as you can. The false king is not your only enemy and certainly not the most dangerous."

"What do you mean?" I ask alarmed as I stare into the beautiful face of the goddess, whose forehead is scrunched in worry. It´s the most agonizing grimace I´ve ever seen.

"Adales is not what the legends make him out to be. There is not enough time to tell you about all the cruel things he did—
"

"He took your lover, didn't he? The king said he killed Kaycen and that he killed all of you how is it even possible that you two are here?" I say blinking confused at them. Tension builds in my body as if I'm pulled towards something.

"He didn't just take my mate, he took a lot of lives. He tried to kill us but he didn't succeed. We all went into hiding in between the realms so he is not able to find us. But with what Cassian did things will change."

"Change how?" I urge them but instead of focusing on them, I clutch my stomach as the pulling sensation appears again. Nausea tumbles through me.

"We don't have much more time left," Demetrus murmurs to his sister while I put my palm against the ground trying to stabilize my body. It hasn't been long but it seems like I just had little time in this transitioning state. Aerwyn suddenly squats down and takes my face into her hands. It's a weirdly humane gesture so unlike a goddess.

"Adales is more powerful than you could ever imagine but you can stop him. You are the only thing in the realms that he fears that is why we hid you."

A harsh breath escapes me.

"Are you crazy what can a human do against a god? Not just a god but the god of all gods?" I breathe out confused as my head starts to spin.

"You need to leave Aerwyna, it doesn´t matter how but Carina—listen you need to leave this kingdom and look for the Fatums."

The what? She must be joking.

"The Fatums are a legend." I press out making Demetrus chuckle.

"Just like we are." He says and I give him that point. Usually, I am not this trusting but something deep inside me, something that has been slumbering for way too long tells me that I can trust them.

"Where do I find them?" I ask Aerwyn to see her blurring in front of my eyes.

"Try to travel to Demeter. . .help you. . .Carina?" Her words are like a puzzle as my eyes flutter. I get sick at the sensation of a pull at my navel but I try to focus again. My vision sharpens and I see both gods squat down in front of me.

"King Ronan Moreau will help you. . .don't trust. . .powerful." Aerwyn sounds urgent but I can´t seem to focus. It´s like I´m dropping in and out of consciousness.

My eyes flutter again my vision blurring.

The room starts to spin destroying my orientation. I don´t know if I´m on the floor or at the ceiling, the temperature drops around me rapidly. My skin turns to ice, the feeling enveloping my whole body like a bubble.

"I might be sick." I choke out as I try to stay awake.

"Fuck. It´s too late." Is that Demetrus voice?

"I´m sorry. . .Carina, make sure. . .Cas."

"I love you. . ."

The words mix and match into a whirlwind of chaos and before I can try to open my eyes again the ground underneath me crumbles and I fall. I fall right into nothing.

"You were too late. Do you know what that means?"

"That I'm going to kill you."

A sensory overload hits me. My body crashes back into existence, the light feeling vanishes in an instant. I'm back into flesh and bone under the living. There are no soft melodic voices of the gods I was with. They're too loud for my sensitive ears which leads me to flip open my eyes. How long was I even out? It feels like it has been days but when I look around I notice I'm still in the cold dungeons. This time a horrible stench clings to the walls, burning my nostrils. I gag for a moment the scent unbearable.

I try to detect where the smell is coming from and my eyes don't take long before they focus on Lord Romanov, lying on the ground. Gods it smells horrible, worse than the last time. It burns my throat and makes my eyes water while I wonder how much time has passed. A choked sound snatches my attention and washes nausea away. I ignore the lord lying in his blood and notice two other people, with beating hearts. I turn on my side, wincing when white hot pain rushes through me. The pain is nothing compared to the horrific picture that appears in front of me.

The king is pinning Cassian to the dungeon walls, his back scraping against the stone. His whole hand wraps around his delicate throat, squeezing and closing his airways.

A torch illuminates the prince's face, trailing over the hard edges and soft lips. A sharp inhale escapes me when I notice the blood dripping down his chin, painting a stark contrast against his pale skin.

Even from this angle, there is no mistaking that he is the regent of Demetrus, their similarities are weirdly frightening. It somehow makes a creepy shiver run over me. But while the warm feeling swirled openly in my chest when I talked to god, I don't know what to feel now.

There is this dark desire for his touch, the feeling to protect him and prove to him that I'm stronger than he thinks. It is etched into my brain, carved into my skin. But it doesn't overpower the one feeling that appeared tonight. It takes every shine, every positive feeling, and squishes it right under its hold.

Deep betrayal floods my veins as I stare at this somehow familiar and yet strange man. I don't know which words were spoken in truth and which were wrapped around lies.

I don't let whatever feeling grips around my chest stop me from pushing my knuckles against the cold ground and I get up on my feet. Holy hell the world is spinning. I watch as both heads whirl towards me but I ignore their gaze. I rather let my eyes wander down my body noticing the lack of pressure in my chest. The dagger is gone.

My fingers shake when I let them wander over and under the torn material of my suit. To my surprise, they hit soft skin. No wound, not even a scar left.

My eyes fly back up meeting the unbelieving look of the king. Something swirls in his eyes close to fear as if he is seeing the god of death himself.

Aerwyn said Cassian fed me his blood, after all, to ensure that I stay alive. I try to believe it was out of the good of his heart but I'm scared. There is no place for the spark of hope that I feel so I make sure to erase it with every ounce of willpower I have left. I don´t know who to trust anymore which means I am the only one I can rely on. I try to take a step forward, to somehow gain a feeling for this body that has changed.

It feels out of balance but that could just be because I was dead for a while.

"Holy Adales I was right, you are her daughter." The king murmurs but I ignore his words my eyes focusing on the hand that is wrapped around Cassian´s throat. He looks pale and on the verge of death, I can almost smell it.

No, I can smell it. It´s a small realization that dawns on me and it shouldn´t disturb me that much.

But it comes with the realization of a thudding pain in my head that doesn´t seem to be a pain at all. It is the beat of his heart that strums in my head, my ears, and my veins. I´m no healer but the rhythm seems off, slowing down with every passing second.

It´s not the only thing I observe, it seems like my senses have heightened, able to realize many things at once. For example, the fact that Orkiathan fled the scene and is nowhere in sight. A different scent of blood lingers and I hear footsteps approaching. My muscles tighten and it takes not even a second for me to bend my knees, squatting lightly.

For a second I´m distracted by the burning in my teeth, making me raise my hand.

Instead of meeting soft flesh and my usual pairs of teeth, I feel the addition of two more, sharp and hard, silky smooth. Teeth that can cut through flesh as no blade could. Oh gods, what did they do to me?

"Damn it."

The king lets go of Cassian's throat who immediately falls to the ground heaving. Something must've lulled him out of his staring, the alarm blazing presently in his eyes. I didn't think there was something in this world that the king would fear.

"You're not supposed to be here." The king says and I feel someone stepping up beside me. The stale scent of blood is horrific but a soft layer of familiarity lies under it. Iron moves through the air hot and powerful. It's like it pulls at my navel, dark and enticing.

I need to turn towards the person. It is a woman, an unearthly beautiful woman. Her hair is as white as spun moonlight and for a moment I catch myself thinking it might be Aerwyn. But it's icier, there is no glow to it.

Yet it is long and silky, small braids are woven in between, promising to feel smooth under wandering fingertips. The strands fall over a black cloak that covers her shoulders. Shoulders that carry pride and ancient arrogance. Her skin is golden brown and shimmery. I wouldn't dare called it soft or breakable. The muscles are obvious under the skin, tight with anticipation.

My eyes wander over her strong arms before I notice the claws attached to her nails. A surprised breath leaves my lips when I see the black color of them, spreading up her knuckles and it looks like the shadows are disappearing into her skin. A color that has never seen any light, shimmering oily as if death was attached to her hands.

Even though she smells like the worst nightmare I don't feel threatened.

Not even when I dare to look into her astonishingly face.

"Holy Fuck." The words escape me in a small breath, triggering the red irises to turn towards me. The pupil is black and widened, stretching to its surroundings.

It is a horrible color as if her soul is drenched in the deepest pits of blood. It still doesn't take any of her beauty away. I swallow and let my eyes wander over plump, red lips. They pucker lightly as if she was mocking her opponents before her eyes turn to the king.

The latter looks like he wants to run for miles and never come back.

I would too if I received the predatory look in her eyes. As if it was her birthright to ensure his life was taken this exact night.

"I wouldn't call something filthy as that holy." The king murmurs boldly and I narrow my eyes.

Is he really stupid enough to curse this woman? To curse my. . .best friend. Because yes, I do recognize Edlyn under all this change.

There is no denying that it's her straight nose or those beautifully carved cheekbones. Even the smirk that now moves on her lips is familiar. And if I haven't endured everything I did tonight I wouldn't believe it.

Edlyn is a goddamned blood witch. After all, that was revealed it is no surprise that yet again a legend proved itself to be true. They were rumored to live in the woods but I don't remember them to be this enticing. I should've noticed, the way she spoke, the glimmering in her eyes as if something ancient lay underneath it. She covered it all with young naivety, fooling me.

"Don't say that I almost missed this party. It's time to finally get to the climax."

Her voice is like honey, her bared teeth like death. No one answers her; the suggestive tone of her voice stunning is into a stupor.

"Oops, that didn't sound like I wanted it to." Her voice drawls a smirk on her lips and this can't be the Edlyn that I remember. Her cold, red eyes turn to me and for a moment she bows her head. With respect and loyalty. As if all of this was fucking normal.

"Your Highness." She greets me.

It is the same taunting tone as my best friend. The same one that sat with me in the bathroom, giggling about gowns and the prince's, running through the Royal gardens, or annoying Henri when we were little.

It was all a bluff again. Somehow the blade of the king in my chest doesn't feel so awful like this.

"How could you?" the question escapes me before I can stop it.

A grimace meets me, one of guilt and pain. It is the same one Cassian wore. Hot anger blazes through me and I am thankful that she doesn't acknowledge the question. Instead, she turns into a whirlwind of black and white circling the king who has drawn his sword.

My chest heaves as I watch them throw punches and exchange groans. To see her fast pace and cleverness makes my chest burn. She's light and hard at the same time fighting like a warrior.

I now understand why she never wanted to fight with me even though I insisted on training. I thought her interest in herbs was some kind of hobby but I was wrong.

It all clicks into place and when I watch her chase the king up the stairs of the dungeon I don´t feel any worry for her. Not just because I saw the way she fought but because I am fucking tired of this. Fucking tired of everyone lying to me.

"What the actual fuck." I whisper and flinch when I hear another groan looking at the monster that was left with me. Cassian gets up on his feet his eyes black as they focus on me.

"You´re alive." He says relieved but I shake my head. I don´t feel alive. This is not my usual body or my hands. They feel stronger more sensitive, my ears feel larger and when I touch them slowly I feel that they´ve elongated into sharp ends and I cry out. A cold claw wraps around my heart squeezing it to the unbearable.

"You did this to me!" I snap at him making his brows raise confused.

 "I saved you, you were about to die!"

 "So? You should´ve let me die, look at me! I´m a monster."

I claw at my skin frustrated, wanting to get out of this weird state that messes with my head, a dull ache forming behind my eyes but I still notice the prince walking towards me dagger in his hands.

I don´t know why but something slips over my eyes like a red veil, focusing my attention on oncoming danger. "You need to calm down. . ." He starts but his voice does nothing to my panic. Aerwyn said I should run and search for the Fatums. It is my only chance.

"Carina!" His voice booms the deathly fangs forming. The second his green eyes glow I lose it completely. It feels like I'm not in my own body as my hands grip the cold dagger, not even feeling the slice of the blade against my skin. The moment it is in my hands I feel peace. Absolute peace before I swing my hand and ram it straight into Cassian's chest.

The beating of his heart guided me to pierce his skin as he so foolishly stood in front of me. Unprotected and naïve.

We both look at the wound, my hands dropping from the weapon as the sudden rage dissipates.

His eyes widen but instead of dropping to the floor as I anticipated, he freezes. His hand is the only whirl of movement as it reaches out and pulls the blade from his skin.

"You should know that the only thing able to kill an Upyr is bloodstone, princess." The growl in his voice touches the deepest parts inside of me, inflicting downright horror.

I take a slow step back, swallowing.

"Not smart to tell me your only weakness."

I use the snarky remark as my only chance to scan the ground, the dagger of the king lying a few feet away.

I need to move now. His lip curls when his skin starts to appear thinner and yet harder, almost stony. The dark seems to close around him, his eyes glowing.

"It is only dumb if you're facing an enemy. I certainly am not."

A jab against the lack of threat he feels in my presence. I am going to show this bastard what a threat I am.

He traces forwards the intent to kill on his face. No matter what Aerwyn said this is the look of a murderer. I walk in synch with him, every time he takes a step forward I take one back.

I stop the second the heel of my foot comes into contact with the right dagger. I drop down to my knees like a dead body, making his eyes widen in surprise. A moment of hesitance. That´s all I need. I swipe the dagger right from the cold ground before I´m back up.

It doesn´t even take me a second to analyze it. It´s like I can listen to the thumping of his heart, hear the sharp inhale of his next breath as the bloodstone pierces right through his chest.

I tilt my head, my lip curling at his wounded look.

"I hope this is the right blade, Your Highness. Enjoy fucking hell."

The beating of his heart stops.

Epilogue

I always wondered if someone had to choose between the act to be loved or to love, what their answer would be. My answer would've been easy, to be loved. There is no deeper satisfaction than to be admired by a person, to see the devotion shine in their eyes. I'm sure it would've been my brother's answer as well. Zayne bathed in the attention the Moreau family received. If it wasn't for his good looks the women might find him arrogant and vain. I tell him that every day, despite his inherited looks. I viewed him like every little brother viewed their older ones. With love and devotion. An idol, a motherfucking star.

I did everything to gain his approval, to somehow stand higher in his viewings. I knew our parents found it cute, how I ran after him like a lost puppy. How I adored and worshipped him like my own god. Zayne bathed in satisfaction, knowing how much I yearned for his approval. So when I asked him *'Zayne, do you care to be loved or to love?'*

His answer was quick.

'Easy to be loved, any form of affection you could have for someone would pass some time and you would realize it was all spent in vain.'

That was where he was wrong. I knew it the second I saw her, and laid my eyes on her long silky hair. It flowed around her like a curtain, hiding those beautifully flushed cheeks, splattered with freckles.

I knew it the second those big round sapphire eyes met mine in wonder, a soft smile adorning her lips. We were kids, I thought it was a stupid crush. I fought against it, a lot. Fought the way my heart didn't stop humming around her, my hands running clammy every time she gifted me with one of her smiles.

I felt awful, I've gone as far as to tell my parents I was sick earning a hearty chuckle from my father. I knew we couldn't get sick, it made everything much more embarrassing. But the feeling didn't ease not after months, not after years. I only understood it when my father explained the cause.

"It is your blood yearning for her, the ancient magic that flows through her veins just as it flows through yours. You are meant to be at her side, it was written in the stars and painted by the moon."

Whatever his words were supposed to mean I got the order lying under it. Nothing would ever happen to Carina as long as I lived. I grew up with this promise, this oath, knowing that even when her eyes blazed at me in anger, even when those beautiful lush lips told me to go fuck myself that I would do anything. Would move anything and everything to ensure she stayed safe.

That brought me to this day, barely sixteen as I kneel in front of the King and Queen of Demeter. My father holds the oath exclusively, not even Zayne is allowed to watch us. The question in my father's eyes is loud and clear.

Are you ready?

I don´t need to answer, I only lift the dress shirt from over my head, revealing tan skin.

"We shall start with the procedure." The voice of my father is final. Etched into stone and marble in this private hall. The priest scrambles over to me, knife in his hands.

"I will need some of your blood, my prince."

"Go ahead." My voice is restrained when I hold my palms up for him. I know the sensation of bloodstone piercing through my skin. I prepare for the searing pain, a fire destructive and relenting. The shimmery blade cuts through both my palms, the blood sizzling as it comes to the surface. Just like practiced I lay on my side when he lights the candles that envelop us two in a circle.

"You may repeat after me, Your Highness."

I close my eyes for a moment, relishing in the silence. A foreboding picture flashes in front of them. Dark silky hair, flying in seducing waves. Cheeks red with anger and dotted with freckles. It isn´t even a question I asked myself if I could do this.

I know. I know there would be no way for me to live without making sure she is protected. Blame it on our ancestors, or on the stupid beat of my heart that always tumbles over itself when I see her. Blame it on her ancient beauty because, fuck, the princess is beautiful.

She looks like a fucking goddess. May it be one of destruction or peace, it doesn´t matter. I will go down for her in every possible way. My eyes fly back open and meet the priest, who carries a vessel in his hand. Mixed with my blood and the ink that he is going to carve into my side.

"I, Cassian Eliaz Moreau, promise from this day and every day upon—"

I copy his words with a hard tone, staring at the angel-painted ceiling.

"That I will, in death and life, protect Katarina Sebestyen's life and ensure her help. May it be harm caused by others or herself."

I repeat his words while my eyes flicker to my mother's. Soft glistening Jade appears as a tear slips down her cheek. I know she doesn't want this. I train my eyes back to the ceiling.

"I will shed my blood so that hers has never to be spilled. . ."

I half listen to the priest, repeating his words as if I haven't practiced it my whole life. The words aren't the hardest part, it is him tattooing my skin that will burn me from the inside out, inflict her name into my skin and soul.

I can't stop myself from looking back at my mother who is adorned with a tear-stained face. I know it must be hard.

To watch their sixteen-year-old son bind his soul to a girl she doesn't know. But it is easy for me. No matter if she believes the girl is the death of me or not, I will take the risk.

Just for the fact to hear that laugh again, when I listen to her closed doors. Or see the care she takes of those ridiculous flowers. I give it all up.

And when the words are finished and the first needle prick etches her name into my skin, I know. Know that sooner or later she is going to be the death of me.

Hi!

If you feel like talking about books in general or are interested in more of my work my Instagram is mthornewrites! I´d really like your opinion on this book so if you have the time please leave a review it would mean the world to me <3

Stay safe and enjoy many more books!

Acknowledgments

Thank you to everyone who read my first book ever. It was a long journey until I finished this and I appreciate everyone who picked this up and found it worthy to be read.

Thank you to my mom who listened to me rant about the plot and characters even though she hates fantasy and probably doesn´t understand a thing that is going on in this story.

Thank you, dad, for pondering over covers and names even if most of them sounded ridiculous.

A big thanks to my brother, if it weren´t for his rainbow glowing keyboard he lent me, this story wouldn´t exist.

Thank you Rosa that you kept me motivated throughout this story. That you liked Henri the most and that you were very patient and non-judgmental every time I doubted myself.

Thank you, Coca that you listened to me and my annoying worries about things that stressed me out.

To everyone else who helped create this book and the characters inside, I am more than grateful for everything you did!